A DEADLIER BREED

A SLEEPING DOGS THRILLER

Human evolution doesn't stop with Homo sapiens…

COPYRIGHT

writes by complying with international copyright laws by not reproducing, scanning, or distributing any part of it in any form without permission.

ISBN: 978-0-9986117-3-0 PRINT VERSION
ISBN: 978-0-9986117-2-3 DIGITAL VERSION

LCCN: 2018911223
Published by the Falbey Group, LLC
Cover Design: Tatiana Villa at Villa Design

To "Annie", who continues to show me every day what unconditional love and patience truly are. Sweetheart, you are the prettiest, calmest, most well-adjusted person I've ever known. You really don't know how special you are. And that makes you even more special.

TABLE OF CONTENTS

PART THREE
THE PACK IS BACK

FOR THOSE WHO CAME LATE

For Those Who Came Late...

A Deadlier Breed is the fifth novel in the Sleeping Dogs series of international intrigue thrillers.

The following is a brief summary of the action in the first four books in the series: *Sleeping Dogs—The Awakening; Endangered Species; The Year of the Dog*; and *The Dogs of War*.

Sleeping Dogs—The Awakening

In this first book in the Sleeping Dogs series, the president of the United States has been targeted for assassination—by his *own* handlers. The killing must look like the president's political opposition is responsible. Desperate to prevent the crime, the opposition turns to the only force that can stop it this late in the game—a mysterious hunter-killer team known only as the Sleeping Dogs. This darkest of black ops units was formed to carry out America's wettest, most politically incorrect missions abroad.

A seemingly unconnected car crash rapidly escalates into a series of plot twists and a rising body count involving Russian agents, crooked politicians, Ukrainian gangsters, a billionaire international arbitrageur, a secret society of patriots in the military and intelligence communities, the CIA, a doggedly determined FBI agent, and the six deadliest men on earth—the Sleeping Dogs. Brendan Whelan and the other Dogs relentlessly pursue the would-be assassins and their handlers. As they do, they begin to uncover, layer by layer, a plot to bring America to her knees and impose a one-world government on the planet. The enemy is powerful, with access to unlimited funds and the ability to manipulate the rogue nations of the world. The problem? They've awakened the Sleeping Dogs.

Endangered Species

The world is descending into chaos. America is like a rudderless ship—its elected government gridlocked and ineffective. Rogue governments spit on Old Glory and defy a weakened America to stop them. Religious fanatics are dedicated to butchering all the world's citizens who don't convert to their beliefs. And the worst is yet to come. From Russian aggression to worldwide jihadism, from China's designs on Southeast Asia to a morally and financially bankrupt European Union, from violent and expanding drug cartels to Iranian nuclear designs, the members of the Alliance for Global Unity are close to achieving their goal—a single world government with them ruling it.

But a shadow government of old fashioned patriots is working to change the course of events. The key to success is the world's deadliest hunter-killer special ops unit—the Sleeping Dogs. But keeping the six Sleeping Dogs alive is challenging. An outstanding Presidential Decision Directive ordered the men to be terminated with extreme prejudice. An angry FBI agent, believing his wife had an affair with the unit's leader Brendan Whelan, is pursuing him with homicide on his mind. A rogue Russian agent seeks revenge for thwarting his mission to assassinate the president of the United States. And, most chillingly, a huge and mysterious brute named Maksym is systematically hunting the Dogs down individually. The fate of the free world hangs in the balance.

The Year of the Dog

Thousands of Islamic terrorists have set up cells in America, stockpiling weapons, assembling explosives, and identifying soft targets, as well as police and first responder stations, military installations, and the nation's electrical and communications grids. The Chinese are solidifying their dominion throughout Asia and setting their sights on the rest of the planet. The Russian president is intensifying his threat against the free peoples of Europe and beyond. Cyberwarfare is ramping up from Beijing and Moscow to Pyongyang, Tehran, Havana and elsewhere.

It's the eve of a presidential election, but the outgoing administration spent the past eight years, like a modern Nero, fiddling away the country's treasure, seemingly too oblivious or incompetent to recognize the threat. Time is running out, and a shadow government has learned of a pending threat to the U.S. homeland that will render the nation defenseless. It asks Brendan Whelan to reunite the members of the world's deadliest hunter-killer black ops team—the Sleeping Dogs—and try to stop it. The question is, can Whelan get the Sleeping Dogs back together in time?

The Dogs of War

They're here. In America. Thousands of Islamic terrorists committed to a rabid jihad that ends only when they've butchered the last man, woman, and child. Worst of all, they have six nuclear devices. Their plan is to detonate the first one at the Los Alamos National Laboratory where America stores its plutonium supplies. The odds of Western civilization being snuffed out grow stronger each day.

Only the shadow government known as the Society of Adam

Smith, or SAS, may be capable of dealing with this threat. And it desperately needs the skills possessed only by that deadliest of hunter-killer teams, the Sleeping Dogs. But its members each have gone their separate ways. Now, Brendan Whelan must reunite them while recruiting a new member, an Australian. But with his rogue brother, the monstrous Maksym, intent on killing Whelan's family, can he reunite the Dogs in time? Herding cats would be easier.

Heart pounding, non-stop action pulls the reader from one global crisis spot to the next as Western civilization faces its worst onslaught in history.

CAST OF CHARACTERS

A DEADLIER BREED: A SLEEPING DOGS THRILLER

This novel is one of a series. Several characters recur throughout the series. Others from earlier books in the series may be referred to in subsequent books.

Brendan Whelan (WHEY-luhn) – by appearances, an innkeeper in Dingle, Ireland, but also the reluctant leader of the deadly hunter-killer black ops unit known as the Sleeping Dogs

The Sleeping Dogs – together with Brendan Whelan, the most lethal black ops unit in history; genetically evolved—Mother Nature's beta models for humans in future generations:

Sven Larsen – the "Man With No Neck," he is the most physically powerful of the Dogs and closest to Whelan

Marc Kirkland – the "Zen Warrior," he is completely dedicated to mastering every style of martial arts fighting and weapons techniques

Nick Stensen – the "Serial Killer," a loner and certifiably insane; his singular is hunting down and killing criminals who have escaped the punishment of the law

Quentin Thomas – the "Philosopher King," is the best pure athlete of the Dogs and a professor of Eastern philosophies

Rafe Almeida (RAIF al-MAY-duh)– the "Runt Of The Litter," is genetically gifted like the other Dogs, but an inveterate substance abuser and skirt-chaser

Liam (LEE-um) *Stone* – "Lime Stone," is an Aussie who also is genetically gifted like the other Dogs, but is a recent member recruited to the unit

Caitlin (KATE-lin) *Whelan* – Brendan's wife, partner, and mother of Sean and Declan, two young lads who appear to be chips off the old block

Cliff Levell (Luh-VELL) – former Recon Marine officer and CIA operative, now leader of the Society of Adam Smith. The SAS is a shadow government attempting to counter the elected government's destruction of American values and freedoms. Although confined to a wheelchair because of injuries incurred in an automobile accident, he is tougher than most able-bodied individuals

Mitch Christie – an agent of the FBI who originally pursued Whelan and the other Dogs. He experienced an epiphany and joined the SAS

Maksym (Mack-SEEM) *Kozak* – a ruthless killer and, like his brother Brendan Whelan and the other Sleeping Dogs, genetically advanced. He works for the highest bidder

Harland Fairchilde IV – fourth generation scion of an über wealthy family. Leader of the Alliance for Global Unity (AGU), a global organization of financiers and government finance officials seeking to impose a one-world governing structure on mankind for their own financial benefit

Kirill (Keer-REAL) *Federov* – a former Spetsnaz (Russian special ops) colonel serving in the SVR, Russia's external intelligence agency (*believed to be deceased*)

Andrei Ulyanin (An-DRAY Uhl-YAN-in) – former Spetsnaz colleague of Federov's, now pursuing his killers

Tom Murphy – Caitlin Whelan's father and a former member of the UK's SBS; currently *An Garda Síochána* (the Irish National Police force) District Superintendent for County Kerry, Ireland

Padraig (Paddy) Murphy – Caitlin's brother and the Sergeant in Charge of the *An Garda Síochána* station in Dingle, Ireland

Maureen Delaney - chief executive of one of the largest and most successful technology companies on the planet, and Levell's love interest

Luiz Fernando (Nando) Correia (Kor-RAY-ah) – Levell's personal assistant, driver, and bodyguard; a master, or specialist, in *Capoeira Regional* and Brazilian Jiu-Jitsu

The Mueller (MULE-er) *Brothers* (Alfred, Hermann, and Tomas) – billionaire industrialists and patriots who fund SAS operations and provided leading edge technological support

Camila Ramirez (Ra-MEER-ez)– a sheriff's deputy in Albuquerque, New Mexico and Mitch Christie's lady friend

Nadir (Nah-DEER) *Shah* – leader of the Holy Army of the Caliphate, a radical group establishing an Islamic state in the Middle East

Zheng Bao Xun (Zhing Bah-oh Zhun) - the minister of finance for the People's Republic of China

Turan (Ter-RAHN) *Salam* (SuH-LAHM)— a Pakistani Waziri teenager recruited to jihad by Bazir Haqqani, trained in the mountains of North Waziristan for an attack on the U.S. homeland

Carolina (Cah-row-LEEN-ah) *Avila* (Ah-VEE-la)—a teenage neighbor of Turan Salam's in Santa Fe. He's been smitten by her beauty, but she begins to suspect he may be something other than he seems

Bazir (Bah-ZEER) Haqqani (Hah-KAHN-ee)— a Waziri and former Taliban fighter who has pledged his allegiance to Nadir Shah and the Islamic Caliphate. He recruited Turan Salam

Fermin "Frank" Cuellar (KWAY-lar)—a major in the New Mexico State Police and commander of its Special Operations Bureau

David Hidalgo (Hee-DAHL-go) — U.S. Customs and Border Protection agent stationed at the Antelope Wells Border Patrol port of entry and forward operating base (FOB)

HAC—the Holy Army of the Caliphate, the largest and most successful terrorist organization yet. It has declared a caliphate across a large swath of the Middle East and Africa with inroads into Europe, Asia, and the New World.

Prince Bandar bin Nayif al Saud - head of Saudi general intelligence and a close friend of Levell's

Frederick Flagler—president of the United States. He engages Levell, the SAS, and by extension the Sleeping Dogs for a highly illegal operation to recover five nuclear devices possessed by Nadir Shah's Holy Army of the Caliphate and harbored in Mexico

Billy Trupockitt— White House senior advisor on counterterrorism

David Farmer— special counsel appointed by the United States Department of Justice to investigate alleged irregularities in President Flagler's campaign

PROLOGUE

DINGLE PENINSULA, IRELAND

"BE POLITE, be professional, but have a plan to kill everybody you meet."

—General James N. (Mad Dog) Mattis, USMC, Retired

TEN HEAVILY ARMED, well-trained, members of the People's Liberation Army's special operations forces slipped ashore at a little after 2 a.m. They had been specially chosen for this mission on Irish soil. Their goal was to kill a single individual who lived alone in a now-defunct bed-and-breakfast on the edge of the town of Dingle. They had been warned that their intended victim, Brendan Whelan, was an unusually dangerous man and would be difficult to kill. Still, to the commandos, it seemed like overkill. No one man was a match for men such as they. He would be sleeping. They would infiltrate the B&B, called the Fianna House, and kill him in his bed.

Within thirty minutes, the commandos had made their way from the beach to the B&B, breached it, and were dead. All ten of them. To avoid their further bleeding out on the B&B's ancient hardwood floors or expensive carpeting, Whelan stacked their corpses behind the Fianna House. Minutes later, he had showered their gore off his body and was fast asleep.

PART ONE

LONE WOLVES

"A wolf doesn't concern himself with the opinions of sheep."

CHAPTER 1

DINGLE, IRELAND

As ALWAYS, Whelan woke at 5 a.m. But instead of following his usual practice of going to the gym, he made a pot of coffee and two phone calls. The first was to Tom Murphy. As district superintendent of *An Garda Síochána*, he was the top cop in County Kerry. Tom also was the father of Whelan's estranged wife. Because of the early hour, Murphy was still at his home outside Dingle. He answered on the second ring.

"You're up a bit early, Brendan. Is it Caitlin you want to speak with?"

"Not really."

There was a moment of silence as if Tom had hoped for a different answer. "I see. Then what *is* the purpose of your call?"

"There are ten dead bodies behind the inn."

"Holy Mary, Mother of God! I thought all that ended with the death of Maksym. What is it this time?"

"Dunno, Tom. They showed up around two in the morning, and they weren't looking for lodging."

"And you're saying you killed them?"

"Yeah."

"Why? Did they mean to harm you?"

"We've known each other a long time, Tom. Have you ever known me to kill a human purely for sport?"

"No need to get touchy about it. Who were they?"

"Other than being well-equipped and physically fit, I've no fucking idea."

"You killed them three hours ago. Why are you just now calling me?"

"I figured we both needed our beauty rest."

There was another brief pause at Murphy's end of the conversation. "Caitie was planning to stop by the inn and pick up more of the boys' things today. I'll advise her not to do that, the place must be a mess."

"Ten men died violent and bloody deaths inside the Fianna. It's not a good time for anyone to drop by. In a way, it's a good thing we've been closed to paying guests since...." Whelan struggled to find the words. "Since Caitlin moved out."

"Sounds like you're going to need a cleanup crew."

"The sooner the better, it's beginning to stink. Got any suggestions?"

"I do. My cousin Bertie is in that line of work. The *Garda* has used him and his boys a few times in the past."

"Please ask him to drop by. This morning."

"You'll have to pay him."

"I expect to."

"Ah...it's none of my business, but you're providing Caitie and the boys with funds, generous I might add. But with the Fianna closed, how are your finances holding up?"

"That'll be the purpose of my next call."

"Levell?"

"Yeah. In the meantime, those bodies aren't getting any fresher."

"I'll get right on it, but I'm going to need your statement."

"No problem. Just be sure to have your forensics people do a thorough job. I need their reconstruction to support my side of the story."

Whelan was about to end the call, when Murphy said, "I hate to say this, but this new situation is not going to help you and Caitie get back together. It'll just bring back bad memories."

"Yeah, I know. It'll yank the scab off the Maksym nightmare."

"You can't blame her for feelin' that way, Brendan. The bastard tried for a long time to kill you, her, and the boys. As it is, he killed her brother, my boy Pádraig, and nearly succeeded in killing all of you."

"Dammit, Tom, I know that. I've explained countless times that I never should have relied on Paddy and the townsfolk to protect Caitie and the boys. I thought at the time that it was more important for me to find Maksym first and kill him. I was wrong."

Tom lowered his voice and said in a measured tone, "Let me ask you something, Brendan."

Whelan knew what it was going to be but said nothing.

"Do you want to see you and Caitlin back together?"

Whelan said nothing. The wound was still too raw to discuss.

"I see. Well, it may be none of my business, but you'll never find another girl like her. There are none."

"I know."

THERE WAS another moment of silence, then Murphy said, "I'll gather my lads and be there in thirty minutes."

After Whelan clicked off the cellphone call with Murphy, he refilled his coffee mug and went into the small office near the inn's kitchen. A top-of-the-line safe made from half-inch thick ballistic armor with a fingerprint sensor was built into the wall. He put the pad of his right index finger against the sensor. There was a soft clicking sound and the door, hinged on the right, swung open. He removed a modified satphone and punched in a code. The call was routed through a special satellite owned and operated by one of the billionaire Mueller brothers' countless entities. Ostensibly, the satellite was used to stream music for commercial purposes. But it also served a more cryptic use. The phone call was digitally encoded into the music stream. Moments later Whelan heard the call being answered on the other end. He recognized the speaker as Nando, the Brazilian Capoeira master who served as Cliff Levell's valet, driver, bodyguard, and general factotum. A moment later Levell was on the other end of the call.

"You're up early," Levell said in his distinctive rasp. It always reminded Whelan of Clint Eastwood's "Go ahead, make my day" voice. "What's the matter? Having trouble sleeping?"

"No, I'm not an old fart."

"Touché, you prick. What's on your mind?"

"There's a problem."

"That's the trouble with you fucking Irishmen, you're always stirring up trouble," Levell said with, what for him, passed as joviality. "What is it this time? Your local distillery out on strike?" Whelan heard the Old Man chuckle at his joke.

"No, not that bad. Ten men tried to kill me this morning."

Suddenly Levell was fully in the moment.

"Jesus Christ!" The Old Man seemed to recover his composure as quickly as he'd lost it and added, "The dumb bastards, obviously they didn't realize they were outnumbered. Are you all right?"

"Better off than they are."

"You kill 'em?"

"Yeah."

"All of them?"

"Seemed appropriate."

"You're a bright guy. Did it occur to you to leave one alive for interrogation?"

"I did. Briefly."

"Did he tell you who sent them?"

"I think he was trying to, but my Mandarin is a little rusty."

"They were Chinese?" Levell said. "All of them?"

"So it would seem."

"Why would the Chicoms want to kill you?"

"I have no fucking idea."

Levell was silent for a few moments then said, "With Federov and Maksym dead, I thought this shit would stop...at least until we managed to piss off someone else."

"What about your 'one-world' buddies at the Alliance for Global Unity?"

"AGU? Yeah, I suppose that's a possibility."

"It's clear someone wants me dead. Presumably, they'll keep trying. In the meantime, this isn't helping my situation with Caitlin."

"And how's that going?" Levell said.

"What do you think? She blames me for Maksym almost killing all of us. And she's right."

"It'll work itself out. You just have to give it time."

"This latest incident won't help."

Levell shifted the subject. "I may have just the thing to keep you occupied while Caitlin works things out in her mind."

"This ought to be good."

"Shitcan the sarcasm and listen. The new sheriff in town is aware of the Society's role during the previous administration and wants to meet with me."

"In the Oval Office?"

"Probably, but I hope not. With all the leaks in that place, the left-wing media would have a field day. I can see the headlines now, 'President Plots with Alt-right Cabal.'"

"The Society of Adam Smith isn't alt-right. It's a group of well-placed patriots from the military, intelligence, and industrial communities trying to preserve basic democracy and civil liberties."

"I know that!" Levell thundered. "But those weak-kneed sob-sisters on the left are determined to impose statism on us and will use any and all tactics to do it."

"Do you know what POTUS wants to talk about?"

"Yeah, I think he wants the Society...SAS...to work directly with his administration."

"To continue to take the fight to AGU?"

"In a manner of speaking, but I think specifically he wants us to help him reestablish *Pax Americana*."

Whelan said, "He does have grandiose ideas. Is this likely to involve the Dogs?"

"Yes, but for you and the others it also could mean that damned presidential decision directive will be removed."

"It would be nice to be rid of the death warrant that's been hanging over our heads for almost twenty years."

CHAPTER 2

RAPHAEL, MISSISSIPPI

Quentin Thomas's car began to make a strange noise. He glanced at the instrument panel and saw a warning message flashing, "Check Engine." He knew it had to be addressed soon or the motor could suffer serious damage. He smelled the odor of hot engine and eased off the gas, leaning forward to stare ahead into the darkness. The car's headlights struggled to cut through the stygian blackness of the deserted country road. The digital clock on the dash said "10:20 p.m."

Thomas suddenly regretted taking what had appeared to be a shortcut on Google Maps. It connected Mississippi state road 679 with 693, which in turn intersected Interstate 10 just west of his destination, Gulfport. *I should have known better when I saw the name of this road: Nathan Bedford Forrest Lane. The first Grand Wizard of the Ku Klux Klan.* But he was behind schedule and looking for ways to make up time. His only sibling, a younger sister, was getting married in the morning to her Seabee fiancé in Gulfport. Their father had died years ago and she had asked her big brother to walk her down the aisle.

Thomas hadn't seen any towns or villages since he'd turned off Interstate 59 near Nicholson, Mississippi. In fact, he hadn't seen any signs of habitation. He glanced again at the warning message and his brow furrowed in concern. He had no idea where he was nor how much time he had before the engine became inoperable. He'd picked up the rental car at the airport in Memphis. He didn't belong to or have insurance in, any organizations that provided emergency services. Thomas didn't want to call his sister and add one more concern to her night-before-the-wedding jitters.

He pulled the car onto the shoulder of the road and dug out his cell phone. Unfortunately, the maps accessible on the Web didn't show much detail. Then he had another idea. He tapped in a phone number he had memorized a long time ago. After two rings, it was answered by a man with a Latino accent.

"Hey, Nando, it's Quentin. Is Cliff there?"

Moments later Levell was on the other end. "What's a health nut like you doing up this late?"

Not sure how to respond, Thomas forced a laugh then said, "Yeah, well, I have a problem I'm hoping you can help me with."

"It's tough to feature someone like you having a problem. What's your situation?"

Thomas explained and said, "I'm hoping your sophisticated electronics can help me."

"Are you suggesting that I might have some means of knowing where you are twenty-four-seven?"

"Yes, and Whelan and the other guys, too."

Levell laughed mirthlessly. "Considering our government has been chasing all of you for nearly twenty years, it seemed like a good idea to keep tabs on you."

"Including now, I hope."

"Yes. You're almost halfway between Nicholson and Gulfport, Mississippi, stopped on a country road in the middle of no-fucking-where. Bad time to have engine problems."

"Is there any place up ahead where I might get help? I know there's nothing behind me."

Levell was silent for a few moments as if studying a map or similar materials.

"You might be in luck...I think. There's a flyspeck of a town named Raphael about a mile down the road. Not much information on it, but it seems there's a combo gas station-car repair place. Other than that, you're fucked until morning."

"Can't wait for morning. I have a wedding I have to get to."

"Then good luck in Raphael. You might need it."

"What does that mean?"

"I'm not sure, but what little intel I can find on the place doesn't indicate it's a warm and welcoming town. It's in the Deep South and you're Black. Keep your eyes open.

CHAPTER 3

SANTA FE

CAROLINA AVILA WAS eighteen and a freshman at Santa Fe Community College. For financial reasons, she still lived at home in the same house her parents had owned since before she was born. There were other reasons, too, such as the absence of on-campus student housing. But the primary reason was fear. Ever since Islamic terrorists had detonated a nuclear weapon, destroying nearby Los Alamos, Santa Fe had been a city paralyzed by anxiety. Would it happen again? When? Where? In Santa Fe itself? Her aunt Soledad and uncle Ernesto, both employed at the Los Alamos National Laboratory, had been vaporized in the explosion. As a result, Carolina's parents were reluctant to let their only child stray too far from the nest.

It was a typically cloudless, blue-sky January day, the kind the Santa Fe Chamber of Commerce prayed for. Even better, it was unseasonably warm with the high around seventy, although the wind created a chill, particularly in shady areas. But if one could get into both the lee of the wind and the open sunlight, it was a perfect day. Carolina had found such a place in the backyard of her parents' home on Santa Inéz Road. She was lounging in a deck chair and reading a homework assignment. But it was beginning to bore her.

She closed the textbook she'd been reading for Biology 202, a three-credit-hour required course in genetics for the school's associate's degree in Biological Sciences. It was a precursor for a pre-med curriculum in a four-year university, a step toward her goal, medical school. Resting the book on her stomach, she closed her eyes for a few moments and thought about a video she and some of her friends at school had seen. Although it had quickly been removed from YouTube, it reappeared immediately on the Dark Web, that part of the Deep Web accessible by networks such as Freenet, 12P, and Tor. The video showed the ringleader of the Los Alamos attack having his heart ripped from his chest by a man using only his bare hands. Some of her friends had been horrified, but Carolina, still grieving the loss of her aunt and uncle, thought the punishment was justified. She wished all of the terrorists involved in the act would suffer the same fate.

She thought of the young man who had called himself Tomás. She had no idea what his real name was. *Probably Mohammed or Abdul or Yusuf.* But he definitely wasn't Latino. He had been a part of the terrorist cell that had smuggled the nuke into the United States and participated in its placement. She admitted to herself that, at first, she'd been attracted to him, believing he was what he said he was, a boy from Argentina. He was cute, shy, and kind of sexy. They'd hit it off from the beginning.

Suddenly, despite the warmth of the bright sunlight, she felt a chill and shivered. Tomás…whoever…was a coldblooded killer. She remembered the last time she'd heard from him. It was a few days after the explosion. He'd been on the run and called her hoping to convince her that he hadn't known what his people had been planning, claiming he would never have participated if he had known. *He was a liar as well as a killer.* The air seemed chillier now. She wondered if her thin, brightly colored tights and sky-blue cable-knit sweater were enough.

Her cellphone rang, and Carolina reached down to pluck it from the ground beside the deck chair. She looked at the number and didn't recognize it. But she'd exchanged numbers with most of the people in her classes. *Maybe one of them is calling about a homework assignment or class project.*

"Hello," she said pleasantly.

"Hello, Carolina."

She recognized the voice instantly, and an icy fear swept through her. She was unable to speak.

"I'm back," Tomás said.

When he heard no response, he said, "Please speak to me, Carolina. I have something I need to say to you."

After several additional long moments of silence, Carolina finally was able to respond. Her initial reaction, a strong one, was to get rid of the phone, pitch it over the backyard fence. But she, too, had something she wanted to say.

"You bastard. You murdering, lying bastard. How dare you ever call me again. You murdered my aunt and uncle and thousands of other innocent people. You deserve a special place in hell."

"I understand your anger, Carolina, and your grief. I hate what happened, and I hate that I was part of it. But, please, before you hang up, I want you to know that I'm going to do everything I can to try to make things right."

"There's no way on God's earth you can ever undo what you've done."

"Perhaps not, but that's not going to stop me from trying."

"I couldn't care less what you're going to do." Her voice was heavy with loathing, anger, and contempt.

"Wait. Please don't hang up. I need your help in trying to atone for my involvement."

"You really are insane to think I'd help you in any way at all."

"Please, just listen for a moment then I promise I won't ever bother you again."

After a moment's hesitation, Carolina said, "What is it?"

"Los Alamos was just the first nuclear weapon. There are five more planned to be detonated in your country."

"Oh my God! Where?"

"I don't know...yet. I think I can find out, but I'm going to need to speak with people in your country who are working to find the terrorists."

"I'm a college student, I have no idea who those people are or how to find them."

"Yes, but your mother works for the New Mexico State Police. You told me her boss is the man who runs their Special Operations Bureau. He will know who I should speak with. Please help me do this, Carolina."

She was struck by the sound of sincerity in Tomás voice. Still, he was a terrorist and a mass murderer. She struggled with the dilemma of whether to just hang up or try to get him to turn himself over to the authorities.

Finally, she said, "I hate you. I don't know why I should do anything to help you unless it's to see you go to prison. But here's what I will do. I'll ask my mom to arrange to have you taken into custody. After that, you're on your own."

CHAPTER 4

DINGLE, IRELAND

THE ODD, yet unmistakably sickly-sweet, smell of death hung in the air. Hordes of flies swarmed around the stiffened and bloody corpses. Tom Murphy's police crew loaded them into body bags and stacked them in the back of a lorry. Even though the Fianna was closed, at Whelan's request the truck had been parked around the back where it was less likely to attract attention.

"Any idea why these ten bloody Chinamen wanted to kill you?" Murphy said.

"Because I don't like egg rolls?" Whelan said.

"A straight answer would be appreciated. Could it have anything to do with your late brother Maksym?"

"Doubtful. No one liked Maksym enough to avenge his death. More likely, there was a lot of celebrating going on."

"Well, forensics is wrapping things up inside," Murphy said. "You can send Bertie and his crew in to start the cleanup."

"It's a fucking mess in there. I don't know if it'll ever be the same."

"Don't underestimate Bertie's crew. They've been doing this

kind of work for a long time, since the Troubles," Tom said in reference to the bloody internecine strife between Irish Catholics and Protestants. "Besides, you're the one who chose to kill those blokes inside your own home."

"What was I supposed to do? Invite them outside for tea, then off them on the lawn?"

"There's no need for sarcasm. What I'm saying is you might have considered killing them in a less bloody manner."

Whelan said nothing, just locked Murphy with a baleful stare that spoke volumes. His unblinking glacial blue eyes unnerved even the tough, longtime cop, a man who had seen the worst side of human savagery.

"That would be the silent side of sarcasm," Murphy said. "How could I forget. The Good Lord created you and your Sleeping Dogs colleagues as the damnedest hunter-killers on the planet. I reckon when someone comes into your place of residence intent on harming you, you've a right to kill 'em any damn way you choose. Do you mind telling me how you managed to kill ten professionals?"

"Quickly and quietly. Are you going to tell Caitlin about what happened?"

Murphy shrugged. "Doesn't matter. Dingle's a small town. Everyone knows everyone. There are no secrets. She'll hear about it whether I tell her or not." He paused. "Maybe it's best if you tell her yourself." He arched an eyebrow inquisitively.

"You're probably right."

"Your boys are in school and Caitlin's mother is visiting her sister Gráinne in Tralee this afternoon. Caitie will be alone if you want to stop by."

ALTHOUGH HE'D BEEN in Tom and Ciara Murphy's home on countless occasions, it had always been with Caitlin by his side. Now they were estranged and it felt palpably uncomfortable to know that she and their two sons were living there. He tried to read her attitude when she met him at the door and led him into the living room. It didn't escape his notice that she chose to sit in a chair and waved him to a small sofa across from it. She hadn't sounded cordial when he'd called earlier, but neither did she seem aloof or distant. As usual, she was stunning in a white blouse, an above-the-knee black pencil skirt, and black wedge pumps with an ankle strap. Her dark hair was thick and lustrous, framing bright, emerald green eyes.

"Would you like something? Coffee?"

"No thanks, Cait."

"Alright, then I suppose we should get to the point of your visit if it's not to see the boys." She glanced at her wristwatch.

"Got somewhere you have to be?"

She stiffened visibly. "I don't believe that's any of your business."

"Have you forgotten we're married?"

"Have you forgotten we are no longer living together as husband and wife?"

Whelan sighed in frustration. "I didn't come here to fight with you, Caitlin."

"Why did you come here?"

"Two reasons. Some men broke into the Fianna last night with the intention of harming me."

She gasped and sat suddenly forward. "My God, it's still happening." There was genuine anguish in her voice. "Why are you telling me this?"

"Because it did happen and I wanted you to hear it from me

first. I don't want there to be any secrets between us. It's not who we are."

"I'm no longer sure who we are, Brendan."

The words sliced into his heart. "But the second reason I'm here is to try to find a way to mend things between us, to put things back together the way they were."

She slowly sat back in the chair. "I don't know if I want that, Brendan. And just so you hear this from me first, I've begun seeing someone."

CHAPTER 5

KEY BISCAYNE

HARLAND FAIRCHILDE WAS the billionaire beneficiary of dynastic wealth, but he feared the unpredictability of life could change that abruptly and without advance warning. He held an unshakeable belief that one could never have enough money. The only reliable way to preserve wealth, indeed enhance it, was to assert total control over the political environment. And not just the local scene, but globally. The only safe path was to eliminate not only the potential for threats to one's wealth, but also any possibility of competition for it. This meant destroying the old order and replacing it with one controlled by a handful of the world's leading financiers. That was the role of the Alliance for Global Unity or AGU.

Fairchilde considered his life's work to be extremely challenging. Despite the fact that he'd been born into one of the wealthiest families in America, and old money at that, he had plotted, schemed, and politicked his way into the chairmanship of the most powerful organization in the world, AGU. The organization had been formed in the early part of the twentieth century by an international group of wealthy, progressive-minded individuals. In their wisdom—and greed, they had realized that the surest way to maximize wealth and power was to concentrate it in the hands of the few—them. The means for doing that was to subsume societies and cultures under a one-world government, in which the members of AGU would have absolute control over all things financial.

AGU now was a century old and had become immensely powerful, particularly under Fairchilde's stewardship. Most of the world's major financiers, as well as the finance officials of most governments were members of the organization. And Fairchilde ran it all like a personal fiefdom. One of the reasons he was in Miami Beach was to attend the quarterly gathering of the International Forum on Global Economics. Ostensibly, the Forum's goal was to facilitate agreements and offer business opportunities. In that vein, it promoted an exchange of views and perspectives on pressing economic issues among world leaders and business executives. But its underlying purpose was to address the major governance challenges of the impending new world economic order.

Fairchilde's other reason for attending was to meet privately with Zheng Bao Xun, the minister of finance for the People's Republic of China. He considered Zheng to be an important ally.

The meeting was being held at the new and über posh Hotel Oro d'España on Key Biscayne near Miami. Fairchilde sat at a small table in a secluded alcove in the hotel's bar, La Tasca de la Isla. He took in his surroundings while waiting for Zheng to arrive. Located off the resort's best dining room, the bar reproduced a 1940's Havana motif with high ceiling fans, rich-dark woods, wood floors, and sultry ambiance. The deep blue of the Atlantic, visible through a wall of windows, was complemented by soft shades of blue, green, and gold. An iconic painting of

Hemingway's home near Havana, *Finca La Vigía* or Lookout House, hung in a conspicuous place behind the bar.

Zheng arrived just as Fairchilde was ordering shots of Samaroli Demerara 1988 from Trinidad and Rhum JM 1997 Vintage from Martinique.

Zheng slid gracefully into the table's only other chair and said, "Is one of those drinks for me?"

"No. I don't presume to know another person's taste in food or beverages."

Zheng looked at the server, a pretty young Latina. "We're in a tropical paradise, what would you recommend?"

She flashed a dazzling smile. "Everyone raves about our Mojito Kalinago. It's named after the indigenous people of the islands. They were also known as Caribs."

"Thank you so much for the lesson in sociocultural anthropology." Zheng returned her smile. "That is exactly what I shall have."

He turned back to Fairchilde. "I'm curious. If you don't mind me inquiring, why did you order two different drinks at the same time?"

Fairchilde sniffed. "Well, I'm certainly not an alcoholic if that's what you're implying. I simply wanted to do a taste comparison with two of the more expensive Caribbean rums."

"Ah, so." The Chinese minister of finance smiled his famously inscrutable smile.

The two men made small talk about the day's events involving the Forum until the server returned with their drinks. When she'd left, the subject changed abruptly.

Fairchilde leaned in conspiratorially toward Zheng. "What is this exciting news you wanted to share with me?"

Zheng took a leisurely sip of his mojito before answering. "You recall Nadir Shah complaining that his forces, the Holy

Army of the Caliphate, had been demoralized by what happened to one of their most admired heroes, Bazir Haqqani?"

"Yes, it was those damned Sleeping Dogs. Despite being in a heavily guarded hospital in Qatar, a nation sympathetic to Shah's efforts, Haqqani had his heart torn from his chest by one of those Dogs using his bare hands. The video went viral immediately. So, what of it?"

"The message was not lost on Shah's ragtag fanatics. They understood that it means none of them will ever be safe anywhere in the world."

"Yes, yes, what's your point?" Fairchilde took a small sip of the Samaroli Demerara and rolled it around on his tongue. He cleansed his palate with water, then took a sip of the Rhum JM.

Watching with amusement, Zheng said, "And the winner is?"

Fairchilde frowned. "They're both quite excellent. It's going to take a bit longer to determine which is the better of the two." He motioned for Zheng to continue.

"In addition to Shah's concerns, these same special operators have destroyed much of the apparatus that's been used to smuggle Islamic terrorists into the United States. And those five remaining nuclear weapons as well."

A sour expression spread across Fairchilde's face. "Yes, I know that. I'm hardly senile, you know. My late employee, Maksym, was supposed to dispose of those bastards. But he failed to do so before his own demise."

Zheng plucked a maraschino cherry from his cocktail, placed it in his mouth, and pulled the stem out between his teeth. "Actually, Maksym may not have been up to the task regardless of circumstances."

Fairchilde looked at the other man expectantly.

"Rather than experience additional problems with these Sleeping Dogs, I chose to take action myself. As Maksym said, they probably would be quite ineffective without their leader, that Brendan Whelan person."

"So, you unilaterally decided to take matters into your own hands? What exactly did you do?"

The Asian shifted uncomfortably in his seat. "I sent ten of the People's Liberation Army's special operations forces, top commandos, to kill Whelan. They were specially chosen from our navy's commando team known as the *Jiaolong*."

"Jiaolong? What does that mean?"

"Sea Dragon."

"And the outcome?"

Zheng appeared to be studiously examining his drink. "Unfortunately, there has been no contact from them in some time."

"What, precisely, are you saying?"

"They infiltrated from a PLA submarine near Whelan's home in Dingle, Ireland. We had credible intelligence that he was at home alone. The commandos should have carried out their mission very quickly and contacted the ship for exfiltration, but they have not been heard from."

"Meaning?"

"Meaning we believe they are dead."

Fairchilde sat up quickly. "Dead? All ten of them?"

Zheng nodded cheerily.

"These were ten of your military's best soldiers?"

Zheng nodded again, still smiling.

"Whelan must have had assistance."

"We believe he acted single-handedly."

Fairchilde slumped back in his chair, picked up one of the snifters of rum and knocked it back. He placed the empty glass heavily on the table.

"My God, these people appear to be unstoppable!"

"So it would seem, Harland."

"Then why the fuck are you smiling?" Fairchilde said.

"Because I have discovered another way to be rid of these Sleeping Dogs."

Fairchilde sighed and said, "At this point, I'm willing to listen to anything, Mr. Minister."

CHAPTER 6

RAPHAEL, MISSISSIPPI

QUENTIN THOMAS NURSED the ailing car another mile through the darkness until he saw a sign announcing "Welcome to Raphael." The word "Welcome" had been badly marred, as if someone had tried to remove it. There wasn't much to the village, just a tired-looking mom-and-pop motel, a rundown two-pump service station, and a saloon. He eased the car into the service station and killed the engine. The station was closed. It had the look of a place that had been closed for a long time. He shifted his gaze to the motel. The ancient neon pylon sign in front said "ancy." The letters "v," "a," and "c" were unlit. Thomas shrugged and walked over to the dismal-looking lodge.

The office smelled musty with traces of unidentifiable food in the air as if countless fast food meals had been eaten by whoever manned the registration desk at mealtime. There was no one behind the scarred and battered desk, so he rang the night bell. Several seconds later, a scrawny old man limped slowly through the doorway from a back room. He stopped dead in his tracks when he saw Thomas.

"Ain't got no rooms left," he said with a slow drawl. The distinct odor of a body too long unwashed had entered the room with the old man.

"The sign says vacancy.' Thomas pointed to it. "Or at least it's trying to."

The old man flipped a switch on the wall behind the desk. The sign went dark. "Now it don't say nuthin." He turned to leave.

"Hey, hold on a minute. I'm having car trouble and need a mechanic. Is there one in town?"

The desk clerk turned back toward Thomas. "He ain't available."

"My sister's getting married tomorrow and I need to get to Gulfport."

"That ain't my problem."

"Will the mechanic be available in the morning?"

The desk clerk shrugged. "Guess you'll have to wait and see."

"Fine. In the meantime, where am I supposed to spend the night? In the backseat of my car?"

"Do that and the sheriff will arrest yore black ass. This county don't cotton to no vagrants, 'specially black ones."

"Shit," Thomas said in disgust and walked out of the motel office. He looked across the street and saw there was activity at the saloon. He studied the place for a couple of moments. The structure was as old and rundown as the service station and the motel. It was as if nothing new had been built, or even renovated, in the village in well over fifty years or more. The saloon looked like it had been made out of old barnwood and had a steep tin roof. Its few windows were darkened with age and the accumulated detritus of the decades. A few of them were boarded over. Country music spilled loudly through the swinging double doors. *Might as well get a drink or two while I figure out my next move.*

He strolled into the place and paused just inside the doorway to look around. Three-foot fluorescent strip fixtures hanging from the ceiling provided light. The place reeked of tobacco smoke, stale beer, and unwashed bodies. There were about twelve people, all of them white, scattered around the place. Some sat at a battered old bar to the right of the entrance. Others were seated at equally beat-up and mismatched tables. As if in unison, all turned and stared at Thomas. Each face had the same look—pure hatred.

Thomas suddenly got a bad feeling about the place and the people in it. As he turned to leave, he was violently shoved from behind. It caught him off balance and he staggered a few steps deeper into the room, almost falling. Thomas was a big man, six-two, two hundred thirty pounds. He turned to see who could have had shoved him with such force.

His assailant was a giant of a man, a good six inches taller and close to a hundred pounds heavier. He had long hair matted with dirt that framed a face badly scarred from a history of brawling.

"Look, I was just leaving," Thomas said. "I'm not looking for any problems."

A voice from behind him said, "Waal now, boy, you shoulda oughta thought of that afore you come in heah."

Thomas turned to face the speaker. He was a stocky man in western wear with a straw cowboy hat. It had a braided black leather band studded with silver-tone conchos. He had long, thinning hair and a full, but scraggly beard. His shirt was unbuttoned to the waist revealing a sizable beer belly. There were sweat stains under the arms.

Thomas was aware of the situation developing around him. It

was like something out of an old movie. *Deliverance* came to mind. In this day and age, he thought, people no longer acted out such blatant racism. It was illegal, among other things. This must be a joke of some kind. Some good ol' boys having fun at the stranger's expense. Still, it seemed real enough that he didn't want to stick around.

"Look, I'm having car trouble and just came in to get a beer. But I've changed my mind. I'll be leaving now." He turned to go but the giant still blocked the doorway, his mouth drawn back in a snarl. Several teeth were missing and the remaining ones were chipped and badly discolored.

The others in the bar had all gathered around the Cowboy, who said, "Reckon you gotta convince Eddie Jack to let yore black ass through that door."

There were snickers from the others. The expression on the giant's face eased into a grin, but malevolence still shone in his eyes.

Thomas wasn't concerned for his own safety. He had a rare genetic construct that gifted him with speed and strength possessed by only a few other men. And none of those present. He detested using his gifts to harm Norms, or normal human beings, unless they were on Levell's kill list. But he realized he was going to have to make a statement in order to get out of the place. That statement was going to have to involve Eddie Jack.

He took a step toward the door and Eddie Jack took two steps toward him, closing the gap. With inhuman speed and power, Thomas crushed a devastating right hook into the giant's solar plexus. Eddie Jack's mouth shot open as the volume of air in his lungs exploded from him. His massive body flew backwards knocking the saloon doors off their hinges. There was a loud thud as he landed on the sidewalk outside, then momentary silence.

Thomas turned to face the men in the bar and made a motion as if dusting off his hands.

"Well, 'gentlemen,' you have a nice evening." He smiled and turned back toward the door just as two men with shotguns entered. The guns were aimed at the center of Thomas's chest. He turned and looked at the Cowboy and the others in the bar. They all had revolvers or pistols in their hands.

"Waal, now, boys," the Cowboy drawled. "It looks like we got us one big ol' badass nigra. Reckon we gonna have us some fun."

Now, Thomas was concerned for his safety.

CHAPTER 7

SYDNEY, AUSTRALIA

RAFE ALMEIDA SIGNALED the stunning blonde bartender for another round. She set a beer in front of Liam Stone and a beer and shot of tequila in front of Almeida. As she did, he leaned across the bar and, to be heard above the disco music, shouted, "Hey, beautiful, how would you like to have the most intense orgasm of your life?"

Her lips widened into a dazzling smile that wasn't matched by the look in her eyes. "If you only knew how many times I've heard that line." She scooped up his money from the bar and strutted toward the cash register.

Almeida nudged the Stone, the big Australian next to him and said, "What's a guy gotta do to get laid in this place?"

Stone was talking to another pretty blonde. He turned toward Almeida and said, "For starters, a better pick-up line would help."

"What was wrong with that one? I was just cutting through the usual bullshit, getting right to the point, you know?"

The Aussie threw an arm around his friend's shoulders and

said, "Don't take it personally, mate. That poor sheila's working her gorgeous arse off. It's Friday night and this is one of the busiest clubs in Sydney. Besides, not all sheila's dig Yanks."

"Shit, what I am gonna do? I can barely understand that fuckin' Strine you people speak."

Stone laughed. "Don't worry, mate. It's early yet and this is one of the best pick-clubs. It pulls in a huge percentage of the hottest sheilas in town. You're gonna score." He turned back to the young blonde, then leaned back toward Rafe. "The odds are in your favor. The dating scene in the Big Smoke is brutal on women over twenty-five. All the AMOGs are hitting on the younger ones."

"AMOGs? What the fuck is that?"

"Alpha Male of Group. That includes just about every Ozzie male. They won't hesitate to get verbally aggressive with you when a young sheila is involved. Physical too."

"So, you're saying I should chase skanky old broads because some fucking punk-assed Norm might get in my face?"

"No, mate, no Norm or group of Norms stands a Buckley's in a barney with you. I'm just sayin' why bust your arse trying to cop a root with someone who barely knows what her wad is for. Sheilas twenty-five and older are much better at doin' the nasty." He turned back to the blonde on the bar stool next to him.

Almeida straightened up and looked around the noisy, crowded place. The Club Nowhere was located in The Rocks, a historic section of Sydney near the harbor. In recent years, it had been gentrified and become a popular club scene. He snickered at the name of the club. *When a guy goes home and his wife asks him where he's been, he can say "Nowhere."* He pulled his cell phone out and checked the time. It was past midnight. Stone had told him about the lockout laws. The bars were required to stop admitting patrons at 2 a.m., and last call was at 3:30.

His eyes swept the room again, assessing the female population. Many of them appeared to be in their mid-twenties to early-thirties. His gaze came to rest on a corner table where six attractive, well-dressed blondes were sitting. *Is every chick in this fuckin' country a blonde?*

He grinned broadly and walked over to the table, assessing their ages to be thirtyish. "Evening ladies, do you know whose lucky night this is?"

The women looked at each other. A couple of them giggled. One said, "Whose?"

Almeida opened his arms and said, "All of ours."

This brought more giggles, and he thought he saw a twinkle in the eyes of a couple of them. *As usual, Rafe Almeida is irresistible. The line forms on the right, ladies.* He leaned over the table. "I'm Rafe. How about we start things off with me buying a round of drinks?"

"We already have drinks," one of them said with a flirtatious smile.

"The night is young, you'll need refills anyway."

The women introduced themselves and one of them said, "You're a Yank?"

"Guilty, and damn proud of it, too."

Another one of them with bright blue eyes, flawless skin, and impressive cleavage, said, "So, what's your plan? Try to lure one of us from the group then ignore the rest of us?" She said it with a playful pout.

"One of you? Hell no, I plan to make all six of you very happy women."

Another blonde, slim with elegant painted fingernails that matched the shade of her eyeshadow, said, "What if we don't want to be 'shared'?"

"Then you'd be missing out on the best night of your lives."

The blonde with the cleavage said, "You Americans always talk big. Do you really believe you can fully satisfy all six of us?"

Almeida's smile widened like a spider inviting the fly into its web. "Well, why don't you ladies call my bluff and we'll find out." With his left hand, he made a sweeping gesture toward the entrance.

The women glanced at each other. A couple of them shrugged. The slim blonde with the immaculate fingernails gathered her small purse and said, "What have we got to lose? It wouldn't be the first time a man failed to live up to his claims of sexual prowess."

The other women giggled and stood up to follow Almeida out of the club. Before they got to the entrance, three men stopped them.

The man in the middle was a big man, taller than Almeida, but not as heavily muscled. "What's the rush? Where's everyone going? The party's just about to get started." He tried to move between Almeida and the women.

"They're with me. Go find your own women."

"A fuckin seppo," the man said scornfully and looked at his friends. They snorted derisively. One of them said to the women, "You're not planning to do the nasty with this stinking seppo are you?"

"What the hell's a seppo?" Almeida said and looked at the women.

"It's a derogatory term for Yanks," the busty blonde said.

"It's short for septic tank," another woman said.

Almeida scowled at the three men. "Excuse me for a minute, ladies, while I haul these AMOGs to the trash."

He took a step toward the tall man in the middle.

"Hold up, mate." Stone said from behind him. He walked up

to the tall man and stood an inch away from him. At six two, Stone was as tall as the other man, but vastly more muscular.

The man swallowed. "This doesn't involve you, mate."

"But it does. This bloke's my cobber. You got a problem with him, you got a problem with me."

That was when three of the club's bouncers arrived. Their leader's eyes suddenly opened wide as if in recognition. "I've seen you before, I think, mate," he said to Stone. "If you're who I think you are, these bloody fools," he motioned with his head toward the three troublemakers, "are about to have their heads ripped off and shoved up their arses."

Stone nodded.

"We don't want that kind of trouble in here, mate. Me and the boys will show these gentlemen to the street."

"Not necessary. I believe my mate and … his lovely friends," he smiled at the six women, "were about to leave." Stone reached back and took the hand of the blonde girl he'd been talking with at the bar, pulling her gently around beside him. He looked at the head bouncer. "Have a g'day, mate."

STONE AND ALMEIDA were staying in a two-bedroom suite at a luxury hotel in the heart of Sydney's central business district about one and a half miles, or a little less than 2 and a half kilometers from the Club Nowhere. It was seven o'clock the next morning when Stone pushed open the door to Almeida's room. There were five naked women sleeping in various places around the room. The sixth one, also naked, was just beginning to scream out her latest orgasm.

Stone took it all in with an impressed look on his face. "Sorry to interrupt the festivities, mate, but something's come up."

"Yeah, and it's still up," Almeida grunted without looking around or missing a stroke.

Undeterred, Stone said, "We just got a call from Cliff. He wants us back in the States p.o.q."

As the woman's orgasm abated, Almeida rolled over and looked at Stone, whose lady friend from the previous evening was standing beside him, her petite, voluptuous body lost in one of his XXL shirts. "I don't give a flying fuck what Levell wants. We're on R and R. I'm nowhere near my fill of fuckin', fightin', and drinkin.' Besides, Levell and his candyass SAS owe us big time for what we went through in Doha with those ragheads."

"Party's over, mate. Tickets are waiting for us at the Qantas desk at the airport. Plane departs in two hours."

Almeida glanced at the clock on a bed table. "For chrissakes, it's barely seven o'clock in the morning. What kind of asshole calls at that hour?"

"It's four o'clock yesterday afternoon where Cliff is." Stone paused to smile mischievously, then said, "Kiss the ladies good-bye. And don't forget to thank them."

"Shit, they should be thanking me."

CHAPTER 8

KEY BISCAYNE

THERE WERE a few more people in the hotel's bar, La Tasca de la Isla, than when Fairchilde had entered. But the alcove where he and Zheng were seated was sufficiently separated from the other tables and booths that their conversation remained private.

Zheng Bao Xun drained his cocktail glass and signaled to their attractive server for another drink. "The young lady was right about the mojito. It's excellent."

Fairchilde's remaining shot of rum was about half finished. Periodically, he would pick up the snifter, put his nose into the glass, and inhale. After several moments of reflection, he would take a small sip and roll the liquid around on his tongue. He always followed it up with a drink from a glass of water before repeating the process.

The server placed the fresh mojito in front of Zheng.

"Our Mojito Kalinago is fabulous, isn't it?" she said with a big smile as she removed the empty glass.

"Indeed, you were most kind to recommend it," Zheng said unctuously.

When the girl had left, Fairchilde said, "Tell me more about your idea for dealing with our adversaries in the Society of Adam Smith, particularly their rather effective special operators, the Sleeping Dogs." He looked at the drink in front of Zheng with various types of fruit and flowers crowning the liquid and thought that it looked like a cocktail designed for a randy tourist.

Zheng took a sip and placed the glass precisely in the middle of the doily that bore the logo of La Tasca de la Isla. The motion wasn't lost on Fairchilde.

"Now that Maksym's talents are no longer available to us, I believe I may have found a means for dealing with those Sleeping Dogs."

Fairchilde motioned for the finance minister to continue, and said, "This should be interesting, given that for whatever reason they are almost superhuman in their strength and quickness, as well intellect."

Zheng removed a piece of pineapple from the rim of his glass and nibbled at it.

Eventually, he said, "They definitely are unique. But do you know why?"

Fairchilde shrugged. "I don't know whether that's even relevant. They are what they are."

With an enigmatic smile, Zheng said, "It is relevant if they are not the only ones of their kind."

Fairchilde stared at him blankly. "I don't understand. Are you telling me there are more of them? If so, where?"

"Some of our astute genetic scientists at the Beijing Genomics Institute made an interesting discovery. They came upon an article in an obscure academic journal published years ago by two American geneticists."

Zheng paused to take another sip of his drink, smiled, held

the glass up, and looked at it admiringly. "This really is most excellent."

"Yes, yes, of course. Get on with your story. What, if anything, does it have to do with the Sleeping Dogs?"

"Ah, but that is the point, Harland. It seems that the article was based on research and discoveries made by the two geneticists, doctors Horowitz and Nishioki. They developed a theory based on the fact that European Early Modern Humans were as large as humans today, and more powerful and physically robust. And their brains were one-eighth larger than modern man's. The geneticists discovered that some humans still carry elements of this genetic code designed to produce stronger, faster, smarter humans in response to a hostile environment. They theorized that on those rare occasions when a male carrier mated with a female carrier, there was a potential for one or more of their offspring to be more advanced genetically. And most interestingly of all, they apparently discovered a rare genetic marker that identifies it. They developed a means for testing for this marker in bodily fluids such as saliva." He paused and nibbled on a slice of orange from the rim of his glass.

Fairchilde slid forward to the edge of his chair. "Dammit, you can eat later. Get to the point."

Zheng smiled indulgently. "Coincidentally, our foreign intelligence service, the Ministry of State Security, penetrated the CIA's computer system and learned that the CIA engaged Horowitz and Nishioki on a top-secret project."

Fairchilde interrupted. "Which was to identify individuals possessing this rare genetic trait."

"Exactly. They cross-referenced academic achievement, such as grade point average, with athletic prowess. Using tests on the candidates' saliva, they were able to detect the marker. Those individuals were recruited and trained by the CIA and the special operations arm of the military."

"And," Fairchilde said, "they became the Sleeping Dogs unit."

Zheng smiled triumphantly. "Indeed!"

Fairchilde leaned back in his chair and stared thoughtfully into space for several moments, then said, "So you're telling me that we, you, have the ability to seek out other such individuals."

Zheng nodded.

"There are over a billion Chinese. You should be able to identify and recruit quite a few."

"Sadly, no. This genetic marker is unique to individuals descended from early human ancestors that inhabited Western Europe."

"I don't understand how that can be. One of the Sleeping Dogs is a black man. Another is descended from Eastern European Jews."

"That is correct, but was it so unusual for black slave women to bear children of white plantation masters? And the Jews have been a nation of wanderers for countless generations. It is highly likely that those two men have ancestors who were descended from early Western Europeans."

"But that's still a large universe for us to search. During the Age of Discovery, the French, Spanish, Portuguese, Dutch, and English, among others, spread colonies around the globe."

"True."

"But how do we go about conducting a search? We're talking about a massive geographical area containing countless individuals."

"Ah, but I already have people assigned to it. The search is not as difficult as you think. For the kind of people we would want, there is one sure place to look."

"And that is?"

"Prisons."

CHAPTER 9

SANTA FE

CAROLINA AVILA DIDN'T HAVE classes at the community college that morning. Her mother, Marisol, brought Carolina to her workplace, the New Mexico State Police headquarters at 4491 Cerrillos Road in Santa Fe. Marisol was a twelve-year veteran of the force, the last nine of it in the Special Operations Bureau currently headed by Major Fermin "Frank" Cuellar.

This was Carolina's first visit to her mother's office in all those years. She knew her mom was a good cop, but had no idea how impressive the bureau and its operations were. The walls looked like they had been freshly painted. The floors gleamed as if they had just been cleaned and polished. The staff members were well-groomed and polite. The officers all appeared to be spit and polish cops, just like Marisol. There were no clusters of people gassing near a water cooler. No one was idling or nursing a cup of coffee in the immaculately clean lounge area. There seemed to be a place for everything, and everything seemed to be in its place. The people in motion were moving swiftly and smoothly from one point to another. Those at their desks sat ramrod straight speaking on a phone or working with their computers.

"Is it always like this?" Carolina asked.

"Yes, why do you ask?"

"It's so…it's so…"

"Dynamic?"

"Well…, yes. Everyone is so active, so involved and focused. I don't think I've ever been in a place like this before."

"You're young, *cariña*. You've yet to enter the work world fulltime. It can be a very serious place, especially when it concerns situations as critical as the ones we deal with."

Marisol stopped in front of an open office door. The sign beside the door said "Major F. Cuellar." The room was large, but modestly furnished. There was a desk with only a computer on it. Behind it was a credenza that had a single framed photo of a man, a woman, and two middle school-aged children on it. Two armchairs were positioned in front of the desk, and a bookshelf lined the wall to the right of the entrance. A large, stocky man with close-cropped salt and pepper hair was sitting behind the desk, focused on his computer. He looked like the man in the photo.

"Major Cuellar," Marisol said, "is this a good time?"

The man looked up from his computer and smiled broadly. "Yes. You called earlier, I've been expecting you." He paused then said, "Is this beautiful young lady your daughter?"

Carolina blushed, but her mother merely smiled indulgently, as if she was used to such compliments. Marisol was strikingly beautiful, and Carolina thought she probably did get her share of comments on her looks.

"Carolina, this is my boss, Major Cuellar. He's the head of NMSP's Special Operations Bureau. Yes, Major, this is my daughter Carolina."

"Please, call me Frank," Cuellar said as he stood and shook Carolina's hand. "Your mother has told me many wonderful things about you, but she didn't tell me how beautiful you are. It obviously runs in the family."

Carolina didn't know how to respond, and blushed a deeper shade.

"And," Cuellar said, "I, and so many others in law enforcement, owe you a deep debt of gratitude for helping us identify the terrorists who attacked Los Alamos."

He waved the women to the chairs in front of his desk."

Marisol said, "Actually, this has to do with those terrorists." She turned to Carolina. "Cari, tell Major Cuellar about the phone call."

Cuellar had been sitting back in his chair with a smile on his face. Now, he sat forward and the smile disappeared. "Was it from the same boy? What was his name…Tomás?"

Carolina nodded her head vigorously. "Yes."

"When was this?"

"Yesterday…about two in the afternoon."

"What did he want?"

Carolina hesitated.

"Go ahead, Cari," her mother said firmly.

"Well, he said he was back."

"Back?" Cuellar said. "In Santa Fe?"

"Yes. He said there are five more nuclear bombs. And they'll be detonated somewhere in America."

A shocked look burst across Cuellar 's dark-skinned face. "Did he say where or when?"

"No, he said he didn't know, but thought he could find out."

Cuellar slumped back in his chair and rubbed his chin with his right hand.

His knuckles were scarred and Carolina wondered if he had been a fighter. She thought he looked like he probably had been.

"Why did he tell you this, Carolina?" Cuellar said.

"He said he wanted to atone for what he'd done, that he wanted to speak with the proper authorities." She looked at Marisol. "Mama said you were the one I should tell."

Cuellar looked at Marisol then back at Carolina. "I know this is a tough question, but how did he sound? Sincere or like he was trying to set us up?"

"He…he sounded real…but he *is* a terrorist and a murderer. And he's lied to me in the past."

"How did you leave it with him?"

"He knew about my mom, where she works. I told him I'd ask her what to do."

"What was his reaction to that?"

"He seemed okay with it. He said he'd call again to find out what to do, after I spoke to Mom." She paused momentarily, then said, "If he does, you will arrest him, won't you? He killed my aunt and uncle and so many others. He should be in prison."

Cuellar nodded his head. "I understand your feelings, Carolina. What he did is inexcusably evil, but I don't make the ultimate decisions in a situation like this. It's possible that this 'Tomás' is offering to help us find the other terrorists who have the remaining nukes."

"So, if you don't mind me asking, what will you do with this information?" Marisol said.

"If Tomás does want to turn himself in to cooperate in tracking down the other weapons, I'm inclined at this point to turn him over to a good friend in the FBI."

"Would that be your friend Special Agent Christie?"

"Yes."

"But he was gravely wounded, almost killed in a shootout

with Tomás and the other terrorist. What sort of condition…has he recovered?"

"I spoke with his fiancée the other day. She said he's making excellent progress and should make a full recovery." Cuellar hesitated. "But it's not Mitch I had in mind for the dirty work. He's just a conduit."

Marisol inquisitively arched a perfectly shaped eyebrow. "Are you saying you don't want state or federal authorities involved?"

"It pains me to say this, but my years in law enforcement have taught me that with state or federal agencies this thing could go totally FUBAR in a heartbeat. Even a best-case scenario would mean that years would pass before justice finally was served. But it seems Mitch has a connection with someone who has access to certain 'assets' that can go places and do things that law enforcement cannot."

"Did he say who or what these 'assets' are?" Marisol said with a puzzled expression.

"He said only that they're deadlier than we are capable of imagining. Smarter, faster, stronger than anyone any of us has ever known or heard of. He called them 'the deadliest sonsof-bitches on the planet,' and said they can go anywhere and kill anyone."

CHAPTER 10

BOURBON STREET

NEW ORLEANS WAS NOT much of a tourist town in January once the Sugar Bowl game was over. It was cold, wet, and windy. The town didn't come back to life until Mardi Gras, or Fat Tuesday. The earliest it could roll around was February 3, depending on the date of Easter Sunday in any given year. Large portions of the town were below sea level. Generations of the dead were buried in aboveground crypts because the water table was barely below the surface. A pernicious dampness permeated everything, contributing at times to a malodorous stench that hung over the oldest parts of the town. Mildew, rot, and mold thrived in the environment. It was a popular background for tales of vampires and other gothic horrors. The FBI's Uniform Crime Report revealed the murder rate in New Orleans was many times the national average. According to the report, the city had almost forty victims per one hundred thousand residents.

Daylight hours in New Orleans were in short supply in January while the sun vacationed south of the equator. Business was slower in the bars and clubs along Bourbon Street. The old city seemed to hold its fetid breath, as if saving its energies for the looming madness of Mardi Gras.

Despite being the slow season, the city's most famous venue, the French Quarter, hosted a modest crowd of party-seekers. It's main drag, Bourbon Street, housed a seemingly endless collection of seedy bars, strip clubs, souvenir shops, and other assorted tourist traps, as well as the occasional landmark.

Marc Kirkland sat at a small table in the corner of one of those bars. He was flirting with a cocktail waitress who was dressed like a high school cheerleader in a tight blouse and short, pleated skirt. The blouse was unbuttoned to her waist and her ample cleavage was well displayed. A name tag said "Delilah." She appeared to have lived about thirty rough years, but was still comely.

Simultaneously with the conversation, Kirkland took in everything and everyone in the place. There were thirty-three people in the bar including two bartenders, three cocktail waitresses, and one bouncer who was leaning against the wall just inside the doorway. The customers were mostly men. Like Kirkland, a few of them were loners, but many were in groups of two or three. There were two couples with dazed looks on their faces as if they had no idea what they were doing in the place. Blaring background music alternated between New Orleans blues and Dixieland jazz.

Kirkland saw one of the bartenders glaring in Delilah's direction and nodded toward him. "The barkeep looks unhappy that you're spending so much time talking with me."

She glanced at the man and shrugged. "Screw him. It's a slow night. Besides, he has the hots for me and gets jealous when I spend time with a fine lookin' man like you." She spoke with a modest drawl. Given that she'd told Kirkland she was from Ohio, he assumed it was affected.

He didn't like attracting attention, and held up his glass. "Maybe it would be a good idea if you brought me another beer."

She leaned over and took the glass, giving him a close-up view of her breasts. "Sure, I'll be right back," she said and flashed him a sexy smile that resonated in his crotch. *Tonight, was going to be fun.*

Delilah sashayed toward the service section of the bar, as Kirkland's eyes followed the gentle swing of her hips. He felt one of his two cellphones vibrate in a pants pocket. It was the special one, the one that was used only by Cliff Levell.

He fished it out and said, "I'm about to get laid, Cliff. Don't do anything that will spoil it."

On the other end of the call, Levell chuckled. "I thought you were celibate, a spiritual soul who was above the temptations of the flesh."

"That won't happen as long as I'm breathing. If not longer."

"I hate to throw cold water on your hoped-for intimacies, but I need you and Stensen now."

"Now? Right now, not a couple of hours from now?" There was a touch of irritation in Kirkland's voice.

"Yes, right fucking now!"

"Why Nick and me? Why not one or more of the other Dogs? Shit, Cliff, I haven't been laid in a while."

"Because you two are the ones closest to where I need you to be. And why isn't Stensen with you? What the fuck's he doing wandering around the French Quarter?"

"Maybe he is here with me."

"Alright, wiseass, then let me speak to him."

"Maybe he went to take a leak."

"You're sitting in a dive in the six hundred block of Bourbon Street, and Stensen's in a seedy apartment three-and-a-half blocks away at St. Louis and Burgundy Streets."

It never ceased to amaze Kirkland and the other Dogs that Levell always seemed to know exactly where each of them was at any given time. Kirkland was the most technologically savvy of them all. He'd taken the special phone apart on several occasions, but had never found any locator or tracing device. He, Thomas, and Whelan had speculated that the Old Man, as they referred to Levell affectionately, had had some sort of device implanted in each of the Dogs many years earlier when they were being trained to become the deadliest black ops unit on the planet.

"Why don't you just call Nick on his 'special' phone? We've all got one."

"Because the sonofabitch never answers."

"Well, I can't help you there." Looking up, Kirkland saw Delilah heading his way with a fresh beer. He held an index finger up to signal that he needed a moment, then pointed at the phone.

He shifted gears with Levell. "What the hell's so important that you need Nick and me to jump right on it?"

"First, you tell me what Stensen's doing at that apartment."

"Maybe he's getting laid, too."

"My information says the person who lives there is Leonie Fontenot, the former wife of Paul Fontenot."

"Really?"

"Don't play dumb with me, Kirkland. You, Stensen, and the other Dogs were tight with Paul. He was one of your martial arts instructors. When his little hot pants wife got tired of cheating on Paul and dumped him, he lost his edge. Ultimately, it got him killed. I figured it was only a matter of time before one of you… most likely Stensen, avenged Paul."

Kirkland didn't like where the discussion was going. "Nick

doesn't share his agenda with me. More to the point, you owe me an explanation. What's the purpose of this call?"

"One of our own, Quentin Thomas, is in deep shit about an hour's drive from where you are. He needs your help, and he needs it fast."

CHAPTER 11

YANASU, ALASKA

Chapter 11—Yanasu, Alaska

JAKE MULLALLY STOOD at the window in his second-floor office that overlooked the makeshift village square below. The world outside was green and white, a typical January day in Alaska's Chugach Mountains. His attention was focused on an octagonal structure in the middle of the square. It was open to the elements, its sides made of chain-link fencing that enclosed an elevated platform. The canvas that covered the platform was stained with the blood of men who had fought and, on occasion, died there.

The fights were one of Yanasu's two claims to notoriety. The other was its reputation as the worst place to live in Alaska, a state renowned for having an exceptionally large number of towns commonly deemed dangerous and miserable places. The FBI's Uniform Crime Report, which summarized the number of property crimes and violent crimes in each city per year, listed

Alaska as the only state with a rate over six hundred violent crimes per one hundred thousand residents. And the mining village of Yanasu was the worst of them all. It had the highest rates in the state for murder, violent crime, school dropouts, and poverty. Not surprisingly, it also had the roughest bars in the state. Many surmised that the absence of females in the area only compounded the pervasive misery.

Mullally watched the workmen making the final adjustments to the fencing. It had to be able to resist the force of the bodies that would be slamming into it later that night. He swelled with pride as he congratulated himself for having created the concept of the Baddest Badass competition. As he'd hoped, it brought needed money to the town in the form of fans, many from far away, who traveled to Yanasu each month to witness the blood-iest spectacle on any continent. The crowds were steadily growing larger. The temporary facilities meant to house them were giving way to a hotel currently under construction. Best of all, ticket sales were increasing rapidly.

His assistant, a short, pudgy man with a failed comb-over of gray-brown hair, stepped into the doorway. "Does everything look ready for tonight?" he said.

Mullally turned away from the window. "Seems to be. What's the latest head count for the fighters?"

"Eighteen so far. One or two more could show up unan-nounced or not show up at all. That's happened before."

"Just as long as Kruchinkin is here."

"He wouldn't miss, I'm sure. After all he's the defending champion and undefeated since he first showed up."

"He's the main draw. A brutal sonofabitch, most people want to see him get his ass kicked."

"I don't like to watch the fights," the assistant said. "But from what I've heard, there's not much chance that will happen."

Mullally shrugged. "Never can tell. Any local boys? They're usually crowd favorites."

"A couple of them, but the audience keeps coming from farther and farther away as word spreads."

"Anyone special?"

The assistant paused then said, "There is an Asian guy here, a spectator. Seems to be involved with the Chinese government."

"And you know that...how?"

"He's staying at the boarding house my cousin runs. Waldo saw his passport when he checked in. Actually, every place in the area is full, doubled up in most cases."

Mullally smiled as he thought of the potential gate. "The fighters come from all over, too."

His assistant bobbed his head. "Tonight, we have a Turk, that Russian, Kruchinkin, an Egyptian, the usual contingent from the Lower Forty-Eight, as well as a Brit and an Aussie. Plus, there's a mystery man."

"What do you mean?"

"He didn't list a nationality or a home base."

"Maybe he has something to hide. What name did he use?"

"Just Sven. I don't know if it's a first name or a last."

SVEN LARSEN HAD BEEN LIVING with a smoldering anger fueled by a need he would never be able to fulfill. But that didn't stop him from trying. It was what had brought him to the oddly named town of Yanasu. He'd learned earlier that day that it was a corruption of the Tlingit words *ya-naa* (dead) and *xóots* (brown bear). It was an odd place, not really a town, more like a collection of small placer mining operations in an area with a total population of twenty-five hundred rugged, dangerous souls. To reach it, one had to fly about two hundred fifty miles southeast from Anchorage to the thirty-five-hundred-foot gravel airstrip in McCarthy. From there it was a bone-jarring sixty-mile ride deep into the Chugach Mountains on twisting, rutted mud and gravel roads in a four-wheel drive vehicle. For those able to meet the price, helicopter service was available from McCarthy. The choppers were used to haul the mined gold to the airstrip in McCarthy. Ground transportation invited certain hijacking of the precious ore. In fact, the fifty-five-gallon drums used to haul the gold by chopper usually arrived a few pounds lighter than when they had left Yanasu.

Larsen had heard about Yanasu's monthly no-rules, winner-take-all fights. He fully expected to win, but that wasn't what brought him here. Money wasn't an issue. He had always earned substantial sums on missions for Cliff Levell and the Society of Adam Smith, and he still could if he chose to. Instead, he had come here to kill a man, someone who deserved to die, a cold-blooded killer who had caused misery and sorrow for countless people. This man actually was a stand-in for a person Larsen couldn't kill because that person was already dead. The fact that his intended victim was still alive was testament to the man's ruthless nature and innate toughness. Larsen had no doubts that this man expected to win tonight, and likely would cripple or kill some of the other contestants in doing so. *But the sonofabitch has never met anyone like me.* Larsen smiled his bad smile, the one that caused brave, strong men to lose sphincter control. His other smile, the good one, merely caused women and children to faint. With any luck, maybe this time Larsen would be able to exorcise his own demons.

It turned out that there were sixteen competitors. One contestant had been injured in a training session the previous day, and one had changed his mind about entering the Octagon. That made it easy for Mullally to organize the fight into eight preliminary bouts. The survivors became quarter-finalists. Those four qualified for the semis, and the two winners would fight for the prize—one-hundred-thousand dollars. But more importantly, the winner would be deemed the Baddest Badass on the Planet. At least until the next month's fight.

Sergei Kruchinkin had first entered the now-famous Yanasu Octagon two years ago. Since then he'd returned every month to defend his title. In the process, he'd seriously injured most of his opponents, even killed a few. It was these exploits that had quickly propelled the Baddest Badass competition to major event status on cable television. The programming head at a previously obscure network heard about it on a hunting trip near the old Kennecott mines close to McCarthy. He'd checked it out and, although personally shocked by the violence, saw the potential. As the show's popularity had grown, so had Kruchinkin's notoriety. Eventually, reports surfaced that his day job was that of chief enforcer for several Russian billionaires, each one the czar of a major industry in Putin's Russia. Larsen heard about Kruchinkin and that was all it took for him to come to Yanasu.

Kruchinkin sounded like exactly the man he'd been looking for; more than that, exactly the man he needed. Larsen was virtually consumed with anger and a huge measure of shame. He had failed at only one thing in his life. It had been the most important one and the failure haunted him hour by hour, night and day. Redemption wasn't something he desired, it was mandatory. Without it, he had no will to live. He had been existing on a day-to-day basis ever since he and Brendan Whelan had been defeated and nearly killed by Maksym Kozak. That wasn't supposed to have been possible. Whelan and Larsen were unique beings, genetic freaks—faster, stronger, smarter than ordinary human beings. The two of them should have been able to handle

Maksym, even though they had been nursing wounds from a recent gun battle in Doha. But they didn't and Maksym had actually toyed with them before Andrei Ulyanin unexpectedly shot him. If not for Ulyanin, Larsen and Whelan wouldn't be alive today.

Initially, Larsen had expected to go one-on-one with Maksym and kill him with his bare hands. Even among Whelan and the other Sleeping Dogs—Thomas, Kirkland, Stensen, Stone, and Almeida—he had always been the most powerful. But Maksym had also been a genetic freak, and somehow better.

Maksym had killed Larsen's entire family. A thirst for vengeance had driven him for more than a year. He had wanted nothing more than to rip Maksym into small pieces. Now, he not only had to endure the shame of having been bested by the man, but Ulyanin's act had robbed him of any opportunity for a second chance. And then, he'd heard about Kruchinkin. The Russian certainly had proved he was a powerful and dangerous fighter, but he was no Maksym, no genetic freak. What he was, however, was a vicious and cruel thug who enjoyed killing for his Moscow employers as well as in the Octagon. It was finding and punishing people like Kruchinkin that gave Larsen a reason to live.

ANY FIGHTING COMPETITION that was designed to end in the serious disabling or killing of a contestant was challenging enough. But it was January in Alaska and the fights were held outdoors. The competitors were required to fight bare knuckled and bare-chested. The area had a subarctic coastal climate which caused the weather to be moderate in comparison with the Alaskan interior. But the Chugach Mountains forced the westerly winds off the North Pacific upwards, cooling the air mass and causing clouds and precipitation. This resulted in greater snowfall in the Chugach than anywhere else in the world, an annual average that exceeded six hundred inches. It made for long, snowy winters that weren't particularly cold. The average high for January was at or just below freezing.

The lands on which the fights were held, along with the mining interests, were owned by the Chugach Alaska Corporation, or CAC, one of thirteen Alaska Native Regional Corporations. It owned all of the surface and subsurface or mineral rights; thus, the fights were under tribal jurisdiction. Otherwise, the laws of the State of Alaska or the federal government might have prohibited the competition. The tribe provided security for the events and participated with Jake Mullally in the gate receipts and payments received from the cable network that broadcast the fights.

Before the evening's elimination matches had been set, Mullally made it a point to check out this mysterious one-named man, Sven. What he saw impressed him, and he'd seen a lot of large, powerful men since he'd started the Baddest Badass competition. The man who had impressed him the most was Sergei Kruchinkin. But this Sven character was packed with even more muscle than the Russian. In fact, his trapezius, deltoid, and scalene muscles were so large and dense that he appeared not to have a neck. His head seemed to sit squarely on his massive shoulders.

Going on his promoter's instinct, Mullally had arranged the draws so that Sven and Kruchinkin were in separate brackets and would not meet until the finals. He had seen the Russian in the Octagon enough times to realize that he wasn't like ordinary humans. Something told him that Larsen wasn't either. If things went as he expected, their match should easily surpass anything yet. He even suspected there could be a new champ before the night was over. *Think of what that would do for the ratings!*

THERE WERE NO RULES, no trainers or cornermen, no rounds. Each fight lasted uninterruptedly until one of the competitors was tossed over the Octagon's eight-foot high sides, disabled beyond the ability to continue, or killed. The preliminaries went as expected. Kruchinkin and Larsen easily dispensed with their opponents in the rounds of eight and four. The nature of the fighting notwithstanding, Larsen had dealt humanely with his first two opponents. Moving methodically, if not particularly swiftly, he had simply picked up each of the large men as if they were rag dolls and slung them over the chain-link fencing into the crowd. Neither man had suffered serious injuries. The crowd had booed Larsen's efforts. They were used to maiming and worse.

Kruchinkin, on the other hand, had toyed with his challengers like cat's-paws, eventually snapping the spine of the first one and crushing the skull of the second one with repeated blows to the head. The man had died in the Octagon, sending the crowd into a frenzy of bloodlust.

Now it was time for the championship match. The fighters faced each other waiting for Mullally's signal to engage. Larsen looked around the crowd. The TV cameras had been strategically placed so as to not miss a drop of blood. The air was filled with the screams of the crowd and the smells of whiskey, tobacco smoke, and the sweet odor of cannabis. Sitting in the front row was a large, well-dressed Asian man. He sat calmly and straight, almost rigid, his expression impassive, as if oblivious to the closeness of the crowd, the noise, and the cold. From his bearing, Larsen suspected the man had a military background.

It was a little past nine p.m., Alaska Standard Time and the temperature in Yanasu was five degrees above zero and dropping. Large snowflakes had begun to fall. The contestants in the Baddest Badass competition were restricted to wearing only a pair of tight Lycra shorts: no shirts, footwear, gloves, or headgear. The purpose of the rule was to encourage them to fight like hell in order to generate heat as well as to end the fight as quickly as possible. Only Kruchinkin seemed to enjoy prolonging the matches. He mugged for the TV cameras.

Mullally, sitting in an elevated chair and wrapped in a thick fur coat signaled for the action to begin. Kruchinkin had watched Larsen's previous two matches and assumed he wasn't particularly quick. The Russian charged him with speed that few had seen in a human. But Larsen had seen it. Still, he wasn't expecting it from anyone who wasn't a member of the Sleeping Dogs. It caught him by surprise as Kruchinkin rammed a shoulder into his ribcage, drove him into the fencing, and wrapped his arms around the neckless man in an effort to break his spine.

Larsen had other plans. He slammed the palms of his thick hands mightily against the sides of Kruchinkin's head. Momentarily stunned, the Russian's knees buckled slightly. Larsen head-butted Kruchinkin then jammed his knee forcefully into his groin. The Russian sagged to the canvas, his face beginning to bleed profusely. Though freezing, Larsen was in no hurry to finish the Russian. He had come too far, waited too long. He wanted to savor his exorcism.

Kruchinkin climbed painfully to his feet, a puzzled look on his face, as if he couldn't understand what had happened to him. He began to move slowly around the Octagon in a clockwise direction. Larsen, standing in the middle, watched him with a look of disinterest on his face. Eventually, Kruchinkin began to move toward the neckless man. He appeared to be staggering slightly. He reached out tentatively with his left hand, as if trying lamely to engage his opponent.

Larsen moved almost casually to swat it out of the way, but Kruchinkin suddenly yanked the arm back, swiftly stepped forward, and grabbed Larsen's wrist with his right hand. Adding his left hand to the grip, he yanked Larsen's arm up and around. It caused Larsen to rotate backward in the air to avoid having his shoulder dislocated. He landed heavily on his back and managed to roll to his left to avoid the Russian's foot, which was aimed at his head. Even so, the blow caught him on the shoulder with such force it temporarily went numb. The already deafening noise of the crowd increased several decibels.

Larsen sprang to his feet and backed away from the Russian, rubbing his injured shoulder with his good hand, trying to restore feeling. He wasn't cold anymore. In fact, he was beginning to sweat.

His opponent was moving toward him, a sneer on his bloodied face. One of the benefits of the Octagon was the absence of corners. There was no place for an opponent to trap you unless you foolishly backed against one of the eight sides. Larsen kept circling as feeling began to return to his shoulder.

No one had ever hurt Kruchinkin, let alone bested him. The look in his eyes said he wasn't going to let it happen tonight. He began to move directly at Larsen, who continued to move, first one way then the other. His face was expressionless. The crowd screamed at the Russian to finish him. Seemingly responding to their encouragement, Kruchinkin faked a sudden dash at Larsen, who ignored it. The second time, it wasn't a fake and with a snarl the Russian leapt at his opponent. But Larsen was faster. He met him halfway and delivered a devastating right hook to Kruchinkin's solar plexus. Stunned, temporarily unable to breathe, the Russian staggered backward.

Larsen instantly pursued him, grabbing him by the neck with his left hand and almost crushing it. He lifted Kruchinkin until his feet were off the mat. The Russian clawed desperately at the offending hand, his eyes beginning to bulge. Larsen drove an enormous punch into Kruchinkin's ribcage, snapping a couple of ribs. The crowd went completely silent.

For a moment, there were no sounds at all. Then three gunshots rang out.

CHAPTER 12

RAPHAEL, MISSISSIPPI

THE BLOOD DRIPPED STEADILY from Quentin Thomas's smashed nose. His eyes were swollen almost shut. His lips were split open in a couple of places and his tongue told him a few of his teeth had been loosened. The savagery of the beating had driven him briefly unconscious on three occasions, but he was awake now and acutely aware of the pain. It wasn't just his face and head that ached. His ribs, shoulders, arms and legs had been battered by crazies wielding baseball bats.

He was tightly bound, hand and foot, by chains to a heavy metal chair. Thomas was an exceptionally strong man, a physical freak, and had tried to break free from the restraints. With a growing sense of dread, he realized it wasn't going to happen.

Thomas raised his head as best he could and squinted though the slits formed by his swollen eyelids. He thought, from the surroundings, he was in some kind of basement or cellar. It was damp and cold, and had a musty-sour smell from the greenish mold thriving on the wet walls. The floor and walls were unfinished and the ceiling was supported by bare, cobwebbed beams.

A half-dozen light bulbs dangled from electric cords. On the far side of the room, a rail-less set of steps led up to a doorway. He turned his head slowly, painfully and apprised his situation. He counted a dozen men in the room and heard the voices of at least a few more behind him. The ones he could see looked like the same men that had been in the saloon. All wore jeans and most wore long-sleeved flannel shirts. Many of them had ball caps bearing the logos of various farm or construction implement manufacturers. Work boots seemed to be the most popular choice in footwear. The ones that still had hair wore it long and oily-looking. To a man, they had scraggly, unkempt beards.

"Hey, looka heah," one of them said, pointing to Thomas. "The darky done come to."

Eddie Jack lumbered into Thomas's view, a dark scowl on his scarred face. He hauled back and threw a punch at Thomas, who dipped his chin down at the last moment. The giant's knuckles slammed painfully into the top of the victim's forehead, and Thomas saw flashing lights for a few seconds.

"Ow, goddam, that nigra done that on purpose." He yanked a bat out of the hands of another man and raised it high above his head.

"Now, you just hold on there, Eddie Jack. First off, we don't take the Lord's name in vain. That there is sacrilegious. And second, we don't wanna go and kill this sonofabitch just yet. He ain't nearly paid for the sins of his black brethren."

Slowly, begrudgingly, the giant lowered the bat, finally flinging it in anger at the wall on the other side of the room.

Through teeth clenched in pain, Thomas, in a voice that was barely more than a croak, said, "What sins?"

The man who had spoken to Eddie Jack didn't answer immediately. He walked slowly around from behind Thomas and stood in front of him.

"We talkin' about all them innocent white women you nigras done raped over the years. Somebody got to pay for that."

Thomas shook his head slowly. The motion sent bolts of pain shooting through his skull. He took a deep breath and slowly said, "What the hell's the matter with you people? I've never raped anyone. No one I know has raped anyone. What you're doing here violates federal and Mississippi laws. Are you living in the Dark Ages?"

One of the other men said, "Get rid of all the darkies, they won't be no Dark Ages. Ain't that right, Preacher?"

The man standing in front of Thomas said, "That is right, son."

"Preacher? You're a man of God?" Thomas said.

"Indeed, I am and damn proud of it. I done brought the word of the Gospel to all these heah folks. Done showed them the error of their ways, and saved them and their loved ones from hellfire and damnation."

"By teaching them to kill other people?"

"Not other *people*. Nigras."

Thomas's anger overrode much of the pain. "You're all bat shit crazy. Black people are no different than the rest of you. We're citizens, patriots, hard-working, just trying to achieve the same things you are."

"That ain't true. None of *us* wants to rape a *black* woman. Ain't that right boys?"

There was a chorus of "Yeahs and Amens."

Thomas was silent for a few moments. "So, you're all planning to kill me only because my skin color is different from yours?"

"Nah," Preacher said. "We gonna kill you because you nigras ain't even human." That brought cheers and guffaws from the others.

Thomas shook his head slowly, painfully. "Did it ever occur to you that you're all going to be arrested for murder and spend the rest of your lives in prison? How is that going to help your families?"

"There ain't gonna be no arrests," a voice said from the back of the room. The speaker walked forward and stopped beside the Preacher.

Thomas was shocked to see that the man wore a badge and uniform.

"This heah is Sheriff Crosley. He's the *only* law in this heah neck of the woods," Preacher said with wide grin. "Now, what was you sayin' 'bout prison?"

"You people just don't get it. When I don't show up for my sister's wedding in Gulfport tomorrow, she'll alert the authorities. In addition, I told the man I work for about my car problems and he directed me here. Bottom line is that the feds will get involved and they'll put pressure on everyone around here, including the ones in this room. Sooner or later, someone is going to break and give the rest of you up to save his own ass. The feds will find what's left of me and send all of you away for the rest of your lives."

The shit-eating grin was still on the Preacher's face, only wider. "Well, do tell. That there is a real interestin' story. For a fairytale. Truth is none of these ol' boys is gonna say shit to nobody. Them there feds will be lucky not to end up like you're gonna. It ain't like yore the first nigra we ever done this to."

"Shit, boy, you jes' one of many," the sheriff said. "Over the years we done kilt a dozen of y'all, maybe more'n that."

Thomas's face scrunched up in confusion. "I don't get it. Why are you doing these things? Hate crimes are at the top of federal law enforcement and prosecutors' lists. How do you get away with it?"

"Pretty simple. We do it 'cause it needs doin'. This damn country has gone communist and pro-fag. White people built this here country, and now we're treated worse than second class citizens. Shit, America ain't even a shadow of what it once was. Somebody got to fight back, and that's what we doin'."

"So, all the black men you've killed over the years and no traces of them have ever been found? Yet?"

"Yeah," the sheriff said, "there ain't never anythin' left to find."

A cold chill spread through Thomas. "Why is that?"

The Preacher turned to Eddie Jack. "You wanna tell 'em 'bout Ol' Hitler?"

Now it was the giant's turn to grin. It was filled with pure malevolence. "Yeah, I'll tell 'em." He leaned his bulk down and brought his face to within inches of Thomas's.

"We got us a gator down to Stump Crick. Biggest ol' motherfucker anybody ever seen. Got to be eighteen foot and more'n a thousand pounds. Sumbitch is always hungry."

"And," Preacher said, "he don't ever leave no leftovers."

CHAPTER 13

BOURBON STREET

A BLOCK further down Bourbon Street from the bar where Kirkland was flirting with Delilah, the cocktail waitress, a dark-haired, hard-looking but attractive woman rounded the corner from St. Louis Street. Smoking a cigarette, she strode purposefully north in the five hundred block of Bourbon Street. The sidewalk was littered and uneven, paved with red bricks. The ancient and narrow street was lined with tired three- and four-story buildings adorned with ornate wrought iron balconies. Seedy-looking bars and lounges occupied the ground floors of most of the buildings.

The woman's walk was as provocative as her attire. Despite the cold weather, she wore a very short black skirt and tight ivory sweater with a steeply plunging neckline. Her breasts were large and mostly on display. Fishnet stockings, a black leather purse slung over one shoulder on a long strap, and black shoes with six-inch stiletto heels completed her dress. The casual observer might assume she was a hooker trolling for her next john.

Midway up the next block, the woman entered a bar. She

smiled at the bouncer and ran her hand slowly across the front of his pants on her way inside. He shook his head and smiled. "Nice to see you too, Leonie."

Inside, the bar was purposely kept very dark to hide its indiscretions as well as those of its patrons. It stank of decades of cheap whisky, tobacco, rot, and stale human odors. The woman took a seat at the midway point of the scarred bar that spanned most of the back of the room. It was her favorite spot. From it, she could survey the entire room. She looked around. Tonight, there was a young couple at a table, obviously tourists visiting the city during one of the cheapest times of the year. Two old men sat at another table, nursing their drinks and ogling the young waitresses wearing little more than two pasties and a skimpy thong. A chanteuse with a worn-out voice was trying to sound enthusiastic about the rock songs she was bruising. Not only had her voice seen better days, but so had her body and the low-cut, short shimmery cocktail dress that stretched over it. On raised platforms on either side of the room, bored-looking topless women gyrated listlessly around slim metal poles.

The bartender, a thin, dark man with bad teeth, a pencil mustache and a receding hairline, walked up and leaned toward her over the bar. "'Evenin', Leonie." He looked her up and down, his eyes coming to rest on her cleavage. "You're looking good tonight. I get off at two. Wanna play?"

She hid her disinterest well. "No thanks, Sugah. I plan to get off well before then." She smiled slyly.

The bartender nodded. "Well, if things don't go the way you planned, keep my offer in mind. I'll show you a real good time." He winked. "The usual?" She nodded and he wandered down the bar to make her cocktail.

Leonie was aware of movement beside her. She turned to her

right and smiled provocatively at the tall, muscular man taking a seat on the stool next to hers. He returned her smile.

"Hi, Sugah, I'm Leonie." She held her hand out coyly. The stranger was handsome in a rugged way. She turned up the wattage in her smile.

The man took her hand, squeezed it gently and held it for a moment longer than usual. She liked it. Their eyes locked and he said, "I'm Tom."

Tom appeared to be in his late thirties, with short, darkish blond hair and long sideburns and a mustache. He was wearing jeans, running shoes and a gray sweatshirt. And, despite the darkness of the room, he was wearing sunglasses.

"I haven't seen y'all in heah before, Tom. Where y'all from?"

The bartender returned with Leonie's Bourbon and Branch and set it on a small cocktail napkin in front of her. He stared sullenly at Tom. "What's it gonna be, pal?"

"A Restoration ale," Tom said. He turned on his stool and faced Leonie, his right arm resting on the bar. She reached over and put her hand on top of his and began gently stroking it.

"So, Tom," she said, "are y'all wearin' them sunglasses 'cause you got an eye problem or you jes' tryin' to be cool?" She was smiling when she said it.

He laughed easily. "A little bit of both, I guess."

The bartender returned and put the bottle of beer down in front of Tom hard enough to slop a small amount on the bar. He didn't offer a glass or a cocktail napkin. "You payin' for hers too?" He nodded at Leonie.

"Yeah, I'll take care of it."

"Twenty bucks," the bartender said.

Tom peeled off two tens and a five from a roll in his pocket and laid them on the bar. "Use the change to buy yourself a better attitude."

"You sonofa…," the bartender started to say. He cut it short when he saw the look on Tom's face. He scooped up the bills and retreated to the far end of the bar.

"You're funny," Leonie said. "I like that in a man." She drank the remaining swallow in her glass and said, "This place is kinda' expensive. Why don't we go back to my place and get to know each other better?"

"Stole the words right out of my mouth," Tom said.

They left the bar and strolled hand in hand on their way to Leonie's apartment a few blocks away.

"Tell me about yourself, Leonie. Where are you from? What brought you to the Big Easy? You know, the whole life story thing." Tom said.

She tilted her head back and ran her free hand through her thick, dark hair. "There's not much to tell. Ah' grew up over in Houma, 'bout fifty miles from heah. Shitty little hick town. Nothing much for a girl to do there but find her a guy, get married and have a shit load of screamin' little brats."

"Sounds pretty bad. How much of all that did you do?"

"I got to the married part, but it wasn't for me. God put me on this earth to have fun." She looked at him. "Fun means men. God, I love men!"

"So, you're saying you weren't exactly faithful to your husband."

"Sugah, I managed to be cool for most of the first year, but after that I tried not to miss a single opportunity."

"Did your husband catch you?"

"Naw, he always kinda suspected, but he didn't really wanna know. Funny thing is, he was the prize catch of that little hick town. Marine war hero in that shit in the Middle East. Good lookin'. Smart. Pretty much everything most girls would want."

"But not you?"

Her voice took on a tinge of a whine. "He didn't pay 'nuff attention to me. Spent all his time teaching martial arts in that *dojo* of his." She paused and said, "That's one of them karate places."

"I know. Did you ever talk to him about your needs, Leonie?"

"Shit, a lot of good that woulda done. He was always wore out from that *dojo*. And besides, I was getting' all the lovin' I could handle from jes' about everybody else in town."

"I take it he wasn't the one who wanted the divorce."

"No, Sugah, that was mah idea. I needed out of that damn town. I needed to enjoy life to the fullest." She paused then said, almost wistfully, "He shore was a helluva guy, though. A nicer, gentler, more kindhearted man than you could find jes' about anywhere."

"How do you suppose this affected him?"

"How do ya think, Sugah? The poor man was devastated. Practically gave his *dojo* away and went to work up north some-where for an old Marine Corps friend."

They reached her place, a small apartment on a corner above a boarded up former grocery store. The building was faced with rough red bricks. A rather plain wrought iron railed balcony ran along the two street sides of the building.

As she was unlocking the door, Tom said, "Do you ever miss him?"

"Who?"

"Your former husband."

"No. He's dead. Got hisself killed playin' bodyguard." She opened the door lock. "I don't wanna talk about Paul, my ex, no more. Ah jest wanna get to know *you*, Sugah,…real intimate. You know what ah mean?"

When they were inside, she said, "Wanna drink or somethin', Sugah?"

"No, Leonie. Right now all I want is you."

"That's mah man," she said with a squeal of delight. She gently removed his sunglasses. "You won't need these in heah." She looked at his eyes. The brilliant, glacial blue immediately appealed to her.

"Mah," she said, "yore eyes are jes' beautiful. I only seen eyes like them once before. On a gorgeous hunk named Whelan. He was tall and muscular like you. You any relation?"

Tom shook his head. "Never heard of him."

There was something even more unusual about Tom's eyes; there seemed to be tiny red dots in their centers. The unusual excited Leonie, and this was no exception.

In moments, they were undressed and standing at the foot of her bed. She pressed her full breasts against his chest and tried to kiss him, but he moved his head away. "Plenty of time for that in the afterglow," he said. "I just really want you. Turn around."

Leonie turned, leaned over, and rested her elbows on her bed. She spread her feet wide apart on the scuffed hardwood, and waited excitedly for him to enter her. Instead, he put his left hand on the back of her head and his right hand around her chin. With a sudden powerful twist, he snapped her neck. Her lifeless body collapsed in a loose heap. Like none of her bones were connected.

For the next hour, the killer carefully scrubbed the scene. In his stocking feet and wearing thin rubber gloves, he vacuumed the areas where he had been and wiped down the few places he'd touched. He had been careful not to exchange saliva, semen or other body fluids with her. When he was through, he put the disposable vacuum bag in a plastic grocery sack that he withdrew from one of his pockets.

Before leaving, he stood over Leonie's corpse. "Paul Fontenot was a friend of mine; a good man. He deserved a lot better. Because of you, he put himself in harm's way and it got him killed."

He stepped off the carpet at the top of the stairs, and put his shoes on at the bottom. With the rag he'd used upstairs, he opened the door and stepped out into the quiet, deserted street. He took the rag and the plastic bag that held the vacuumed hairs and fibers with him.

Closing the door softly behind him, he casually strolled away. Within minutes, Nick Stensen had vanished into the dark, wet night.

CHAPTER 14

YANASU, ALASKA

WHEN THE SHOTS WERE FIRED, Larsen instinctively dropped into a crouch, his left hand still clamped around Kruchinkin's throat in a death grip. Like all of the Dogs, his sensory perceptions were more acute than those of Norms. His ears told him the shots had come from behind him and to the left. Was it some drunk celebrating the outcome of the fight? Or someone trying to alter it?

He turned to look in the direction the shots had come from. When he did, the Russian managed to kick him in the side of the head. Hard. Momentarily stunned, Larsen lost his grip on the man's throat, and Kruchinkin struggled to crawl to the section of the fencing that also served as a gate to let contestants into and out of the Octagon. He didn't get there. Larsen sprang on him, focusing his two hundred sixty-five pounds on his right knee as he landed on the small of the Russian's back. The sound of extreme pain exploded from Kruchinkin's mouth. Larsen flipped him over and locked his legs around Kruchinkin's waist. He wrapped his right arm around the man's neck, locking his throat in the area between his mountainous bicep and thick forearm, and squeezed.

Kruchinkin thrashed wildly on the mat and clawed desperately at Larsen's arm. It did him no good. Larsen wrapped his left hand around his right wrist and pulled the hold tighter and tighter. Despite the noise, both men were oblivious to the raucous activities around them. Just as the Russian began to lose consciousness, the gate to the Octagon burst open and several armed men rushed in, surrounding the two combatants. Some of the men wore Alaska State Trooper uniforms and carried Colt AR-15A4 rifles, others carried Remington 870 shotguns. There were other men with guns, but they were wearing heavy jackets with the initials "IRS" on the back. Some carried M&P15s, the Smith & Wesson version of the AR-15 semi-automatic rifle. Others had Remington 870s.

The IRS agents seemed to be in charge. One of them, a tall, lean man with thick salt and pepper hair, pointed his M&P15 at Larsen and said, "Release that man, spread out on the mat, and stretch your hands out in front of you."

Larsen, wearing only Lycra shorts, was suddenly aware of the cold. He swiftly weighed his options. There really weren't any, so he followed the man's orders.

Kruchinkin had rolled over and climbed to his hands and knees. He was struggling to breathe. The man gave him the same order. When he was slow to comply, a large state trooper put a foot on his butt and shoved him.

At the same moment, two additional IRS agents entered the Octagon with a handcuffed Jake Mullally between them.

He was in a belligerent mood. "I demand to know what authority you have to arrest me and interrupt the entertainment."

"Two answers, smart guy. First, you've never paid federal taxes on the income generated by this...entertainment. That constitutes evasion of taxes. Second, as the state troopers will soon advise you, you failed to obtain a concert promoters license as required by the statutes and regulations of the State of Alaska."

"That's bullshit! These are Indian lands. You don't have any fuckin' jurisdiction here! I demand you release me immediately; otherwise, I'm gonna sue the livin' shit out of you and everyone else involved in this fuckin' travesty."

The tall IRS agent shook his head and said, "U.S. citizens are subject to all U.S. laws even if they also have tribal citizenship, which you don't. In addition, most Indian land is held in trust by the United States. Federal law regulates the political and economic rights of tribal governments." He stared at Mullally for a long moment then said, "You can save anything else you've got to say for your arraignment. He motioned to the two troopers to remove Mullally.

"What about me?" Larsen said, teeth clenched against the bitter chill. "Other than participating as a contestant, I don't have anything to do with this fight business."

The tall man looked at him and said, "As far as I know, the federal government has no particular interest in you. You'll probably be released, but that call ultimately is up to the Staties."

"In the meantime, I'm freezing my ass off out here."

The IRS agent motioned to one of his agents. "Take him inside somewhere so he can find some clothes."

"What about him?" Larsen pointed to Kruchinkin.

The tall man looked long and hard at the Russian. "As I understand it, he has a reputation for killing men in these 'contests.' I think the State of Alaska may have some issues with him, but he's not my concern." He turned and walked away.

An agent led Larsen toward a wooden storefront across from the Octagon. Wading through calf-deep fresh snow encouraged

Larsen to move quickly, too quickly for the agent. He pointed his M&P15 at the barefoot man and said, "What's your rush?"

Larsen forced himself to slow down, but said nothing. Instead, he made a mental note to beat the man within an inch of his life if the chance ever presented itself.

Little more than an hour later, the tall IRS agent returned and officially released Larsen with the admonition that he make himself available, if needed, to testify in proceedings against Mullally and his operation.

"What about that big Russian guy?" Larsen said.

"Krushev? Krushinsky?"

"Yeah, him."

The agent shrugged. "The Staties may consider him a person of interest, but they didn't arrest him."

"So, he's still around here?"

The agent shook his head. "Last I saw of him he was boarding a chopper with some Chinese guy."

"How do you know he was Chinese? There's a lot of Asian-looking people around."

"This guy had diplomatic papers. He's attached to the Chinese Consulate General's Office in San Francisco. The papers said he was a colonel in the People's Liberation Army.

CHAPTER 15

RAPHAEL, MISSISSIPPI

"Any problems with Leonie?" Kirkland said, as he and Stensen sped east on Interstate 10.

"Of course not," Stensen said.

"So, tell me, were you tempted to bang her before you killed her?"

"I admit, she looked hot as hell, all naked and ready. But no, any interest I might have had was overridden by contempt for who and what she was."

"Picky, picky."

"And she wasn't my type."

"What *is* your type?"

Stensen shrugged unconsciously. "Definitely not sluts and tramps."

"Like I said, too picky. Those kinds of women are the easiest ones. Hell, they're aggressively looking to get laid. Won't take no for an answer."

"Yeah? What about you? Did you score with the waitress, what was her name, Delilah?"

"I would have if the Old Man hadn't interrupted our mating ritual."

Stensen made an amused snort. "You've got to learn to move faster."

"Speaking of faster, are you aware that you're doing thirty miles an hour above the posted limit?"

"It's a frigging Interstate. Everyone goes fast."

"It's three o'clock in the morning and there are no other cars in sight. That makes it easier for cops to spot you. If Levell is right and Quentin's life is at stake, we won't be much help cooling our heels in the county lockup."

"No, they'll just cite us. We'll let Cliff pay the fine."

"Fine, my ass. If they look in the trunk, and they always do, they'll find our arsenal and throw us under the jail."

Stensen glanced at Kirkland. "And how is it, anyway, that the Old Man always seems to know precisely where each of us is and what the situation is?"

Kirkland shook his head. "That truly is one of nature's great unsolved mysteries."

"Think there's a tracer in our phones?"

"No, I've torn the damn things apart on several occasions. If there was a bug there, I'd have found it."

"He hid it someplace else, maybe? Like an implant?"

"No dice there either. I've purposely had two MRIs to try to find an implant. Nada."

"Maybe he has people following us twenty-four-seven."

Again, Kirkland shook his head. "Who on this planet has the skills to be able to follow us if we don't want to be followed?"

"Good point."

The two men traveled in silence for the next thirty minutes. Finally, Stensen said, "Is that our exit up ahead?" He pointed to a large green highway information sign announcing Exit 13 and the intersection with Mississippi state road 43. He flipped on his right turn signal and veered onto the off-ramp. When he reached the traffic light, he turned left and headed north on 43. Two miles later he turned left on a country lane called Nathan Bedford Forrest Road.

"Do you know who the guy was that the road's named for?" Stensen said.

"Yeah, a confederate general and leader of the Ku Klux Klan."

Five miles further on Kirkland said, "See that little sign on the right?"

"The one that says 'Raphael'?"

"Yeah. Pull the car off into those trees over there. We'll hoof it from here."

There was a deeply rutted dirt road that wandered off into the scrub pine trees and undergrowth. Stensen followed it. When he rounded a bend and the paved road was out of sight, he stopped the car.

The two men went around to the rear and Stensen opened the trunk. Levell had cautioned them that the situation looked like it would involve close-quarters combat. Accordingly, he'd provided a small arsenal. They began pulling out the equipment they would need: bullet-resistant vests, suppressed SIG MCX SBR assault rifles with five polymer magazines per man each loaded with thirty 7.62 mm subsonic hollow-point rounds. The combination of suppressor and subsonic ammunition produced minimal noise when fired. The rifles had single-shot, three-round burst, and full-auto capability.

Kirkland also carried a suppressed Heckler & Koch USP9 Tactical semi-automatic 9 mm pistol and two fifteen-round magazines. Stensen holstered a suppressed FNX-45 Tactical Handgun with a raised 3-dot night sight for use with the suppressor. He shoved two fifteen-round magazines in the pockets of his cargo pants.

Each man grabbed three of the latest versions of stun or flash-bang M84 grenades. They produced a "bang" of 180 dB causing immediate, but temporary, deafness. That level of noise not only deafened the victim, it also disrupted the fluid in the middle and inner ear that regulated the body's balance. It ruptured tympanic membrane which caused the victim to become dazed and disorientated. The "flash" function produced an intense burst of light approximating 13.5 million candelas.

Each man also donned enhanced night vision goggles. The ENVGs also were the latest version and had an interlayer of a gel-like substance between its two layers of glass. The substance reacted to the flash produced by the grenades by instantly blocking all light for a two-second period.

Stensen sheathed a full-size black Marine version KA-BAR knife at his waist. Kirkland, who had mastered virtually every form of martial arts and weaponry, slid his beloved katana, which he had named *doragon no chi* or "Dragon's Blood," into its *saya*, a lacquered wood scabbard, and slipped it between his belt and cargo pants. He stuck several razor-sharp shuriken, sometimes called ninja or Japanese throwing stars in breast pockets.

When they finished their preparations, the two men looked at each other. Stensen said, "Let's party."

They activated their ENVGs and moved off in a westerly direction paralleling the road. Despite the goggles, the going was challenging. The scrub pine and other stunted trees grew in close profusion, and the dense undergrowth added to the struggle. After three hundred yards, they came to a swampy area where the vegetation changed. The trees gave way to tall, densely clustered marsh flora. The soggy earth sucked at the soles of their booted feet, and the odor of decaying plant life assaulted their nostrils. There were sounds of creatures slithering in the darkness around them. Eventually, they reentered the scrublands and came upon the cleared area that Levell had told them about. There was a structure in the middle of it.

Kirkland pulled out his satphone and called Levell. "We have the objective in sight."

"Describe it."

"Tall, rectangular, white frame and stucco structure. Sits on a stem-wall that puts the slab about three feet off the ground. Wooden staircase that leads to double entryway doors."

"Twin leafs," Levell interrupted.

"What?"

"Never mind. Continue."

"A few stained-glass windows. Steep tin pavilion roof with a steeple in the center. Obviously, a church of some kind, or was."

"Yes, that's the place."

Kirkland glanced at Stensen, then spoke into the phone. "And you know Quentin's in there…how?"

"That doesn't concern you. Suffice it to say he's in there, and I have positive proof of it. Your mission is to get him out. And in one piece, understand?"

"Roger that. What about anyone else?"

"When you see what those bastards put Thomas through, there'll be no such thing as collateral damage."

"Roger that, too. Got an idea how many bad guys are in there?"

"Heat images show sixteen. One of them isn't moving. That will be Thomas."

"So, fifteen of them and two of us. Those poor bastards are badly outnumbered."

Kirkland terminated the conversation and turned to Stensen. The pinpoints of red light in the center of his startlingly blue pupils were beginning to dilate. A cruel smile of anticipation tugged at the corners of his mouth. Kirkland knew from experience that it was going to be a bloodbath. It was never any different with Stensen.

"I don't see any sentries, Nick, at least not outside."

Stensen shrugged. "Could be one or more in the back. I'll circle around and give you the sitrep." He slipped away in the darkness.

A few minutes later Kirkland's satphone vibrated. He fished it out. It was Stensen.

"There's a rear entrance. A bandit was sitting on the stairs having a smoke."

"How do you know he was a bandit?"

"He was armed."

"And now he's not?"

"Roger. Suddenly gave up smoking, too."

"A wise decision on his part. It's bad for one's health."

"It was for his."

"What else do you see?"

"Mostly quiet, at least outside. But there are a couple of windows in the stem wall. They're frosted over, maybe painted, but there's light behind them."

"Sounds like there's a basement. Instinct tells me that's where Quentin is."

"I'll take the back entrance and move through the building in case there's a sentry inside the front entrance."

"Roger that."

A few minutes later, the leaf on the left side of the front door swung open and Stensen gave Kirkland the all-clear sign.

QUENTIN THOMAS HAD BEEN unconscious for the fourth time that night. Then the bucket of icy water hit him in the face and he wasn't unconscious anymore. The first thing he noticed was the pain. It was everywhere, from the follicles of the hair on his head to his toenails. It hammered him in many ways: spasming aches, pounding throbs, stabbing, searing, burning sensations on his skin as well as deep within his body. He stared at the blood puddling beneath him. His blood.

At first, he was confused. Where was he? Why was he bound? What had happened to him? Then he gradually became aware of people around him and the fog began to lift. He was a prisoner of white supremacists deep in the backcountry of Mississippi. He had been beaten savagely and told he was going to be killed. Thoughts of a monstrous-sized alligator slipped through his mind. He slowly opened his eyes. The light, although not particularly bright, brought more pain. He blinked several times, trying to erase the veil caused by the blood that had run into his eyes. Suddenly a hand slapped him hard and painfully on the side of his head. He nearly passed out again. When he was able to open his eyes again, he saw the Cowboy standing in front of him.

"Looky heah, fellers, our 'guest' done woke up from his beauty nap."

"Yeah?" Someone else said. "He don't look too beautiful now, does he?"

"Aw, he don't look that bad," a third person said. "Maybe we best stomp the shit outta him some more."

Thomas opened his mouth to speak. The effort caused his split and swollen lips to burn as if sulfuric acid had been poured on them. He grimaced and that caused even greater pain. When he spoke, it came out in a raspy whisper.

"What are you waiting for? Why don't you just go ahead and kill me?"

The Cowboy said, "What's the matter, boy, you in some kind of a hurry to die?" There were snickers from several of the others in the room.

"No, I'm just tired of all this and want to get it over with."

"I wouldn't be in such a big hurry to meet Ol' Hitler, if I was you, nigra."

Thomas looked at the speaker and his memory produced a name: Eddie Jack.

"Well, maybe *we* ain't ready to call it quits yet," the Cowboy said. "Maybe you done forgot, but you told us a while back that you got you some kinda important friends, real badasses, who was gonna come and make us pay for what we was doin' to you." He looked smugly around at the others in the room.

"Tha's right," Eddie Jack said. "Personally, I wanna meet them sumbitches."

The Cowboy shook his head in mock sadness. "I do hate to be the one to tell you this Eddie Jack, but there ain't no such people. Look at him, he's a nigra. Any of you fellers ever knowed a nigra that knew anyone important?"

"Then," Eddie Jack said, "let's kill this black sumbitch."

KIRKLAND AND STENSEN stood in the old church's vestibule, just inside the front entrance.

Stensen softly said, "There's no one up here. I think the action is in the basement."

"How many access points does it have?"

"Only one that I've found so far. There's a small room behind the altar with a door that says 'Basement.'"

"How convenient."

Stensen prowled quickly around the vestibule. "Nothing here."

"You said you saw a few windows in the stem wall around back."

"There are two along the side, too."

"Also frosted?"

"Yeah."

"How big are they?"

"Big enough for one of us to fit through, if that's what you're getting at."

Kirkland nodded. "Here's how we'll handle this."

Minutes later, Kirkland was hunkered down beside one of the basement windows along the side of the old church building. It was about two feet high, three feet long, and had been frosted over from the other side to prevent anyone on the outside from being able to see in. He could hear men talking inside.

Kirkland waited until he knew Stensen would be in position in front of the door marked "Basement." Using the butt of his SIG MCX, he smashed the glass then lobbed two flash-bangs through the hole where the window had been. There were deafening explosions and brilliant white flashes. He followed that by emptying a thirty-round magazine into the basement, one rapid shot at a time to provide cover for Stensen. He was careful to aim toward the ceiling of the basement to avoid hitting Thomas or Stensen, who would come bursting down the stairs as soon as the flash-bangs detonated.

He replaced the spent magazine. When he heard the sound of Stensen's SIG MCX, he slung his rifle over a shoulder and swiftly dropped through the window frame into the basement below. He landed cat-like in the smoke-filled room and drew his katana. He smiled coldly and licked his lips in anticipation. *Let the killing begin.*

Disoriented and dazed, in seconds twelve of the men in the basement had been decapitated by *doragon no chi* wielded by Kirkland or picked off by headshots from Stensen. Having collapsed when the M84s detonated, the Preacher, the sheriff, and Eddie Jack, confused expressions on their faces climbed slowly to their hands and knees. A large and rapidly thickening pool of blood surrounded them. While Kirkland freed Thomas, Stensen savagely kicked the three survivors into the center of the room.

Thomas rubbed his legs to restore the sensation that had gone missing from sitting tightly bound for a long period of time.

After a while, he said, "Do you rednecks remember me warning you about my friends?"

The three prisoners looked at each other and bobbed their heads rapidly.

"Didn't I advise you to let me go? That you'd never seen anyone like them? That they would do things to you that you couldn't begin to imagine?"

The heads bobbed again.

"It turns out I was wrong."

Stensen and Kirkland looked at each other and grinned.

"They're not going to kill you. I am."

"There goes your reputation as a softie, Quentin," Stensen said.

Thomas stood up slowly, grimacing from the pain. "Understand this. I'm not going to kill you because of what you've done to me."

"Maybe he's still a softie after all," Kirkland said.

"No, I'm going to kill you for what you've done over the years to an unknown number of innocent black men, men whose only misfortune was the color of their skin. But more than that, I'm going to kill you for ruining my little sister's wedding by turning the man she chose to walk her down the aisle into Frankenstein's twin."

Thomas paused with his eyes closed as he waited out a sharp spasm of pain. When he was able, he said, "I'm going to feed two of you to Ol' Hitler. The one who won't be is the one who tells us where to find him."

Without hesitation, Eddie Jack blurted out, "He's down to Stump Crick. It's no more'n a half a mile north of here. They's a dirt road out behind this heah church that goes right to it. I'll lead you mysef'. Just please don't kill me. I never meant you no harm. It was them fellers." He pointed at the Preacher and the sheriff. "I had to play along so they didn't think I was a nigra-lover."

"You sonofabitch," the sheriff said and gave Eddie Jack a murderous look.

"You're a damn traitor to your own kind, Eddie Jack," the Preacher said. "If we stick together and keep our mouths shut, won't none of us get fed to that damn gator. Use yore head, boy!"

"If you don't lead us there, Eddie Jack," Thomas said, "I'll let my friend Nick here kill you his way." He looked at Stensen and said, "Why don't you tell them about it."

The three prisoners looked at Stensen and gasped. The pupils of his eyes were almost entirely red, a deep, fiery blood red.

"It's simple. I'll flay you."

The three men returned a blank look.

"For those as ignorant as you three, let me simplify it. I'll skin you alive, and it will take a lot longer to kill you than that gator will."

"No," Eddie Jack shouted. "I done tole you, I'll take you there. I ain't lettin' these two ol' fools get me killed."

An hour later Ol' Hitler had worked up an appetite with the Cowboy and the sheriff as apéritifs. Thomas looked at Kirkland and Stensen and nodded. They each took one of Eddie Jack's arms, and with no apparent effort, tossed the big man into the huge waiting jaws.

Eddie Jack screamed all the way. "You said you wouldn't kill me."

Stensen smiled at Thomas, the red centers in his eyes had begun to contract. "You're such a bullshitter, Quentin."

PART TWO

A RIVAL WOLF PACK

"What frightens us today is exactly the same sort of thing that frightened us yesterday. It's just a different wolf." —Alfred Hitchcock

CHAPTER 16

POTUS

NANDO CORREIA DROVE Levell from the Lodge in the thick deciduous forest near Fairview Beach, Virginia, to the headquarters of the Central Intelligence Agency in Langley. To old hands like Levell, the CIA was known as the Company. The weather was surprisingly pleasant for the time of year, but the heavy traffic on I-95 was an unwelcome counterbalance. Near Springfield, Nando navigated an intersection with the Capital Beltway Outer Loop. It was the concrete version of the Gordian Knot. He emerged on I-395 and drove northeasterly before changing to South Washington Boulevard just south of the Pentagon. At the Potomac, he merged smoothly onto George Washington Memorial Parkway. Moments later he exited onto four-laned, divided Chain Bridge Road-Dolley Madison Boulevard. He headed south over rolling hills covered with the trees gone nude for the winter. The large colonial style homes in brick or clapboard, hidden in summer, were helplessly exposed to the traffic on the highway. Shortly, he saw a sign just before the intersection with Highway

193. A road curved off to the right. The sign warned of a restricted government area. Nando turned right.

The car entered the two-hundred-fifty-eight-acre CIA campus known officially as the George Bush Center for Intelligence. Colloquially, it was simply known as Langley. Immediately, it passed the Route 123 Memorial to two fallen CIA operatives. After passing through two checkpoints in less than a mile, Nando was directed to a parking space at the CIA's headquarters in Langley, Virginia.

The trip from the Lodge had taken an hour and forty minutes, giving Levell plenty of time to reflect on his memories as a Para-military Operations Officer in the Company. He'd been recruited from the Marine Corps after his service in Nam. Together with his best friend, the late Marine Corps general Roscoe "Buster" McCoy, and a handful of others, he'd been tasked with the most challenging mission of his life—identifying, recruiting, and training some very unique young men—the Sleeping Dogs.

Levell remembered working out of cramped space in the Original Headquarters Building. Its lobby was a testament to the CIA's history, going all the way back to its origins as the Office of Strategic Services in World War II. A statue of its leader "Wild Bill" Donovan was to the left of the entrance. On the white marble floor of the lobby was a sixteen-foot-diameter inlaid granite replica of the CIA's seal. The north wall of the lobby displayed Memorial Wall, containing one-hundred-twenty-five stars, one for each the CIA officers who had made the ultimate sacrifice. Levell had known some of them. Below the Memorial Wall was the glass-encased Book of Honor. It listed the names of ninety-one of the one-hundred-twenty-five who had died. The other thirty-four officers remain unnamed for security purposes.

Levell was surprised by the feeling of nostalgia that overtook him. He sensed the moisture in his eyes. *Maybe*, he thought, *it's better that the meeting is being held in the New Headquarters Building. Besides, the president called this meeting. He gets to hold it anywhere he chooses. Comes with the job.*

At the second gate, Nando had been instructed to circle around to the left of the NHB and OHB to one of the enormous parking lots. At the entrance of the lot, a uniformed security officer motioned them to a parking place. He also checked the men's identification and escorted Levell, who was being pushed in his wheelchair by Nando. The man issued the two men visitors' cards. Each had a large orange V and the words "Visitor Escort Required." He led them into the lobby of the NHB, a six-story twin-tower across from the older building.

Because it was built into the side of a hill, the NHB's entrance lobby was on the fourth floor. Inside, was a huge skylight ceiling. At the other end, the entry corridor opened to a spectacular view of the OHB. The lobby itself hosted a collection of artwork commemorating the Company's contributions to securing the Free World and a plaque honoring the late Director of Central Intelligence William J. Casey. As he and Nando were led across the lobby, the one-sixth scale models of various photoreconnaissance aircraft were suspended from the ceiling of the four-story, glass-enclosed atrium. He recognized the U-2, the infamous spy plane of the '50s and '60s. It brought back old memories of Francis Gary Powers and the international incident caused when the Soviets shot his plane down over Russia in 1960. *He was lucky to have survived, but we had to swap Rudolf Abel to get him back, and Abel was one of the Ruskies most capable spies.*

Levell was impressed, but also discomforted by the obvious sums of tax dollars that had been poured into what he considered to be unnecessary extravagance. But then, he thought, even the Company was the province of bureaucrats, a species that had long since mastered the art of spending limitless amounts of other people's money.

The security agent ushered the two men into a sleek looking elevator and pushed a button with the numeral 1 on it. The car descended smoothly and soundlessly to the bottom floor of the building. The agent swiped a card in a slot at the rear of the car and a door opened. Levell and Nando followed the agent down a wide, brightly-lit corridor to a small windowless but luxuriously appointed conference room.

There were three people seated around a round, highly polished mahogany table. Levell recognized all three. One was an influential former senator from a western state, now the newly confirmed Secretary of the Interior. He had long been an important member of SAS. The second man was a top White House advisor. The last man was tall with long, oddly-colored blond hair combed in an unusual sweep—toward his forehead then back over the top of his head. The hair on the sides also was long and combed back. It was parted on the left. He was in the process of making a point and using his hands to underscore it. It was the president of the United States, Frederick Flagler.

He motioned for Nando to position Levell at a place at the table from which a chair had been removed. As he did so, he rose and came around the table with his hand stretched out to Levell, who took the hand. When he did, the president squeezed firmly and pulled, almost yanking the older man from his wheelchair.

"Cliff," he said, "thank you for coming. I appreciate it." He rocked back on his heels and looked down at Levell. "I hope you weren't too inconvenienced." He pointed to the wheelchair. "Although I did agree to meet you here, instead of at the White House. But any future meetings are going to be in the Oval Office. I mean, what the hell's the sense in having it if I don't use it?"

"No inconvenience at all, Mr. President. I got used to this damn baby buggy a long time ago." He turned to Nando and said, "I understand the generous taxpayers of this nation have provided a very nice cafeteria for this facility. I'll call you when the meeting ends."

Nando nodded and left the room escorted by the security agent.

"I believe you know Secretary Talley," the president said. "But have you met White House senior advisor Billy Trupockitt?"

Levell eyed Trupockitt impassively. "I've seen him in the news media."

"He's a good man, one of the good guys. I depend on him for a lot of things. Off the record things. I'm counting on the two of you working well together." The president returned to his seat.

"Working? I've been retired from the Company for several years."

"Oh, come on, Cliff, I'm the President of the United States. I know everything. People tell me everything. There are no secrets from me."

Levell was aware of the president's infamous ego. He threw a quick, but piercing glance at Talley, then said, "I'm not sure what you're getting at, Mr. President."

"Well, Talley here, being the true patriot he is, has shared information with me about your organization, the Society of Adam Smith. Right, Talley?" Flagler tilted his head back, pursed his lips, and with squinty eyes looked down the bridge of his nose at the former senator.

Talley squirmed in his seat and examined his perfectly manicured fingernails. "Well...ah...yes, Mr. President." He looked momentarily at Levell then resumed studying his nails. "I see an opportunity, Cliff, for the Society to work with the new administration, one that shares our values. It will enable us to emerge into the open, to more effectively pursue our goals of restoring this nation to a position of preeminence."

"And you did this without consulting anyone else in the SAS?" Levell said.

"Aw, don't be too hard on Talley. He wants to help me make America great again," the president said. "He attended a dinner at the White House the other night for the Israeli prime minister. I'd heard rumors that there was a secretive group of people from intelligence, the military, and corporate America. Supposedly, they had been working behind the scenes during the previous administration, trying to counter or contain the damage caused by my traitorous predecessor. From Talley's background, I figured he might be a member or know something about it.

"I asked him to speak privately with me in the Oval Office after dinner. He made a good decision." He glanced at Talley, then turned back to Levell. "I commend you on your group's efforts, Cliff, but let's face it, they were amateurish." The president's lips curled in a momentary, mirthless smile. "But with the power of my administration involved, it will be big league. What do you say, Cliff?"

Levell looked pointedly at each of the other men. "Frankly, I don't know what to say. We've clearly lost the benefits that anonymity provided. Now that we've been 'outed,' so to speak, I'm not sure what we can do that various civilian and military intelligence operations can't do, given that there's been a change in administrations and governing philosophies.

"And you having knowledge of, let alone participating in these extra-legal activities could cause problems in addition to the ones you're having with the special counsel looking into alleged irregularities in your recent campaign."

The president closed his eyes, shook his head, and waved one hand, as if dispelling Levell's comments. "No, no, Cliff, you're not on the same page with me. We don't want your organization to work in the open. What Talley told me will go no farther than me and Trupockitt. Nor should it. And, as for that special counsel, David Farmer, he'll get his soon enough. Let me deal with him."

Levell, ordinarily anything but a patient man, said nothing, just stared at Flagler, eyebrows raised quizzically.

"You'll continue to work behind the scenes, but you'll coordinate with Billy. He's my senior White House advisor on counterterrorism. You'll do what you've been doing, but this time you'll have the full resources of the White House behind you." Flagler paused, leaned toward Levell, and, squinting his eyes and pursing his lips in a pseudo-pout, said, "I don't want another Los Alamos! I'm counting on your sources giving us timely intel. And I'm counting on your people working with us..., through Billy, to stop anything cold before it becomes a problem. Understand?" He sat back, slouching in his chair, lips still pursed.

"I think so, but what is Mr. Trupockitt's role in this? How much of our day-to-day operations have to be passed through him?"

Without hesitation, the president said, "All of it."

"What if urgent action is needed and he's unavailable at the moment? Also, how much of the mundane should we bother him with?"

Flagler sat forward quickly. "Dammit, Cliff, he doesn't need to know when you or someone in your group takes a crap. Use your discretion. If it's something that could involve action for or against the well-being of the country, tell him. Include him in your planning processes. Got it?"

Levell nodded. "Got it." *This is a hell of a development.*

The president sat back and smiled. Holding up his right hand with thumb and forefinger making the "ok" sign, he said, "Then let's get to the interesting part. Talley tells me you've got a bunch of super ninjas. Go anywhere, kill anybody. If they're real, they might be the best secret weapon we've got. Is this true?"

Levell winced at the thought of where the discussion might be going. He stared unwaveringly at the president and thought carefully about his next words. "We do have a small group of well-trained paramilitary operatives. Super ninjas or anything of the sort is hyperbolic. They're just men who are good at what they do."

"They're called what…the Sleeping Dogs? How'd they get that name?"

"When we originally recruited and trained them, they were to be the ultimate weapon against America's enemies, only used if all other avenues failed. We took the name from an expression originally attributed to Chaucer, 'let sleeping dogs lie.' Meaning if someone wakes these dogs, they'll destroy whoever did it."

"Is there any chance these guys can clean up the border? Save us the cost of that tall, beautiful, southern border wall between the U.S. and Mexico? The one I promised during the campaign. I mean, the damn thing is supposed to cost twenty-one billion, probably a lot more before it's over. And I don't really see the Mexicans paying for it."

"In all due respect, Mr. President, in addition to the fact that there are only seven of them, that's not what these guys do. They're hunter-killers, the best ever, not fucking patrolmen. That would be a complete waste of their unique skill sets."

Flagler gave Levell a long, hard stare then relaxed back into his seat. "What makes these guys different from everyone else?"

"Twenty or more years ago, two gifted geneticists were researching an anomaly in the DNA of us modern descendants of early European hominins…humans. They discovered we still carry elements of a genetic code designed to produce stronger, faster, smarter beings in response to a hostile environment. They theorized that if a male carrier mated with a female carrier, there could be a potential for one or more of their children to be more genetically advanced."

"You mean," Trupockitt said with a sneer, "like a race of Supermen?"

Flagler laughed. "Don't be an asshole, Billy. Let Cliff finish."

Levell gave Trupockitt a long, cold stare before saying, acidly, "No. These people don't wear tights and capes. Bullets chew through them just like they do you and me."

"So, how do you explain these guys? Flagler said.

"It's nature's way of furthering the evolution of the species. It involves creating genetic mutations in advance of the need for a particular trait," Levell said.

"Sounds like voodoo bullshit to me," Trupockitt said. "How in hell could a genetic mutation occur *prior* to an event?"

"I'm not a geneticist. I can't offer you an explanation for that, but I can give you an example. In the middle of the fourteenth century, the Black Plague killed one hundred million or more in Europe alone, more than half its population. Yet, as contagious and devastating as the disease was, not everyone who was exposed to it became infected despite living with and among those who were. Those survivors eventually repopulated the continent."

Trupockitt said, "So, you're telling us that the fact these guys are here means some cataclysmic event is going to happen?"

"Look around you, what do you think? Every pissant country is trying to go nuclear, and some are already there. None can be trusted not to use it aggressively. Religious fanatics are dedicated to destroying civilization. And they're close to taking power in many European countries, including some that have nuclear weapons. The dictators running two of the most powerful nations are working to bring the West down. Here at home, the inmates are very close to running the asylum. Even Mother nature is throwing more shit at us than we can handle."

Flagler said, "If these Sleeping Dogs aren't supermen, then what are they?"

"They have different muscle fiber. It's denser. It gives them much greater strength. Their nervous systems transmit signals faster in their brains and throughout their bodies, and their hearts and lungs are larger, giving them the ability to process oxygen faster. As a result, they're a lot quicker, faster than the rest of us. Their bones are thicker and stronger too."

"Are they *Homo sapiens* like us?" Trupockitt said.

Levell slowly shook his head back and forth. "No. Jake Horowitz and Bill Nishioki, the researchers who discovered their genetic trait, named them *Homo maximus*, the next step in human evolution."

"So, how come I never heard of these guys? Wouldn't they be dominant athletes, world champions?" Flagler said.

"Yes."

"And we never heard of them because…?" Flagler said.

"Think about what life was like for these guys. As young children, they were vastly superior to their playmates, but didn't know why. It frightened the other kids, and adults, too. As a result, these guys were treated cruelly, like freaks, like Frankenstein's monster. They became guarded. They learned to display a certain level of athleticism and intellect, but nowhere near the maximum. They became frustrated and, over time, angry that they were different and had to constantly monitor themselves and their environment so as not to reveal those differences. In some ways it warped them."

"Meaning?" Trupockitt said.

"Loners. They don't play well with others. Aggressively intolerant of bad guys and bullies. Puzzled by the penchant for fuckups we 'lesser' beings seem to have. It's why marriage doesn't seem to work for them. Hell, they don't even like each other some of the time."

Flagler regarded Levell with narrowed eyes, then rubbed his hands together and said, "I like these guys already. When do I get to meet them?"

CHAPTER 17

DINGLE, IRELAND

To Whelan, the Fianna still smelled of death. A lot of men had been killed there in recent months. He had slain five a year earlier, men who'd come to kill him and his family. One had been shot-gunned and another partially flayed in the usually pristine kitchen. A week ago, he'd stalked and killed ten Chinese commandos. All in all, there had been substantial blood loss throughout the old bed and breakfast.

He'd worked tirelessly to clean it. Several women from the village, mostly those with eligible female family members, had offered to help, but he'd politely declined. The townsfolk were well aware that he and Caitlin had separated and that she was currently dating another man. The assumption was that Whelan, whether he liked it or not, was soon to become the most desirable bachelor in southwestern Ireland, maybe all of Ireland.

He'd gone online and researched cleaning products. Many "guaranteed" to remove all stains and odors. Maybe he just had an overly acute sense of smell, or maybe it was the memories of the killings, but nothing seemed to work. He was glad when he heard one of his phones ring, giving him an excuse to take a break from the endless scrubbing.

It was the special satellite phone, the one only Levell used. *Now what?*

He punched the icon and said, "Yeah?"

"Good, you answered. I won't have to wait for a call back."

Whelan sighed wearily and stretched his back. "In that case, get right to the point. I'm busy."

"So much for the social pleasantries," Levell said in his familiar raspy growl. "I've got good news, bad news, and news I don't know what to make of."

"Start with the bad news."

"John Talley, the recent senator from Wyoming and currently secretary of the interior, told the new sheriff all about SAS, including the Dogs."

"Flagler, the new president?"

"Yeah."

"Talley's a member of SAS. Why the hell would he do that?"

"Sucking up to his new boss, maybe. Hell, I don't know what possesses politicians and bureaucrats to do dumb fucking things. Maybe it's a defective gene." Much more of a growl this time.

"And it's bad news because it outs SAS?"

"Not necessarily. Flagler says it's staying in-house, just him and one of his advisors, guy named Pickpocket or Trupockitt or some kind of fucking pocket. Says he wants SAS to continue, but with his support."

"So where is the bad news in that?"

"He wants to meet the Dogs."

"Flagler?"

"Who the fuck have we been talking about? Yes, Flagler."

"That's a very bad idea."

"Hell, yes, it is. And it's not going to happen. Not on my watch."

"You may have your work cut out. From what I've read and heard about him, he seems to believe he's entitled to get whatever he wants."

"You let me deal with him. In the meantime, the good news is all the Dogs are once again accounted for and traveling to a rendezvous I've arranged."

"Not all of them, Cliff."

"What are you saying?"

"I'm not going anywhere. I've got a marriage in shambles and I'm trying to salvage it."

"And how's that working out?"

There was a long pause. "Caitlin's seeing another man."

"Seeing? You mean dating?"

The answered caused a tightening in Whelan's chest and his stomach felt a little queasy. "Yeah."

"Does it look like anything serious? Maybe she's just angry at you and this is her way of punishing you a little."

"I don't want to think about how serious it might be."

"Good plan. If you dwelt on the possibilities, you'd hunt the sonofabitch down and kill him slowly in ways too horrible to imagine. You wouldn't be much use to us rotting in some Irish prison. In fact, rejoining the Dogs for the upcoming mission is just what you need to get your mind off things at home. Give her a little time to sort things out. She'll come around. Hell, there are no other men like you on the planet. Anything else is settling for second best, if that."

"I'm staying right here, Cliff. It was the previous mission that led to the problems she and I are having." Whelan changed the subject. "You said you had other news you didn't know what to make of. What is it?"

"I got a call from Mitch Christie."

"Mitch? How's his recovery?"

"Definitely on the mend, he's about to resume his duties."

"Has he recovered enough to marry that beautiful fiancée of his?"

"Not yet. He wants to be fully capable of traveling so they can be wed in Camila's hometown. He called to tell me he'd gotten a call from a cop buddy of his in Santa Fe, a guy he worked with on the Los Alamos terrorist attack. The guy told him one of the terrorists was back in the States and wanted to cooperate with authorities. Says he may know where the other five nukes are. The cop knows how bureaucrats function. Or don't. Anyway, Mitch had hinted to him that he knew people who could act extralegally outside bureaucracies and actually make things happen."

"You're suggesting the Dogs interdict the suspect and interrogate him."

"I talking rendition. Grab his ass before the authorities fuck things up. Take him somewhere isolated. Find out where the nukes are and contain them. In the process, I trust you and the other boys will send as many ragheads as possible to rendezvous with their apocryphal virgins."

Whelan could imagine the sinister smile on Levell's leathery face. "I told you I'm not going, Cliff. The other six are more than sufficient to handle this. Let Larsen or Stone or one of the other guys lead the team for a change."

"That's easy to say, but the reality is different. Larsen is Larsen. Good guy to have at your back, but wants no part of leading. Stone is the new guy. No one's ready to follow him. Stensen's crazy. Almeida's a fuck-up. Thomas gets queasy at the prospect of collateral damage. And Kirkland's picture is in the dictionary under the word 'loner.' You're the natural leader of these crazy bastards, always have been."

"Not gonna happen, Cliff. Not this time."

There was a pause. Whelan could sense Levell's frustration and disappointment.

Levell said, "I understand your situation. But I want you to think about it. We can talk again in a day or two." He disconnected the call.

CHAPTER 18

SHENZHEN, GUANGDONG, CHINA

CHINA'S HARBIN Z-9 helicopter was a licensed variant of the French Eurocopter AS365 Dauphin. This particular one used the rooftop landing pad to deposit Zheng Bao Xun and his guest, Harland Fairchilde, IV, at the Beijing Genomics Institute (BGI). Located southwest of populous Shenzhen, China, it was housed in a windowless multistory, terraced building. Although Shenzhen is situated in the floodplain of the Pearl River Delta, the BGI had been built on a rocky outcropping high above the floodplain and with the capacity to withstand a magnitude-7 earthquake. The facility was a global leader in DNA sequencing and related genetics research. That was what brought the two men to the facility.

They had been attending a meeting on international financing issues in neighboring Hong Kong, a mere forty-five kilometers away. The aging but serviceable helicopter had covered the distance in less than fifteen minutes despite encountering turbulence.

Although he traveled frequently, the Chinese minister of finance wasn't fond of air travel, especially in small, light aircraft. The short, rough hop from Hong Kong had left him agitated and a little green around the gills. And he didn't like heights. He moved shakily across the roof to the elevator door. Once inside the operator began the descent. Zheng took a deep breath and exhaled slowly.

"Practicing Zen, are we Xun?" Fairchilde said snidely. His smile indicated he was enjoying Zheng's discomfort.

The Chinese man glanced at his tormentor out of the corner of his eyes but said nothing. His eyes were unusual, hazel with dark green around the edges and minute gold flecks scattered throughout the irides. He had brought Fairchilde to this facility to show him something that would shock him, but in a positive way.

The elevator reached the appropriate level and the operator opened the door. His two passengers exited.

As Zheng led the American down the wide, sterile, brightly-lit corridor, Fairchilde said, "Flying in, I couldn't help but notice this is a most impressive structure. It looks almost secure enough to protect the People's Republic's darkest secrets." He smiled at his own effort at humor.

"But that is not its purpose."

"What is its purpose, if I may ask?"

"Do you remember that conversation we had in the cocktail lounge of the Hotel Oro d'España on Key Biscayne a few weeks ago?"

"Yes, I recall you admitted taking unilateral, unapproved action against that Whelan person. And you failed." Fairchilde's voice indicated he took some satisfaction in Zheng's failure.

"This is true, but at least I was taking action, not wringing my hands over Maksym's inability to complete the task."

"So, what does our being here have to do with that?"

Patiently, Zheng said, "If you will recall, I told you our scientists had uncovered research conducted by two American geneticists."

"Yes? Something to do with the genetic makeup of those damn Sleeping Dogs, as I recall."

"Very good, Harland. The Americans discovered a rare genetic marker possessed by an exceptionally few individuals. They developed a means for testing for this marker."

"And your scientists have duplicated this test? That's what this facility is for, isn't it?"

"That and much more. But it's the rediscovery of this marker that concerns our visit today."

The men navigated a labyrinth of corridors and ultimately came to a hermetically sealed sliding glass door. Two armed military guards stood sentry on either side of it. Anticipating the arrival of their minister of finance and his guest, one of them punched a series of symbols on a screen beside the door on the right. There was a barely audible click and the door slid open. The guard politely motioned for the two visitors to enter.

Once inside, they were met by a tiny Asian woman wearing a white lab coat and wire-rim glasses. She held an iPad in one hand and bowed politely to Zheng then glanced briefly at Fairchilde. The American thought he detected an attitude of disapproval of his presence in the top-secret facility.

Zheng motioned toward the woman and said in English, "This is Dr. Youxin-Xie Ling. She is one of our very finest research geneticists."

Turning back to the scientist, he spoke Mandarin. "Thank you, Doctor, for taking time from the demands of your busy schedule to discuss your work with us."

Youxin-Xie nodded, but the stern expression on her small face never softened. She again looked at Fairchilde.

"You are not to concern yourself with this man, Doctor. I personally vouch for him. He is chairman of a very wealthy American foundation interested in funding research into genetics." A well-practiced master of deception, the lie flowed smoothly from his disarming smile.

The woman's expression never changed. She nodded again and motioned for the men to follow her. She led them across the room to another hermetically sealed sliding door. This one was made of heavy gauge metal with a window, two feet by two feet, set into the right side. The window was half-inch thick polycarbonate, the kind used in detention facilities because, unlike other types of ballistic glass, polycarbonate flexes and rebounds when struck. It wasn't suitable for stopping bullets, but firearms generally aren't found in detention facilities. Instead, it was superior at stopping chairs, tools, and other heavy objects thrown at it.

Dr. Youxin-Xie paused in front of the door and raised up on her tiptoes to see into the room on the other side. Zheng and Fairchilde stood close on either side of her and stared through the glass too.

The room was large and brightly lit. It clearly was some kind of workout facility. Weights and impressive fitness equipment were situated throughout the space. Several very large, thickly muscled, heavily tattooed and scarred men were working out. Some were lifting prodigious amounts of weight. Others were grappling with each other on mats. Two men, using martial arts techniques, were sparring in a ring set in the middle of the room. There were trainers and coaches everywhere.

After a few moments, Fairchilde said, "Is this what I think it is?"

"To paraphrase Shakespeare, 'fight fire with fire.' Our previous efforts to eliminate the SAS's assets, the Sleeping Dogs, have failed," Zheng said. "What you see indeed is our own version of the Sleeping Dogs."

"I must admit I had my doubts about your ability to pull this off. Are these men equal to the Sleeping Dogs?"

"They are their equals genetically. While they no doubt are far more vicious because of their backgrounds, they presently lack the same level of skills in weaponry and hand-to-hand combat. But, as you can see, we are training them in an effort to close that gap."

"This is extraordinary. How did you find them? Where did you find them?"

A smile of satisfaction appeared on Zheng's dark, round face. He motioned toward the geneticist standing between them. "Dr. Youxin-Xie and her colleagues assembled a team of genetic scientists. They followed the trail blazed by the Americans Horowitz and Nishioki, and rediscovered the genetic marker that identifies men like these. After that, it was relatively simple.

"The team knew the marker was originally developed in people of Western European descent. So, they concentrated on the criminal element and prison populations in those countries."

"Was that a problem? I mean interviewing or testing those who were being incarcerated by various states?"

"Not at all. The whole thing was conducted under the guise of a scientific study to determine if there was a genetic marker that predisposed certain individuals to a life of crime. We were able to secure the release of some of those who tested positive by claiming a need to do further substantial testing in our special lab specifically designed for such purposes." Zheng paused then said, "It seems we were a bit disingenuous."

"There's that Oriental inscrutability," Fairchilde said.

Zheng gave him a strange look but said nothing.

"So, how many are there?"

"Ten."

"When will they be ready?"

"As soon as we deem them fit for our purposes."

Fairchilde seemed aggravated by Zheng's answer. "Can't you at least give a ballpark estimate of when that might be?"

Zheng returned a cold smile. "Perhaps you'd like to meet these men?" Without waiting for a response, he turned to Youxin-Xie and, in Mandarin told her to take the two men inside.

She punched a code into the access control pad beside the door. It slid open almost soundlessly. She walked quickly into the room and approached an older Chinese man wearing a white lab coat and making notes in a notebook computer.

"Dr. Cai," she addressed him in Mandarin. "These men," she motioned toward Zheng and Fairchilde, "would like to observe our operation." After a brief pause, she leaned close to the older man and whispered, "The smaller man is Mr. Zheng, the minister of finance for the People's Republic."

Cai turned, smiled, and bowed respectfully to Zheng. He gave a perfunctory nod in Fairchilde's direction.

"Welcome, Minister Zheng. We are honored by your visit. I am Dr. Cai Wu, director of this project."

"It is our honor to be your guests. We are most interested in learning about this significant work you and your colleagues are doing." He turned toward Fairchilde. "As this gentleman doesn't speak Mandarin, I will translate your words for him." He paused and smiled at Cai. "But perhaps not all of your words."

Cai nodded and briefly described the nature of the project and its purposes. He explained the basics of how the genetic testing was developed and applied, then covered the highlights of the training program and its ultimate goal of producing extraordinary special operations warriors—stronger, faster, smarter than any others. When he was finished, he asked Zheng if there were any questions he could answer.

Zheng capsulized Cai's comments for Fairchilde, including the question at the end.

Without hesitation, Fairchilde said, "Who is their Brendan Whelan?"

There was a brief exchange between Zheng and Cai.

Cai motioned for the two visitors to follow him. He led them across the room on a twisting route that wound between exercise equipment, the massive men using it, and their trainers. On the far side, a man was doing repetitive bench presses with three hundred kilograms, more than six hundred fifty pounds. Sweating profusely, his face contorted into a snarl, he grunted loudly with each repetition. His musculature was massive, and thick veins and sinew stood out like cables just beneath his skin.

When he sensed Cai and his party approaching, he replaced the barbell on the rack and sat up. His head was shaved, displaying gang tattoos. In fact, his bare chest, shoulders, arms, and back were covered with similar skin graffiti. His body also was covered with scars. Some looked like they had been made by knives or razors. Others appeared to be old bullet wounds. There were scars on his face and part of one ear was missing. His appearance was made more sinister by the chill in his eyes and menacing sneer on his face.

With glacial blue eyes, he slowly, carefully took the measure of the two men who were with Cai. The shorter of the two was Asian with dark brown hair instead of the usual black. His companion clearly was a Westerner. He looked to be about six-two, but lean and wearing an expensive-looking suit and what appeared to be custom-made shoes. The quintessential dilettante.

The sneer on the weightlifter's scarred face widened, further flaring his nostrils and curling his upper lip back.

As Cai approached, he continued to sit and said nothing.

The project director stopped in front of him and turned to the two men accompanying him. "I believe this is the man you inquired about. His name is Sergei Kruchinkin."

CHAPTER 19
THE OVAL OFFICE

LEVELL HAD NEVER BEEN INVITED to the White House. He didn't know whether to feel honored or apprehensive but was leaning toward apprehensive. He knew the meeting was happening because President Flagler expected an answer from him. And he expected that answer to be a positive one. But, Levell didn't have that answer. Yet. When he'd discussed the president's request to activate the Dogs with Whelan, the Irishman had rejected him. Levell had tried to reach him again two days later, but it appeared Whelan was avoiding the conversation. *Shit! It's Murphy's Law at work again. If anything can go wrong, it will.*

Nando had driven Levell up yesterday from the Lodge to his home in Georgetown. This morning Flagler had sent two Secret Service agents to pick him up in a ubiquitous black Suburban and drive him to the White House. The driver pulled the SUV under the covered portico of the West Wing entrance off of West Executive Avenue NW and stopped. Levell looked around nervously and was relieved to note that there were no cameras or news people present. They were almost as bad as squatters, occupying that territory on an almost 24/7 basis.

The agents assisted Levell into his wheelchair and pushed him past the two marine guards in full dress uniform flanking the double-doored entry on the ground level. They passed through a narrow foyer with a large framed mirror and console table on either side. There was a fern arrangement on one and a figurine of some Nineteenth-century politico on the other. Just beyond the foyer was an elevator. Levell and the Secret Service agents took it to the first floor.

A White House functionary joined them as they entered the Oval Office Corridor and passed between the Vice President's and White House Chief of Staff's offices. After going past a few White House advisors' offices, the Roosevelt Room, and the Dining Room, there was a slight jog to the left and the corridor opened into a small waiting area in front of the entrance to the Oval Office.

The functionary stepped around Levell and rapped on the office door, then swung it open and stepped aside as the agents wheeled him in. He was now in the most important non-religious site on the planet—the seat of incredible power and might. Levell couldn't feel weakness in his knees, but he felt something. It was powerful and emotional. He felt a catch in his chest. Moisture formed in the old warrior's eyes. How many had fought and died to create and maintain the great democratic republic symbolized by this semi-sacred spot?

He looked around, taking the room in as a pilgrim might do upon arriving at a shrine. There was the large, intricately carved *Resolute* desk, a gift from Queen Victoria to president Rutherford B. Hayes in 1880. Seven United States presidents, including Levell's icon Ronald Reagan, had used the desk while in office. It had been built from the English oak timbers of the British

Arctic exploration ship HMS *Resolute*. Behind it, tall muntined windows overlooking the Rose Garden were framed with bright yellow curtains. The marble floor was overlaid by a huge oval-shaped carpet with the Presidential Seal woven into the center of it. Small bookcases had been built into the walls. Opposite the desk, two large sofas faced each other. There was a long narrow coffee table between them. A large bowl of fresh apples was positioned in the middle of the table.

Billy Trupockitt, his long, lanky frame sprawled on one of the sofas, was munching an apple.

Flagler, seated behind the desk, took his time looking up. He gave Levell a blank look then smiled and stood. Coming around in front of the desk, he stretched out his hand. "Cliff, thanks for coming by. What d'ya think of the digs? Pretty cool, huh?"

Levell remembered the greeting from their initial discussion at Langley. He took the president's hand and squeezed hard. At the same time, he braced for Flagler's famous tug and thwarted it.

Flagler seemed surprised and stared at Levell for a few moments, then grinned and sat down across from Trupockitt.

"Have you thought over the possibilities that these Sleeping Dogs of yours can be a great asset in protecting this country from its enemies?"

Levell nodded. "Yes, I have, Mr. President. My colleagues on the governing board of the Society agree that we can play a role in helping your administration make the situation safer for Americans."

"Good. I was confident you'd see things my way."

"But," Levell said, "we need details on what it is you expect from us."

"Fair enough. Let's talk about that." Flagler looked at Trupockitt and said, "Billy?"

"I think we all remember the recent disaster at Los Alamos," the advisor said, talking and chewing bites of the apple simultaneously.

Flagler's head bobbed up and down. His well-coiffed mass of oddly yellow hair never moved.

Levell said nothing, just studied Trupockitt. He didn't like people who talked with food in their mouths.

"Our intel suggests there are five more of those nukes still in the terrorists' hands." Trupockitt looked quizzically at Levell, as though expecting a confirmation.

Levell gave no response.

"Soooo, then, we need to find those nukes, recover them, and terminate the bastards that have them. And we want it done in such a way that it will send a message to the rest of their little pals wherever they are," Trupockitt said.

Levell said, "And you expect our role to be…?"

Trupockitt had finished eating the apple and threw the core back into the bowl with the other apples. "What we expect is that these hotshot killers of yours will carry out this mission. And quickly, before those camel jockeys can set off any more of their fucking nukes. Any questions?"

"Yeah, as a matter of fact, I do have a question. These guys don't play well with other people. You and everyone else need to stay in the background. I…the Society will handle the Sleeping Dogs."

"Now, hold on a second, Levell. I don't—"

"Don't get your panties in a knot, Billy," the president interrupted. "Ol' Cliff here is the official den mother of these boys. He's been dealing with them for years. Knows them better than anyone. As long as he runs everything by you, I don't see a reason to cause needless issues."

Trupockitt started to respond, but Flagler cocked his head to the side and stared balefully at him. A pout spread across Trupockitt's face. He slouched back into the sofa and didn't say anything, just glared at Levell.

"Another question," Levell said. "What kind of intel do you have regarding the possible location of these nukes and who might have them?"

"If we had that intel, we wouldn't need you, would we? We'd just send our own special ops whizzes and let you vegetate in that log palace of yours in Tidewater country." Trupockitt laid the sarcasm on thickly.

Levell's eyes narrowed and he smiled a thin, cold smile. "Good. We'll gather our own intel. But understand this, we will not share our sources or the nature of the intel with anyone else. That includes the White House." He looked at Flagler.

The president pursed his lips, put his hands together and looked up thoughtfully toward the ceiling. After a moment or two, he looked at Levell and said, "Fair enough. Anything else?"

"I do have a concern. This guy Farmer, the special counsel investigating your campaign. He's clearly expanded beyond the original scope of his mission. It looks like he's trying to get any dirt he can on you, regardless of its nature. As I said at our first meeting, if he were to get wind of any of this, it likely would bring down your administration."

"Dammit, Levell, I told you I'll deal with that prick. Your only concerns are to ensure the success of the mission and keep it all on the Q.T. Understood?" Flagler sat forward and rested his elbows on his knees. "Now, anything else?"

"A condition, not a question."

Trupockitt sat up suddenly as if goosed. "A condition? A condition? Who the fuck are you to place demands on the President of the United States of America? Perhaps it's more than just your legs that don't function properly."

"Whoa, Billy, that's going a little too far," Flagler said. "I mean, Cliff's proven that he's a patriot, a good American. This is his operation. If he needs something that I can provide, let him ask."

He turned back toward Levell. "What were you about to say, Cliff?"

"There's a nearly twenty-year-old Presidential Decision Directive issued by a former occupant of this office. It calls for the termination of the members of the Sleeping Dogs with extreme prejudice. I want it rescinded immediately."

Flagler looked pensive for several moments. Again, his lips were pursed and he stared at the ceiling. One hand was rubbing his chin. Finally, he looked at Levell and said, "You know I'm a businessman, right? I pride myself on being a terrific negotiator. One of the keys to negotiating successfully is never give anything away." He stared at Levell with a slight grin on his face.

"I'm aware of your background, sir. And I understand that you are renowned as a negotiator of business deals."

"Well, Cliff, this, too, is business. It's the nation's business. Pretty important stuff."

Levell waiting patiently for the president to come to the point.

"So, here's the deal, Cliff. You get your guys to grab those nukes and neutralize the bastards that have them. Afterward, I'll see that the damn PDD is rescinded in full. Hell, I'll even issue a full presidential pardon for each of them. What d'ya say?"

Levell nodded his head slowly. "Sir, I'm on board with the rescission, but, as much as I'd like to accept the full pardon for those men, it would have the effect of acknowledging their existence. And that would be the worst possible thing that could happen to them."

CHAPTER 20

DINGLE, IRELAND

FOR A CHANGE, Whelan was having a good time. He'd come to watch his teenage sons Sean and Declan practice American-style football for the local team, the Dingle *Tuath Dé*. In Irish Gaelic, the name meant "tribe of the gods," a supernatural race in pre-Christian Irish mythology. The team was a member of Ireland's Junior Football program. At seventeen and sixteen, respectively, Sean was the team's starter at running back, while Declan was its top wide receiver. The boys were much like their father, ridiculously fast and powerful. Most of the top teams in the Irish American Football Association were anxiously recruiting the boys in advance of their eighteenth birthdays.

Even more fascinating were the feelers coming from universities in the United States, among them Power Five Catholic schools such as Notre Dame and Boston College. But it was a wasted effort. There was only one school that interested the boys. The U. Their father had been recruited by every major college program in America. He'd never wavered in his desire to play at the University of Miami. And he'd brought Sven Larsen and Quentin Thomas with him. Although they had run roughshod over the best players in America in spring practice, they'd never played a down in regular season for Miami. Clifford Levell and Buster McCoy had persuaded them to put those plans on hold and use their unique talents to serve their country first.

Whelan paced the sideline, enjoying watching his sons practice and chatting amicably with other spectators. Everyone on the Dingle Peninsula knew Brendan Whelan, knew of his strength, speed, and intelligence. His reputation alone kept the peace. But the locals also knew about his troubles with Caitlin and were careful not to go there.

The head coach called a break and the players trotted to the sideline to hydrate.

He walked over to Whelan and said, "Nice to see you, Brendan."

They shook hands, and the coach said, "You must be quite pleased with your lads. They're phenomenal athletes."

Whelan smiled proudly.

"No question that they take after their da." The coach paused briefly. "If you're willin' to do it, it would be a big help to all the lads to have you scrimmage with us. What say ya'?"

"That would be quite an honor, Donagh, but they're just lads."

"You worried about hurting them, or the other way around? We're just scrimmagin' in shorts and helmets, but I can put a red jersey on you, so they'll know to avoid even incidental contact." Donagh smiled tauntingly.

"Well, truth be told, I believe I can still hold my own."

"I'm sure you can." The coach blew his whistle and motioned the players back on the field.

WHEN THE PRACTICE ENDED, Whelan took his sons to dinner at one of Dingle's fifty-two pubs. Although it had been an exhausting scrimmage, the boys were excited that their dad had not only watched them play, but also gotten involved.

"Da, did you see me outrun Conor O'Byrne and Dermot Madigan on that touchdown? What was it, sixty yards? I'm the fastest player by far," Sean said.

"I'm as fast as you are," Declan said. "Faster."

"In your dreams, Pee Wee." Sean made a dismissive motion with his hand.

"Pee Wee? I'm as big as you are…well, almost. But I will be soon." Declan turned to his father and said, "Did you see how open I was on that touchdown pass you threw to me? There was nobody within ten yards of me. No one is as fast as me."

"I," Whelan said.

"I what?"

"No one's as fast as I…am. Not 'no one's as fast as me am.' You're beginning to sound like a Yank."

"Will you be at our game on Friday, Da?" Sean asked eagerly. "It's against Tralee. We're tied for first place with them."

"That's my plan, if your mother doesn't object."

The boys looked at each other.

"Well, she won't. She can't," Declan said anxiously. "That wouldn't be fair."

"We'll ask her when I drive you home."

AFTER DINNER, Whelan drove the boys to Caitlin's from the practice field, *Páirc an Ághasaigh*, also known as The Fort Field for an old stone ring fort that had occupied the site for centuries. It was the home field for CLG *Daingean Uí Chúis*, the Dingle Gaelic Football Club. For a small annual fee, the club allowed the local American football team to use the facilities. Ironically, it was only a few hundred meters from the Fianna House.

Caitlin had rented a small cottage from a family friend in an area called Knocknahow. It was about three kilometers west of the center of Dingle. She and the two boys had moved there from her parents' home a week earlier.

As Whelan turned into the gravel driveway from the one-lane paved road, he saw a car he didn't recognize. Its number plate indicated it was registered in Dublin.

"Did the use of a car come with the house?"

Sean and Declan exchanged quick, worried glances. They said nothing.

"Something up?" Whelan said, as he pulled to a stop behind the other car.

Sean said, "Um…um…I think I left some of my equipment back at the pitch. I mean field. We'd better go back there before someone steals it."

Whelan locked eyes with the older boy. "I loaded your gear, all of it, in the boot. What's going on, Sean?"

His son wagged his head slowly back and forth. His mouth was open but no words came out.

"I take it your mother is having company."

Declan, head down, said in a soft, quiet voice, "Yeah."

"It's alright. She told me she was seeing someone else."

"Seeing?" Sean shouted, anger flashing in his eyes. "She's doing a lot more than…" He stopped in mid-sentence.

He didn't need to finish it. Whelan suddenly felt a cold sense of dread of losing something special. Simultaneously, there was a hot surge of sudden rage.

"He was supposed to be gone by the time we got home, Da," Declan said.

"What are you going to do?" Sean said anxiously.

Whelan didn't answer for several moments, calming himself and considering the right response. Finally, he said, "I'm going to see you boys safely inside, then I'm going back to the Fianna."

Sean said, "Aren't you going to beat the bloody hell out of him, Da?" His tone was one of disappointment.

"I have enough problems with your mother as it is. Harming her 'friend' would only make matters worse."

"But she's still your wife!"

Through clenched teeth, Whelan said, "She left the marriage, Sean. She's a grown woman and can make her own decisions, good and bad." He opened the driver's door and stepped out. "Now, let's be going."

Reluctantly, the boys climbed out and trudged to the door.

Whelan rapped on the front door. More than thirty seconds went by with no response. He started to knock again, when the door suddenly opened.

A disheveled-looking Caitlin stood there clutching a robe to keep it closed. The loose ends of its belt dangled at her sides. Her hair was wildly tousled and she seemed a little short of breath.

Whelan recognized her state from their own countless love-making sessions. A murderous rage engulfed him and he stepped toward the door.

Caitlin quickly placed both hands on his chest and pushed against him as hard as she could. Ordinarily, the same action by a five-hundred-pound sumo wrestler wouldn't have slowed Whelan.

"Brendan, don't!" Caitlin said. "Not in front of the boys."

"We don't care," Declan said.

She glared at her two sons. "Go to your room. Now!"

They looked at their father.

Whelan nodded. "Your mother's right."

Sean and Declan sighed in resignation and plodded slowly toward the room they shared.

"Cait, what the hell's the matter with you, shacking with some guy in front of our teenage sons?"

She crossed her arms under her full breasts. When she did, the robe loosened and one of her spectacular legs was revealed. And something more intimate as well. Whelan felt his passion surge, and with it the pain of what was happening to their relationship.

"What I do is none of your business," she said defiantly.

"You're my wife! That makes it my business."

"At this point, our marriage exists only because Irish law requires a minimum separation of four years before it can be dissolved."

"And you're still my wife for those four years."

She gave him another defiant look and said, "It's a stupid law. I'm a healthy, passionate woman. I have no intention of frustrating my needs and desires for four years."

"Even to the point of indulging them in front of the boys?" Whelan felt the anger increase.

Caitlin lowered her head. "That …that was an accident. I… lost track of time." She raised her eyes and looked at him, her defiance returning. "I'll be more discreet. It won't happen again."

A man's voice came from the back of the cottage. Whelan assumed that was where Caitlin's bedroom was. "Whoever it is, luv, get rid of them and come back to bed. We were just getting' to the good part."

A touch of red colored Caitlin's cheeks. She put her hands gently on Whelan's massive chest and firmly pushed him outside. "Go home Bren. I'll gladly share the boys with you, but you're not to involve yourself in my life."

He started to respond, but she put a finger on his lips.

"You need to remember the failure of our marriage is your fault. In choosing between protecting your family or serving that Levell person, you made the wrong choice. And now, I'm making choices."

CHAPTER 21

SANTA FE

Turan Salam was a skinny, orphaned Pashtun teenager turned legendary warrior in the Holy Army of the Caliphate. His fame came principally from participation with the late Bazir Haqqani in smuggling a nuclear device into the United States. It was used successfully by a suicide team to obliterate the Los Alamos National Laboratory. The act had brought acclaim and support for the HAC, the largest and most successful terrorist organization yet. Although it had been defeated militarily and lost the large swath of land it had declared as a caliphate across parts of Africa and the Middle East, it had made inroads into Europe, Asia, and the New World. The destruction of the Great Satan's nuclear bomb-making facility at the LANL had spurred recruitment of many thousands of new jihadi soldiers.

HAC's leader, a man who called himself Nadir Shah, was planning to multiply that success several times over. Shah personally had appointed Turan as the successor to Haqqani, and instructed him to oversee the smuggling of the remaining five nuclear devices into the United States.

But Turan was no longer a true believer. He'd had an epiphany. He had gotten to know some of the citizens of America and realized they weren't evil. They weren't really any different than his fellow Pashtuns. They had conquered a country at least as challenging and formidable as his native Waziristan. They had utilized their country's natural resources and their own rugged individualism to raise the standard of living to unparalleled heights. They did all this without instituting a caste system, suffering the dictates of an oppressive central government, or the need for chieftains and warlords. In fact, they had developed a system in which those from the lowliest circumstances of birth could attain great stature and wealth through education and industriousness.

To Turan, this was not the mark of a nation of Satans. If anything, its people were to be respected, admired, befriended, and emulated. It was one of the reasons for his epiphany, but not the principal one; that was a raven-haired beauty named Carolina Avila. The thought of her caused a weakness in the pit of his stomach and an ache in his heart.

He silently cursed himself. Unintentionally, he had been complicit in the deaths of Carolina's aunt and uncle, incinerated in the nuclear holocaust at Los Alamos. In planning the attack, he had considered the intended victims to be abstract figures, impersonal members of the Great Satan's masses of infidels. Too late, he'd realized what he'd done. Now, he intended to try to atone for it.

He realized that Carolina had only begrudgingly agreed to help him contact American authorities through her mother, Marisol, who worked for Major Fermin "Frank" Cuellar, the person in charge of the New Mexico State Police Special Operations Bureau. The meeting had been set up through Carolina because the only contact with Turan was through his promise to call her for instructions about a meeting.

The young Pashtun had the Uber driver drop him off at the Inn and Spa at Lorreto, a resort founded on the site of the historic Our Lady of Loretto, a Catholic girls' school run by the Sisters of Loretto. He wandered around the premises for several minutes, as if he were a curious tourist. In reality, he was carefully observing his surroundings for any sign of a tail. Next, he paid the entrance fee and toured the Loretto Chapel and appeared to spend more time admiring its famous "miraculous staircase." Again, he was looking for signs of surveillance.

The chapel had been completed in the late 1800s. Unfortunately, its builders neglected to include a means of accessing the choir loft twenty feet above ground level. Allegedly, the Sisters prayed to St. Joseph, the carpenter father of Jesus. Immediately, an unknown carpenter appeared on their doorstep. After working in secret for three months with only primitive hand tools, he emerged and disappeared. He left behind an enduring mystery— a twenty-foot tall, helix-shaped spiral staircase constructed without nails or center support.

During the time Turan appeared to be exploring the Loretto site, he continued to scan the surroundings for any sign that he was being tailed. Eventually, satisfied that he wasn't he began strolling casually east on Old Santa Fe Trail. At the end of the block, he jogged briefly left on East Water Street and continued east on Old Santa Fe Trail. Most of the buildings along both sides of the street had been built in the Santa Fe style, meaning there was minimum use of glass at street level. He crossed to the east side of the street and came upon a few shops that had plate glass windows. He paused and used them to surveil his surroundings. Eventually, he came to the intersection with East San Francisco Street. He paused briefly on the corner and stared across at the Santa Fe Plaza with its historic obelisk monument marking the terminus of the old Santa Fe Trail.

He felt his heart begin beating faster, and despite the chill of the January air, he began to sweat. Turan carefully looked around again but didn't notice anyone staring at him or seeming to approach. He swallowed hard and slid his right hand into the pocket of his leather bomber jacket, wrapping his fingers around the butt of the stubby Ruger EC9S. With a deep breath, he stepped off the curb and walked slowly across the street toward the Plaza.

THE SANTA FE PLAZA was the historical center of the town, dating from its original Spanish colonial days. It was roughly an acre and a half in size and square in shape with the controversial American Indian War Memorial Monument at its center. Walkways crisscrossed it beneath leafy bowers. A myriad of benches dotted its ancient surface. Despite the brisk temperature, groups of two or more tourists strolled the Plaza reading the information plaques, resting on one of the many benches, or tossing bits of food to the fearless and greedy head-bobbing, in-toed pigeons. To the north, across West Palace Avenue the ubiquitous row of Native Americans sat blanket-wrapped beneath the vigas-studded portico that ran along the front of the Palace of Governors. Displayed on the sidewalk in front of them were their wares— jewelry, rugs, blankets, carvings, and more.

Three people sat on one of the benches nearest the obelisk in the Plaza. Carolina Avila was flanked by her mother and her mother's boss, Major Frank Cuellar, who kept nervously glancing at his wristwatch. His actions were beginning to make Carolina nervous too.

"What time is it?" she asked Cuellar.

He reflexively looked at his watch again. "Three-twenty-two."

Another minute or so passed, and Cuellar turned to Carolina. "You're sure this was the place he picked? And the day and time?" It was the third time he'd asked those questions in the past twenty or so minutes.

"Yes, I'm sure."

Cuellar squirmed as if the bench was becoming uncomfortable for his bulky frame. "Then where is he? Did he chicken out, or maybe he was BS'ing us all along?"

His head swiveled around as he searched the area for the man he was seeking. He pulled the worn selfie Carolina had taken from his shirt pocket and stared at Turan Salam's youthful face. He held it in front of Carolina and said, "This is what Tomás or Turan or whatever the hell his name is looks like, right? Would he have changed his appearance?"

Marisol Avila sighed and said to her boss, "Major Cuellar, please, you're interrogating the poor girl. He either shows up, or he doesn't. Maybe he's running late. Maybe he's checking us out to make sure we didn't bring additional law enforcement personnel with us. It really just depends on how long you're willing to wait."

The metal bench was hard and cold. It was a blue-sky day, but an icy wind from the northwest was whipping through the narrow canyons of the old town. Carolina wiggled deeper into her long puffer jacket. She had mixed emotions about this whole operation. She wanted justice for her deceased aunt and uncle, but she recognized that she still harbored feelings of some kind for Tomás/Turan. She wasn't deceiving him or setting him up for a trap. He had asked her to arrange this meeting. But he was late.

Was he coming at all? Had he had second thoughts? A sudden gust of wind made her shiver.

Cuellar had begun tapping his foot impatiently. He looked different to Carolina. It was the first time she'd seen him out of his New Mexico State Police uniform. That had been part of the terms Tomás…Turan had set—only the three people on the bench, and no uniforms. She was to be in the middle with her long, thick, dark hair down so he could more easily spot her. And absolutely no one else. Cuellar had agreed. Other than Marisol, no other law enforcement personnel—local, state, or federal— knew about the meeting.

Cuellar seemed about ready to call it off when Carolina felt a presence. She looked at the nearby obelisk. A small group of tourists was bunched together reading the controversial commemorative plaque. A young man, taller than she remembered, was standing near them looking at Carolina. He wore a watch cap, a brown leather bomber jacket, faded blue jeans, and work boots. Although his eyes were shielded behind sunglasses, she recognized him immediately. Tomás. She wasn't cold anymore, as a surge of tension engulfed her.

She nudged her mother, and whispered, "He's here."

"Where?"

She pointed at him and reflexively made a small waving motion with her hand, as if in greeting.

Turan looked carefully around the area, then approached the three people who had stood up and now faced him. He kept his hands in the pockets of his jacket and his eyes focused on Carolina's expressionless face, looking for any sign of betrayal.

THE FOUR OF them had walked about five hundred feet from the Plaza to the Inn of the Anasazi on Washington Avenue. Turan, hands always in the pockets of his jacket, stayed close to Carolina, as if he knew there would be no sudden, violent actions with her in the line of fire. Once inside, they settled into the lounge area that adjoined the restaurant and bar. It was midafternoon and the area was deserted, just as Cuellar had promised. He had previously spoken with the hotel's manager, a good friend, and arranged for privacy.

The manager had met them at the entrance and seated them in an alcove. Turan purposely waited until the others sat down, then chose a seat on a rawhide covered sofa. With its back to the wall, he could see the whole room. It was furnished Southwestern-style with lots of leather and wood. Silence prevailed while the manager brought a silver tray with three coffees and a hot cocoa for Carolina. He placed them on a long, low wooden coffee table with granite inserts and departed.

Turan, of course, knew who Carolina and Marisol were. He stared at the third person, knowing he had to be Cuellar, the representative of the legal authorities.

Cuellar introduced himself, then said, "I...we appreciate the risk you're taking by being here. I want to assure you that, as you instructed, there are no other members of law enforcement involved in this meeting."

Turan said nothing. He looked at Carolina briefly. She seemed to be purposely looking away from him, a cold expression on her exquisitely beautiful face and smoldering anger in her dark eyes. The intensity of the feeling that flooded through his chest surprised him. He swallowed hard and looked away, scanning the room.

"You asked for this meeting," Cuellar said. "Is it your intention to surrender to authorities?"

Turan turned his gaze slowly back to Cuellar. "No. It's my intention to work with the appropriate authorities to prevent additional nuclear weapons from being detonated in this country."

Cuellar seemed uncertain. "And what is it you expect in return for these…ah…services?"

Turan looked at Carolina.

"You just hold on, Mister," Marisol said heatedly. "If you're thinking my daughter is going to be a part of this, you're delusional. This isn't the Middle East, where women are mere chattel to be given away as a part of deal-making. There will be no deals where she's concerned!"

"That's not what I'm thinking, Turan said, slowly shaking his head back and forth.

"What *are* you thinking?" Carolina said.

"Simply that I want to try to atone for my role in the incident at Los Alamos."

"Incident!" Marisol said. "Call it what it was—mass murder! My sister and her husband were incinerated in that…'incident!' There's no way on God's earth that you'll ever be able to atone for that."

Cuellar quickly said, "We just need to be clear about your expectations in the event you're successful in helping us find and recover those other nukes. I…we don't want you to assume that you'll be given a carte blanche when it's over."

"Will you be in charge of those efforts?" Turan said.

Cuellar hesitated and glanced away, then said, "No."

"Then what is your role? Why are you here?"

"For this, the initial meeting."

"Then what? Who will I be working with?"

"People that I'm told are the scariest bastards on this planet. They are able to go places and do things that law enforcement people can't."

"Why aren't they here?"

"I wasn't given the specifics, only to meet with you and try to determine if you're the real deal."

"The real deal?"

"It means legitimate, sincere in your offer to work with us."

Turan looked at Carolina again, then back at Cuellar. "Are these 'scariest bastards' the ones who killed Bazir Haqqani by ripping this heart from his chest with their bare hands?"

Cuellar nodded.

"When do I meet them?"

"Soon, but we'll need to be able to communicate that information to you."

"I'll be in touch with you though Carolina."

"Like hell," Marisol said.

"Those are my terms. I will not work through anyone else."

"It's alright, Mama," Carolina said, looking at Turan.

He stared back at her and felt a sudden rush in his chest. There was something different in her eyes now, not as much smoldering anger. And something else…interest?

CHAPTER 22

THE OVAL OFFICE

PRESIDENT FLAGLER LOOKED up from his chair behind the *Resolute* desk and motioned Senior White House Advisor Billy Trupockitt to take a seat on one of the two large sofas that faced each other in the middle of the room. Flagler came around the desk and sat opposite Trupockitt.

"Refresh my memory. Did we have a meeting scheduled?"

"No, sir."

Flagler shrugged. "No matter. One of the things that brought me such tremendous success in business was having a free-wheeling schedule. Very informal. What's on your mind?"

Trupockitt grabbed an apple from the large bowl that was positioned in the middle of the table separating the two sofas. "Something's bugging me about this whole set up with that Levell character."

"Before you get started, did you see my tweet this morning?"

"The one where you told the North Korean regime that you never sleep and the red button is never out of your immediate reach?"

"Yep," Flagler said with a satisfied smile.

The president slid forward near the edge of his seat, folded his hands between his knees, pursed his lips, and said, "What is it about Levell that bugs you? Cliff has access to some off-the-record badasses. I think that's just what we need to find those other nukes and eliminate the problem. You know, keep everything off the radar screen, don't panic the American public."

Trupockitt took a bite of the apple and starting speaking. "Yeah, that's all well and good, Mr. President, but I think we could be playing with fire here."

Flagler frowned. "Didn't your mother ever tell you not to talk with food in your mouth?"

The other man paused in mid-bite, then began chewing again.

"So, what's your problem with Levell?"

The advisor grimaced and shook his head. "I don't know. There's just something about the old bastard I don't trust. He's acting entirely on his own. What if he fucks up? What if it all comes back on us? I mean on you? The media would have a field day. The ensuing shitstorm could easily bring down your administration. Especially now that the sonofabitching special counsel has broadened the scope of his investigation to cover the number of times you take a leak."

Flagler wrinkled his nose, wagged his head, and made a similar motion with his hand. "From what I understand, this guy Levell is an old hand at clandestine operations. And this group of super ninjas he runs is supposed to be everybody's worst nightmare."

"Yeah, supposed to be. But at the end of the day, they're human too. And Levell is an old fart. Is he really up for something like this? I mean, these hotshots of his may have to go extraterritorial in searching for the nukes, as well as tracking down the perps and terminating them. There's always a possibility, probably a big one, that things could go totally FUBAR in a heartbeat. Then what? Our allies and other nations have had more than enough of the U.S. violating their territorial rights as well as their cyber secrets. And that goddam Farmer, the special counsel, will be throwing indictments at us as fast as he can print them."

"So, what are you saying? That we should call off the whole operation?"

"No, not at all. That would leave the country still exposed to the threat of these bombs."

Flagler pursed his lips, squinted his eyes, and stared silently at Trupockitt.

The advisor shifted nervously in his seat and put the partially eaten apple back in the bowl. "I'm just suggesting there's a better, less risky way to accomplish the goal, and have more control over the operation. After all, these badasses of Levell's aren't exactly trustworthy types. They've been subject to a Presidential Decision Directive for damn near twenty years. It calls for them to be executed on sight. Anywhere, anytime. These don't sound like the kind of people you should be associated with."

"Meaning what?"

"Maybe the best course of action would be to set them up, then carry out the PDD. Use U.S. military special operators for the mission."

Still squinty-eyed, Flagler offered a thin smile and said, "Do I detect professional jealousy on your part, Billy?"

Trupockitt shook his head vigorously. "No! I mean, why would there be?"

"Because you're my senior advisor on counterterrorism, including all off-the-radar activities. Maybe you're unhappy that, in your opinion, I've handed some of your perceived territory over to Levell and his people."

"No, you were clear with Levell that he has to coordinate everything through me."

"Fine, if it turns out he's not doing that, tell me. I'll straighten it out. Until then, let's not cause waves, when there isn't any storm."

Flagler stood, and Trupockitt scrambled to his feet too.

"Thank you, Mr. President," he said and started toward the door.

"Oh, and one other thing, Trupockitt. The next time you help yourself to an apple, don't put it back in the bowl once you've taken a bite."

CHAPTER 23

ALBUQUERQUE

IF THE WELL-KNOWN ANAPODOTON, "If looks could kill," spoke truth to power, the fire and anger in Camila Ramirez's dark eyes would have eviscerated Turan Salam on the spot. They were sitting in the cramped living room of a small house in the Nob Hill section of Albuquerque. The aging pueblo-style adobe home was located about one mile from the University of New Mexico Hospital. It was because of that proximity that she and Mitch Christie were renting it. His rehabilitation program required him to attend several physical therapy sessions per week at the hospital.

Cliff Levell had called Christie and asked him if he would be willing to accommodate a meeting at his home. Camila had vigorously opposed the venue for the meeting. Memories of the shootout with Turan and Haqqani that had nearly taken her fiancé's life were still vivid. The meeting included Levell, Christie, Camila, Frank Cuellar, Turan, and Marisol and Carolina Avila. The ever-present, ever-expressionless Nando stood silently behind Levell's wheelchair. Turan had insisted he would not attend the meeting if Carolina wasn't there.

Marisol had argued just as adamantly that her daughter should not be there. Even Cuellar had been unable to change her position. In the end, it was Levell who had called her and stressed how important it was to neutralize the remaining five nuclear devices in the hands of the jihadi terrorists. Only Turan could provide the information necessary to locate the weapons and the people who possessed them. Ultimately, Marisol had conceded the point, but insisted that she would be at Carolina's side every second.

"Like me, everyone here has some place else they need to be, so let's get to the point," Levell said. He looked at Turan. "You're Nadir Shah's point man for the five nukes, yes?"

Turan took his gaze off of Carolina and looked at Levell, then Nando behind him. Even with his inscrutable expression, the Brazilian exuded a menacing aura. Turan was uncomfortable enough in the tiny room, knowing that Christie, his captivating fiancée, Cuellar, and Marisol all were cops and probably armed. Levell and Carolina weren't threatening, but Levell's personal attendant gave Turan the impression that he didn't need a firearm to kill someone in an instant. He had the Ruger EC9S in the right-hand pocket of his bomber jacket, but, in the interest of appearing non-threatening, purposely had kept his hands where everyone could see them.

He looked back at Levell. "Yes."

"You look awfully young to be entrusted with such a major assignment."

Turan shrugged. "It was because of my involvement with the Los Alamos mission…" He glanced quickly at Carolina who sat rigidly on a tattered loveseat next to her mother. She stared unwaveringly at a point on the far wall. Turning again to Levell,

Turan said, "And Bazir Haqqani was no longer available to lead this one."

An icy smile creased Levell's leathery face. "Yes, Haqqani. Do you know how he died?"

Turan nodded again.

"You should never forget that you will be working with the same men who tracked him to a supposedly safe haven. One of them ripped Haqqani's heart out of his chest with his bare hands."

"I'm aware of the dangers," Turan said calmly and looked at Carolina again. She didn't return his gaze.

Christie said, "Do you know where the nukes currently are?"

Turan shook his head. "No."

"You're not much good to us without that knowledge," Levell said. "That's your only get-out-of-jail pass. Without that information, we've no reason not to take you into custody and prosecute you for the Los Alamos terrorism, an act that resulted in the murder of thousands of people."

"I know that. I wouldn't have exposed myself if I wasn't confident that Shah will provide that information to me."

"When?"

"I don't know exactly, but I believe it will be very soon."

"How will that happen?" Christie said.

"I have a cell phone that is to be used only to receive that information, then destroyed. The text will be encrypted in one of al-Mutanabbi's poems."

"Al who?" Cuellar said.

"He was one of Islam's greatest poets."

"What are you supposed to do until you receive that message?" Christie said.

"Lay low, as you in the West would say. Avoid involvement in any situation that might call attention to me."

For the first time, Carolina spoke. "So, what *have* you been doing?" There was no warmth in her voice or her expression.

"Mostly staying in a small motel near Santa Fe, watching television and reading books and newspapers."

"Books? What kind of books?" Camila said.

"Mostly about America and its people, where its greatness comes from, warts and all."

"Why the interest in America? After all, you very recently were part of an organization that is dedicated to destroying us." Camila said.

Turan's gaze dropped to the floor momentarily. "Yes, I know. I was mistaken. You are not the Great Satan. It is men like Nadir Shah who bring evil into this world. I hope to atone for my deeds…." He looked at Carolina. "If that's possible."

"Who's to say what's possible," Levell said. "Assuming you're not a double agent and are fully committed to helping us stop all further nuclear attacks, your life will be at risk no matter how the cards fall. If Shah's people discover you're a traitor, you know what they'll do to you. As horrible as that would be, it's nothing compared to what my people will do. Ripping Haqqani's heart out was merciful in comparison."

"Even worse than that will happen to you if you're harboring any thoughts about Carolina," Marisol said.

Levell looked at Marisol, then at Carolina, then at Turan. He and Christie exchanged glances.

"You said you expect to hear from Shah's people soon. When you do, what is supposed to happen next?" Levell said.

"The message will provide information for five contacts. They are members of the Holy Army of the Caliphate."

"These are people who are already here, in the US?"

"Not yet, but thy will be. They each lead a group. Each group will be responsible for moving a bomb to its intended location."

"And detonating it?"

"Yes."

"Do you know where these locations are?"

Turan shook his head. "Only the leader of each group knows the intended location for their specific bomb. That's done purposely for internal security. If one group is captured, they won't be able to give up the other groups."

"So, even you won't know the locations?" Christie said.

"Possibly not."

"Shit!" Christie said.

Levell leaned back in his wheelchair and smiled a cold, hard smile. "That clearly makes the task more challenging for us, but the people we're using will just have to get to these bastards while the bombs are still in a single location."

Christie and Cuellar exchanged glances, then Christie said to Levell, "So, you are going to use the Dogs for this?"

Levell nodded. "It's what they were born for."

CHAPTER 24

LOWER MANHATTAN

HARLAND FAIRCHILDE WAS the principal partner and largest
shareholder of one of the oldest and most successful investment
banking firms on Wall Street. It had been founded by one of his
ancestors in the mid-1800s. His personal office occupied almost
a quarter of the top floor of one of the city's tallest and most
prestigious office towers. From this exalted perch, he could see
most of the five Boroughs and beyond.

The telephone intercom on his desk buzzed.

"Yes?"

"Mr. Ulyanin has just arrived, sir." His executive assistant
said. "Shall I send him in?"

"Please do, Rosalynn."

A moment later the door to his office opened and Andrei
Ulyanin entered the room. Fairchilde waved him to a client chair
in front of his massive desk.

Ulyanin paused for a few moments before sitting. His gaze
took in the sheer size of the room, the incomparable view, the
furnishings and accessories. The room temperature and

humidity felt perfect. There was no noise from beyond the glass walls. There was a faint, but pleasant scent in the air. Finally, his eyes fixed on his host and he casually slid into the chair.

"I hope you'll excuse me if I forego the usual social conventions and move directly to the point of this meeting," Fairchilde said. "I regret doing so, but I have a busy schedule this morning."

Ulyanin shrugged dispassionately. "You sign my paycheck."

"Ironically, this has to do with your employment."

Ulyanin's expression of complete disinterest faded a little and he shifted slightly in his seat. "What about my employment?"

"I want to be very certain that you and I are on the same page. Despite having been very well compensated, it's clear that your late friend Kirill Federov was not loyal. And I fear that the recently departed Maksym Kozak wasn't either."

Ulyanin said nothing. His demeanor conveyed nothing.

"It seems that Maksym had two employers, me and the Chinese minister of finance, Zheng Bao Xun. Were you aware of that, Andrei?"

Ulyanin gazed steadily at Fairchilde. "It may have come to my attention."

Leaning back in his chair, Fairchilde tilted his head slightly and looked down his long, thin patrician nose at the Russian for several moments. Finally, he said, "I'm disappointed in you, Andrei. It appears you're being disingenuous."

Ulyanin's expression still betrayed nothing. "How so?"

"Shortly after the death of Maksym—at your hand, as I recall —you met with Zheng in Zürich. I believe it was in the lounge of the Dolder Grand Hotel, was it not?"

"I might have. Let's cut to the chase. What's your point?"

Fairchilde sat forward, placed his elbows on the desktop, and steepled his fingers. "It's a simple point, really. I must have absolute loyalty from my employees, especially from someone who is handling very sensitive matters for me."

"Are you suggesting that I'm disloyal?"

"I'm not suggesting, I'm stating fact. Like Maksym before you, you have agreed to work for Zheng while ostensibly working for me at the same time."

"Why would I do that?"

"I can only think of one reason. In spite of his air of inscrutability, Zheng clearly intends to take control of the Alliance for Global Unity once I have achieved our goal of one-world governance."

Ulyanin shrugged. "Why would he do that?"

"You are continuing to be disingenuous, Andrei. Zheng has shared with you his intention to usurp control of his nation's government. With China as the only surviving superpower following the fall of Western nations, he will be able to realize his dream of total Chinese world dominion."

Ulyanin said nothing.

"You're wondering how I know these things."

"Perhaps you are paranoid."

Fairchilde smiled coldly. "I didn't consolidate my power in AGU by being careless or trusting foolishly, Andrei. Are you familiar with the aphorism, 'keep your friends close; keep your enemies closer?'"

The other man nodded.

"That is what I have done with minister Zheng. I have had him under surveillance since he became a member of AGU." Fairchilde paused for effect, then said, "I have tapes of his conversations, including the one he had with you in Zurich. Let me play a portion of it for you."

Fairchilde tapped a button on a recording device on his desk and Zheng's voice came through the speaker.

"I need a replacement for Maksym, and you, Andrei, seem the perfect candidate."

"How so?"

"You already are employed by Harland Fairchilde and are familiar with the workings of the Alliance for Global Unity. You would continue in that role, except you actually would be working for me, reporting everything Fairchilde says and does, who he meets with, that sort of thing."

"Because?"

"It is China's destiny is to rule the world, and we are using AGU to help pave the way."

"How so?"

"AGU has strong relationships with America's enemies—the various jihadi organizations, North Korea, and others. Their actions serve to weaken America and other Western powers, making our path easier."

"What about my 'homies', the Russians?"

"That's become a bit more confusing with the new American president in the mix. We're working on a strategy to drive a wedge between the Russian and American presidents."

"Yeah, good luck with that. How much does this job pay?"

"Twice what Fairchilde is paying you."

"And I'll still get paid by Fairchilde too?"

"Of course."

"When do I start?"

Fairchilde stopped the recording and looked at Ulyanin. "Your disloyalty seems rather obvious, don't you think?"

"Are you firing me?"

"Given the circumstances, the damning evidence, wouldn't you say you deserve to be terminated?"

Ulyanin said nothing.

Leaning slowly back in his chair again, Fairchilde said,

"Actually, this may be your lucky day, Andrei. If you can reestablish your allegiance to me, you would be a unique position to keep me informed of Zheng's activities."

Ulyanin's eyes narrowed, as if in deep thought. After several moments, he said, "What you're proposing is that I be what the spy people call a triple agent. I work for you, but Zheng thinks I'm working for him by reporting on you, while I'm really working for you and reporting on him."

"Triple agent, how clever. Yes, I like that."

"You can't let Zheng go on indefinitely. What is your plan for him?"

Fairchilde smiled again. "I've maintained a complete dossier on his treacherous intentions with regard to China. I'll see that it's delivered to China's president at the appropriate time."

CHAPTER 25

DINGLE, IRELAND

UNCHARACTERISTICALLY, Whelan hadn't shaved for several days and his work clothes, though clean, were unironed and wrinkled. His thick brown hair was uncombed. He'd closed the Fianna House and cancelled all pending reservations. He didn't have the same interest in running it now that it wasn't his family's home. The emptiness of the rambling inn mirrored the vacuum in his soul.

He sat at the table in the kitchen, days' worth of dirty dishes piled in the sink; testimony to the solitary meals he had eaten. Most of those had been prepared meals he'd picked up at the SuperValu grocery or from local pubs. He didn't like going out and tried to slip in and out of those places with a minimum of social contact. Still, everyone knew him. Some respected the struggle he was going through; yet others seemed intent on discussing the state of his marriage to Caitlin. It was more than embarrassing. His wife had left him and was now openly living with another man.

Tall, handsome, and blessed with speed, strength, and intellect possessed by almost no other men, Whelan was accustomed to women literally swooning over him. He was having a difficult time adjusting to Caitlin's loss of interest in their marriage and infatuation with a lesser being. He accepted that she blamed him for the death of her brother and the near loss of her own life and those of their two sons. But the shock of the disintegration of their marriage was overwhelming.

It was midafternoon, and he sat with a tumbler in his hand. A half-empty bottle of Kavanagh twelve-year-old, single malt Irish whiskey was on the table next to it. He remembered his late father saying on many occasions that the "drinking lamp" was lit at five in the afternoon. Any drinking before then was a bad sign. *Well, Da, I hope you're not too disappointed.*

Just as he lifted the tumbler and brought it to his lips, he heard the special ringtone of the satphone Levell used for SAS calls. He'd left it on the small desk in the cramped office space that was just off the kitchen. He ignored it and took a sip. It wasn't his first one that day, but the finely made paragon of the distiller's art still filled his mouth with a pleasing warmth followed by a long, smooth finish.

The satphone stopped ringing, but his cell phone started. He let it ring too. Eventually, the call went to voicemail, and the ringing stopped. It was followed shortly after by a sound that let him know he'd received a text message. On its heels, came another tone that indicated he'd received an email.

Whelan shook his head and smiled. No doubt all the attempts were from the same source—Levell. *The Old Man is persistent, I'll give him that. He must be really anxious to speak with me.* He took another sip of the whiskey. *Whatever he wants, I'm not interested.*

THE PHONE CALLS, text messages, and emails kept up their annoying arrivals all afternoon. He locked the satphone in the special safe in the office. That stopped its interruptions, but he couldn't turn off or mute the cell phone. A family member might call.

He cleaned up, shaved, and put on some decent clothes, then walked down the street to the soccer pitch. Sean and Declan's American football team was hosting the team from Tralee. Whelan didn't feel much like being social, but forced himself to smile and nod to the many folks who called out to him. He found a spot against the chain-link fence near the twenty-yard line and watched his boys toy with grown men. By halftime, the game was well out of hand for the visiting team. Sean had scored on three long runs, and his wide-open younger brother had snared two touchdown passes in the end zone. Watching them made Whelan feel as though he was watching himself almost twenty years earlier.

Late in the third quarter, after the play was dead, Declan was blindsided by a hulking player from Tralee. Whelan could see the blow had injured his son. All eyes in the stands focused on Whelan, as if expecting a violent reaction. His initial instinct was to bolt onto the field and, with his bare hands, separate the offender's head from his shoulders. There must have been a tele-pathic communication between him and his oldest son. Sean, leaning over his fallen brother, spun around and stared at his father. Sean's expression said "No!" He even subtly wagged his head back and forth.

The team physician checked Declan over, and helped him get to his feet. The youngster shook his head as if to clear it, and slowly trotted off the field. In a few minutes, he seemed to have recovered. Just for good measure, late in the game, Sean laid the offending player out with a vicious cutback block that knocked the man unconscious. Whelan smiled with a deep sense of satisfaction and thought: *The apples don't fall far from the tree.* Declan chest bumped Sean as he came off the field.

After the game, Whelan took the two boys to one of Dingle's many pubs for dinner. As they waited amid the tantalizing aromas for the server to bring their meals, Whelan checked his phone again. As he'd expected, he'd received even more email, voicemail, and text messages from Levell. But there was something else. A text from Caitlin: "I have to see you. Please."

He looked at the boys. "Is everything alright with your mother?"

They didn't look at him, just fiddled with their water glasses.

"Boys, I asked you a question."

Declan looked at Sean.

The older boy sighed and said, "I dunno, maybe." He still didn't look at Whelan.

At that point, the server arrived with their dinners.

Whelan waited until she left.

"I got a text from your mother saying she wanted to talk with me. Sounded kind of urgent. What's going on?" He looked pointedly at Sean.

The young man shifted uneasily in his seat. "She's been kinda sick lately."

"And Rodney, the guy from Dublin, he's gone," Declan said. "Maybe she wants to get back with you, Da."

"Don't be pinning your hopes on that happening, son."

WHEN HE DROVE the boys back to Caitlin's cottage after dinner, he noticed the car with the Dublin number plate was not there.

Caitlin came out to the car as soon as he pulled into the driveway. Her hair was a mess and she wasn't wearing makeup. Her eyes were puffy and red and looked as if she'd been crying. She had on a heavy cable knit cardigan. Her arms were crossed, pulling it tightly around her.

"We have to speak," she said, "but not here, not now."

"When and where?"

"Tomorrow. I'll come by the Fianna about nine." Caitlin turned abruptly and walked back to the cottage.

CHAPTER 26

LOWER MANHATTAN

BILLY TRUPOCKITT, the president's special advisor on counterterrorism, exited the cab in front of a Georgian-style six-story building on East 14th Street. It was where Gramercy Park transitioned into Irving Place. The street was typically clogged with New York City foot and vehicular traffic. At ground level, an endless number of narrow commercial bays hawked every conceivable product or service. Most of the buildings on this section of the street housed offices on the upper floors. Rusted fire escapes further blemished some of the aging facades.

Trupockitt glanced furtively up and down the street. The Expeditionary Club was one of the oldest private clubs in the city, established following the Civil War by the wealthiest members of the financial community. Harland Fairchilde's great-great-grandfather had been one of the founders, and membership had included each succeeding Fairchilde generation. Most of the other venerable private clubs founded in that era had moved more than once and now called Midtown Manhattan home. The Expeditionary Club was traditional if nothing else.

A liveried doorman admitted Trupockitt to the foyer, where a receptionist checked her records and found his name on the guest list. Another employee materialized through a doorway behind the receptionist and led him to a classic and ancient elevator. It creaked slowly to the fourth floor. The guide showed him to a small, elegantly furnished room and closed the door as he left. There was a musty smell, as if the air in the room hadn't circulated since the Civil War.

There was a sole occupant other than Trupockitt, a tall, lean middle-aged man wearing an immaculately tailored suit was sitting at a small coffee table. He looked up from the newspaper he was reading and said, "You're precisely on time, Trupockitt. I appreciate punctuality. That's not always easy to achieve in this city." He motioned at a chair on the opposite side of a coffee table. "Won't you have a seat. Would you care for coffee or some other refreshment?"

"No, thank you, Mr. Fairchilde."

"Please, call me Harland. The Club is an oasis as far as formalities are concerned." He paused, then added, "It's also an ideal place to hold discussions of a sensitive nature."

As he sat down, Trupockitt said, "I appreciate your seeing me on short notice, Harland."

"Not at all. The message you sent me through that obsequious bastard Mort Solomon was most intriguing."

"You don't care for Senator Solomon?"

"As this state's senior senator and a progressive ideologue, he has his occasional uses. Let's just leave it at that."

Trupockitt nodded.

"In this instance, Mort said you had some interesting information you wanted to share with me. Something to do with that boorish oaf in the White House and illegal plans to wage war in other countries?"

"Yes, I'm deeply disturbed by it."

"As we all should be. But why, exactly, is it that you want to share this with me?"

Trupockitt moved to the edge of his seat and rested his elbows on his knees, leaning toward the other man. "I've... always wanted to join the Alliance for Global Unity, AGU. I was hopeful that if I can prove useful to its cause, I might be invited."

"Yes, well, depending on the extent of this 'usefulness,'" Fairchilde said carefully, "I may be able to put in a word for you." He looked at his guest and motioned with a hand to start talking.

"We have intelligence that the terrorists who destroyed Los Alamos have five more nuclear devices." Trupockitt waited as if expecting Fairchilde to display shock.

Instead, the other man smiled thinly and said. "I know."

With disappointment in his voice, Trupockitt continued. "I was under the impression that that information was highly classified. How could you know about it?"

"Given AGU's many members and contacts within the deep state, there isn't much I don't know. But the question is, does Flagler know where the devices are?"

Trupockitt smiled as if sensing an opening. "Not yet, but he's working with someone named Levell—"

"Levell! Clifford Levell?" Fairchilde sat bolt upright.

"Yes. I take it you know him?"

"Only too well, unfortunately. What has Levell told Flagler?"

Trupockitt's eyes narrowed ever so slightly, as a calculating thought entered his consciousness. *I may have just found my entry pass into AGU.* "Levell apparently has some sort of patriotic organization—"

"Yes, yes, I know all of that. They call themselves The Society of Adam Smith, or SAS."

"Well, apparently Levell controls a unit of special operators who are superior to—"

"Normal human beings. Yes, they're genetic freaks. What are he and Flagler planning to do?"

"Levell says he's gotten information about one of the terrorists who was involved in the Los Alamos attack. He says the man wants to work with us…with our authorities, as a mole. When he learns of the location of the other five bombs, he'll share that and the identity of those who are to place and detonate them."

"And Levell's so-called Sleeping Dogs will neutralize the threat."

"That's the plan."

"But at this moment, SAS doesn't know who they are or where the nuclear devices are, correct?"

"That's my understanding."

"Do we know who the mole is in the terrorist organization?"

Trupockitt shook his head. "I'm sure Levell knows who it is, but he hasn't shared that with me."

Fairchilde stared thoughtfully at Trupockitt for several seconds, then said, "You've done AGU a very important service, Billy. But, going forward, we'll need you to be our eyes and ears where this program is concerned. I want to know instantly when anything develops, and in particular the identity of this 'mole.' Understood?"

"Yes, of course. But things are likely to happen quickly from this point forward. Trying to contact you through another party, like Solomon, won't do."

"No, it won't. I'll see that you're provided with a properly encrypted communication device. You are to use it only to contact me. No take-out orders, no Uber rides, no chats with lady friends, no anything."

CHAPTER 27

NEAR KARAGANDA, KAZAKHSTAN

SERGEI KRUCHINKIN TOYED with the Belarusian special forces soldier. The man was as tall as the Russian, but almost one hundred pounds lighter. He was young, quick, and well-conditioned. And he had a combat knife. Kruchinkin did not. With the Russian's genetic gifts, it didn't matter. He easily slipped the Belarusian's attacks, laughing derisively as he did.

Although exceptionally well-trained, the soldier's frustration began to override his judgment. He feinted to his right, then attacked straight ahead as swiftly as he could. Kruchinkin was faster. He pivoted to his right and clamped his right hand on the wrist of the other man's arm that held the knife. Using his opponent's momentum against him, the Russian yanked the man off his feet and began spinning him around his head like a cowboy with a lasso.

The Belarusian's shoulder dislocated. He screamed in pain and dropped the knife. After several rotations, Kruchinkin released the wrist. The young soldier's body rocketed twenty feet through the air, coming to a sudden halt when it collided with the concrete wall of a building. It bounced off the wall and crashed to a motionless heap on the ground.

The large crowd that moments earlier had been raucously cheering for one or the other of the combatants fell silent. Medics rushed to tend to the Belarusian. After several moments, one of them looked toward the judge's stand and slowly shook his head. It provoked an uproar from the crowd and fistfights began to break out.

Kruchinkin, with a wicked grin, raised his arms above his head in triumph and slowly swept his gaze across the crowd.

A single gunshot rang out and silence returned. An older man in the uniform of a Kazakhstani general strode from his seat in the middle of the panel of judges to the VIP section of spectator seating. He stopped before a small, well-dressed Asian-looking man.

Speaking passable English, he said, "Minister Zheng, you are well aware that these are training exercises and friendly competitions. Was it not made clear that there was to be no intentional harm to any of the contestants?"

"My sincerest apologies, General Temirov. I shall deal with the offender personally."

"And who will deal with the Belarusians? Your undisciplined killer has ruined this annual competition between special forces units from around the globe. And it has created a diplomatic problem between my government and that of Belarus."

"I am personally acquainted with President Kovalev and consider him a friend. I will speak with him and assure him that Kazakhstan did everything in its power to prevent this occurrence. I will withdraw our team from the remainder of the competition and return to China at its conclusion. Needless to say, the perpetrator will be severely disciplined." Zheng smiled placatingly.

Temirov was silent for several moments, as if struggling with his next words. Finally, he said, "My opinion is that we should retain that individual, try him and punish him here in Kazakhstan. But, in respect of the relationship between our two nations, I will let you deal with that."

"I will see to it immediately. Thank you for handling the situation so well."

"To be clear, Minister Zheng, I want you to remove your entire team from my country by this evening. Is that understood?"

THE AIR ASTANA chartered flight covered the less than five hundred miles from Karaganda to Almaty, the former capital of Kazakhstan and its largest city, in ninety minutes. From there, a PLA troop transport helicopter ferried Zheng and the rest of the Chinese special forces team and trainers the remaining one hundred and seventy miles to Ili. The town was in the Xinjiang Uyghur Autonomous Region, the largest Chinese administrative division and the eighth largest country subdivision in the world, spanning over 640,000 square miles. Ili, itself, was located between the Altai Mountains and the main range of the Tian Shan, in the Dzungarian Basin in northern Xinjiang.

Because of the variety of rugged terrain surrounding the area, Zheng had chosen it as the site of the training facilities for a small group of special operators. Including Kruchinkin, there were ten men in the unit. The nearby alpine Sayram Lake, formidable mountains, dense forests, and trackless Taklimakan Desert made it the perfect location for training special operations forces in all conceivable conditions and situations.

Zheng didn't need these men to be the best on the planet. He just needed them to be able to kill the Sleeping Dogs. The fact that they had the same genetic benefits as the Dogs was the most important factor.

Back at their camp on the high ground above Ili, Zheng called a meeting. Only the ten trainees, including Kruchinkin, were invited.

"I have something important to say to you," Zheng said in English, the only common language among them. "Please stand and pay close attention." Only Luka Dragović, the Croatian, stood. The others lounged insolently. All were burly, thickly muscled men who dwarfed Zheng. He was infuriated by their insubordinate attitudes but masked it. "You each have a paycheck coming in a few days. You would do well to humor me."

Slowly, the other nine stood.

Zheng looked pointedly at each man, saving Kruchinkin for last. "Thanks to you, Sergei, it may be some time before a Chinese team is invited back to the annual special forces competition."

"Competition?" Kruchinkin said with disdain. "Maybe is for pussies, yes? But not for Sergei Kruchinkin." Many of the others snickered.

"The point, as I repeatedly told all of you, was not to reveal your extraordinary talents until the appropriate time. The point was to continue your training by practicing with other special operators. At. Their. Level."

"So? Now they know they are inferior. Where is harm?"

"We recruited you and are training you for a special mission. Knowledge of your existence could ruin the element of surprise."

"So?" Kruchinkin looked around at his comrades. "We don't need no surprise. Look at us. Who has chance against us, surprise or no?"

The Spaniard, Ignacio "Loco" Montero, slapped the Russian on the shoulder. "Sergei is right."

"Yeah," said Alard Deschamps, one of the two Frenchmen, "what's all this secrecy shit? Just show us who you want us to kill."

"And have your bank standin' by." The Englishman, Gage Stark, said. It brought cheers from the others.

Zheng remained patient. "The praying mantis waved its arms angrily in front of an approaching carriage, unaware that it is incapable of stopping it. Such was the high opinion it had of its talents."

Horst Geissler, one of the two Germans, said, "Sun Tzu?"

"Close, but no. It was Zhuang Zhou."

"So, what's it bloody fuckin' mean?" said Stark.

With an enigmatic smile, Zheng said, "Overconfidence can get you killed."

"You're not overconfident when you are the best," said the Turk, Mehmet Karga.

"Ah, but you presume there are no others with your skills. You are wrong, and that is what will get you killed," Zheng said.

"What does that mean? Are you saying there are others like us?" Kruchinkin demanded.

"Yes. They are better trained and have been working together for many years. But they don't know you exist, at least before today." Zheng looked pointedly at Kruchinkin. "They will be your target. To defeat them, you will need to have surprise on your side."

"Bullshit!" Kruchinkin said. "I have never even been close to losing a fight. I am the undefeated champion of the famous Baddest Badass competition. No one can beat me."

"Not so," Zheng said softly. He pulled out his smartphone and pressed a key.

The door opened and a large Chinese man wearing a PLA colonel's uniform stepped inside. He bowed slightly toward Zheng.

"Do you recognize Colonel Zhao?" Zheng said to Kruchinkin.

The Russian stared at the newcomer uneasily. "Maybe I see him somewhere."

"Indeed, you did. He was in the front row at the last Baddest Badass competition. He helped you get out of town when the authorities raided it." Zheng turned toward the colonel. "Mr. Kruchinkin was defending his title in the finals. How did that go for him?"

Zhao looked unwaveringly at the big Russian. "As Westerners would say, he was getting his ass whipped. If the raid hadn't occurred when it did, he would have been beaten, perhaps killed."

"Bullshit," Kruchinkin said without much conviction.

His fellow genetic freaks all looked at him.

"Your opponent that night was a man named Sven Larsen," Zheng said. "There are six more like him. They're called the Sleeping Dogs, and they are the ones I mentioned a moment ago. At this point in time, they are better than you are. They also are a threat to plans that are important to me. Your purpose is to kill them before they cause any further problems."

The ten men stirred uneasily. One of them, Màriu Sanno, the Sardinian, said, "You say they better than us. Then how we kill them?"

"With proper training and the right opportunity, all of which we will provide."

"And you pay big money for this, yes?" Sanno said.

Zheng nodded. "More than you can comprehend."

CHAPTER 28

WASHINGTON, D.C.

DAVID FARMER REFLECTED WISTFULLY on the days when windows actually were made to be opened. Today would have been a good day to crack a window and let some wintry air slip into the office that felt overly warm to him. HVAC was impersonal. It didn't care how comfortable or otherwise the occupants were. It just maintained whatever temperature had been programmed. In this case, one setting controlled the whole building. Even a special counsel appointed by the United States Department of Justice had no say in the matter. His office was heated or cooled at the same temperature as the entire building. Personal comfort and the limitless capabilities of modern technology had been overridden by budget-minded bureaucrats.

He loosened his tie and rotated his chair to peer out the large window behind him at the cold gray sky. It gave every appearance of a pending snowfall. Farmer wondered if the weather would affect the plans of the man who was traveling from New York City to meet with him today. He didn't know the man personally, but certainly knew of him. Harland Fairchilde IV was one of the wealthiest men in the country. And definitely one of the most politically influential.

He glanced at his watch. It was almost 10:30 a.m. Farmer hadn't been advised otherwise, so he assumed the meeting was still on. He stood and walked to a coat tree near the entrance to his office, slipped into his lined trench coat, and left the building, advising his executive assistant that he needed some fresh air. Farmer drove the little more than two miles through the midmorning traffic to the Four Seasons Hotel in Georgetown. Fairchilde was waiting in a small private dining room.

As Farmer entered the room, the older man stood and extended his hand. "I appreciate your seeing me under these circumstances, Special Counsel Farmer."

"Please, call me Dave, Mr. Fairchilde." He shook the offered hand and sat down.

Fairchilde poured a cup of coffee from a carafe and handed it to Farmer. "Turnabout is fair play, as they say. You must call me Harland."

Farmer was honored and delighted that a man of Fairchilde's stature wanted to be on a first-name basis with him. He took a sip of the coffee. "Your office said something about you having potentially valuable information regarding the current investigation into the president's campaign activities."

"That's correct, but it may only be indirectly or tangentially connected with the original parameters of your investigation."

"How so?" Farmer put the cup down and leaned in toward Fairchilde.

"You're looking for any links or coordination between a certain foreign government and individuals associated with the president's campaign, and whether any crimes were committed as part of those activities. But the latitude afforded your investigative efforts could easily encompass other illegal activities or affiliations involving this administration, correct?"

"Possibly." Farmer leaned back in his chair and gazed thoughtfully at the other man, as if wondering where the conversation was going. "Is there something in particular you wanted to discuss?"

Fairchilde nodded and in a grave tone of voice said, "I fear this president is engaging in an illegal activity, one that will place this nation in great peril."

Once again, Farmer leaned forward in his chair. "Is this speculation, or do you have proof?"

"I have the strongest kind of evidence...someone on the president's staff, a senior advisor."

"Are they willing to discuss this with me?"

"Yes, but only in the strictest confidence, of course."

"And what's the nature of this...illegal activity?"

"The president plans to use a private security force, answerable only to him, to assassinate foreign interests he deems a danger to this country."

Farmer slumped back in his chair. "My God."

CHAPTER 29

DINGLE, IRELAND

WHELAN HEARD the car pull into the motor court of the Fianna House. He had been using his iMac and glanced at the upper right corner of the screen. It was 9:01 a.m. *If nothing else, the girl is punctual.* A feeling of foreboding came over him as he rose to go to the door. He wasn't sure what she wanted to discuss, but something told him it wasn't going to be positive. He took a deep breath and exhaled slowly.

She rang the bell just as he reached the door. He thought how odd it was that not so long ago she had lived here as his wife. Now, she was almost a stranger, ringing the doorbell at what for years had been her own home. He opened the door slowly so as not to startle her.

They stood silently on the threshold for a few moments looking at each other. Whelan didn't know what she saw, but he knew what he did. Kate appeared very different from the woman who had lived at the Fianna with him. He'd always thought her long, silky, dark auburn hair was the most beautiful he had seen on any woman. Today, she had it pulled back in a ponytail, held in place by a green rubber band. She used to brush it a hundred or more strokes each day. Now, frizzy and lifeless, it looked like she hadn't brushed it, maybe even washed it, in a while. The sparkle was gone from her emerald green eyes. Her once beautiful skin looked pale and lifeless, and lines were showing around her eyes and mouth. He noticed too that she wasn't wearing her usual minimal makeup. She wore a short jacket over an untucked blouse, jeans, and slippers. The girl he'd married had been meticulous, if informal, about her appearance. Looking at the woman on his doorstep, he wondered if she'd even glanced in the mirror before she'd left her house.

Whelan stepped aside. "Come in, Cait."

He led her to the B&B's kitchen. Less than twenty-four hours earlier it had been a disaster area, but the occasional housekeeper, Mrs. Thornhill, had helped him clean it up. The stack of dirty dishes was gone from the sink, the countertops and cabinets polished, and the floor vacuumed and mopped. The room now looked serviceable. Whelan didn't ask if Caitlin wanted coffee. She looked like she did. He used the Keurig machine to brew two mugs. While he did, she sat silently at the kitchen table. When the coffee was done, he placed a mug in front of her and took a seat on the opposite side of the table.

"I think your words last night were 'we have to speak.'"

She sat stiffly, her hands clenched in her lap, staring at her coffee mug. "Yes."

"You're tense, Cait," he said, as gently as he could. "Is it the boys? Have they been acting up?"

She moved her head from side to side slowly. "No."

"If we 'have to speak,' your reticence is making that difficult."

She was silent for several moments, but her body English spoke volumes. She began twisting her hands in her lap, and a

large teardrop started a slow glide down one of her softly
rounded cheeks.

Whelan resisted the strong urge to speak, to offer comforting
words.

After a minute that seemed an eternity, she said in a whisper,
"I've been so very stupid."

She seemed to be having trouble continuing. Whelan
thought he knew what she was going to say, but knew it had to
be expressed by her, in her own words. He said, "In what
way?"

The tear was nearing the corner of her mouth. She reached up
and swiped at it, still not looking at him.

He waited for her to continue.

"I...I was so angry." She closed her eyes and swallowed
hard. "I even thought I hated you for what you'd done. I felt
betrayed."

She kept her eyes closed, and her lower lip began to quiver.

"Because of Maksym."

"Yes." She was silent for several more seconds. Whelan
waited.

"Yes, Maksym. And Levell. That whole situation." The
words began to tumble out as her upper body began to tremble.
"You knew Maksym had sworn to kill us, that one day he would
come for us. Yet you left us alone, guarded by ill-prepared
friends and neighbors. Maksym killed some of them, including...
including my brother Padraig...and came within seconds of
killing our sons and me." She began sobbing uncontrollably as
she relived those terrifying moments.

It was difficult, but Whelan refrained from offering comfort.
He knew she needed to confront her grief, to get it out of her
system, as much as that was possible.

After another minute or so, her sobs began to abate, but she still didn't look at him. "I was so angry with you that I...did something impossibly foolish."

"Took up with another man."

Caitlin's sobs returned, and she covered her eyes with her hands. When she regained control, she said in a barely audible voice, "I was so stupid, Bren, to throw away what we had. Can you ever forgive me? Is there any chance we can rebuild our marriage?"

In a voice that had the chill of an ancient tomb, he said, "Before we cross that bridge, I think there's more to your story, isn't there?"

She pulled her hands away from her face, and stared at the floor. "Why do you say that?"

He said nothing, just sat motionless, looking at her without expression.

Caitlin looked down quickly and began to cry again. "Yes, there...is...more," she said jerkily between sobs. "I'm pregnant."

"With his child."

She bobbed her head rapidly up and down.

"What do you plan to do about the situation?"

She shrugged. "I don't know. I'm still in a state of shock. I mean, I thought I was past having more children. Not physically, of course, I'm only thirty-seven. But we have two beautiful boys and I was satisfied with that."

"Then *what* happened?"

She sobbed a bit more, then said, "I was so foolish, so blinded by anger and a desire to hurt you. I threw myself at the first attractive man that came along, and...well, things happened. Oh, God, Bren, I feel like such a slut." She doubled over as if in pain and sobbed harder than ever.

As much as he wanted to console her, he knew it would only make matters worse in the long run. She would interpret it as an expression of his desire to be with her again. That desire was absent. He stood and went to the Keurig again. He made another cup for himself, but noted she hadn't touched her original one.

When he sat down again, she wiped her eyes and looked at him for the first time since their conversation had started. There was fear in her eyes. Not fear that he would harm her; fear that he didn't care.

"Have you told the father?"

She shook her head. "Not yet."

"What are you waiting for? Don't you think he should know? Or are you afraid that he'll do the gentlemanly thing and offer to marry you..., when our divorce is final?"

"I don't want to marry Rodney. I don't love him. I never did. Besides, I don't think he would do it. He's more of a playboy than he is marriage material."

Whelan was silent for a moment. "That didn't seem to stop you from sharing your most intimate moments with him."

"I don't blame you for being angry with me. You have every reason to be. I can't believe I behaved so stupidly, so recklessly. I can't believe that I could ever hurt you, damage our extraordinary relationship. You're the only man I've ever loved." Her words tumbled out.

"I'm not angry with you, Caitlin, more like disappointed." He took a swallow of his coffee. "I'm not sure what you're asking me to do. Offer you advice? If that's it, go marry Rodney. He if refuses, I can have a come-to-Jesus talk with him that will convince him otherwise. It would be a way for you to regain a portion of respectability. This is, after all, a small town." He paused. "For that matter, have you given thought to moving away?"

She sat slumped in her chair, hands folded in her lap again, head down. Very softly, she said, "That's not what I want. I want you. I want us."

"And the baby?"

She shook her head again. "I don't know. Abortion is now legal in Ireland, but it's still frowned upon. I could go to another country, but I don't believe in that vile practice."

"That leaves only one alternative—have the baby. But that raises the question: then what?"

"Put it up for adoption," she whispered.

"That would never happen, Caitlin. Your motherly instincts wouldn't allow it."

She nodded almost imperceptibly.

Silence enveloped the kitchen for several seconds. Eventually, she raised her head and looked at him. "There isn't going to be an us again, is there?"

WHELAN SAT at the kitchen table for hours after Caitlin left. Eventually, he switched from coffee to Redbreast 21-year-old Irish whiskey. It was single pot stilled and matured in sherry and bourbon casks. Whelan considered it to be the epitome of Irish distilling skills. He sipped it slowly, almost reverently.

Finally, he rose and went into the cramped office off the kitchen. He placed his thumb against the reading screen of the small wall safe. After a moment, there was a clicking sound and its door opened. He removed the satphone and went back to his seat at the table. Moments later, he heard Levell on the other end.

"You Irish bastard! It's about time you returned my calls. I've been reaching out to you for days. Tried texts and emails. Left voicemails. I was about to call the damn *Garda* and ask them to drag your ass to a phone and link you up with me. Where the hell have you been?"

"Easy, Levell. I'm in no mood for any shit."

"Must have something to do with Caitlin." Levell's tone of voice had moderated considerably.

"That's none of your fucking business."

"Fair enough. What *is* the purpose of your call?"

"Get a Mueller brothers' jet to Farranfore airport."

There was momentary silence, then Levell said, "I thought you were planning to sit this one out."

"You thought wrong."

PART THREE

THE PACK IS BACK

"The wolf, which hunts in a pack, has a greater chance of survival than the lion, which hunts alone."
--Christian Louis Lange

CHAPTER 30

BIG PINE KEY, FLORIDA

THE DE HAVILLAND Canada DHC-2 Beaver equipped with amphibious floats touched down smoothly despite the moderate chop in Bahia Honda channel. The plane could accommodate up to six passengers, but there was only the pilot and one other man on board. The pilot taxied to the small, strand of rocky shore on the east side of No Name Key where State Road 4a dead ended. It was high tide, enabling the pilot to navigate close to the rocks that were covered in green slime.

Whelan opened the door on the passenger side and slid easily onto one of the floats. He reached behind his seat and pulled out the large, olive drab canvas duffel bag. He nodded at the pilot, stepped down into the shin-deep water choked with loose, decaying turtle-grass, and waded onto the rocky, vestigial shore, the remnant of a recent hurricane.

The only thing the man who walked forward to greet him was missing was green skin; otherwise, he could have been a clone of the Incredible Hulk. The impossibly muscled man appeared to have no neck.

He extended a hand. Whelan gripped it in a matching vise.

With his free hand the man slapped Whelan on the shoulder and said, "You look well rested for someone who just flew all the way from Ireland."

"I was able to sleep almost all the way to the Bahamas. It was a seven-hour flight from Farranfore." He didn't mention the dream that had been haunting him repeatedly: a very pregnant Caitlin surrounded by countless toddlers of both genders and various races and ethnicities, all calling her "Mama." Through it all, she sat silently, a sweet-sad Mona Lisa smile on her lips and a single teardrop slowly caressing her cheek.

"Bahamas? Did you stop off for some skin diving?" The man-with-no-neck said with a smile. It was his good smile—no one would die. Probably.

"Sure," Whelan said and patted the duffel bag. "I've got spiny lobsters for everyone."

"I'm thinking you've got underwear and socks in there, and the stop in the Bahamas was to slip through customs and change from a Mueller brothers' luxury ride to that puddle jumper that brought you here."

Whelan shook his head and with mock sincerity said, "And some people, think you're slow to connect the dots."

"Tell me who said that, and I'll kill them," Sven Larsen said with his bad smile.

A third man stepped forward as they reached dry ground. He extended his hand toward Whelan. "It's good to have ya' back at the station, mate."

"Thanks, Stoney, but you're in America, not Oz. Here, we say back at the ranch."

Liam Stone grinned and embraced Whelan in a bear hug. "Now," he said, "we can really shift into kick ass mode."

"Aw, I think you guys missed me," Whelan said, this time with mock sarcasm.

"What I miss, mate…hell, what we all miss, is the action."

"True," Larsen said, almost wistfully, "none of us are cut out for the nine-to-five shit. It's not who we are."

Whelan nodded. "Not to worry, with Levell calling the plays, things will never be routine."

The three men picked their way through a tangle of coral boulders and saplings that had been downed by the recent hurricane and followed a crushed rock path through white mangrove scrubs that transitioned into stunted buttonwood. They emerged on the beginning of a narrow, paved road that ran west straight as an arrow, disappearing into the distant glare. A navy-blue Chevrolet Silverado crew cab was parked near the trailhead. They climbed into it with Larsen behind the wheel and drove back up the road, crossing a long bridge that spanned Bogie Channel. A small cluster of anglers leaned against the rail staring into the clear blue waters below, as if trying to wish the catch onto their hooks. Moments later, Larsen slowed and turned into a gravel-topped parking lot.

It was the middle of the day and the lot was nearly full. It ran through to the next street and was lined on one side with a row of one-story, tin-roofed, yellow cottages with aqua trim. A similarly painted, but larger building was on the other side of the narrow lot. Although the building was on Big Pine Key and not neighboring No Name Key where Whelan had deplaned, the sign affixed to its roof announced it as the No Name Pub. There were several aqua and yellow picnic tables partially shaded by colorful umbrellas near the entrance. A pair of tiny Key deer, the smallest deer in North America and found only in the Florida Keys, were snacking on popcorn someone had left behind.

The three men entered the bar with Stone in the lead. Whelan instinctively checked out the surroundings, as they looped around a U-shaped bar. The walls and ceiling were covered with thousands of one-dollar bills, most of them inscribed with the names of the patrons who'd hung them there. A section of one wall was covered with shoulder patches from numerous police and fire departments from around the country. Most of the bar stools were occupied, as were the tables tightly crammed into the small area.

Whelan and his companions crossed the scuffed floor and exited through a side door onto a patio, much of which was lined with red brick pavers. A dozen yellow and aqua picnic tables were scattered across the pavers. They were shaded by umbrellas advertising a popular craft beer. The vertical board fence was painted the same shade of aqua and enclosed the paved area and a sandy space of about equal size. There was a Sea Grape tree at the far end and a scattering of gumbo limbo and palm trees.

Four large, muscular men were sitting at the table farthest from the building, near the edge of the brick-paved area. Marc Kirkland, Nick Stensen, Quentin Thomas, and Rafe Almeida.

Almeida, surrounded by shot glasses and empty beer bottles, looked up and saw the three men approaching. He expelled a loud belch and said with a grin, "Party's over. The boss man is back."

After a round of bear hugs and fist bumps, Whelan, Larsen, and Stone joined the others at the table.

While they waited for their food and beverages, Kirkland said, "Any problems getting back in the country?"

"No," Whelan said.

"Mueller brothers provide the ride?" Kirkland said.

"Yeah, a new G650.

"Now, that's traveling first class," Thomas said.

"Cruises at about four hundred ninety knots."

"That's around five hundred sixty miles per hour," Larsen said.

Whelan nodded and smiled. Larsen had an ability to do conversions in his head faster than anyone he'd known. "Yeah, even so it took almost seven hours from Ireland to the Bahamas."

"Any runway takeoff or landing problems in a bird that fast?" Stone said.

"It only needs three thousand feet for landing, but takeoff is close to double that. The strip at Hamish Cay is fifty-eight hundred, but the plane was at minimum weight when it left there."

"Where the fuck is Hamish Cay?" Almeida said, and tossed back another shot of tequila.

"It's a private island in the Bahamas. About two hundred fifty miles from here."

"Don't tell me," Thomas said. "Levell knows the owner."

"Close. The owner's an intimate friend of the Muellers."

Thomas shrugged. "Same thing."

"Yeah," Almeida said, his mouth full of conch fritters, "they're all old farts."

"Speaking of Levell," Stensen said to Whelan, "did he fill you in on our activities here?"

"Mostly. But it wasn't clear why we're in this particular place."

Stensen wiped some beer foam off his lips and said, "An SAS member high up in NSA told the Old Man about some chatter they'd picked up involving HAC people. Something about the five nukes being in a place that's coastal and very swampy."

Whelan nodded. "Good to know. This area is mostly mangrove islands. Good place to train. Is our crib somewhere around here?"

"Yeah," Larsen said, "SAS is putting us up in a house about a klick from here."

Stensen said, "At the tip of Doctor Point, on Calle Aqua."

"Sounds like easy ingress and egress by boat," Whelan said.

Stone smiled. "As long as you don't run aground, mate."

"Not much chance of that," Larsen said. "Brendon spent a lot of time in the Keys, knows how to read the color of the water. He showed me how to SCUBA dive, spearfish, and catch lobsters when we were at The U. Remember, Quent?"

Thomas nodded. "The dude's definitely in his element here."

Whelan looked up and saw a party of four attractive women entering the patio. There was something strangely familiar about one of them.

CHAPTER 31

WASHINGTON, D.C.

SPECIAL COUNSEL DAVID FARMER stepped from the cab at the
intersection of New York Avenue NW and 9th Street NW. He
clutched the collar of his heavy trench coat tighter around his
neck and walked quickly to the entrance to the restaurant. The
attractive young hostess greeted him with a practiced smile and
an air of boredom.

"I'm meeting another gentleman here. His name is Mr.
Trupockitt," Farmer said.

The hostess picked up a menu. "Yes, he's already here.
Please follow me." As he did so, Farmer enjoyed the aroma of
Cajun cooking that filled the well-appointed restaurant.

The dining room was long and narrow. The young woman led
him to a booth in the very rear. It was occupied by a man Farmer
recognized from the news media, White House senior advisor
Billy Trupockitt. When Trupockitt rose to greet him, Farmer was
surprised by his height. The special counsel was a little more
than six feet two inches, but the other man was at least two
inches taller.

The men shook hands and Trupockitt waved Farmer to a seat opposite his. "Thank you for agreeing to speak with me under these rather clandestine conditions."

"Well, when a senior White House advisor says he has something to discuss that pertains to my current investigation, how can I refuse? Besides, this restaurant is one of my favorites. Even if our discussion leads nowhere, the meal will be worth it."

"I assure you, the discussion will not disappoint."

A server glided up to the table, introduced himself as Isaac, explained the evening's dinner specials, and took their drink orders.

When he'd left, Farmer said, "For a Washingtonian, I'm not much for small talk. Can we get to the reason for this meeting?"

Trupockitt grimaced. "Actually, given the sensitivity of what I'm about to disclose, I was hoping to have that drink first."

Although he'd never met the man before tonight, Farmer became aware that Trupockitt seemed edgy and tense. He glanced at his watch. "Perhaps we should have ordered doubles."

"Perhaps."

The two men engaged in a disjointed discussion of the weather until Isaac returned with their drinks. Farmer said to him, "We'll signal you when we're ready to order dinner."

When the server was out of earshot, he looked at Trupockitt and said, "I'm all ears."

"I'll tell you upfront that I don't believe you'll find any evidence that Flagler or anyone in his campaign consorted with agents of a foreign power."

Farmer stared at him. "We'll see."

"But I can tell you that there is evidence that he's involved in something far more sinister."

Trupockitt had lowered his voice, and Farmer leaned in toward him. "What would that be?"

"He's engaged with members of a shadow government to seek out those who he deems to be enemies of this country and eliminate them."

Farmer thought about his recent discussion with Harland Fairchilde at the Georgetown Four Seasons hotel. "And you know this...how?"

"The president assigned me to work with the leader of this shadow government."

"You said 'enemies.' What enemies? Eliminate them how?"

"This shadow government has a group of special operators, apparently quite a fearsome lot. They were described to me as the deadliest, most ruthless hunter-killers on the planet. Flagler and I have been told there are five more nuclear devices, like the one used at Los Alamos. He wants these special ops guys to find them and kill whoever has them."

"Other than the obvious legal technicalities of using a private, off-the-records force to perform these services, I can't say I don't like the idea. Recovering the remaining weapons and punishing those responsible certainly has merit."

"Yes, but where will Flagler stop? If he can do this, he can use these killers to do anything...consolidate power, eliminate opponents, perhaps even constitute himself president-for-life."

Farmer had a pensive look on his face. "I do see your point and share your concerns. It has frightening possibilities."

Trupockitt exhaled slowly and sagged back in his seat. "Exactly. It has to be stopped."

"True, but those terrorists also must be stopped and the nukes recovered."

"That's counterterrorism, that's my field. We'll do things the proper way, with military and intelligence operatives, not a bunch of loose cannons who aren't answerable to any authority."

"You said Flagler assigned you to work with the leader of this 'shadow government.' Who is that person?"

Resting his weight on his elbows, Trupockitt leaned across the table and lowered his voice. "You didn't hear this from me. I'll deny it vehemently. I damn sure don't want those hunter-killers coming after me."

Farmer looked him in the eye. "I always protect my sources, Mr. Trupockitt."

The White House advisor glanced quickly around the room. "His name is Clifford Levell," he whispered.

CHAPTER 32

BIG PINE KEY

WHELAN and the other Dogs had just finished their lunches at the No Name Pub and ordered another round of drinks. He glanced at the growing army of empty shot glasses and dead soldiers in front of Almeida. It was a sometimes recipe for trouble. He was reassured to see Larsen and Kirkland flanking Rafe, just in case.

The server had just placed an IPA in front of Whelan when he heard a woman's voice say, "Oh my God, is that Brendan Whelan?"

He looked up and saw a woman with a blonde ponytail wearing shorts and a halter top headed his way. It was the one he'd noticed entering a few minutes earlier with her three friends. She appeared to be in her late thirties and was beautiful. There definitely was something familiar about her—the way she walked, her extraordinary legs and slim hips, the fullness of her breasts. But it was the dazzling smile with white, perfect teeth that triggered recognition. He stood as she rushed up to him. She threw her arms around his neck, pulled her breasts tight against his chest, and kissed him full on the lips.

He was aware that everyone on the crowded patio was staring at them, especially the other Dogs, all of whom were grinning from ear to ear. He looked into her pale blue eyes and didn't know what to say. Finally, he struggled with, "Nice to see you again, Brooke. What's it been? Nearly twenty years?"

"It's been way too long," she said, not taking her eyes away from his. "Where have you been? What have you been doing all this time? Why didn't you ever call or write or come to see me?"

"Yeah," Almeida said without taking his eyes off Brooke's butt. "What the fuck's the matter with you, Whelan? Ask her to join us."

Nick Stensen immediately slid over to create a spot at the table.

"Oh, I'd love to, but," she made a little grimace, "I'm here with some girlfriends."

Whelan glanced up and saw the other three attractive women staring at them.

Almeida leaped up and grabbed a second picnic table nearby. There were two couples sitting at it.

"Hey," one of the men said, "we're using this table."

"Use the other end if you don't want your asses kicked." Almeida grabbed one end of it, occupants and all, and dragged it effortlessly until it abutted the end of the table the Dogs were using.

The disgruntled customer took one look at the seven powerfully built men, especially the one with no neck, and motioned his wife and the other couple to move to the far end of the table.

Brooke waved her three girlfriends over. They all were about the same age, pretty, and had the aura of wealth about them. They all were wearing wedding bands, as was Brooke. She introduced them and Whelan reciprocated with the Dogs.

"Now I remember you," Larsen said with his good smile.

"You were captain of the freshman cheerleading squad at The U. You and Brendan dated."

"Dated? Hah, I was his steady!" She was seated so close to Whelan she was almost in his lap, both arms wrapped tightly around his massive bicep. "Ooh, you're even bigger and stronger than you were in college."

She proceeded to tell the other girls that Whelan, Larsen, and Thomas were the recruiting coup of the century, the three most heavily recruited football athletes in the country. And they'd all committed to the University of Miami.

Nicole, one of the other women, said, "You certainly look big enough. Were you famous in college?" It wasn't said provocatively. In fact, the other women seemed far less enthusiastic with the unexpected seating arrangements than Brooke.

"Would have been," Thomas said. "We enrolled early, in the spring term, so we'd be familiar with the system when the season opened in the fall."

"You said 'would have been.' What happened?" another woman, Kellie, said.

Whelan, Larsen, and Thomas all glanced at each other, then Thomas shrugged. "It's complicated. We didn't think the coaching staff was using us to our full potential."

"So, you quit?" Kellie said.

Whelan said, "No, we got a better offer, a different kind of recruitment."

"We thought we could always come back later," Larsen said.

"How did that work out?" Nicole said.

"That's even more complicated," Whelan said, thinking about the Presidential Decision Directive that called for them to be shot on sight.

"Forget this football shit," Almeida said impatiently. "I wanna know which one of you hotties wants to spend the night with me. Maybe all four of you? It's the closest thing to heaven there is without really dying."

"You're kind of obnoxious," Brooke said. "For your information, we're all married."

"Yeah? Married? Looks to me like you're damn near dry-humpin' Whelan."

Larsen made the barest of movements with his elbow, but it nearly cracked Almeida's ribs.

"Ow, shit! Why'd you do that? I was just sayin,' is all."

Larsen gave him his bad smile. The women gasped, and Almeida struggled painfully to his feet. "I gotta go pee." He staggered off toward the men's room.

Whelan felt the warmth of Brooke's body against his, smelled the clean scent of her hair. Her skin was smooth and clear. The closeness of her body aroused him. Intimate memories of their previous relationship began to stir. He recalled that she was one of only two women he'd known who were multi-orgasmic. The other one was Caitlin, memories of whom now seemed distant.

Brooke tilted her head up and whispered in Whelan's ear, "Can I talk to you…in private?"

Whelan gave her a quizzical look. "Yeah, sure."

They rose and walked toward the back of the fenced-in patio area. Brooke continued to cling tightly to his arm. He felt the firmness of her breast pressed against it. And liked it. The other Dogs and Brooke's three friends followed them with their eyes.

There were catcalls from some of the Dogs, and Stone jovially said, "Don't mess this up, mate."

When they were about twenty-five feet away from the others, Brooke pulled him around to face her. "I can't believe I've run into you. What are you doing here?"

He lied. "The other men and I are just here for some R and R. You know, fishing, diving and stuff."

"Are you staying nearby?"

He hesitated, wondering where she was taking the conversation, then said, "Yeah, we're renting a house on Calle Aqua."

"Oh my God, I live only two blocks from there. How long are you going to be here?"

More hesitation. "Just a couple of days, I think."

"I want you to come over for dinner tonight. We have soooo much to catch up on."

He looked at the two gold bands, one with a huge diamond, on the ring finger of her left hand. "Dinner with you and your husband?"

The seductive smile vanished from her face. "No! He won't be there."

"Is that a good idea? I mean, you and I were lovers. And there's still a lot of heat there."

"He and I…it's a long story."

"I'm listening."

She looked away from him briefly, her eyes narrowing grimly and her lips tightening into a thin line.

"Frank, my husband, flies for a commercial airline. Like so many of his buddies, he sleeps around every chance he gets."

Whelan slowly ran his gaze from her face down to her feet. "From where I'm standing, he must be first-class fool."

The corners of her lips twitched upward in a brief smile. "Thanks, but I don't think he sees me that way. Or he wouldn't be so abusive."

"Abusive? Emotional or physical?"

"Both. I've tried so hard to be the best wife possible, but no matter what I do, it doesn't change anything. I've always been such a good person, a goodie two-shoes. I deserve better than this."

"Have you tried counseling?"

She snorted. "Of course. He refuses to go."

"Have you considered divorce? Or is it a matter of money or children"

"This is Florida. It's a wife-oriented state. If I fought for it, I could get the house, lifetime alimony and custody of our daughter. Frank's made some very good investments over the years; he's worth millions."

"Then why haven't you filed?"

"There's a stigma attached to divorce."

"Not in the twenty-first century. How many of your girl-friends over there have been divorced?"

"All of them. Nicole's on her third husband, a rich builder."

"Then what's your problem?"

She turned and locked eyes with him. "I wasn't sure until today." She paused for a moment. "I never got over you."

"I'm not sure how to take that."

"It's a compliment. No one's ever treated me the way you did. You were my first love. No one else ever measured up after that, treated me the way I deserve to be treated. Our chemistry is so incredible."

Whelan felt uncomfortable, almost embarrassed. "I don't know what to say."

"Just say you'll come over for dinner tonight." There was a pleading note in her voice.

He smiled. "Only if I can bring dessert."

Brooke leaned back at the waist and looked up at him, pressing the lower part of her body against his. "I think I know what it will be."

CHAPTER 33

LOWER MANHATTAN

THE NON-STOP JOURNEY from street level to Fairchilde's massive and richly appointed office suite on the top floor of the glass and steel building took thirty-one seconds. With no stops available at any of the lower floors, the elevator traversed the one thousand feet at a speed of twenty-two miles per hour. He was the only person in the building who had access to it. The other members of his firm had to use the bank of elevators in the center of the structure, forced to rub elbows with the great unwashed masses.

He stepped into the foyer of his office suite and nodded at his executive assistant, Rosalynn Mercator. Passing her desk, he said, "No calls or other interruptions until I say otherwise."

"Certainly, Mr. Fairchilde."

He closed the door to his office and walked to his desk. Removing a ring of keys from a pocket, he used one of them to unlock a drawer and withdrew a small phone. Heavily encrypted for secrecy and restricted in use, it could only access one other phone in the world. That one was in the possession of Zheng Bao Xun, the minister of finance for the People's Republic of China.

He pressed the call icon and waited for Zheng to pick up. As he did, he turned and gazed out the wall of glass behind his desk. It was a clear day and he could see most of the five Burroughs and beyond. Then he had a disturbing thought. If, for some highly unlikely reason, he was being surveilled, his lips could be read, negating any advantage of the phone's encryption. He turned and faced away from the glass.

After a few moments, Zheng came on the line. In impeccable English, the minister said, "How nice to hear from you, Harland. I wasn't expecting your call. I trust there are no disturbing issues."

Fairchilde knew Zheng was a paragon of political correctness and generally didn't immediately cut to the purpose of a call. He assumed Zheng's time was limited. "I have some information that should be of great value to our friend Nadir Shah."

"Given the uninterrupted string of defeats his caliphate has suffered, he certainly needs something positive."

"What he needs is to detonate those remaining bombs in America. Bring that kind of massive destruction and slaughter to this country, and it will change America's attitude toward the war in the Middle East."

"A tautological statement, Harland. Does your call pertain to the nukes?"

"Yes, it does. I had a conversation with someone who is a trusted advisor in the White House. It appears that Flagler has asked him to work with our old adversary, Clifford Levell."

"Now, that *is* fascinating." There was a definite note of interest in Zheng's voice.

"This source tells me that Levell and the SAS have managed to plant a mole in Shah's operation, specifically the group in charge of the bombs."

"Did this 'source' identify the mole?"

'Unfortunately, no. Levell, as usual, is playing things very close to the vest. But, he did say it was someone who had been directly involved in the Los Alamos operation. That should narrow the list considerably. Let Shah figure out who it is."

There was a brief pause at Zheng's end, then he said, "You don't have direct access to Shah, as I do. I'll pass this information along to him and trust he will be able to deal with the issue successfully."

NADIR SHAH WAS ENRAGED by Zheng's message. Now that the forces of the Western powers had mobilized against him, his dream of commanding a vast caliphate was in tatters. It was so dangerous for him in the Levant and North Africa that he'd moved his headquarters to that bastion of neutrality-at-a-price, Geneva, Switzerland. His best hope for reversing his fortunes was the five remaining nuclear weapons. And now there was a traitor in his organization who threatened to destroy even that aspiration.

He summoned his young aide, Jibril, into his office and told him to get Ali Sayad Kazemzadeh, the top general in Iran's Quds force, a special unit of their Revolutionary Guards, on the encrypted phone. Kazemzadeh was the mullahs' top military advisor to Shah's forces.

"'Caliph,'" the general said when he came on the line. There was a certain measure of sarcasm in his voice. "How may the Islamic Republic of Iran serve you today?"

Shah explained the situation.

"I hope you know the identity of this bastard, Nadir."

"He was described to me as someone who participated in the

first detonation, the one at Los Alamos. Only one person survived that mission."

"Ah, yes, the one you called a hero to the cause. What was his name? Salam?"

"Yes, Turan Salam!" Shah seethed with anger. "I did praise him as a hero. Bazir Haqqani, a *genuine* hero, begged me on his deathbed to put Turan in charge of this mission. And Salam did seem to be the logical choice…the traitorous bastard!"

"Clearly, you do have a problem. You need to detonate those devices as planned. What is it you think I can do?"

"The bombs are in Mexico. The traitor is across the border in America waiting for me to direct him to them. Instead, I will mislead him, send him elsewhere. You have Hezbollah allies in Mexico. I want them to trap him, extract whatever information he has, and kill him. Very slowly and painfully."

CHAPTER 34

BETHESDA, MARYLAND

Mitch Christie had returned to work at Bureau headquarters in Washington on a part-time basis. Because of his status as a former naval officer, his rehabilitation continued at nearby Walter Reed National Military Medical Center. He and Camila had rented a small, single-story, brick and stone bungalow on a rolling, tree-lined side street in an older residential section of Chevy Chase. Most of its neighbors were split-level or two-story structures, but his physical therapists didn't want him climbing stairs yet. It was convenient to the medical center and FBI head-quarters. Walter Reed was three miles to the northwest. The Metro station in Friendship Village was two-and-a-half miles to the southwest. It was a quick ride from there to Union Station. Christie had a therapeutic walk of one mile from the station to Bureau HQ. For Camila, it was half that distance to her office with the Capitol Police.

The house was old, but comfortable and in good condition. The only thing about it that bothered Christie and Camila was the presence of their housemate. Turan Salam. When they had moved from Albuquerque, Levell had prevailed upon them let Turan live with them until he was contacted by Nadir Shah. The purpose was twofold: provide the young Pakistani with a safe house and keep him under surveillance. At first, Camila had all but broken off their engagement over it. But eventually, after many heated discussions, she conceded that Turan was the only lead to the missing nukes. Begrudgingly, she accepted the living arrangements, but prayed each day for the call from Nadir Shah to come. Less than a week after they moved in, her prayers were answered.

It was midafternoon. Christie and Camila were at work in D.C. Turan was sitting on a well-used sofa sipping a cup of green tea and reading a biography of George Washington. The burner phone Shah had given him made a sound that indicated a text had come in. He fished it out of a trouser pocket and read the text. It was a passage from a poem by al-Mutanabbi. Turan immediately dialed a phone number from memory. When he heard it being answered, he spoke in Arabic, initiating the password sequence.

"The weather is much better at home."

"It always is."

"I'm eager for the nutmeg to be harvested."

"Yes, this will be an exceptional year."

Satisfied that it was Shah, Turan said, "I await you orders, Caliph."

There was a brief pause then Shah spoke. His voice sounded tight, as if he was struggling with some kind of emotion. "The time is right. The teams are in place. Now we will punish the Great Satan for waging war against Allah."

Turan wasn't sure how to respond. He shifted nervously on the sofa and simply said, "Whatever you require of me, Caliph. I await your instructions."

"You are a good man, Turan." The words sounded like they

were being wrung out of Shah. "You are in a place called Chevy Chase, yes?"

"Yes, Caliph," Turan said hesitantly. *How does the man know where I am?*

"You are curious how I know that," as if reading Turan's mind. "We have been tracing the phone we gave you."

Turan said nothing, unconsciously holding his breath.

"It is very clever of you to hide near the heart of the Great Satan. I was not pleased when you first arrived in America and chose to live so close to the site of our first nuclear explosion. But then I realized you were being clever in choosing that spot. After all, the Americans knew you had escaped to Doha and beyond. Santa Fe, like their nation's capital, is not some place they would expect you to be."

"May I assume you're ready for me to initiate my mission?"

"Yes, the leaders of each team await you in Tampico. Go to the airport immediately and fly to Brownsville, Texas. You will be met there by our agents. They will have your identification which will enable you to cross into Mexico."

"Mexico? The remaining nuclear weapons are in Mexico?"

Shah ignored the question. "These people will take you to a place on an island called Isla El Idolo. The bombs are there. You know what to do from that point."

"Yes, oversee the moving of the weapons into position." Turan hesitated a moment, then said, "Have you determined the target locations?"

"Yes!" Shah said sharply. "Why would we move them if we didn't have the locations in mind? Do you think I'm an idiot?"

"I'm sorry, Caliph, I didn't mean to insinuate anything. I just believe that I can do my job better, be more effective, if I know where the devices are to be located."

"Really?" Shah said mockingly. "You will be told what you

need to know, when you need to know it." He abruptly terminated the call.

TURAN PACKED his scant belonging in a well-worn rucksack and waited for Mitch Christie to return home. He was nervous. Something in Shah's attitude and voice raised a red flag. *Are they on to me?* The biography no longer held his attention. He surfed around various channels on the TV in the living room, but couldn't get into any of the game shows, soap operas, and news broadcasts that hammered away at the same political issue they'd been covering for several days while waiting for the next one to develop. He wanted to go outside and try to walk off his nervous energy, but Christie had told him to stay inside out of sight. It seemed an eternity before he heard the car bringing Christie and Camila home from the Metro station in Friendship Village.

They had picked up Chinese takeout on the way home. Camila went into the kitchen to dish it up. Christie and Turan settled into seats in the living room.

"You look a little edgier than usual, Turan. What's up?"

"It happened today. I heard from Shah."

Christie quickly sat forward. "Tell me what happened, start to finish, everything."

When Turan finished describing his earlier conversation with Shah, Christie glanced at the rucksack on the floor at the other man's feet. "Brownsville? Immediately? Looks like you're ready. Have you checked flights?"

"Yes, there is a flight from Reagan at 5:30 tomorrow morning. With an hour layover in Dallas, it gets into Brownsville at about eleven."

"And Shah said you'll be taken directly to the nukes?"

"Yes." He hesitated briefly, then said, "You will be tracking me all the way?"

"Of course, we'll put a tracer on you. We'll be able to track you everywhere you go."

Turan frowned. "These people are not amateurs. They will be very sophisticated in checking for these devices. If they find it, they will kill me, then we won't know where the bombs are."

"What do you suggest?"

"I was instructed to destroy my phone after Shah's call. They didn't want anything that could be traced back to them. But that's not to say that I wouldn't have a phone of my own, one that your people can track."

"Yeah, I can see that as a possibility. The Bureau has malware, a Trojan horse. We can infect your phone and it will force it to continue to emit a signal even when it's turned off. Just don't remove the battery. No electricity means it will stop communicating with cell towers. We'll only know where it was at the time it was powered down, not where it went after that."

Christie fired up his iMac and activated Google Earth. He took several measures with the onboard ruler, then did some calculations with a smartphone app. After several minutes, he said, "That damn island is approximately seventeen square miles, mostly swamp. We need to pinpoint the location of the nukes. We'll have a preset speed dial button. As soon as you find them, hit it and Levell's people will handle it from there. You'll just need to get your ass someplace safe until it's over." He looked at Turan for several seconds. "You're taking a hell of a risk. HAC's followers are a crazy-cruel bunch. If they suspect anything, it won't go well for you."

"I know."

"Are you sure you want to go through with this?"

"If I don't, they will detonate the remaining five bombs.

Thousands, hundreds of thousands, maybe millions of innocent people will die. It'll be so much worse than Los Alamos."

Camila came out of the kitchen with the takeout food on a platter and placed it on the coffee table. "Is it those potential victims that motivate you or is it Carolina?"

She, hands on hips, and Christie, still seated at the computer, looked at Turan.

He exhaled slowly. "It's both."

CHAPTER 35

WASHINGTON, D.C.

THE ROOM WAS SMALL, its freshly painted walls bare and glaringly white in the harsh light cast by the LED tubes above. It was crowded with several uncomfortable looking chairs. While his disability was a source of frustration, Cliff Levell was grateful that he had his cushioned wheelchair as an alternative. The room was empty. Nando had been required to wait in another area of the federal building.

Levell had been waiting for more than two hours, yet no one had come by to check on his comfort or indicate when he would be called into the grand jury chamber. He used the time to reflect on his long and demanding career, beginning with his service as a member of the Marine Corps Force Reconnaissance element. He'd served well, being awarded both the Silver Star and the Navy Cross for valor in combat. And there was the Purple Heart with three oak leaf clusters signifying the times he had been wounded in combat.

His fearlessness, patriotism, and unmitigated resolve for success brought him to the attention of the Central Intelligence

Agency, specifically the National Clandestine Service back when it was still known as the Directorate of Operations. In particular, it was the Special Operations Group (SOG), an element of the Special Activities Division (SAD), that recruited him. SAD was a paramilitary arm of the U.S. government that conducted covert operations the government didn't want to be associated with. Again, his skills and dedication were such that he had been awarded the Distinguished Intelligence Cross, the highest decoration awarded by the CIA. It was considered the Company's equivalent of the military's Medal of Honor.

And now here he was, subpoenaed to testify before a federal grand jury empaneled by special counsel David Farmer. The GJ's original purpose had been to investigate alleged improprieties committed by a foreign power in influencing the last election. The suspicion was that Frederick Flagler's campaign team had colluded with this foreign entity to wrest the election away from his heavily favored opponent. Levell snorted. *Heavily favored? Only in the eyes of the fawning, adoring news media. In truth, she was probably the most despised and distrusted candidate her party could have nominated.*

Levell and others hadn't voted for Flagler so much as they'd voted against his opponent. But Flagler, a businessman who was as unorthodox as could be for a nonmember of the elite political establishment, had the economy in recovery mode with regulatory deregulation and tax reform, as well as a growing body of constitutional constructionists on the bench and a strengthening military. Yet, here was special counsel Farmer expanding beyond alleged election irregularities, widening the net grotesquely into dark corners never intended to be within his original jurisdiction.

Where had Farmer gotten his information about SAS, the existence of the Sleeping Dogs, and Flagler's plans to use them to find the five missing nukes and those who possessed them?

Was it someone in SAS? Not likely, as very few members other than himself and Christie knew about it. Christie's fiancée? Cuellar, the cop in Santa Fe? Maybe that Turan kid was a double agent despite obviously being gaga over young Carolina Avila. Or maybe the leak was in the White House. It wouldn't be the first one in the Flagler administration's short time in office. Hell, maybe it was Flagler himself. The sonofabitch's ego knew no bounds. Maybe he'd inadvertently bragged in the presence of the wrong person.

In his mind, Levell went over once again the conversation he'd had with his legal counsel, Irv Weintraub, after being subpoenaed as a witness before this grand jury:

"A SUBPOENA? What the hell is this guy Farmer up to, Irv? I already spoke to him voluntarily. Now, he's subpoenaed me as a witness. A witness to what? Isn't he overstepping the boundaries of his investigation?"

Weintraub, short and heavyset with a perennially sad smile on his face, shook his balding head. It caused his heavy jowls to quiver. "No, Cliff, in the grand jury forum, the prosecutor's powers are much broader than that of a trial jury. Unfortunately, the defendant's and the witnesses' rights are far fewer."

"Meaning what, exactly?"

"For one thing, the jurors are not screened for bias. For another, they don't determine guilt or innocence. They decide whether there is probable cause to believe that a crime may have been committed. It's a lower standard of proof than 'preponderance of the evidence,' used in civil cases, and much lower than 'beyond a reasonable doubt,' the standard needed for a conviction in criminal trials. And it doesn't require a unanimous decision from all members of the jury in order to indict."

"It sounds to me like a free pass to conduct a fishing expedition. Given the political leanings of the people Farmer has assembled on his team, it's clear the whole damn thing is political and they're simply after the president."

Weintraub smiled his sad smile and nodded.

"They questioned me about Flagler's involvement with a paramilitary group. Supposedly, he wants to send them on an extraterritorial operation to retrieve some bombs or some such and kill those who possess them. They questioned me about my involvement in this pipe dream. I told them I didn't know anything about it, that it was a mystery to me. Next thing I know, I get this damn subpoena. That's when I called you."

Weintraub smiled again. "I appreciate that, Cliff. You know I'll do anything I can to help."

"Then how do I get out of this damn thing?"

"First, do you have any knowledge of the things they're questioning you about?"

"Of course not," Levell lied. "The whole thing sounds like these bastards have been smoking funny shit. It was a fucking mistake to legalize pot."

The lawyer eyed Levell through thick, rimless glasses for several seconds before saying, "Assuming you're being candid with me, you may be okay. But, if Farmer's team has developed evidence that indicates otherwise, or casts doubt on your testimony, you could be indicted on perjury charges."

Levell squinted his eyes and studied Weintraub for a few moments, as if running scenarios through his head. "In that case, aren't I entitled to plead the Fifth?"

Weintraub wagged his balding head slowly back and forth. "While that is a constitutional right every citizen has, it generally doesn't work in a grand jury proceeding."

"Why the hell not?"

"Because the GJ can arbitrarily grant you immunity, which has the facility of removing the argument of self-incrimination."

"Doesn't matter, I still can't answer the questions they're going to ask."

"Sadly, it does matter. If a witness refuses to testify once the threat of self-incrimination no longer is a factor, he or she can, and probably will, be held in contempt."

"WHAT?" Levell shook his head in disbelief. "What has justice in this country become, the Court of the Star Chamber?"

"It's similar in many ways, I'm afraid."

"So, if I claim my rights under the Fifth Amendment and refuse to testify, then I'm arbitrarily granted immunity from prosecution for self-incrimination. By continuing to refuse, I'm guilty of contempt and what, jailed?"

"Yes, unfortunately that's how it works in a grand jury forum."

"You're going to be in there. Isn't there some legal magic you can work to prevent this? Raise objections or something?"

"Again, this kind of proceeding is quite different from what most of us think of as a civil or criminal trial. Witnesses subpoenaed to testify before a grand jury don't have a right to have their attorneys present in the grand jury room. They can consult with their attorney before testifying. They also, prosecutor willing, may have an attorney outside the grand jury room and step outside the room to consult with the attorney before answering any questions."

"But the prosecutor, or whatever the bastard is called, can have free rein to hammer the defenseless witness?"

Sad smile still firmly in place, Weintraub nodded. "'Fraid so.

. . .

LEVELL'S THOUGHTS were interrupted by the sound of the door being opened.

The special counsel, David Farmer, stepped into the room. "I trust you've had enough time to recognize the difficult situation you've put yourself in, Mr. Levell."

Levell said nothing.

"Incidentally, I'm aware of that so-called Lodge in Tidewater Virginia. A large number of interesting people come and go on a frequent basis, like an exclusive club of some sorts."

Levell said nothing.

"I would love to have a look inside, but, regrettably, it seems to be a consulate for a foreign nation. Oddly, one in which the Mueller brothers have made very generous investments over the years. As much as I'm tempted to raid the property, I can't. Pursuant to Article 31 of the Vienna Convention on Consular Relations, the host nation is prohibited from entering consular premises. Equally as frustrating for those of us who are pursuing justice, it appears to be invulnerable to probing techniques available to us. But then I'm sure you're aware of that." Farmer smiled, but it looked more like a sneer.

Still, Levell said nothing.

Finally, Farmer sighed a long and deep sigh of frustration. "Why don't you save me a lot of time and yourself the damage to your rather sterling record, Mr. Levell? Otherwise, I have no option than to have you incarcerated for contempt."

Levell raised his hands, palms up, and said. "Does that mean I don't get to pass Go or collect two hundred bucks?"

CHAPTER 36

CAYO HOMBRE MUERTO

IT WAS late afternoon as Whelan left the stilt house he was sharing with the other six Dogs. He strolled the less than two blocks to Brooke's house, knowing how the evening was going to go. She had made that clear without saying a word, as only women can do. He wondered if it was part of the fabled "feminine mystique."

The weather was perfect with a cloudless sky and a warm breeze out of the southeast. Still, something didn't feel right. While he'd had innumerable opportunities as a married man, from shy flirtations to bold propositions, he'd always brushed off the interests of other women. Since he and Caitlin had met, she had been his only sex partner. And, until recently he'd been hers. He winced at the thought of what had happened to them since the near-deadly meeting with Maksym. Whelan kicked angrily at a small coconut lying on the shoulder of the road. He focused on the weather again. It looked like there would be perfect conditions for the practice run later that evening.

Brooke's vacation home, like most of the other houses in the area, was built on pilings so that residential sections were above flood stage with parking underneath. He climbed the stairs and rang the doorbell. She answered it in seconds, throwing it open with a breathless squeal of delight and gracing him with a beautiful, seductive smile, hands on hips. Though it was almost twenty years later, she looked even better than she had as captain of the freshmen cheerleading squad. With her short, pleated skirt and narrow crop top, she still looked the part of a cheerleader. Her long blonde hair was divided into two braids, the same way she had worn it at The U. She had on just the right amount of makeup. Whelan couldn't take his eyes off of her.

"You haven't changed much, Brooke, maybe gotten more beautiful."

She grabbed his arm and all but yanked him inside. "I have nosy neighbors."

"Is that a problem?"

"What do you mean?"

"Are they likely to tell your husband?"

"Screw him!"

"Things not going well at home?" He raised an eyebrow.

"I told you earlier he's a bastard."

"Why'd you marry him?"

She shrugged. "You had dumped me and I was feeling sorry for myself. He was cute, came from money, and seemed like a good catch at the time."

"Speaking of 'catch,' is he likely to wander in while I'm here?"

Brooke grinned coyly. "Why? Isn't it okay for a wife to have an innocent dinner with an old college friend?"

"Dressed the way you are and looking as good as you do, I doubt we'll spend much time with dinner. I just don't want to get shot by an angry husband."

"I told you, he flies commercial. He's in Europe for the next two days. Besides, he never comes down here. He's too busy screwing every female in Florida and Europe and every place in between."

She slid her hand down the front of his water shorts. "Umm, someone's ready to play." She took him by the hand and led him into the master bedroom.

As they desperately tore at each other's clothes, Whelan's mind was a confusing whirl. The sight of her near-perfect body flooded his head with memories of the great sex they'd enjoyed as eighteen-year-olds. It made him even harder. But other thoughts and memories crowded in, thoughts and memories of Caitlin. He wondered for an instant if he was simply doing what she had done to him, rushing into the intimacy of sex with another out of anger, as a means of punishing the other spouse. Then Brooke was on her knees in front of him. He groaned with pleasure and his mind emptied instantly.

She'd been very skillful all those years ago, but now she was even better. After a long while, he pulled her to her feet and pushed her onto the queen-size bed. She lay back and spread her legs wide. He returned her favor and quickly brought her to a screaming orgasm. Again, and again. Finally, gasping for breath, she said with an air of desperation, "I need you inside me. Now. Please."

He slid atop her as she grabbed him and guided him, and then he was in her. Brooke's eyes opened wide, as if startled, then they closed with a flutter as she moaned. Their bodies began to move in rhythm, slowly at first then at a quickening pace. Thoughts of Caitlin began to creep back into his mind. To dispel them, he began to thrust into her harder and faster. She raised her hips to meet each stroke. They both began to breathe hard from the exertion. Then, she screamed her way into and through another orgasm. And on it went. For hours.

It was almost midnight and they were still in the sweat-soaked bed. Their legs were entangled. He had an arm around her, enjoying the sensation of her perfect breasts pressed tightly against his chest. What wasn't so perfect was the conversation. It was really a monologue, all Brooke. It seemed as if she didn't even pause for breath. She went on and on about what a bastard her husband was. How he mistreated her. How her alcoholic parents had mistreated her. How everyone in her life except Whelan had mistreated and abused her. Even the women who had been with her at The No Name Pub, girls she'd known for years, were described as petty and spiteful.

Interspersed along the way were assessments of her own saintly nature. She had always been polite to everyone, even those countless souls who treated her abominably. She had been friendly to everyone, had never cast the first stone. Or subsequent ones. Maybe everyone hated her because she was so beautiful, so accomplished, so superior to everyone else.

Unable to get a word in edgewise, Whelan listened. He was amazed at what he was hearing. *It's a combination of "Oh, poor me" and "It is all about me, isn't it?" No wonder she has no real friends or caring family members.* He was beginning to feel some sympathy for her husband, Frank the Bastard. Maybe he wasn't the abusive one in the family after all. Maybe he stayed away from home as often as he could as a matter of self-defense.

Whelan remembered her parents. Dad was an executive with a major cruise line headquartered in Miami. Her mother was extremely active in civic and charitable causes in South Florida. They didn't seem like the kind of people who were closet drunks and child abusers. Old memories began to surface. They had started dating the first week of college. It seemed destined to happen. He and Larsen and Thomas had been the most coveted high school football players in the nation. Brooke was the reigning Miss Teenage North America. While the attraction was electric from the beginning and the sex off the charts, he began to recall that they had fought constantly. Thinking back, he realized she had been the same Brooke then too. His passion for her had marginalized it at the time. But now he wondered if she might be a poster girl for celibacy.

The reality, then and now, was that anyone who wasn't physically in her presence got no kind words from Brooke. He was struck by the contrast. How could someone of incomparable physical beauty be so devoid of any positive qualities of character? He thought about Caitlin once again. Now, there was incomparable physical beauty combined with genuine warmth and grace. Except for her affair with Rodney. But maybe he was beginning to understand how that had happened too. He took a deep breath and let it out slowly as Brooke babbled on.

He was relieved when his phone rang suddenly. It was Larsen's ringtone.

The noise startled Brooke, interrupting her oral autobiography. "What was that? Is someone calling you here?"

"Yeah, it's one of the guys who's down here with me. You met him at the bar." He rolled out of bed and picked up his pants off the floor where he'd hastily discarded them. He thumbed the icon and said, "Yeah?"

"Did you lose track of time, lover boy?"

"Something like that."

"Think you can pull yourself away from reminiscing with hot little Brooke long enough for a boat ride?"

"Boy, can I. I'll be there in a minute." He had pulled his pants on while speaking with Larsen. He slipped into his shirt and shoes and headed for the door.

"Wait," Brooke said. "Where are you going?"

"Long story. We were planning a late-night fishing trip. Tonight's the night. Gotta run."

She sat up in bed, her back ramrod straight. It thrust her high, firm, proud breasts straight out. "Sounds like fun. Can I come too?"

"Not this time, it's a guy thing."

Her full lips drew into a mock pout. "You dumped me once before. You *are* coming back, aren't you?"

"How could I resist?" he lied.

CAYO HOMBRE MUERTO was midnight black against the ebony water surrounding it. Low and flat, it was mostly a tangle of twisted, gnarled red mangroves, their roots intertwined in the shallow water like a huge Gordian Knot. The islet was nine and a half nautical miles out Big Spanish Channel from the stilt house they were renting at the tip of Doctor Point. It sat right on the edge of the Gulf of Mexico where the water quickly begins to deepen. In daylight, the color would change dramatically from a translucent lime green to a deep blue.

The Dogs had arrived in two INMAR Rapid Response, Military Series Inflatable Boats powered by Torqeedo Deep Blue 80 TXL outboards. The minimal noise created by the eighty horsepower electric motors had been further damped by the use of technology originally created for stealth helicopters. But the technology hadn't made the ride any smoother. A stiff breeze from the northwest had created a strong chop and the boats had bounced over the surface like a bicyclist on a cobblestone road. To compound the difficulty, there were few channels with any depth. They'd nearly run aground several times. Ordinarily the color of the water was a good indicator of shoals and mudflats, but on this moonless night the differences could barely be distinguished even with enhanced night vision goggles.

It was 2 a.m. and the area was silent and empty. They had gotten as close to the islet as they could. At this point their crafts were in barely six inches of water.

Whelan, in the lead inflatable said, "Time to hike, men."

The Dogs were wearing comm gear, heavy body armor, and carrying backpacks with water, medical supplies, and spare magazines for their suppressed SIG MCX SBR assault rifles. They each carried five polymer magazines loaded with thirty 7.62mm subsonic hollow-point rounds. The combination of suppressor and subsonic ammunition would produce minimal noise if the training exercise had been a live operation. The weapons had single-shot, three-round burst, and full-auto capability. Each also had a TANGO6 4-24X50MM scope mounted on the pitcatinny rail. Whelan usually chose this particular rifle for its tactical advantage in close quarters combat such as jungle warfare.

"Hey, Whelan," Almeida said, "what the hell is the name of this place again?"

"Cayo Hombre Muerto."

"Is that Spanish?"

"Yeah."

"What's it mean?"

"Dead Man's Key."

"No shit? Hell, that ain't very inviting."

The men climbed out of their respective craft and began to wade toward the mangroves. It was tough slogging in the deep mud and uneven bottom, particularly with the added weight of their gear. A couple of the Dogs almost fell before they made it to the edge of the mangroves.

"There's no dry land in there," Whelan said into his comm gear, "just water and tree roots."

"Shit, I ain't afraid of no water or tree roots," Almeida said. "I'll take the point." He stood motionless, staring into the trees.

"What's the problem, *Mr. Point Man*?" Stensen said.

"These fucking trees are the problem. There's no way in."

"What, no garden path? Imagine that," Kirkland said.

"You volunteered to take the point," Whelan said, "so make a damn path. But do it silently. This is supposed to be a warmup for the real thing."

"Yeah," Thomas said, "that's when there'll be bad guys with guns waiting for us. Got to be silent."

Almeida studied the impenetrable maze in front of him for a few more seconds, shook his head then stepped forward. He placed his weight on a prop root and tried to lean forward, but his pack got hung up on a mangrove. It pissed him off. He twisted and tried to yank the pack free. His booted foot slipped on the slimy root and he fell into the tangle of roots and branches. "Ow!" he screamed, "I've been cut. Get me the fuck out of here." He struggled to hold an arm up in the thicket. It was bleeding heavily, blood running onto the SIG.

Whelan reached in and grabbed the weapon, tossing it to Stensen. "Somebody give me a hand getting him out of there."

Stone instantly stepped forward. He and Whelan were able to get enough of a grip on parts of Almeida that they eventually worked him loose. Blood was flowing freely from a long, deep gash on Almeida's forearm.

"What the hell happened to him, mate?" Stone said to Whelan.

"Oysters. They attach themselves to the roots. Sharp as razors."

Whelan did a quick assessment. "He may have nicked the

ulnar artery. Stoney, put some pressure above the wound. We'll get him back to the inflatable then put a tourniquet on it."

"I take it the exercise is over for the night," Thomas said.

"Yeah, give Stoney a hand getting Rafe in the boat. We're out of here."

Larsen was standing nearby grinning his good grin. "Gonna pick up where you left off with Brooke?"

"Get your ass in the boat."

FALSE DAWN, the transient light that precedes sunrise, was beginning to glimmer in the east by the time the Dogs had cleaned and repacked their gear. They'd deflated the boats and stowed them and the motors away in a tow-along trailer that could be hitched to one of the Silverados. Kirkland, the team's unofficial medico had stitched the ugly gash in Almeida's forearm. The wounded man had complained ceaselessly about his injury, blaming everyone he could think of from his fellow Dogs, to Levell, to the State of Florida for its regulations protecting mangroves, to the trees themselves for harboring oysters.

Finally, unable to tolerate any more, Thomas had shoved a bottle of cheap tequila and a six-pack in Almeida's hands and banished him to the elevated deck that ran along the outside of the rented house's second story.

Stensen self-imposed sentry duty and went for a stroll through the quiet neighborhood. Kirkland and Thomas hit the sack for a few hours of sleep. Whelan, Larsen, and Stone sprawled on the rattan furniture in the living room. Larsen sipped a cup of tea. The other two drank beer.

"You think Levell knew what he was doing when he dreamed up this exercise?" Larsen said.

"Probably never saw real mangroves. Had no friggin' idea how impenetrable they are."

Stone took a long pull from his bottle, then said, "It was a fizzer, mates, a real fizzer."

Larsen looked at him with squinted eyes. "What's that mean in Aussie?"

"A bloody fiasco, mate."

Whelan stretched and yawned. "The challenge now is what do we do? If Cliff believes he's sending us into a hot zone in that kind of environment, where and how do we train for it?"

"Maybe we don't," Larsen said. "Maybe we have to come up with alternative tactics for approaching and taking down a target in that kind of situation."

Whelan could feel exhaustion pressing down on him like a huge weight. Adventures with Brooke. The travel. The situation with Caitlin. He shook his head to clear it and took a deep breath. "I don't know what else to suggest. We can't risk a jump. We'd either end up in the drink or so entangled in the damn mangroves it would take a team wielding chainsaws to get us out."

"If the target is surrounded by water as shallow as what it is at Dead Man's Key," Stone said, "we'd get picked off trying to wade ashore."

It was silent for several minutes, each man lost in thought. Finally, Stone got up and grabbed two more bottles from the refrigerator and the teapot for Larsen. On his way back to his seat, he opened the screen door and checked on Almeida. The wounded man was slumped in a canvas and aluminum beach chair, head back, mouth open, snoring softly. There were six dead soldiers at his feet. The tequila bottle also was empty.

He handed a beer to Whelan and popped the cap off his own with a thumbnail. "So, what's our next move, mate?" he said to Whelan and took a long pull.

Whelan shrugged. "Guess that's up to Levell, but we're not going to crawl around mangrove islets again."

"Any idea how long we'll be here?"

"Why?"

"I think that sheila, Nicole, your girlfriend's chum, took a fancy to me."

"She's not my damn girlfriend." Whelan's voice sounded tired, even to him.

Stone and Larsen glanced at each other and grinned.

"I dunno, mate, if a sheila who looked like her wrapped herself around me the way she did you in that pub, I'd bloody marry her." He laughed, Larsen along with him.

Whelan shook his head and exhaled. "You have no idea what you're talking about. Things aren't always what they seem."

Larsen's eyes narrowed. "I seem to recall that you two fought a lot back at The U. Both of you went to Georgia with Sharon and me and stood up for us when the JP married us." He paused and his eyes narrowed further. "The two of you argued all the way up and all the way back. Except when you were screwing."

"She had issues, still does."

"I remember. She would hound you to get engaged, then turn chill. Not exactly stable. Sharon didn't like her. Said she talked about herself constantly and put down anyone who wasn't present."

Whelan nodded. "Tell me about it. I was there, remember?"

"Sounds like Cliff did you a favor when he recruited you for the Dogs. Did you ever try to contact her again after that?"

"No. Never looked back."

"Until yesterday."

"That was a mistake. One I won't make again." Whelan slowly stood up. "I'm going to take a shower and get some rack time."

Stone looked at his 5.11 Tactical Field Ops watch and said, "The bloody No Name will open in a couple of hours. Want us to wake you up so you can join us?" He grinned wolfishly.

"Yeah, you're bound to run into someone you know from your misspent youth. Think how much fun you'll have." Larsen's grin matched Stone's.

"Assholes. You're worse than teenagers. I'm not going anywhere near that place, and don't tell her where I am." There was a growl in his voice.

"Can we bring you something?" Larsen said with mock innocence. "I mean, besides Brooke."

"Keep it up, motherfucker."

Larsen and Stone busted out laughing. It was a guy thing.

"No, seriously, fair dinkum, do you want some grub?" Stone said.

"Yeah, they make a great Cuban."

"We'll probably be there a while," Larsen said. "We don't want you starving on us. We'll ask Brooke to bring it over."

Whelan snatched up a pillow from the sofa and flung it at them, as they ran out the door laughing like schoolboys.

CHAPTER 37

TAMIAHUA, MEXICO

THE RIVER KNOWN as the Rio Grande in the United States and
Rio Bravo in Mexico divides the two countries from a point three
miles northwest of El Paso, Texas, all the way to the Gulf of
Mexico. Near its terminus, its waters, the color of split pea soup,
pass between the cities of Brownsville, Texas, and Matamoros,
Mexico.

Turan caught an early morning flight from Reagan National
to Brownsville/South Padre Island International Airport with a
short layover in Dallas. Two men approached him in the terminal. They were dressed like indigenous Latinos and spoke fluent
Spanish but had the distinct appearance of Middle Easterners.

"Señor Salam?"

"Sí."

"Had the snow turned to rain when you left?"

"Yes, it formed black ice."

Passwords exchanged, the men moved to either side of Turan
and escorted him toward the main entrance of the terminal. One
of the men spoke briefly with someone on a cell phone. When

they exited, a dark blue Kia Niro pulled to the curb in front of them. One of his escorts took Turan's rucksack and tossed it into the rear compartment. The three of them climbed into the second row of seats with Turan in the middle. Two other swarthy men occupied the front bucket seats.

No one spoke as the car wound through alternating densely packed residential neighborhoods and cheerless commercial areas for about five miles. Eventually, they came to the Veterans International Bridge border crossing station. The driver paid the nominal fee and they crossed into Mexico.

The change in jurisdictions seemed to relax the other five men and they began speaking with each other in Lebanese-accented Arabic. Everyone ignored Turan. The driver eventually turned onto Avenida Pedro Cárdenas Gutiérrez which became Mexico Highway 101. They stayed on it, moving in a southerly direction through mostly agrarian countryside dotted with occasional villages and hamlets.

They angled to the southeast and onto Highway 83 just north of the city of Ciudad Victoria. The farmlands began to share the scenery with massive flat-topped hills covered with green scrublands. Outside an unnamed small village, the road changed again and became Highway 81. The farms and mesas gave way to mostly barren lands until they neared the town of Gonzalez, where the driver took another left onto Route 80. None of the other men offered to spell him, and he didn't ask them.

Many miles further on, they passed the vast marshy area of Champayán on the right near the city of Altamira. Turan could smell the odors of the sea blowing in from the Gulf of Mexico only a few miles to the east of the city. Ten miles later they arrived in Tampico. They had been traveling for more than six hours and covered over three hundred miles, with only one quick stop along the way. Six hours of being crammed between two beefy men who hadn't bathed in quite a while. Six hours of being pointedly ignored by the others. Even the one stop they'd made was uncomfortable. Turan had been allowed out of the SUV only to use the toilet. The two men accompanied him into the tiny, filthy room and watched him urinate. They stuffed him back into the Kia and gave him a candy bar to eat along with a small bottle of water.

When they rolled into Tampico, the driver pulled into a gas station and refilled the tank. Turan said to the man on his right, "This is Tampico. Isn't this our destination?"

"The man examined him through narrowed eyes. "You don't speak."

"Yes, but the caliph told me..."

He was painfully interrupted as the man on the other side cuffed him hard on the side of the head. "Like he said, you don't speak."

Turan's ear hurt like hell and concerns of more than discomfort began to creep into his consciousness. *What's going on here? Has my cover been blown? Does Shah know what my real purpose is? If so, what do I do?* He settled nervously back in his seat as the driver pulled out into traffic. The temperature of the air flowing through the vehicle's open windows was warm but refreshing because of the proximity to the Gulf. Turan began sweating heavily.

It took a little more than three hours to cover the one hundred miles from Tampico to Tamiahua. It felt like a lifetime to Turan. The other four men in the car said very little during the ride. If they paid any attention at all to Turan, it was to glare at him. The highways had been four-lane divided thoroughfares at first. They had been reduced to well-marked two-lane roads until they reached Naranjos. From there, they downgraded into paved, but mostly unmarked highways. Toward the end of the journey, as they neared Tamiahua, the road deteriorated into a country lane barely two cars wide. It was poorly paved by the time they turned onto Avenida Benito Juarez and rolled into the coastal fishing village of Tamiahua.

The weather had changed. It was warmer and more humid. They drove almost to the end of the town of about twenty-three-thousand souls and pulled into a parking area at a boat basin. The men climbed out of the dusty Kia and stretched. Two of the men went into a large open-ended metal structure that looked like a giant Quonset hut where a few men were working on a couple of small, ancient fishing boats.

The other two men took Turan out to the dock area and put him in a well-used twenty-foot bay boat with low gunnels. He thought it probably was used for crabbing. Except for the small, aged outboard, it looked like it could have been around since biblical times. The two men climbed in after him. One started the antiquated motor. The other cast the lines off and they moved out to the middle of the basin quickly entering the channel and swinging to a northerly bearing. Still, no words were exchanged. They continued in silence for about five nautical miles. Their path took them up a narrow estuary into a wide, shallow lagoon. Eventually, they came ashore at a sandy beach on a large, swampy island otherwise covered in red mangroves. There were three cabins along the small beach. They looked like they'd been deserted for a long time. It was eleven o'clock at night.

MITCH CHRISTIE's phone rang on the nightstand beside his bed. He tried to grab it quickly in hopes it wouldn't wake Camila lying next to him. Instead, he managed to knock it off the stand. As he swore and reached for it, she sat up.

"Who is it?" she said sleepily.

"Don't know yet."

He thumbed the answer icon. "Christie."

The voice on the other end was that of a former Green Beret who now worked for SAS. His job at the moment was to monitor the signal from Turan's cell phone using military grade GPS. "Hey, Mitch, it's Ron Waddell. Sorry to call so late, but something's up with our boy, Turan."

Christie rolled into a sitting position on the edge of the bed, rubbing sleep from his eyes with the other hand. "What is it?"

"Not sure, but his phone went dead a couple of minutes ago."

"Dead? Like what does that mean?"

"We're no longer picking up a signal. It just stopped suddenly."

Christie tried to shake the cobwebs of sleep from his head. "We infected his phone with a Trojan horse that forces it to continue emitting a signal even if it's in standby mode."

"Yeah, it's supposed to continue communicating with nearby cell towers...unless the battery was removed."

"Even so, we should be able to trace it to the location it was in when it was powered down."

"Yeah, we do have that."

"Where was he?"

"Looks like it's an island in the Laguna Tamiahua."

"Where the hell is that?"

"About sixty-five miles due south of Tampico, Mexico. The island's called Isla El Idolo, it means Island of the Idol."

"Keep trying to pick up the signal, Ron. Get back to me if you're able to do it." Christie ended the call and continued to sit on the edge of the bed.

"What is it, Mitch?" Camila said.

"Turan. We lost his phone's signal."

She was quiet for a few moments. "That poor kid. What are you going to do?"

"Frankly, I'm not sure. Ordinarily, this would be Levell's call, but he's basically incommunicado in the Central Detention Facility on a charge of contempt of the grand jury."

Camila shook her head. "That's just not right. He's an old man and he's physically handicapped. They could have confined him to a hotel room, that's what's usually done."

"Farmer's being a prick, wants to put all the pressure he can on Cliff in hopes of breaking him, so he can get at Flagler."

"Knowing what I do about Clifford Levell, that could involve a long wait. In the meantime, he placed you in charge That makes this your call, Mitch."

"I know, dammit," he said. "But I don't have his background and connections."

She pursed her full lips pensively. "I thought he ultimately was going to use those Sleeping Dogs people to follow up on Turan's intel, yes?"

"That's the plan."

"Then maybe you should let them know what's happened. Do you have contact information for them?"

"Cliff said Nando has it. I'll get it from him."

CHAPTER 38

LOWER MANHATTAN

HARLAND FAIRCHILDE ENJOYED a full measure of satisfaction whenever he used the special phone Zheng had provided him. He took particular pleasure in the fact that the NSA couldn't trace it. Especially because his conversations with Zheng concerned the destruction of the United States and its Western allies. The resulting chaos was necessary in order to establish a one-world government, one in which he and other members of the moneyed class would run all things financial.

Zheng wasn't truly a financier, but he was the minister of finance for the People's Republic of China, and recently had been appointed vice premier and charged with overseeing all of China's economic policies and financial issues. That put him one step away from the office of president. Fairchilde knew that China's current president aspired to hold office for life and to exert his nation's control over the entire globe. He also was aware that Zheng intended to usurp the president's role and establish China's global dominion for his own purposes.

But Fairchilde had other plans for Zheng. In the meantime,

the Chinese official was a valuable tool for AGU's global ambitions.

Fairchilde smiled when he heard Zheng connect on the other end of the phone call. "Mr. Minister, I trust you have good news."

"Indeed, Harland. Things are working out well for AGU."

"That is exciting. Please fill me in."

"I just spoke by phone with our friend Nadir Shah. He advises that the HAC has captured the mole we warned them about, a young Pakistani. As a result, his plans to detonate the five remaining nuclear devices in the American homeland remain on schedule."

"That's most refreshing to know. I wonder if the 'caliph' feels any sense of gratitude toward us."

"Frankly, Harland, I don't care whether he does or not. He and his Islamic fanatics are simply a means to an end. We have always planned to eliminate them when they are no longer useful."

"What about those bastards, the Sleeping Dogs? They've been a major impediment to our actions for quite some time." There was a petulant tone to his voice.

"Not to worry, Harland," Zheng said soothingly. "Our own version of 'Super Ninjas' have finished their training regimen and are to be sent to intercept and ambush the members of the Sleeping Dogs. That should rid us of that problem permanently."

"Where is this to take place?"

There was a pause at Zheng's end, as if he were considering his response. Finally, he said, "I'm not sure you truly have a need to know and having too many people in possession of vital infor-mation is not a wise move. Nevertheless, considering your role in the greater picture, I'll share it with you. Shah arranged to have his Iranian friends working through Hezbollah in Mexico capture the mole. Hezbollah is using members of the gang MS-13 to do the heavy lifting."

"However they do it, whomever they use, it doesn't matter so long as they achieve those nuclear detonations. That's imperative in destroying Americans' confidence in their government."

"Agreed."

"When will our so-called Bad Dogs take down Levell's hounds from hell?"

"Very soon. The trap has been set."

"One last item. Speaking of Levell, you are aware, aren't you, that he's been effectively neutralized, at least for a while?"

Fairchilde could almost see the smile on Zheng's lips when he heard him say, "Indeed, he's between the proverbial rock and a hard spot. He can't testify before the grand jury without destroying SAS while also causing the termination of Flagler's presidency. And, as long as he refuses to testify, he will remain incarcerated for contempt of that grand jury. He can't operate SAS effectively from jail."

"Yes," Fairchild said, "life is good."

CHAPTER 39
GENEVA, SWITZERLAND

THE NEWLY RENOVATED glass-skinned office building was located on the rue du Rhône and the rue du Marché. The ground floor was occupied by an assortment of luxury goods retailers, the five floors above it housed office tenants. *L'Association pour la paix au Moyen-Orient*, or the Association for Peace in the Middle East, leased the top two floors, about fourteen hundred square meters or fifteen thousand square feet. It was a small footprint for an entity that had once controlled a sprawling swath of land that stretched from Libya to Iraq. It was known as the Holy Army of the Caliphate, or HAC, and commanded by a man born Omar Kamel al-Bakr. Bakr had taken the name Nadir Shah in honor of his idol, a Turkic Afshari who, in the eighteenth century, created a vast empire stretching from Turkey to India. The original Shah often was described as "the last great Asian military conqueror" and the "Second Alexander".

A Libyan by birth, the ersatz Shah was a former general army officer in Mubarak's Egypt. Fearing for his life when Mubarak's regime fell, he'd fled to Riyadh and ingratiated himself with certain ambitious members of the Saudi royal family. Fed by their endless supply of petrodollars, along with additional funds from the UAE, Qatar, and other oil-rich Middle Eastern nations, he had raised an army of veteran jihadi warriors. He'd grown their numbers with thousands of disgruntled young Muslim men who had no jobs, educations, or hopes of ever getting them. Their ranks were supplemented by defiant young middle-class Muslims from around the world. The withdrawal of Western powers from Iraq and the troubled Middle East had created just the kind of political vacuum that would nurture the birth and growth of the caliphate.

HAC had enjoyed an impressive albeit short, brutal lifespan before the Western powers returned and allied themselves with moderate Muslim forces in the region. Routed decisively at every turn, HAC's decimated and debilitated army eventually had melted away into the night. Most of its members had returned to their homelands. But Shah still had access to funding, and he still had that dream of a caliphate. With a price on his head, he had taken refuge in Geneva hiding behind *L'Association pour la paix au Moyen-Orient*. It was ostensibly an organization for developing solutions that would bring peace to that troubled part of the world. In reality, it was a front for the remnants of HAC.

Shah's office in the center of the top floor of the building encompassed one hundred square meters or almost eleven hundred square feet. No expense had been spared in furnishing and decorating it. He was, after all, the caliph. He enjoyed a northward view across a small pocket park to the Rhône river and beyond. The beauty of Geneva with its rich history of art and culture only fed his visceral hatred for all things Western. It served to inspire him in his quest to destroy it.

He'd been staring thoughtfully out the glass wall at the river for a long time. Now, he turned and summoned his aide, Jibril, into his office.

"Yes, Caliph." The young man of twenty had an almost feminine beauty about him. Shah had felt an attraction to him from the moment they had met in Mosul.

"I wish to speak to General Kazemzadeh's Hezbollah contact in Mexico. You have his number, yes?" He stared at the young man's large, soft brown eyes.

"Yes, Caliph, of course. His name is Abdel Sabbah. I will get him on the telephone for you." Jibril returned to his desk in the outer chamber. A few moments later he returned and handed Shah an encrypted phone. "He's on the line."

"Abdel, my brother, is that you?"

"It is, Caliph. How may I be of service?" The slight note of disrespect in Sabbah's tone wasn't lost on Shah. Hezbollah, like their Iranian benefactors, were Shi'a Islamists. Shah and his followers were Sunnis. So great was their mutual desire to destroy the Great Satan and its allies that they were able to cooperate on a limited basis.

"As you know, our allies, the Chinese, entrusted us with six nuclear weapons the first of which we deployed with extreme success."

"The Chinese are also our allies. They insisted those weapons be transported and safeguarded by the Islamic Republic of Iran," Sabbah said sternly.

The comment rankled Shah, but he chose to ignore it in the interest of expediency. "It has become necessary to move the nuclear devices to a different location in Mexico preparatory to their imminent deployment against the Great Satan. Pursuant to General Kazemzadeh's instructions I need your men to relocate them." He didn't want to explain that the move was necessitated because HAC had discovered that Turan was a mole.

"I thought you were going to smuggle them across the Mexican border with the United States as you did the first one."

Shah resented any challenges to his authority, but again chose to let it pass. "Given the effect of the first device at Los Alamos and the strengthening of the border by that new president, Flagler, that plan must be changed."

"And your new plan is?"

"We're going to smuggle them out of Mexico using a commercial fishing boat from a port on Mexico's east coast. Once the ship is well out into the Gulf of Mexico, we will transfer them to five individual vessels. Each of them has a separate destination in the United States."

"And you want me to transport them from Chihuahua to this port."

"Yes."

There was a brief silence on Sabbah's end of the line, then he said, "It may be just as risky moving the devices across Mexico as moving them north to the border like we originally planned."

Shah's patience was at an end. "Are you going to move them or not? Or is it necessary for me to engage General Kazemzadeh and the Chinese in this discussion?

Sabbah's chilly tone grew even colder. "No, of course not. Why would you suggest such a thing? What is the destination?"

Shah smiled in satisfaction. "It's a small fishing village called Las Higuerillas about sixty-five kilometers south of Matamoros."

"Matamoros? That's a very long drive from Chihuahua."

"So, what if it is?"

"It will involve passing through the territories controlled by rival drug cartels. We usually use members of MS-13 for something like this. Because they work with the cartels, they have passage through their respective territories."

"Whatever, my brother, just get it done. And the sooner the better. We have a tight window of opportunity and it won't be open for long."

CHAPTER 40

THE LODGE

SEVERAL MEN and one woman sat around the long, highly polished mahogany table. It was located in a wine cellar beneath the well-appointed library of a huge log structure called The Lodge. It was close to the small, isolated town of Fairview Beach in the Tidewater country of Virginia. Called the War Room, wine cellar's state-of-the-art security against every form of eavesdropping, electronic and otherwise, was amazing. Perfect acoustics, no intrusion of sounds from beyond its walls. No musty smell, just clean, fresh seventy-two-degree air circulating throughout. Equally important, The Lodge was under a long-term lease to a foreign government for use as a consular operation.

Bottles of fine wine were stacked in specially crafted shelving designed to keep each one in a prone position so its contents could work on the cork. The Lodge was owned by a company that was owned by another company that, in turn, was owned by yet another entity, and so on through a mind-boggling chain of domestic and foreign shell corporations. It was impossible to unravel. The ultimate owners were three billionaire brothers with a hardline conservative bent. Alfred, Hermann, and Tomas Mueller also were among the founders of the Society of Adam Smith.

No one other than the Mueller brothers could have created The Lodge, or the entire SAS operation for that matter. Their almost unfathomable wealth, coupled with their control of many of the top technology, electronics, and weapons research and development companies on the planet, put them in a unique position to fund and sponsor a shadow government—the Society of Adam Smith. Christie was struck by the irony. The biggest customer for the Muellers' products and R&D efforts was the U.S. government. The very entity that the SAS was working to reform. The big question was whether it was still possible, at this stage, to reverse the government's destructive behavior instituted by the preceding administration.

There was a note of desperation in Mitch Christie's voice, as he looked around the table. "We've got a real dilemma on our hands. We have good intel that the five rogue nukes are in play, but Cliff Levell's being confined in the Central Detention Facility."

"Poor bastard," said Tomas Mueller, the youngest of the brothers at seventy-nine. "That place is a far cry from what he's used to."

"What's the matter with that Special Counsel, what's his name? Farmer?" Maureen Delaney said angrily. She was chief executive of one of the planet's largest and most successful technology companies that wasn't a part the Mueller brothers' empire. She also enjoyed a romantic relationship with Levell. "Cliff isn't a young man and he's confined to a wheelchair."

Air Force general Parkes DuBois, a member of the Joint

Chiefs, reached over and gently patted Delaney's hand. "They're trying to break his spirit, Maureen."

"Well, good luck with that. He's as tough as they come." Anger flashed in her green eyes.

"We've got the best legal minds in the business working on it, Maureen," Tomas Mueller said. He shook his head. "A grand jury's power really is formidable. Who would have thought such a thing could exist in the Land of the Free?"

"Let's refocus on the most pressing issue," Christie said. "We're essentially rudderless. Cliff can't be replaced, but we should have had a succession plan in place for instances like this."

Mueller looked at Christie for several seconds then swept his eyes around the table. Some of the top members of SAS were present. "With those nuclear devices in play, we don't have any choice. We have to take appropriate action." He brought his gaze back to Christie. "It's no secret that Cliff was grooming you to one day take his place, Mitch."

Christie shifted uncomfortably in his chair. "The operative phrase is 'one day.' What I'm doing with the Bureau now is important to our purposes at SAS. We need to get Cliff released."

"Everything that can be done is being done, Mitch," Mueller said. "Unfortunately, the judge assigned to the matter doesn't like the concept of SAS and seems to believe the country's in a better situation with Cliff in confinement."

"But look at the situation Cliff's in. He's not getting any younger. The longer he refuses to answer Farmer's questions, the longer he sits in jail. But if he testifies, all members of SAS— government, military, private sector participants—will be identified and prosecuted for treasonous activities during the prior administration. It would fatally cripple this country by leaving it without a means for checking unconstitutional and anti-democratic activities, such as those of Flagler's predecessor.

"And it could result in the execution of the Presidential Decision Directive and the elimination of our most effective weapon, the Sleeping Dogs. Essentially the terrorists would be unobstructed in their effort to detonate those remaining nukes."

"Mitch is right," Maureen Delaney said. "We can't afford to wait while lawyers play legal games. The clock is ticking, isn't there some way to speed up this process?"

"What about these super soldiers, these Sleeping Dogs?" said Wilson Druckenmiller, the senior senator from Georgia. "Can't they just break Cliff out, take him by force?"

"Possibly," Mueller said, "but it's probably worse than the current situation. Cliff could be injured, or God forbid, killed in the attempt."

"Plus," General Dubois said, "Farmer has Cliff under heavy guard. So, someone must have alerted him to the possibility. Is that the odor of Fairchilde and the AGU I smell?"

"Not to mention," Mueller said, "the action, even if successful, would ruin one of their best advantages—anonymity."

"And Cliff would have to go into hiding, probably forever, and that would impact his effectiveness in leading SAS," Delaney said.

Finally, Christie said, "What about the proverbial elephant in the middle of the room?"

All heads swiveled to stare at him.

"A presidential pardon."

"Wait," DuBois said. "Can the president pardon someone who hasn't been convicted of anything yet?"

"Of course. Ford pardoned Nixon before he'd been tried and convicted in the Watergate scandal," Mueller said. "It was done, as in this instance, to refocus the country's interest on more important matters."

The room was silent for several moments as its occupants looked at each other. Finally, Tomas Mueller spoke. "On its surface, that may sound like an ideal solution. In reality, it's probably impossible."

"Why?" Delaney said angrily. "He's the one who got Cliff involved in this mess. He's obligated to get him out of it."

"True," Mueller said, "but his purpose was admirable—stop those bombs in the most expeditious fashion even if the methodology violates the rule of law and may infringe on the sovereignty of other nations, not to mention it exceeds the scope of his presidential authority."

"And that's where the problem lies, isn't it?" Druckenmiller said. "Pardoning Cliff would effectively block special counsel Farmer's efforts to indict the president for his extralegal actions. That would make it look like Flagler really did have something to hide, which of course he does."

"But, dammit, those nukes have to be neutralized," DuBois said. "Without Cliff, how do we make that happen?"

There were several moments of silence then Christie said, "There may be a way. We have an agent who's a part of the jihadist group planning to detonate the nukes. Through him we hope to locate them before they're deployed. Once we had that information, Cliff was going to send the Sleeping Dogs to neutralize the threat."

"Can we do it despite the situation Cliff's in?" DuBois said.

"Maybe," said Christie. "We lost the agent's tracking signal, but we know where he was at the time. Hopefully, that's where the nukes are."

"If Cliff was going to unleash the Dogs on that spot, can you do it instead of him?" Mueller said.

"That will depend on whether I can contact those men, the Dogs."

"Cliff's being held incommunicado. Is he the only one who has the ability to communicate with them?"

"Maybe not. I suspect his associate, Nando, knows how to reach them."

CHAPTER 41

BIG PINE KEY

WHELAN WAS ENJOYING the solitude and watching the last light of day creep silently away to the west. The other Dogs, as usual, were at the No Name Pub. He was sitting on the raised deck of the stilt house Levell had rented as a base for the Dogs training exercises on Cayo Hombre Muerto. Intuitively, he felt as if he was facing west, but the sunlight was off his left shoulder, although slowly fading to black. So, he knew he was facing north. The Florida Keys were infamous for disorienting mariners, divers, and fishermen.

Spreading out before him into the distance were mudbanks covered with seagrass, and shallow waters that ranged from nearly colorless in clarity to every pastel shade of green and blue imaginable. But the colors all were darkening rapidly in the ever-advancing dusk. Almost straight out from him, the mangrove islet of Porpoise Key straddled the waters of Bogie Channel and Big Spanish Channel. Beyond it he could see the dimming outlines of Annette Key, Mayo Key, Water Key, Little Pine Key, and the westerly tip of No Name Key. Beyond them, he knew, were dozens of other sandbars, mud flats, and mangrove infested islets. All were part of the countless low-lying dots, many of them under water at high tide, which curved more than one-hundred-twenty miles southwesterly from the tip of Florida, separating the Atlantic Ocean from the Gulf of Mexico.

He also knew from studying the maps, charts, and Google Earth aerials that if he could draw a line due north from the spot where he sat, it wouldn't find dry land again until it came ashore at Everglades City roughly eighty miles across Florida Bay.

All of the Dogs seemed to be enjoying their stay on Big Pine Key. None of them, including Whelan at this point, had ties to anywhere else. The weather was good, the hospitable No Name Pub was a few blocks away, and the living accommodations were comfortable. But lately they'd been remarking to each other that it was strange they hadn't heard from Levell. Whelan had tried to call the Old Man to discuss alternatives to training in the mangroves, but Levell hadn't picked up or responded to voice-mails. Whelan knew the silence wasn't Levell's vengeance for Whelan having been purposely incommunicado in Dingle. He and the others were worried that something had happened to the Old Man. The major flaw in the SAS setup was communications involving the Dogs. Everything went through one point—Levell. There were no alternative routes, not even through Christie.

He stared out across the darkened waters and let his mind drift. Thoughts of Sean and Declan bubbled up. He missed watching their relentless development into strong, good young men and wondered how long it would be before he could return to Dingle. He purposely filtered out thoughts of Caitlin. Nothing positive would come from dwelling on what was.

His reverie was interrupted by the ringing of his satphone. It was on the coffee table in the living room. He stood up and went inside to answer it. *Levell. It's about time.* No one else had access to Levell's phone, and it was the only one that would connect with Whelan's.

He used his thumb to depress the connect icon. "You been on vacation or what?" He was surprised at the response.

"Hey, Brendan, it's Mitch," Christie said.

Whelan instantly recognized the major departure of protocol. *Something must have happened to Cliff.* "I wasn't expecting to hear from you, Mitch. What's going on?" There was an edge of concern in Whelan's voice. "Is Cliff okay?"

There was a brief hesitation at the other end of the line, then Christie said, "Yes and no. Physically he's fine. But he's in jail."

"Jail? How can that be? The Old Man has more clout than the Joint Chiefs."

"Well, he seems to have met his match." Christie went on to explain the situation with the special counsel, David Farmer, and the citation for contempt of grand jury.

Whelan felt his anger rising. "Do we need to go get him out? And disabuse the special counsel of his actions?"

"Would that you could, but that might be a fool's errand. At least for the present. You and the others are too valuable an asset to risk losing any of you. Not to mention it would blow your cover of anonymity, and that's of paramount importance."

"What then? Bask in the Florida Keys until we eat so much seafood we grow gills?"

"Cliff did mention once or twice that you can be a sarcastic bunch."

"Got an alternative in mind?"

"Same plan as before. Neutralize those fucking nukes and the terrorists that have them."

"Our crystal ball is at the cleaners. You have any idea where the damn things are?"

"Yeah. We have a mole with the terrorists who have the nukes. We had a tracer on him."

"Had? What the fuck does that mean, Mitch?"

"Umm…well, that's a small problem. We lost him… temporarily, I think."

"That's the problem with you fucking bureaucrats, Mitch. You're up to your nostrils in a pit filled with alligators and poisonous reptiles and you think it's a small problem."

"Look," Christie said, with more than a trace of irritation in his voice. "We know where he was when we lost the signal. It's an island in a big-ass lagoon in northeastern Mexico, near Tampico. A place called Isla El Idolo."

"The Island of the Idol."

"That's right, Cliff said most of you guys speak a variety of languages. I guess Spanish is one of yours."

Whelan said nothing.

"It makes sense that the nukes would be on that island," Christie said. "It has direct access to the Gulf of Mexico not far from the U.S. The bad guys could load them on fishing trawlers and haul them to heavily populated port cities on America's Gulf and East Coasts."

"What about your mole? Any idea what his situation is?"

"The tracer was in his cell phone. The only way it stops transmitting is if the battery is removed. If the guys he was with did that, then his cover was somehow blown." Christie paused. "If that's the case, we have to assume he's dead."

Whelan detected something in Christie's voice. "Who was this guy? A bureau employee, a co-worker of yours?"

"No, he was just a kid, really. He'd been involved in the Los Alamos disaster, but along the way he was smitten with a local girl in Santa Fe and had an epiphany. He wanted to try to atone for his participation in bombing the national laboratory."

"What was his name?"

"Turan Salam."

"No shit? We chased him and his buddy, Bazir Haqqani, all the way to Doha. I killed Haqqani, but the kid got away. You have some strange playmates, Mitch."

"Whatever. I liked the kid. I think he sincerely wanted to do the right thing."

"If he found the bombs on Isla El Idolo, then he did do the right thing, even if it cost him his life. The question for us is, what now? I assume you've been able to pinpoint the kid's last known location on that island. Presumably, that's where the nukes are. We'll need a lot of intel: maps, aerials, charts of the surrounding waters, locations of the nearest cops and Federales. We'll also need some sophisticated insertion and extraction techniques. And make sure there are multiple exfil scenarios. There have been some fuck ups lately."

"I'll take care of it at this end and get back to you."

"Are you saying you want us to stay here on Big Pine for the time being?"

"Not for long. We'll move you to Texas, maybe as soon as tomorrow."

Whelan terminated the call and put the phone back on the coffee table. He grabbed an IPA from the refrigerator and began slowly pacing the living room. *How was Cliff holding up in jail? How long could he hold out? How long would his health, at seventy-five, hold up? Would the SAS be as effective without him calling the shots? Could Christie pull this off in lieu of Levell? What added risks did this changed situation pose for the Dogs?*

His thoughts and pacing were interrupted by a knock on the frame of the screen door. He looked up and saw Brooke standing there. *Shit!*

Whelan walked to the screen door but didn't open it. She was wearing white short-shorts that looked as if they'd been painted on her tight hips and butt. The striking symmetry of her flawless legs was on full display. The narrow strip of bandeau top revealed almost all of her perfect breasts. Whelan had to force his eyes back up to hers. "How did you know where to find me?"

"One of your friends told me."

Whelan's eyes narrowed. "Which 'friend?'"

"The crude one."

Almeida.

There were several seconds of silence as they stared at each other through the screen door. Finally, Brooke said, "Are you going to invite me in or not?" Her tone implied anger and hurt feelings.

Whelan swung the door open and said, "Sure, come in." *I'm going to strangle Almeida.*

She walked to the middle of the living room and looked around. "It looks like a bunch of guys live here, like a dorm room." Clothes and dirty dishes as well as beer bottles and glasses were scattered everywhere.

Whelan shrugged. "Guys."

"Which bedroom is yours?"

Whelan shifted uncomfortably. "Why?"

"I just want to see it."

He nodded at a doorway to the left.

Brooke walked over and stopped in the doorway, looking around the room. It had two twin beds and a rollaway. "Which is yours?"

"The rollaway."

"Why? I thought you were in charge."

"I am, but I was the last to arrive. That's the way it's always worked."

"Who got the sofa?"

"Almeida."

"Any particular reason?"

"Yeah, no one wants to share a room with him."

"I'm not surprised."

She settled into the rattan sofa's floral print upholstery and crossed one beautiful leg over the other. She patted the seat beside her. "Come sit with me. We need to talk."

Instead, Whelan pulled up a chair that matched the sofa. There was a coffee table dividing them. He looked at her but said nothing. This was an instance where his intuitive abilities told him it was better to let the other player open the game.

"You left in a hurry the other night and didn't come back. And you haven't been around the Pub. Are you avoiding me?"

This was the challenging part for Whelan. He *had* been avoiding her. But if he told her that, it would hurt her and feed into her "oh, poor me" scenario. Besides, he did have a history with her that had been enjoyable in parts. He disliked lying but recognized that sometimes in life discretion truly was the better part of valor. "I've just been busy, that's all. I organized this trip. Between herding these other guys along on fishing and diving jaunts and keeping them out of trouble, I just haven't had free any time."

"Fishing and diving? They're in the No Name from opening until it closes."

Shit! "We've been going at night. Fewer other people out there and no Marine Patrol in case the catch is a little under-sized." He was starting to feel very uncomfortable.

"Really? Where's your boat and gear?"

Double shit! "We hire a captain to take us in his boat, use his gear."

Twin rows of tears began to track slowly down her smooth, tanned cheeks. "You're lying, Brendan. Why? Why don't you want to be with me? We're so good together, I just don't understand. Please help me."

He knew he was being played, but she was very good. It took some deep resolve on his part to resist reaching out to comfort her. But he knew where that would lead. To the bedroom. "We're good together when we're having sex, Brooke, but life doesn't let people have sex to the exclusion of other necessities. It's all those other things where we don't have a common bond."

Her tears were coming hard and fast now. He didn't know what to do, so he just let her cry it out.

After several moments the tears abated to sniffles. She wiped her eyes with her finger tips and her nose with the back of her hand. "I just don't understand why everyone wants to hurt me, why no one ever likes me. I try so hard to please everyone. I always have. What's wrong with me that everyone treats me this way?" She looked pleadingly at him with her big, blue, tear-filled eyes.

It was an Oscar-worthy performance. And it almost succeeded.

Whelan had to look away and push his chair back from the coffee table. "Listen, Brooke, every one of us has people who don't like us for reasons that don't seem to make sense. It's part of the human condition. But you have lots of people who like you."

"Who? Name one."

"Your girlfriends, for starters. You were popular as hell at The U. My buddies here are all favorably impressed with you."

"Your 'buddies' are impressed with my tits and my ass, not me as a person!"

"We're men. Tits and ass always impress us, but we also recognize that there's a hell of a lot more to you than that."

"I don't believe you. I think you just wanted to have sex with me and led me to believe you cared about me as a person, as a friend. You probably think I was easy, that I sleep with every man that comes along. Is that it, Brendan, do you think I'm a slut?"

He grimaced, realizing the conversation was about to go out of control and Brooke with it. "Hell no, I don't think that. For one thing, you're a grown woman; it's none of my business who you choose to sleep with. For another, as I recall, you reached down my pants the minute I walked in your door the other night. But I had the best evening I've had in a long while and wouldn't trade it for anything."

She jumped to her feet, fire in her eyes. "You *do* think I'm trashy! But I'm not. It's you. You're just like all men. You lead women on, get what you want, then dump them to deal with their hurt and pain on their own!"

He shook his head vigorously. "No, dammit, that's not what happened. I do care about your emot—"

"Oh, God, I hate you, you miserable bastard!" She kicked the coffee table hard. It bounced off his shins. "I know you and your 'buddies' are up to no good. I fucking hope you die! All of you."

She stormed out of the house, slamming the screen door behind her, and bolted down the stairs.

As she marched angrily down the street, he grinned and called after her, "I guess this means I'm not 'the only man you ever really loved.'"

Without turning around, she gave him the middle finger and screamed back over her shoulder, "Fuck you!"

Almost feeling guilty about his sense of relief, he walked back inside and got another IPA from the refrigerator. He shook his head. *Some people seem to have no desire to change no matter how unhappy they think their life is.* He took a long pull. *But first things first...that fucking Almeida.*

CHAPTER 42

PORT ARANSAS, TEXAS

ON THE NORTHERN tip of Mustang Island, hard by Aransas Pass the shipping gateway to Corpus Christi, is Port Aransas a town of four thousand souls. Its livelihood has always depended on the Gulf of Mexico that spreads east from its drab, grayish beaches. Sport fishing, commercial fishing, including shrimping, and the tourism its coastal position generates provide its economic underpinnings.

The town and surrounding region were in the process of rebuilding from the devastating effects of a recent Category 4 hurricane. Many of the usual guest accommodations weren't yet habitable, making it difficult for SAS to find lodging for the Dogs especially on literally overnight notice. But Levell's people had come through, even in the Old Man's absence. They had secured, at a steep markup to pre-hurricane rents, a three-bedroom, three-bath condominium unit. It was on the top floor of a massive six-story-over-parking building that fronted on Aransas Pass, a treacherous, shifting channel that accommodated the main shipping traffic for the much larger city of Corpus Christi on the far side of Corpus Christi Bay.

The unit was a little cramped for the seven large and restless men that now occupied it. The main positive was the sole bar to have survived the storm. It was within walking distance of their lodging, a large, multilevel, open-air wooden structure overlooking the Port Aransas Municipal Boat Harbor at Turtle Cove.

The weather was perfect—dry with a high of 70 °F and lows at night around 50 °F. All the more reason to vacate the apartment as much as possible and enjoy the views, ambiance, refreshments, and local ladies at the bar. Six of them did just that. Only Whelan stayed in the unit, speaking endlessly on the satphone with Christie in preparation for the operation on Isla El Idolo. Maps, charts, aerials, and other materials crucial to its success were delivered regularly by a variety of entities. A plan was taking shape, but everyone involved knew time was critical. The bombs had to be located and neutralized before they were individually distributed for their intended targets.

The Dogs would be operating in an asymmetric, non-conventional combat environment on strange turf. It was further complicated by the nature of the location in a remote and primitive area where the impenetrable mangroves made a flanking or surprise assault from the rear impossible. Whelan hoped that disadvantage could be offset to some extent by the use of newly developed, highly sophisticated equipment to be supplied by the Mueller brothers.

He knew that the Dogs would be at a definite disadvantage in terms of the operation's battlespace. The mission was far from finite—locate and neutralize five nuclear weapons. Little, if anything, was known about the enemy they'd be facing. The terrain was anything but familiar. Available time was critically short. Civil considerations were a complete unknown. These all were crucial elements that would unfold once they entered the hot zone. Prior experiences had taught him that this was a recipe for disaster.

All he knew for certain at this point was that the Dogs would sail from Port Aransas in the next day or two aboard a commercial shrimper. It, in turn, would rendezvous with a Mexican counterpart fifty miles or so off the coast of Matamoros at the edge of the continental shelf.

IT WAS late afternoon and the action was beginning to pick up at the bar in Turtle Cove where the other Dogs were killing time. At a table, Thomas was explaining to Larsen the subtleties of the yin-yang as taught by the School of Naturalists during China's Warring States era. The man-with-no-neck didn't have a clue what Thomas was talking about but didn't have anything else to do, so he listened.

The other four were sitting at a bar built into the railing that enclosed the second level, overlooking the boat basin. Stensen and Kirkland had been discussing the finer points of knife-fighting. Stone was checking scores from the Australian Rules football preseason games, known as the JLT Community Series, on his smartphone.

Almeida drained his latest beer and said, "Am I the only one who wants to get laid?"

"Funny you should say that," Stensen said. "considering you're the one most likely not to get laid."

"Why don't you go fuck yourself, Stensen," Almeida said with a snarl. He waved agitatedly in the direction of a cocktail waitress and signaled for another beer.

Kirkland grinned. "What Nick is saying is that no woman is

going to look at some guy with a shiner the size of a full moon and five stitches under his left eye."

"Yeah," Stensen said, "you look like the bride of Frankenstein."

"Good thing they don't let little kids in here. You'd scare the shit out of them," Kirkland said.

"You think I look bad? Ain't nothing like what I'm gonna do to you two fuckers if you keep it up." He tried to look his most menacing as he glared at them.

Stone looked up from his phone screen and said, "Best back off a bit, mate. You already had your arse kicked by Whelan. You don't have a Buckley's with any of these blokes either."

"Bullshit! I can whip any of you candy-asses. Whelan just got lucky. He suckered me."

"Sure didn't look that way to any of us who saw it happen," Stensen said. The red dots in the center of his eyes began to expand. There was blood in the water.

"Pig's bum, mate," Stone said.

Almeida gave him a puzzled look. "Speak fucking English."

"I'm saying you're wrong this time, Rafe. Whelan was just chewing your arse out for sending the sheila over to the house after he'd told you not to."

"That's the finest pussy I ever seen anywhere! I was doing him a favor. Ain't my fault if he's gone queer."

"No, mate. He was clear with all of us that he didn't want to see her. Why, is his business. He was rightfully chewing your arse out when you tried to throw a punch at him."

"Yeah, and why didn't you help me? You're supposed to be my 'mate.'"

"When you do ratbag shit like that, you're on pat malone."

"What the hell does that mean?"

"You're on your own."

Thomas and Larsen walked up.

"What's going on?" Thomas said.

"Rafe's entertaining us with his delusions of grandeur," Stensen said.

Almeida looked around at each of the others. "You know what? I don't need this shit. I'm outta here." He stormed off toward the stairs. On the way, he met the cocktail server, took the beer out of her hand and continued walking.

Larsen wagged his head atop his neckless shoulders. "He can be fun to be around, but sometimes he causes more problems than he's worth." He looked at Stone.

The Ozzie shook his head. "Let 'em go. He really just needs to get full as a goog and find a sheila to do the nasty with. He'll be fine after that."

Kirkland heard his phone ding, pulled it from a pocket, and looked at it. "It's a text from Brendan. He says to drink up and get back home. He's got a plan he wants to run by us."

CHAPTER 43

CHIHUAHUA, MEXICO

THERE WAS no part of Turan that wasn't experiencing agony. His fingernails hurt. His eyelashes hurt. The blindfold was tied so tight it made his head throb. But those weren't his only problems. Several of his front teeth had been broken off. He could feel their jagged edges with the tip of his swollen tongue. His nose had been smashed, leaving him grateful that he hadn't been gagged; otherwise, he would have suffocated. He could sense the dried blood that crusted his face—what was left of it. The skin stung and itched at the same time, but Turan could do nothing about it. His arms were so tightly bound behind him that his one reasonably good shoulder felt as if it was about to dislocate. The other one had been dislocated by a savage kick, one of many. His ribs ached with a sharp, steady pain. He wondered how many of them were broken. Something was wrong with one of his knees. If he tried to move it, the pain almost caused him to vomit. He was terrified and wanted to cry, but feared it would only cause more beatings.

Turan had no idea where he was, only that he was bound and

lying on a cold concrete floor. A dirty one. It smelled of petroleum distillates, as if he was in a garage or similar building. He was lying on his side and wanted desperately to move, to take the strain off of the shoulder that wasn't dislocated, but could muster neither the strength nor the courage.

In his mind, he went over the things he could remember. Being picked up by four men at the airport in Brownsville, Texas, and their unbridled hostility toward him. That was the first red flag. The long, uncomfortable ride to the fishing village of Tamiahua on Mexico's Gulf Coast. He remembered the boat ride from there to the island, Isla El Idolo, with two of the men. That was when one of the men had struck him from behind with an object of some kind.

He remembered falling to the ground, stunned, and being beaten savagely by the two men. One of them had taken his cell phone, removed the battery and thrown it into the nearby lagoon. The man had struck him across the face several times with the now useless phone. That was how some of his teeth had been broken. That phone had been his lifeline. It enabled the people he was working with to track him. They would know where he was at the time the battery was removed, but now he knew he was no longer on the island.

Turan had been so badly beaten he couldn't remember how he got off the island or when, but he recalled snatches of memory of a long trip in the back of a van. It seemed as if it had taken days. He recalled being given some water and scraps of food along the way. And beaten regularly. There had been intermittent lapses of consciousness, but eventually he had arrived at the place he now was.

Finally, Turan remembered that he'd been broken. He'd tried to endure, tried to remain disciplined. But ultimately the beatings, the pain, were too much. He recalled how, through tears and with bloody foam and spittle dripping from his ruined mouth, he'd admitted his betrayal of Nadir Shah and the caliphate. He'd told his tormentors about Levell and Christie and the plan to use a group of special operators to capture the nuclear devices and kill all who were involved. He confirmed what they already knew about the tracer on his phone. But it hadn't stopped the beatings. In fact, they had seemed to intensify in savagery.

He wondered why he was still alive. Why hadn't they killed him? What further use could he be to them at this point? Perhaps, Shah wanted him kept alive for some unfathomable purpose. But it really didn't matter to Turan. Ultimately, they would kill him. At this point, he welcomed the thought of death. Not because he still believed the Qur'anic text that Allah had prepared a place for him in Jannah with seventy-two beautiful virgins. The things he had experienced in his seventeen years had made him skeptical, perhaps agnostic, where religion was concerned. Was the Qur'anic or Biblical version of an afterlife correct? Or, when you breathed your last breath, did you simply slip into an eternal black void?

He had done this for Carolina, in hopes she would forgive him for what he had done at Los Alamos. Now, he knew he would never see her again. A sob convulsed him. The pain it caused pushed him almost to the level of unconsciousness.

Turan's thoughts were interrupted by a sound like a large metal door being moved along tracks, as if being opened. *They are coming back!* His adrenal glands responded immediately, as his heart began to race and his breathing shortened. Because of the echo effect in the building, he couldn't tell how many pairs of footsteps there were, but there was more than one. Instinctively, he wanted to shrink away from the approaching footsteps, but his body wouldn't respond.

"Hey, motherfucker," a male voice said in English with a

strong Spanish accent. "This is your lucky day. We ain't gonna kill you. Yet."

There was laughter that confirmed the presence of more than one person.

"Yeah," a second male voice said. "We s'pposed to keep you alive."

"For a while," the first voice said. "But that don't mean we can't beat the shit outta you."

More laughter, followed by a hard kick to Turan's abdomen. As he gasped for breath, he was afraid he might swallow his swollen tongue and strangle himself.

"What's you name, *chico*?" The second voice said. "Tur-Ban or some shit like that?"

The victim tried to answer. All he could get out was something that sounded like, "T'wan."

"T'wan?" The second voice said. "That don't sound like no camel jockey's name. Shit, that don't sound like no fuckin' name at all."

"Well, T'wan, you gonna go on a little trip. Your raghead bossman wants us to move these fuckin' nukes, and you get to go with them," the first voice said.

"Yeah, *chico*," the second voice said, "maybe you gonna get to ride one of them motherfuckers all the way down, like in that movie…what's it called?"

"Dr. Strangelove," the first voice said.

"Yeah, that's the one."

Both men laughed, then one of them kicked the prisoner in the head, causing him to black out.

WHEN TURAN REGAINED CONSCIOUSNESS, he found himself lying on the bare metal floor in the back of an old and well-worn and windowless extended van. He was sitting up wedged between the back of the passenger bucket seat and the sidewall of the van. There were two men in the front seats. His arms now were bound in front, making the pain on his shoulders a little less excruciating. His injured knee lay against the floor at an odd angle. Because of the commercial vehicle's worn-out springs and shock absorbers, every little bump was intensified, sending bolts of pain coursing through his body.

The blindfold had been removed but his eyes were swollen shut, except for a thin slit between the lids of his right eye. The interior of the van was engulfed in dark shadows and he couldn't make out much about his surroundings, but there were what appeared to be five large rucksacks between him and the rear doors. The van smelled of rust, body odors, cigarette smoke and stale food and beer.

The swelling in his tongue had subsided enough to tempt him to speak. "Where am I?"

A voice coming from the passenger side said, "What difference does it make? Things ain't gonna get no better for you."

A voice from the driver's side said, "Ah, fuck, he's a dead man. What's the harm in tellin' him?"

"Yeah, I guess," the passenger said. "You takin' a little trip, gonna get a tour of Mexico. 'Course you ain't gonna see shit 'cause you inside this fuckin' truck. But if it makes you more comfortable, you sittin' next to five fuckin' nukes, man." Both men laughed heartily.

"Where was I? Last thing I remember I was being taken to an island south of Tampico."

"That's right, *chico*, you fucked up. You crossed that chief camel jockey, what's his name, Nadir Shah?" the driver said. "He had his guys bring you from Brownsville to Tamiahua and beat the shit outta you. Then our guys took over."

"Your guys? What does that mean?"

"You heard of MS-13, *chico*? That's us. We was hired by Hezbollah ragheads to babysit you." Both men laughed again. "See, you been hauled around Mexico and we the only ones can do that 'cause the drug cartels all use us when they got shit goin' on in another cartel's turf. We ain't Mexican. We Salvadorans. We work for whoever pays, so we got relationships with all of them. They let us move through their territories when anyone else, including those Hezbollah ragheads, would be butchered."

"I don't follow what you're saying."

The driver said, "Pay fuckin' attention 'cause I ain't gonna say it twice. You was in the Gulf Cartel's territory on that Island, but to get there, you had to go through the Zetas' turf. Then when you was brought to Chihuahua, you was in turf controlled by the Beltrán-Leyva Cartel. Now we takin' you back to Zeta territory."

"I was taken to Chihuahua? Why?"

"'Cause that's where these fuckin' nukes was being kept," the passenger said.

"Why there?"

"'Cause your old boss, the 'Caliph,' was gonna smuggle them through a little shithole called San Luis, just like he done with the first nuke, the one that fucked up Los Alamos."

Things were starting to make sense to the prisoner. He, Turan Salam, had helped smuggle the first bomb out of San Luis, over the border, and into Los Alamos. Shortly afterward, an off-the-books group of special operators had destroyed the HAC encampment above the village. San Luis, just below the border with the United States, was almost a straight shot from Chihuahua, a large metropolitan area that provided plenty of opportunities for storing the remaining nukes until needed.

"So, why was I taken to Tamiahua in the first place? Why not Chihuahua?"

The man on the passenger side said, "Think about it, *chico*. If you wanna set somebody up, throw the stink off your tracks, you gotta mislead them. Make them think what they're lookin' for is in one place, when it's really in another. Shah, he knows you tryin' to fuck him. So, he makes it look like you went to Tamiahua and found the nukes, but you and them things was really in Chihuahua."

"What do you mean that Nadir Shah thought I was betraying him?"

The passenger said, "How the fuck do I know? He got word from somebody that you was working with the *norteamericanos*, carrying some kinda tracer."

Turan thought about his cell phone. He vaguely remembered that the men who took him to Isla El Idolo had taken it from him when they'd reached the island. Then the beatings had started. He wondered what had happened to the phone but couldn't remember. "What did they do with my phone?"

"Who the fuck knows?" the driver said. "Left it on the island? Threw it in the fuckin' water? All's I know is that the battery was removed and it don't fuckin' work after that."

"So," the passenger said, "whoever been tracing you thinks you and them nukes is still on that island."

"Why? What's the purpose?"

"Settin' a trap, *chico*, settin' a trap."

Turan thought about that for a few moments. "Where are you taking me and these devices?"

"What the fuck difference does it make, *chico*? You gonna be fucking dead after we get there."

CHAPTER 44

PORT ARANSAS, TEXAS

WHILE WHELAN WAITED for the other Dogs to settle their tab and hike the couple of blocks from the bar in Turtle Cove to the condo unit, he dialed up Caitlin's number, hoping to speak with the boys. He was uncomfortable at the thought of having to go through Caitlin to get to his sons. Although she had been opposed to it, he was beginning to think maybe the time had come to get them a cell phone they could share.

After several rings, a recorded message cut in. "The number you are trying to reach has been disconnected and is no longer in service." The line went dead.

Whelan looked at his cell phone as if it had betrayed him. He thought about his next move then dialed the number of Caitlin's parents. Her mother, Ciara, answered. She sounded very pleasant and happy to hear from Whelan, as if her daughter's marriage hadn't broken up and distanced him from her affection and regard. After a short conversation, she told him to call Caitlin at the Fianna's number.

He hung up then dialed it. It went through several rings. Just as it was about to go to voicemail he heard someone connect on the other end. He was surprised to hear Declan's voice say, "Hello?"

"I was expecting your mother to answer, but I'm glad it's you, Declan. I was calling to speak to you and your brother."

"Mum's busy, so I answered it."

Declan sounded sullen. Whelan detected a mixture of anger and resentment in his youngest son's voice. Being a man of direct action, Whelan said, "What's the matter, Declan? Do I detect resentment in your voice?"

"You can detect anything you want. I'll go get Sean."

Whelan heard the sound of the phone being laid heavily on a hard surface.

Moments later, Sean said, "Da, where are you? Are you in Dingle?" He sounded excited.

Whelan hated disappointing him. "No, Sean, I'm still out of the country."

"And you can't tell me 'cause you're on a secret mission, right?"

"Something like that."

"I'll bet those other big, muscled dudes are with you, right?"

Whelan chuckled. "I really can't go into that, but let's just say there's never a dull moment."

"You live the coolest life!" Sean enthused. "I want to be just like you when I finish school. Go do the kinds of things you and your mates do, like hunt down and kill the bad people."

"We need to redirect this conversation, son. How are things at school?"

There was a change in Sean's voice. A note of boredom slipped in. "Ah, it's alright."

"Just alright, huh?" Whelan grinned. "Surely there's at least one young lady to keep things interesting."

"Well, yeah, there's that." His voice perked up.

"So, does this girl have a name?"

"Yeah, Brooke."

"Brooke!" The word exploded from Whelan's mouth.

"Yeah, something wrong with that name? You don't like it?"

"No," Whelan said, as he struggled to backtrack. "It's a beautiful name, and Irish too."

"Did you ever know a girl named Brooke, Da?"

"Uh, yeah, maybe a long time ago."

"Was she pretty?"

"Stunning."

"Prettier than Mom?"

Despite the unit's air conditioner thermostat being kept at 65°, Whelan was beginning to perspire. "Impossible. No one's prettier than your mom. But don't tell her I said that. That's water over the damn at this point."

"Yeah," Sean said, "because of her. She's the one that broke up your marriage, not you."

Sensitive territory. "Don't be blaming your mom, Sean. We both played a hand in that. I shouldn't have left the three of you considering Maksym's threats."

"No, Da, you did what you had thought was best."

"Thanks for the vote of confidence, son, but I was wrong to entrust the well-being of you, Declan, and your mother to friends and neighbors. It only led to heir deaths." He needed to change the subject and said, "Your mother's old phone line was disconnected. Are you living at the Fianna now?"

"We're helping Mom fix it up."

"Fix it up? Is She going to sell it?"

"No, we're going to run it again." A note of enthusiasm had returned to his voice.

Whelan was stunned. "How is she going to do that, I mean with a baby on the way and all?"

Now, there was a chuckle in Sean's voice. "Maybe you should ask her yourself." His voice became muted, as if he had turned away from the phone when he yelled, "Hey, Mom, it's Da. He wants to talk to you." He turned back to the phone and said, "She'll be here in a minute." He paused a moment then, with a sly edge to his voice, said, "Good luck."

Once again Whelan heard the thump of the phone being placed on a hard surface. Now, he began to perspire in earnest.

"Hello. Bren, is that you?"

"Yes."

"I thought you called to speak with the boys."

"I did, but Declan clearly isn't ready to speak with me."

"He's struggling with some issues even though I've told him many times that the breakup was mostly my doing. He's just not ready to accept it yet, but eventually, he will. Just be patient with him. He does love you."

"Well, at least Sean seems not to resent me."

"Oh, don't get me started with that lad," she said.

"Problems?"

"Where do I begin? He's very angry with me for what happened."

"Has he been acting out? Do you want me to speak with him about it?"

"Acting out? He's been a real little shit. Well, big shit actually. He's hit a growth spurt. And, no, don't say anything to him. He adores you. He and I will work it out."

"Speaking of working, Sean tells me you're planning to reopen the Fianna. Are you sure it's wise to take on that burden given your condition?"

"Not that my 'condition' involves you, but you're sweet to be concerned," she said playfully.

"Hell, Kate, it's not like I hate you or want misfortune to befall you."

There was a pause at her end, then "I no longer have a 'condition.'"

"I don't understand what that means."

"I'm no longer pregnant."

"What? Did you have an…"

"No. I miscarried."

"I'm sorry, Cait. That must have been difficult for you emotionally as well as physically."

"It's alright. I prayed and prayed for God to help me find the right resolution. I choose to think that's what happened."

There was silence between them for a few moments, then Whelan said, "I know it's none of my business, but where's Rodney in all of this?"

"Rodney who?"

"I think that answers my question."

CHAPTER 45

THE OVAL OFFICE

FREDERICK FLAGLER, the president of the United States, was a rough, no-holds-barred businessman from New York City. He prided himself in being able to out-tough anyone in high-level negotiations, whether of a business nature or political. He'd come out of nowhere to destroy the presidential ambitions of more than a dozen politicians in his own party. Then he'd done the impossible in the general election and decisively defeated the other party's heavily favored, seemingly preordained candidate. He accomplished it the same way he'd accomplished every success in his life, with politically incorrect savagery and an innate sense of both the opponent's weaknesses and the path of greatest expediency.

The Oval Office comes with more than its share of challenges for any president. But the issue that troubled Flagler most was the opposition party's thirst for his blood. The party that's out of office always looks for any evidence of social or political faux pas that can be used to make POTUS look bad in the eyes of the electorate. This time, however, was different. The opposition party seemed to be possessed by demons to the point where it didn't look for facts, but simply made them up out of whole cloth. But, as the adage goes, "you can't teach an old dog new tricks," and Flagler's I'll-kick-your-fucking-ass-personality only compounded his problems.

Alleged election irregularities supposedly involving collusion between Flagler's campaign people and representatives of a foreign power hostile to the United States had been created by the sore losers on the other side of the aisle and their sycophantic friends in the media. The allegations also implicated Flagler's attorney general. The man had prematurely recused himself and a deputy attorney general had jumped at the opportunity to appoint a special counsel to investigate the supposed irregularities.

This further compounded Flagler's woes because the special counsel had no discernible restrictions on the extent of his jurisdiction. Consequently, that individual, David Farmer, was overturning rocks everywhere in an unflagging effort to pin anything on Flagler that would engineer his downfall.

Flagler knew the allegations of collusion were bogus and lost little sleep over them. What did cause anxieties for him was the new tact that Farmer's investigation had taken. Somehow, he had gotten wind of the president's off-the-records arrangement with Clifford Levell to use a paramilitary group to hunt down the five remaining nuclear devices and eliminate the jihadis who possessed them. POTUS was the most powerful leader on the planet, but he didn't have the authority to send non-government forces to commit hostile acts in foreign jurisdictions. In most situations, he would need congressional approval even to send U.S. military personnel on such a mission.

Throughout his career, Flagler had believed in using the most expeditious methods to achieve a goal, regardless of its propriety.

This had been no exception. After all, if only he, Levell, and Trupockitt knew about the situation, what was the real risk of exposure? Sending the Sleeping Dogs to do it amounted to a false flag operation. And the Dogs wouldn't disclose the mission because he had leverage over them: the revocation of the outstanding PDD calling for their deaths on sight.

Flagler had never been much of a sitter. He believed he did his best thinking on his feet. The *Resolution* desk was historic, magnificent, perhaps even regal, but he only used it for photo op occasions. At the moment, he was pacing back and forth across the Oval Office on its short axis, about twenty-nine feet. He had a visitor waiting to see him. It was Tomas Mueller, the youngest of the three billionaire Mueller brothers. They were the wealthiest individuals in America, probably on the entire planet. Their financial, political, and personal support had been a major factor in Flagler's winning the presidency. Despite their advancing ages, he'd tried to reward them with cabinet positions or choice ambassadorships, but they had politely declined. They preferred to continue to manage their enormous and impossibly complex global network of industries.

Flagler was at a loss for how to proceed with Levell's operation now that Cliff was in jail for contempt of Farmer's grand jury investigation. Worse, he was genuinely concerned that Farmer was going to be able to produce evidence that Flagler had indeed conspired to send a private force to conduct hostile activities on the sovereign soil of a foreign country. At last, he stopped pacing, sighed a long, deep sigh, and buzzed his executive assistant to show Tomas Mueller into the Oval Office.

After the executive assistant had left and closed the door behind her, Flagler waved his visitor to a seat on one of the two large sofas that faced each other across a long, narrow coffee table. At seventy-eight, Tomas Mueller was tall and lean with a thick head of well-trimmed white hair. Like his older brothers, Alfred and Hermann, he suffered from osteoarthritis and took his seat gingerly.

Flagler sat opposite his guest. "I genuinely appreciate your coming on such short notice, Tomas, thank you."

Mueller made a dismissive gesture. "I'm always glad to serve you any way I can, Mr. President."

Flagler made a face. "Please, call me Fred, like in the old days before the damn election."

"I can't do that, sir, it would disrespect the office."

Flagler sighed again and leaned back in the sofa. "I've got a problem that needs a solution quickly. I think I know what to do, but I want to run it by you, get your input. No one has the degree of political savvy that you and your brothers do."

"I'm flattered, of course, Mr. President. I assume this concerns the plight of Clifford Levell."

"You *are* savvy, Tomas." Flagler shook his head in admiration. "Yeah, it involves Cliff. Are you aware of the operation that he and I put together to locate and neutralize the nukes that are still in the hands of the Islamic terrorists?"

"Cliff runs SAS, and we are content for the most part to let him run it his way. But...he is aware of the source of its financing and operational assistance. He's wise enough to always keep us in the loop."

"Of course, you're also aware that he's being jailed for contempt and will remain there until he agrees to testify."

Mueller nodded.

"If he starts talking, I'm toast."

"If he were to do that, it also would expose SAS, it's operations, past and present, as well as the identities of its members, many of whom hold high positions in the government and military."

"It would be a fucking disaster all the way around."

"You mentioned that you had a plan. Do you mind telling me what it is?"

"It's why I asked you here. Although it's far from perfect, and would generate its own set of problems, I don't think I have any choice but to pardon Levell. That would stop Farmer in his tracks."

"It would as far as pursuing Cliff is concerned. But it won't stop Farmer from digging for other sources, other members of SAS, including my brothers and me, who may be forced to offer up evidence that could incriminate you as well."

Flagler thought about that for a few moments, then said, "Shit! What other course of action do I have?"

"Clifford Levell is the toughest man I've ever known. He'll be none the worse for wear if you let this play out for a while longer."

"But where does that leave us with regard to those damn nukes?"

Mueller smiled. "Let's just say that it's in good hands. It probably wouldn't be wise for you to know anything more about it at this point."

Flagler grimaced. "That fucking Farmer. It's a shame something bad doesn't befall him."

"Certainly, you're not thinking of doing something rash?" Mueller's face registered a look of concern.

"Hell no, I'm not a Clinton."

Mueller seemed relieved. "You might consider directing your energies toward learning how Farmer got his information. Obviously, there's a leak somewhere in your administration."

"That's an understatement, Tomas," Flagler said, shaking his head. "There are more leaks inside the Beltway than a dozen sieves could produce."

"Agreed. But someone in particular leaked this information to Farmer. You need to find out who and take appropriate measures."

A grin suddenly lit up Flagler's face. "Hell, in that case, maybe I'm a…, you know who, after all."

CHAPTER 46

WESTERN GULF OF MEXICO

DAWN WAS STILL two hours away, but the light of a full moon shimmered across the choppy water of Aransas Pass. The sixty-foot shrimp trawler, *Miss Sweetcheeks*, chugged steadily southeast, past the ends of the jetties guarding the pass and into the open waters of the Gulf of Mexico. With its hold empty but for the ice, its six-hundred-fifty horsepower, twelve-cylinder Caterpillar diesel engine pushed the ship along at a steady ten knots. Beyond the shelter of the jetties, the chop turned to rolling swells. The crew lowered the outriggers to stabilize the craft and avoid capsizing. Whelan stood at the prow of the ship as it rose and fell in a steady, comfortable rhythm. Comfortable for the crew, certainly, but not all of the seven passengers found the motion relaxing.

Rafe Almeida, despite his claims to have descended from a long line of Portuguese sailors, had proven susceptible to *mal de mer* on past occasions. Whelan smiled at the memories of Almeida's highly exaggerated and often repeated claims to have been a modern-day pirate and treasure hunter. It had happened during the nearly two decades the six original Dogs, including Almeida, had been living under assumed identities as a result of the Presidential Decision Directive calling for their execution on sight. Almeida had persuaded several investors to financially back his scheme to salvage the treasures of a fabled Spanish galleon, the Santa Margarita, lost in a hurricane off Florida on July 17, 1595.

The purported location had been a wild, tequila-infused guess by Almeida—never one to distinguish facts from fiction. He'd used a portion of the investment capital to buy a worm-eaten old shrimper and pissed the rest of it away on booze, whores, and gambling. Almeida-style, he'd named the ship Blackbeard's Cock. When local authorities objected, he'd paid a graffiti artist to paint a rooster on the transom.

The main problem was Almeida's fear of open waters and a predisposition for seasickness. The ship never left port. It didn't take long for the venture to go belly up. The investors sued in an effort to recoup their losses. Unbeknownst to Almeida, he'd had an ace in the hole. Levell, fearful that Almeida's real identity would come out, and with it the existence of the SAS and the other Dogs, bailed him out. He'd been an on-and-off inhabitant of Levell's shit list over the years, but now he was a permanent resident.

As Whelan leaned against the bow rail staring pensively at the dark, boundless sea ahead, he became aware of an approaching presence. Sven Larsen's thick physique materialized beside him. He was drinking a cup of tea and handed Whelan a mug of coffee.

The two men enjoyed the silence for several minutes, then Larsen said, "We on schedule?"

"Yeah, at this speed, it'll take about ten hours to reach the rendezvous point."

"Forty-five miles off the coast?"

Whelan nodded. "Due east of the border."

"It'll take about an hour to transfer the gear to the Mexican trawler, then…?"

"Another thirty hours to the insertion point."

"The Mexican boat isn't going to be in the same class as *Sweetcheeks* here." Larsen slapped the bow rail for emphasis. "Thirty hours on a leaky, smelly fishing boat? Rafe won't be the only one tossing his cookies."

"No shit. But it's another two-hundred-seventy-five nautical miles to Tamiahua from the rendezvous point, and the Mexican boat is older and slower, maybe nine knots. Do the math"

Despite the near blackness surrounding them, Whelan could see Larsen smile his good smile.

"Gonna be a long trip for Almeida."

After a few moments of silence, Larsen said, "Speaking of Rafe, you and him on better terms now?"

Whelan shrugged again. "As good as can be expected after him telling Brooke where to find me."

Again, Larsen's good smile. "You know what they say, you can never go home again."

"Brooke was a smoking hot college girlfriend who still looks sensational, but she was never 'home.' Besides, she's got insurmountable issues."

Larsen took the last sip of his tea. "So, where do you and Caitlin stand at this point?"

Whelan turned his head and looked at the other man. "I have no idea. She's a complete mystery to me."

The wakening sun crawled out of the sea like a hungover drunk and slowly ascended above the horizon. The crew of the *Miss Sweetcheeks* put out a passable breakfast of eggs, ham, hash browns, and toast. With the exception of Almeida, the Dogs ate heartily. Almeida scrambled upwind as fast as he could in an effort to escape the aromas.

The sun had risen at about quarter after seven when the ship was already more than two hours into its voyage. At a few minutes past three that afternoon, the *Miss Sweetcheeks* rendezvoused with a smaller Mexican trawler named *La Diosa del Mar*, the Goddess of the Sea. To the Dogs, it didn't look like their idea of a goddess. More like a barely seaworthy tub.

It took them little more than an hour to transfer their gear from one vessel to the other, then they began the second leg of their journey. Shortly after they got underway, the crew of the Mexican ship positioned otter boards at the ends of the outriggers to hold the nets open while they were being dragged along the sea bottom. This wasn't part of the plan and would only further draw out the voyage because effective trawling required a cruising speed around two-and-a-half knots. Instead of thirty hours, it would take closer to five days. That was unacceptable.

Whelan immediately found the captain. Speaking to him in Spanish, he said, "No shrimping. Just get us to Tamiahua as fast as you can. *Comprende usted?*"

The man, built like a fireplug and with a shaved head and Pancho Villa mustache, tried to argue that the ship would need to have a hold full of shrimp to avoid suspicion when it returned to port at Tamiahua. But Whelan had checked the shrimp hold on boarding the vessel and knew it already was half full. Apparently, the boat had been trawling while waiting to rendezvous with the *Miss Sweetcheeks*. The captain chose to ignore the large, muscular man who was giving him orders on his own boat. A distinct lapse of judgment. Whelan tied him off one of the outriggers and trolled him for a few minutes. The five members of the boat's crew took one look at their seven passengers and decided they'd sooner tangle with Marvel Comics super heroes. When the captain had all but drowned, he was brought back aboard. The brisk dip in the Gulf had disabused him of any further thoughts of trawling on this particular voyage.

The captain, shivering violently from a combination of the frigid water and sheer terror, went below seeking warmth and dry clothes.

Whelan motioned to Kirkland to follow the man. Most commercial fishing boats carried firearms. Territorial disputes weren't unheard of.

"This kind of changes things," Larsen said. "SAS paid the guy well. He didn't need to fill his hold on our dime. Think he can be trusted not to rat us out after we're off the boat?"

"No," Whelan said.

Larsen gave him a questioning look.

Whelan waved Nick Stensen over to a place where the crewmen couldn't hear their conversation. Quentin Thomas saw Whelan motion to Stensen and walked over too.

Stensen was nodding his head up and down as if he already knew what Whelan was going to say, which he always did. It was a characteristic that unnerved all of the other Dogs. Whelan had heard that Stensen had made beer money in college by writing term papers for his fraternity brothers. He would guarantee at least a B-plus regardless of the subject. Supposedly, he would merely hold the course text book to the side of his head for a few moments, then generate a highly successful term paper. Knowing Stensen, none of the Dogs believed the stories were apocryphal.

"Nick," Whelan said, "this has caused a slight change of plans."

The ever-present red dots in the center of Stensen's eyes suddenly expanded. Blood in the water.

"Once we've offloaded in Tamiahua, the captain and crew need to be neutralized. Stuff them in the ship's hold. There's plenty of ice in there. They won't start to stink for a while. Maybe we'll get lucky and exfil before that happens."

"Consider it done."

"What the hell's the matter with you people?" Thomas said angrily. "The captain just got a little greedy, and the crew members haven't done a damn thing. Yet you're going to kill all of them and leave God knows how many dependents, women and children, to starve to death. You're no better than the terrorists we're hunting."

"Alright, Quent, then you're responsible for seeing to it they don't cause any problems for us after we're off this ship but still in-country. If you fuck it up, I'll kill you myself."

"Not if I get to him first," Stensen said. The red centers of his eyes were enormous.

"I'm faster than all of you," Larsen said. He was smiling his bad smile.

Thomas's black skin seemed to grow paler.

CHAPTER 47

ISLA EL IDOLO

THOMAS CAREFULLY BOUND the six Mexicans, including the captain, with flex cuffs and stowed them in the shrimper's hold. Because it was packed with ice to keep the catch refrigerated until reaching port, Thomas made sure the prisoners donned jackets. He checked on them regularly over the ensuing thirty hours. It wasn't entirely out of a sense of humanitarianism. He was concerned about his own well-being if any of them got loose. And it wasn't lost on Thomas that Stensen checked on them too.

At least two Dogs, one of whom had to be fluent in Spanish, occupied the wheelhouse at all times. They operated or monitored the ship's navigation equipment, included radar, radios, LORAN, compass, Global Positioning System, and electronic chartplotter. The last item was critical because it integrated the GPS data with an electronic navigational chart, displaying the position, heading, and speed of the ship, among other things. Without the captain and his first mate, navigation would have been difficult at best if some of the Dogs, including Whelan, Larsen, and Stone, hadn't known how to operate the electronics.

It actually took a little over thirty hours to reach port in Tamiahua because of the effects of a quartering headwind. It was close to midnight when *La Diosa del Mar* tied up at the town's commercial docks. At that late hour, there was no one around. Ironically and unbeknownst to the Dogs, their berthing point was next to the marina where Turan had been placed on a small fishing skiff and taken to Isla El Idolo. Rafe Almeida was the first off the ship and, on his knees, actually kissed the ground. His skin was pasty and eyes bloodshot, but not from drinking this time. It was the almost continuous vomiting since they'd left Port Aransas.

Working quickly, the other six Dogs moved their equipment from the shrimper to an old and well-used Hino box truck. The SAS had arranged for the truck and a driver with local knowledge to meet them at the dock. Before bringing the last load off the boat, Thomas and Stensen went to check on the captain and crew. Thomas made sure Stensen wasn't the last to leave the hold.

When the Dogs were finished offloading *La Diosa del Mar*, the driver looked around and said in Spanish, "Where is the crew?"

"They're staying out of sight on the boat until we're clear of here. It's safer for them in the long run," Whelan said. He made sure the driver saw the SIG 226 tucked in his waistband as he climbed into the truck's cab. The remaining Dogs settled into the cargo area in back.

They exited the dock area, made two right turns and crossed a bridge that spanned the Estéreo Tamiahua, a tidal channel draining the huge Laguna Tamiahua into the Gulf of Mexico. It proved to be a long, dreary ride to their destination, made longer by the barely five miles per hour speed forced on the driver by the condition of the road. Paved in parts, graded in parts, and covered with thick gray mud everywhere else, Whelan suspected it may have had more potholes per yard than any other road he'd ever seen. Considering the places he'd been, that was saying a lot.

The countryside was green and lush but the improvements, if they could be called that, were beyond humble. Many were just roofless concrete block skeletons abandoned before completion for reasons unknown to Whelan. Most of the dwellings that appeared habitable were small, low structures with tin or thatch roofs, dirt floors, and doorways with no doors. Few had been painted in recent years. Those that had, sported pastel colors with dark trim around doorways and windows.

A couple of times, the driver tried to initiate a conversation with his tall, muscular, taciturn passenger. Whelan simply pointed to the road ahead and said *"Maneja!"* Drive! Considering the condition of the truck's springs and shock absorbers and the profusion and enormity of the crater-like potholes, Whelan wondered how the others were faring in back. He assumed they were blaming the driver and drawing straws to see which one of them would disembowel him at journey's end.

The creaking and clanging of the truck wakened the army of dogs that seemed to be a part of each household they passed. Some of them, always skin and bone, chased after the vehicle, howling in mock viciousness at its tires. The occasional chicken fluttered angrily out of the truck's path.

It was the tropics, and the constant high humidity endlessly wrapped the sky in moisture-laden clouds. Even though they obscured the quarter moon, enough light filtered through for Whelan to make note of his surroundings. The road meandered

northward along the edge of the widening estuary, the view interrupted frequently by patches of mangroves.

At points where Whelan could catch a glimpse of the river,
he saw seemingly endless lines zigzagging almost all the way
across the expanding body of water. The area typically was
shrimped with fixed-net systems called charangas. The large V-
shaped nets were set into the lagoon with a series of long palen-
ques or wooden stakes. They funneled schools of shrimp to the
tip of the V, where they were trapped in boxes and later scooped
out by shrimpers. It represented the major part of the local
economy and diet.

Together with the shoals, sandbars, and general shallowness
of the estuary and lagoon, the charangas were a major reason
why the Dogs hadn't launched their inflatables where the *La
Diosa del Mar* had docked. These were unfamiliar waters for the
Dogs and, unlike the Florida Keys, they were an almost mono-
chromatic gray that made navigation virtually impossible for
anyone not brought up in the area.

The road made a sharp right turn for about one hundred yards
to the east, then curved left and continued northerly for almost
three quarters of a mile to a little village called Palo Blanco, or
White Tree. Its homes appeared to be better maintained than
those in Tamiahua and the ones they'd passed along the road.
There even were remnants of a municipal basketball court. The
road was wider, but just as badly rutted. The driver had to
maneuver around an old swaybacked horse standing in the
middle of the street, slurping muddy water from a large pothole.

Beyond Palo Blanco the estuary began to expand rapidly into
the vast Laguna Tamiahua. The lagoon was as much as fourteen
miles wide and nearly sixty miles long. After another one and a
half miles, they passed through a nameless village about the size
of Palo Blanco. Two miles beyond it, they finally reached their

staging point. The driver pulled the truck off the road and stopped near the edge of the shallow lagoon.

When Whelan opened the tailgate, the other Dogs exploded out of the cargo area. Almeida looked even worse than when he'd crawled off the Mexican shrimp trawler.

"Where's the damn driver?" Larsen said wearing his bad smile.

"Forget that, he's mine," Kirkland said. He had unsheathed his ancient katana, *doragon no chi.* Dragon's Blood.

"Leave him alone," Whelan said. "Considering the condition of the road, the guy was doing the best he could."

"Next fucking time, you ride in the back, mate," Stone said.

"Whatever," Whelan said with a shrug. "Let's get this truck unloaded. It's almost two. We need to get in and out before sunup."

"That shouldn't be hard," Almeida said. "It's just a pissant sandbar, isn't it?"

"Eighteen square miles, maybe twice the size of Big Pine."

"No shit?"

For the next thirty minutes, the men performed a drill they'd rehearsed repeatedly in preparation for this operation. They unloaded and inflated the two twelve-and-a-half-foot military-grade inflatable boats, each had been specially modified to be powered by an eighty-horsepower electric outboard engine. Their operating noise had been further dampened by the use of the same technology and materials incorporated into stealth heli-copters.

By the time they finished in the high heat, high humidity, they were drenched in sweat. They were clad in special night time jungle Army Combat Uniforms, or ACUs, with camo paint covering their faces, ears, necks, and hands in lieu of the unbear-ably hot camo balaclavas. Before they shoved off for the island, they would add body armor. All means of identifying the source of their clothing had been removed. None of them carried any identification. They donned sophisticated comm gear that enabled each of them to communicate with the others at all times.

Each wore enhanced night-vision goggles, or ENVGs, mounted on their helmets. They fused image intensification technology with thermal imagery for optimal night operations. New beta models from a Mueller brothers top-secret laboratory, the goggles also incorporated the latest in augmented reality technology.

Just before they shoved off for the waterborne assault on Isla El Idolo, Kirkland launched a drone specially equipped with night vision cameras. Whelan made it a point to remind the truck driver of the large bonus he'd receive by waiting for them to return. Whelan believed they'd need the truck more than ever because of the change in plans necessitated by problems they'd had with the Mexican shrimper. Originally, they were going to reload *La Diosa del Mar* and retrace their voyage to a rendezvous with the *Miss Sweetcheeks*, then return to Port Aransas. He'd purposely withheld that information from Almeida. Alternatively, Plan B called for them to use the truck to get to the border near Matamoros.

With three Dogs in one inflatable and four in the other, they activated their ENVGs and set off for a point on the tip of a peninsula that jutted southwesterly from the island into the lagoon. Specifically, their target was the spot where the last signal from Turan's phone had been detected.

From the shelter of the small cove surrounded by mangroves where the truck waited to the thin strip of white sand beach on the easterly side of the peninsula, it was a distance of almost two nautical miles. During the entire ride, they were in open water, completely exposed to anyone who happened to be looking. Stensen in one boat and Whelan in the other kept their powerful binoculars focused on the target area. The drone hovered above a group of three small cabins, the point of Turan's last signal. Nothing was moving, there were no signs of habitation.

Stone piloted the lead boat with Stensen and Thomas aboard. He eased slowly up to the shore about sixty yards upstream from the cabins. Larsen was at the tiller of the other inflatable. Whelan directed him to run another twenty-five yards northeasterly and parallel with sandy shore to a point where a cluster of red mangroves stretched out into the brackish water. It cut off the line of sight from anyone who might be in the cabins. There was a narrow opening in the mangroves and Larsen nudged the nose of the craft into it.

Whelan slipped over the side of the inflatable and motioned for the others to remain in it. Looking carefully for trip wires, he moved silently along a rudimentary path that had a swampy area to the right. He didn't have to see the swamp, he could smell its unmistakable odor. He heard the sounds of things moving in its dark expanse. To the left, the ground was dryer and overgrown with scrubs, tall grass, and clumps of white mangrove. He paused and whispered into his mike, telling Larsen, Kirkland, and Almeida to join him.

They had just arrived when the silence of the night was shattered by the harsh chatter of automatic weapons. Instantly, the four men hit the soggy turf. They didn't hear anything that sounded like angry wasps traveling past them at warp speed, so they knew the shots weren't being aimed in their direction. They looked at the cabin that was closest to the point of the peninsula. Muzzle flashes lit it up. They also heard the three Dogs from Stone's boat returning fire.

A second later, Stone's voice came over the comm system. "We're taking fire."

"Situation?" Whelan said.

"No one's been hit. Yet. We're hunkered down behind the boat, but it's been compromised and losing air fast. Can you draw their attention away from us?"

"Will do." Whelan turned to the other three Dogs. He pointed in a westerly direction. "Rafe, take a straight line to the beach and pin down anyone in those other two cabins."

"What the fuck? There's crocodiles, water moccasins, and boa constrictors all over this place."

"They're in the swamp, you idiot. Besides, you're armed; if something moves, shoot it. Your teammates are drawing fire. Move. Now!"

Almeida grudgingly moved off, his head on a swivel, looking for dangerous beasties.

Whelan turned to Kirkland. "I'm not seeing anything from the drone that I couldn't see without it. Where the fuck is it?"

"Hovering over the main cabin."

"Too bad it's not armed."

"Next model," Kirkland said.

"Send it to check on Stone and the others. We need to clear the main cabin asap. Take out the shooters, and quick. Spread out twenty feet apart. The cabin is about two hundred feet away. Use the vegetation for cover. When we're set, I'll toss in a couple of flashbangs. Rush the shooters immediately. But remember from the photo what this Turan kid looks like. If he's not a shooter, try not to kill him."

"Should we be worried about a stray slug or the flashbangs setting of those nukes?" Kirkland said.

"Christie says his people told him that couldn't happen."

"Yeah," Kirkland said, "easy for them to say. They're not the ones literally standing on top of the fuckers."

They began to move out.

"Any other prisoners besides the Turan kid?" Larsen said.

"Keep one for interrogation."

"Since it's gonna be close quarters, mind if I use *doragon no chi*?" Kirkland said.

"Slice and dice to your heart's content," Whelan said. "But keep that fucking drone involved."

Envisioning the mayhem that was about to explode, Larsen smiled his very worst smile. All the swamp creatures suddenly went silent.

Each Dog carried a SIG SG 553 Commando compact assault rifle chambered for NATO 5.56x45mm ammunition in 30-round magazines. The weapon had semi-auto and full-auto settings plus an additional trigger module for a three-round burst setting. Whelan had chosen the weapon for this operation because it combined the accuracy of an M16 with the reliability of an AK-47. This was critically important in the wet, muddy environment of the island. The SG 553s also were reasonably good at long ranges and these were fitted with 4x magnification scopes and red dot sights. Each man also carried his knife and sidearm of choice.

Moving quickly through the tall grass and mostly keeping the clumps of white mangroves between them and the main cabin, the three men closed the distance in a matter of seconds. Larsen slipped close to the front of the dwelling, where the shooting was originating, cutting off any chance for escaping in that direction. Kirkland circled around toward the opposite end of the cabin.

Whelan was about to activate and toss the first of the flash-bangs when bullets started flying at them from another direction. This time those angry wasps *were* buzzing close to their heads.

They hit the ground in unison Then, an additional automatic weapon opened up and in a few seconds the others went silent. Whelan lifted his head a few centimeters and looked in the direction the shots had come from. He saw the dark image of Rafe Almeida approaching three prone figures. Almeida paused and put a slug in each of their heads then trotted over to Whelan and Kirkland.

"Nice timing on your part, Rafe," Whelan said. "Thanks."

"Wasn't nothing happenin' in the other cabins except for those three pukes." He nodded at the fresh corpses. "I saw they was so focused on you two they didn't have a clue I was behind 'em. Dumb shits."

Whelan pointed to the rear door to the main cabin. "When I toss the flashbangs, you two rush the shooters inside. I'll cover the side windows in case any of them has a thing for defenestration. Sven has the other end."

Kirkland and Almeida positioned themselves at the bottom of steps leading to the rear entrance.

Whelan slipped along the edge of the dwelling until he was beneath an open window. He activated two flashbangs and heaved them, one after the other into the dark interior. He immediately squatted, covered his ears with his hands and squeezed his eyes tightly shut. He still was very much aware of the loud explosion and brilliant flash of light.

He heard the sounds of men screaming in pain and confusion. In Arabic. He also heard Kirkland and Almeida charge up the steps and into the cabin. That was followed almost instantly by the staccato of their SIG 553s sending slugs ripping into the occupants.

In a panic, one gunman chose to leap through the window above Whelan. He landed off balance and fell. Before he could get up, the Irishman had a hand on the man's neck. With a sudden, crushing squeeze, he destroyed the victim's throat. Then snapped his neck between the sixth and seventh cervical vertebra.

Whelan released the dead man's throat and moved quickly around to the front of the cabin. Two more gunmen tried to escape down the steps leading from the front door. Larsen double tapped both of them and their corpses tumbled to the ground.

"Coming out," Kirkland said. He and Almeida appeared at the top of the steps. Blood was dripping from Kirkland's katana.

"Situation?" Whelan said, nodding toward the interior of the cabin.

"Graveyard mostly," Kirkland said.

"Any sign of the kid?"

Kirkland shook his head.

"Save us a witness?" Larsen said.

"Kind of."

"What the fuck does that mean?"

"It means," Almeida said, "that he hacked a guy up pretty good, but he ain't dead yet." He paused for a second. "But you better hurry if you want to talk to him. He's fixin' to join these assholes." He spit on one of the corpses lying at the foot of the steps.

"Stonie, Nick, Quent what's your situation?" Whelan said.

Stone's voice came over the comm. "Scrapes and minor shit. Nothing serious, mate."

"Like the man said: 'pain heals, chicks dig scars, and glory lasts forever.'"

"I'll wager that bloke was never in a firefight."

Whelan could hear the grin in Stone's voice. "What about the inflatable?"

"It's a bloody bodger, mate."

"Translation?"

"Useless. Full of bullet holes. S'pose they have fuckin' Uber around here?"

"We'll all have to pile into the one good boat. Remove the battery from yours, then rig explosives on what's left. We'll blow it when we leave."

He turned to Kirkland. "Let's go have a conversation with the survivor."

The two men went into the cabin. The interior was thoroughly trashed. The minimal furnishings had been badly singed by the flashbangs. The fusillade laid down by Kirkland and Almeida had ripped holes in more than the three corpses and sole survivor strewn awkwardly across the bloodstained floor. The air was heavy with the scents of ammonium nitrate from the flashbangs and cordite from the expended ammo, all mixed with the smell of lots of blood being corrupted by exposure to the air. There also was the distinct odor of men who had been living in close quarters and had neither bathed regularly nor properly disposed of leftover food.

Whelan and Kirkland knelt beside the dying man whose eyes were wide from a combination of pain, fear, and shock. He was lying in an ever-expanding pool of his own blood. There were several bloody bullet holes in his camo shirt. His right arm had been severed just below the shoulder. Whelan didn't have to ask Kirkland. He'd seen the work of *doragon no chi* in the past.

"He's losing a lot of blood rapidly," Whelan said. "We don't have much time."

Kirkland grabbed the man's jaw and tugged his head up. It caused him to groan piteously.

"Listen, we have the ability to save your life," Kirkland lied in Arabic. "But first we need information."

The man's eyes were beginning to glaze over.

Kirkland withdrew a curved knife with a blade of thirty

centimeters from a small wooden scabbard called a *koshirae* that was tucked in his waistband. The knife was a *wakizashi* and looked like a smaller version of *doragon no chi*. He held it in front of the man's eyes then moved it down his body until the man could feel it pressing against his genitals. "If you don't want to disappoint those virgins who are waiting for you, tell me who sent you."

The man made a gurgling sound in his throat.

Kirkland pressed harder.

In a voice that was barely a whisper, the man said, "Nadir Shah, may Allah bless him."

Whelan said, "Where's the boy called Turan Salam?"

The man's death rattle continued and he attempted to swallow before croaking, "They took him."

"They?" Whelan said. "Who's they?"

"MS-13." The man seemed to struggle mightily to get these last words out.

"What did they do with Turan?"

"You said you'd help me." Now the gurgle was joined by gasping.

"Tell us about Turan and we will."

Even with his glazed eyes, the man knew he was being lied to, that his death was imminent.

Kirkland made a cutting motion with the *wakizashi* and its blade began to cut into the man's scrotum. "Let's not disappoint those virgins."

His eyes locked on Whelan's, the man wagged his head slowly to the left and then to the right. "I don't know where they took him, but they were going to kill him." The man was wracked by a sudden fit of coughing. There was blood in his spittle. More flowed from the stump of his arm.

Whelan looked at Kirkland and nodded.

The *wakizashi* flashed and a wide gap instantly opened across his throat.

The two men stood and walked back outside and joined Sven Larsen and Almeida.

Whelan said to Kirkland. "Break out the Geiger counters. You and Sven split up and look for the nukes."

Stensen and Thomas came trotting up. "What do you want us to do?" Stensen said.

"You go with Sven and be his eyes where booby traps are concerned. Quent, you do the same for Marc."

"What am I supposed to do?" Almeida said to Whelan.

"Since you asked, I want you to look for that kid, Turan."

"Huh? With the other guys sweeping the area looking for the nukes, they'll find him if he's here. I'm more valuable than following along behind them."

"Of course you are, Rafe. That's why I've saved the most important task for you." The sarcasm was unmistakable.

Almeida tilted his head to one side and looked warily at Whelan. "What is it?"

"These dead guys wouldn't have had much use for Turan after they used him to lure us here. It's likely they killed him but wouldn't have left him nearby to stink the place up when the heat, humidity, and bugs got to him."

"Yeaaaah? So, what are you saying?"

"The body's in the swamp. Go follow you nose and confirm it."

"What the fuck! I'm not going in that fucking swamp. It's full of snakes, gators, crocs, and slimy green monsters and shit."

Whelan gave Almeida a long, hard stare. "You go or I'll leave your sorry ass behind."

"This is because you're still pissed that I told that babe, Brooke, where to find you, isn't it?'"

At that point, Stone arrived. "It's alright, mate, I'll go with you." He steered Almeida by the elbow toward the swamp.

As they left, Whelan shook his head. He and the other Dogs didn't understand the bromance between Stone and Almeida. Maybe it had something to do with the similarities in the hardscrabble lives they'd led in their youths. The upside was it seemed to make dealing with Rafe a little easier.

Whelan quickly searched through the clothing on the bloody corpses inside and outside the cabin. There were ten of them. He found nothing of interest. All means of identifying the sources of their clothing had been removed. None of them carried any identification. From their hair, skin, and facial features, they appeared to be Middle Easterners. And they had been speaking Arabic.

As he was finishing, the other six Dogs began returning. Neither Larsen nor Kirkland had found any traces of radiation. "Then, it's just what it appears to be," Whelan said, "a trap."

Stensen said, "I think they were expecting *us*, not just any special operations force."

"Agreed," Whelan said.

"But how could they have known about this operation?" Thomas said.

"Got to be a leak somewhere," Whelan said.

"When we find the sonofabitch, let me kill him," Stensen said. The red glow in the centers of his pale blue eyes flared like twin volcanos.

"No, he's mine," Larsen said with his bad smile.

"Bullshit," Kirkland said. He shook *doragon no chi* and said, "Baby's still thirsty."

"We'll flip a fucking coin *if* we find whoever it is," Whelan said.

Stone and Almeida returned from searching the swamp for Turan's body. They were soaking wet and covered in mud and slime. "Didn't find the bugger, mate. If he was there, something must have eaten him."

Almeida shivered involuntarily.

"Just lots of creepy-crawlies," Stone said with a grin and slapped Almeida on the back.

Whelan felt the vibrator activate on his watch. It was a combat timepiece specifically designed for special ops combatants. It this case, it also had been fitted with a receiver attuned by Bluetooth to his satphone to keep the phone active but silent. He fished the phone from a cargo pocket. "Whelan."

"Christie. From our eye in the sky, it looks like you secured the area, but monitoring your comm indicates no nukes." Mitch Christie and other SAS members had been following the operation via satellite and the Dogs' comm gear transmissions. "No sign of Turan Salam either?"

"No."

"Get ready for strike three," Christie said. "You're familiar with the old saw, 'if anything can go wrong, it will?'"

"That's Murphy's law. Now what?"

"The truck is compromised."

"How?"

"It seems someone found the shrimp boat crew. You can imagine how long it took them to whine to the Federales, probably something along the lines of 'terrorists captured our boat at sea.' I'm sure that big, noisy truck didn't go unnoticed by everyone along its path."

"Shit," Whelan said. "There goes Plan B. You got any ideas?"

"We're working on it, but time is a real bitch. The satellites show the Federales are pounding down to road from Tamiahua to where the truck is. The road doesn't go much farther, there's nowhere for the driver to go."

"He'll likely cut a deal to save his own ass."

"Bet on it."

"I've got an idea, but we have to move quickly. I'll be in touch shortly."

Whelan terminated the call and turned to the others. "Sven, bring the good boat around to the damaged one. We'll pile everyone into it. Stonie, put the battery from the damaged one in it, then blow the ruined craft once we're underway."

He turned to Kirkland. "How much flight time does the drone have left?"

"If it was gas powered, it would be running on fumes about now."

"Bring it in and have Stonie blow it with the other inflatable."

"Are we going to be able to get everyone into a single boat plus that extra battery?" Larsen said.

"It's going to get intimate, but we don't have any other options."

Larsen took off at a fast trot to bring the good inflatable around.

"Where are we gonna go?" Almeida said.

"I remember from studying the area when I was prepping for this operation. There's a small grass strip up the coast beyond where the road ends. A place called Losa. Once we're underway, I'll call SAS and have them send a plane."

"A plane? A small grass strip? How will they get something in there big enough for all of us?" Thomas said.

"Don't sweat it. The Muellers have access to STOL aircraft."

"Stall?" Almeida said. "Ain't that when the fucking plane falls out of the sky?"

"STOL stands for Short Takeoff Or Landing, numbnuts," Stensen said.

"How far is this place?" Stone said.

Whelan looked at him for a few moments, as if debating whether to answer the question. Finally, he said, "Twenty-five nautical miles."

"Crikey, mate, the fuckin' range for one of these floating balloons is barely that, and that's when it's not loaded to capacity."

"Yeah," Kirkland said, "but we're bringing the extra battery."

"Doesn't matter, mate. The capacity is six persons, seventeen hundred pounds. We're seven sizable lads plus the extra battery. That's over two thousand pounds right there. Under normal conditions, the range at full throttle on one of these is maybe eighteen or nineteen nautical miles. These aren't normal conditions and we already used some of that juice getting over here from the truck."

"So, you're saying that even with the extra battery we're at the outer edge of the envelope?" Whelan said.

Stone shook his head slowly. "It's worse than that, mate. With this load, using both batteries, we'll be lucky to make it halfway to twenty-five nautical miles." He and Larsen left to wrestle the extra battery into Larsen's boat.

Whelan turned to the other four Dogs. "Split up and take a quick look through the cabins. Nick and Marc, take the two smaller ones. Rafe, you'll take the main cabin with me. I doubt we'll find anything of value, but it's worth a look."

CHAPTER 48

GENEVA, SWITZERLAND

NADIR SHAH HAD BEEN STANDING in front of the floor to ceiling glass wall staring out at the cold, clear waters of Lake Geneva as it began its long, meandering journey down the Rhône to the Mediterranean. He contemplated how it would be corrupted when its Alpine purity mingled with the saline waters of that ancient sea. It was what was happening to the blood of the faithful, being adulterated by contact with the peoples of the West and Islam's own apostates. Why, he wondered, had Allah not rewarded him and his followers with victory in the form of a global caliphate? Perhaps it was only a matter of using the five nuclear devices against the Great Satan.

At that moment, his young aide Jibril knocked softly on the open door to Shah's office and stepped into the room.

"Forgive the interruption, Caliph, but our contact in Mexico, Abdel Sabbah, is on the telephone. He asked to speak with you."

"Is it the encrypted phone?"

"Yes, Caliph." Jibril handed Shah the phone.

"Abdel, is something wrong? I wasn't expecting your call. Are the nuclear weapons all right?"

"They are fine, Caliph." Sabbah pronounced Shah's title as if it had a bad taste. Their mutual hatred of the West, dedication to its destruction, and reliance on Iran for support made them the proverbial "strange bedfellows," at least for the moment. And that moment included the successful use of the five nuclear devices originally supplied by the Grand Puppet Master, China.

"Have you succeeded in moving the weapons to the new location in Higuerillas?" Shah said.

"Yes, that's the reason for my call. I want to make sure we're on the same page where these devices are concerned."

"Why would you think otherwise, my brother?"

"I'm not your brother." There was an iciness in Sabbah's tone. "I'm just somewhat confused about the matter that happened at Isla El Idolo."

"What of it?"

"I thought your Chinese friends were to provide 'special warriors' to ambush the Americans who were sent to capture these nuclear devices."

"That's not exactly correct," Shah said. "The Chinese have recruited and trained a group of extraordinary men. They are to destroy a force of similarly gifted individuals employed by the Americans. I believe they are called the Sleeping Dogs."

"The ones who raided Isla El Idolo and killed the men I stationed there at *your* request?"

"Unfortunately, yes."

"And why is it that these men trained by your Chinese bene-factors were not there?"

"Because they were always intended as backup in case the trap at Isla El Idolo failed, which it did. I'm disappointed that your men didn't give a better accounting of themselves. We went to great lengths to set the Americans up. They should have been killed. I thought Hezbollah was supposed to have special operators on a par with the best anywhere."

There was a long moment of silence. Shah could hear Sabbah breathing deeply on the other end of the call, as if struggling to maintain self-control.

When Sabbah finally spoke, it was in a tightly measured response sizzling with anger. "Current circumstances may justify a temporary alliance between us Shi'a and you Sunni apostates. But once it no longer is useful, we will hunt down every one of you just as we will the heretics who follow other religions."

As much as Shah was tempted by his own anger to respond by calling Sabbah the apostate and promising to hunt *him* down and kill him, he chose to use a more tactful approach. "I understand your anger at the loss of your men, but I assure you they will be avenged and soon."

"How so?"

"It was always my intention to move the weapons to Higuerillas, not Isla El Idolo. I had hoped the American warriors would be lured to Isla El Idolo and killed. But if they somehow survived the trap, I did not want the weapons to be captured."

"And if these American *djinns* learn that the weapons are in Higuerillas?"

"That's highly unlikely. Their agent who led the Americans to Isla El Idolo has been neutralized. Other than myself, the only ones who know of Higuerillas are a few of my most trusted people...and you."

"What are you suggesting? That there might be a leak at my end?"

"Of course not." Shah had adopted an unctuous tone. "I'm only explaining how safe the weapons are in Higuerillas. It's the perfect location for distributing them by sea to targets in America."

"Perhaps not so perfect."

Suddenly alarmed, Shah said, "What are you saying?"

"It appears your research was faulty. Higuerillas is in the Mexican state of Tamaulipas. Two major drug cartels, the Zetas and the Gulf Cartel, have been fighting a bloody war for the territory for the past decade. As a result, the Mexican military has been particularly active in the area too."

"How does this affect the nuclear devices?"

"If either the drug gangs or the Mexican marines learn of the weapons, they might kill us and take them."

"Our plans are to move the weapons using commercial fishing boats within the next few days. In the meantime, those special operators trained by the Chinese will arrive in Higuerillas by six o'clock tonight, your time. Neither the drug gangs nor the military are a match for them."

CHAPTER 49

ISLA EL IDOLO, MEXICO

WHELAN, Almeida, Stensen, Kirkland, and Thomas had searched the three cabins and surrounding area but found nothing of interest and joined Larsen at the sole operational inflatable. A few moments later, Stone set off the charges he'd rigged in the disabled boat. The ensuing explosion sent a sound wave racing across the surface of the lagoon, as well as a fireball that, unfortunately, would be visible for miles.

Stensen said, "If the Federales didn't know where we were before, they do now."

All seven Dogs wedged tightly into the remaining inflatable along with the extra battery. It alone weighed five hundred sixty pounds They tried distributing the weight several times, but still couldn't get the craft on a plane. It wallowed low in the water, and the outboard strained to sustain thirteen knots. There was a light chop in the lagoon and water regularly cascaded over the bow. The problem was compounded by the need to zigzag around and between the fish traps and poorly marked shoals and sandbars.

Whelan told the other men to start bailing. He pulled the satphone from a cargo pocket in his ACU and called Christie. When the other man picked up, Whelan said, "You still watching us on satellite?"

"Yeah, we're monitoring your situation."

"Where are the Federales?"

"They were 'interrogating' the truck driver but must have seen the explosion. Now, they're piling back into their vehicles and heading north along the road that parallels the lagoon."

"Shit!"

"The good news is that the road, such as it is, doesn't go much farther. Plus, the route you've taken puts the island between you and them."

"With the load we're carrying, we're not even going to get close to the grass strip at Losa. Got any suggestions?"

Christie was silent for a few moments as if he was reviewing maps or similar materials. "Maybe you won't need the boat to get you all the way there. There's a village called Los Nanches about fifteen nautical miles from your current location. A road starts there and runs north to the strip at Losa. If you can make Los Nanches, maybe you can commandeer a vehicle that will get you to the strip."

"Obviously you haven't seen what passes for a road in these parts. How far is it from Los Nanches to Losa?"

"Roughly eight miles."

"And this 'road,' could the Federales be using it to bring cops from the north?"

"No, it doesn't extend much past Losa."

"Could they use the grass strip at Losa to land troops?"

"Maybe, if they had a STOL plane, a skilled pilot, and plenty of daylight. But they don't. If you can move fast enough, you should be out of there before they can get their ducks in a row."

"Easy for you to say," Whelan said. "What're the coordinates for Los Nanches?"

Christie told him, then Whelan terminated the call.

He turned to Stone. "You're our resident expert on these inflatables. Can we squeeze seventeen miles out of it?"

The Aussie squinted his glacial blue eyes and Whelan knew he was running calculations in his head. "Maybe, but doubtful."

Whelan repeated the coordinates Christie had given him and told Stone to try to get as close as he could.

Stone made a slight adjustment in course.

Moments later, the seven men heard the unmistakable whump-whump of an approaching helicopter.

"Betcha that ain't our guys," Almeida said and reached for his SIG 553.

The seven men strained to see the bird in the dark sky, watching as its running lights drew closer. When it was about five hundred feet above them and slightly astern, it rotated to the left exposing the open door and the fifty-caliber machine gun mounted in it. The gunner opened up and a stream of slugs created a long string of rooster tails off to the right of the boat.

The United States military recognizes four levels of shooters: unqualified, marksman, sharpshooter, and expert. All of the Dogs were expert shooters, but Stensen was in a class of his own. It almost seemed as if he could will the slug to the center of the target regardless of conditions.

"Nick," Whelan yelled above the sound of the fifty, "take out the pilot."

Stensen took almost no time in lining up the target, calculating the variables involved, and squeezing off the shot. It hit the canopy precisely in front of the pilot's head but glanced off the curved bulletproof glass.

"That was unexpected," Stensen said, "and disappointing."

He immediately lined up the gunner. An instant later the man's head exploded and his body fell away from the gun. A second gunner stepped up and immediately met the same fate.

"The fucking pilot's going to lead others to us," Kirkland said.

"Worse than that, he's got a twin seventies. One of those rockets hits us, we're fish food," Stensen said.

"Stonie, you flew choppers with Tag West," Whelan said. "Is there a way to bring that bird down?"

"She looks like a bloody Bell Venom. Other than the canopy, she's probably not armored. The best way to stonker it is to take out the engine."

"Where's it located?"

"The CG—center of gravity. It's behind the gunner's door and below the main rotor."

Whelan shouted to the other Dogs, "Empty a mag each into the fuselage behind the door and under the rotor. Lace it good."

Seven SIG 553s opened simultaneously, pumping two hundred ten rounds into the bird in about two and a half seconds. A few moments later, flames could be seen beginning to dance in the dark area behind the gunner's door.

"Must have nipped a fuel line," Stone said, as each man shoved a fresh magazine into their SIGs.

The men watched in silence as the pilot pulled the nose of the chopper up and away from their inflatable. There was a flash, as if something had caught fire. Seconds later the bird exploded in a huge fireball and wreckage began to rain down on the warm, shallow waters of the lagoon.

Their attention was suddenly redirected when the electric motor abruptly died and the boat stopped its forward motion, simply bobbing in the light chop.

"Shit! Sven you're closest. Hook up the second battery," Whelan said. Christie's iteration of Murphy's Law came to mind.

A few seconds later the motor came back to life and the cumbersome craft again began to plow slowly forward.

Less than five minutes later, the second battery died. Herd instinct: the men all glanced at each other, then the motor, then the distant shoreline, then each other again.

Stone was the first to speak. "Shit, mates, I'm beginnin' to think we couldn't organize a fuck in a brothel with a fist full of fifties."

"What?" Almeida said.

"It's Strine for things have gone totally FUBAR," Whelan said.

Stensen pointed into the distance off the starboard side of the immobile craft. "Something's coming."

All seven men grabbed their SIG 553s, aimed them in the direction Stensen had indicated, and squinted through their scopes into the darkness. Less than half a mile away, a boat was making its way toward them. It appeared to be about twenty-five feet in length with a low profile. From the speed at which the boat was moving, it was clear that it had an abundance of power.

"At least they don't look like Federales to me," Almeida said.

"Probably local night fishermen, crabbers I'd guess," Thomas said.

"Not in that boat," Stensen said.

"Pretty clearly coming toward us. You want we should take them out?" Kirkland said.

Whelan stared at the approaching vessel and its two-man crew for a few moments. "No, not yet. They probably saw the explosion and are coming to check it out."

"You thinking what I'm thinking?" Larsen said to Whelan.

"Yeah, Plan D is shaping up." Whelan turned to the others.

"Put the weapons and NVGs out of sight. Don't want to alarm them until they're alongside."

"Then?" Stensen said.

"Then you and Marc take a bead on them. But shoot only if they try to take off. We want that boat."

"And not all slippery with blood, right?" Almeida said with a grin.

Thomas shook his head. "No, Brendan's saying it isn't necessary that we kill every damn living creature that ever crosses our paths." He looked at Whelan and nodded at him, as if expressing his appreciation.

The boat was moving fast and on a high plane, the sound of its engines rumbling across the surface of the vast lagoon. Moments later, the boat pulled alongside the Dogs' disabled craft. One of the newcomers was using what looked to Whelan like a satphone. He spun and looked at the stern. The boat was powered by twin Honda one-fifties.

"Shit, no way they're fishermen," he said. "Take out the guy on the phone."

Without hesitation, Kirkland and Stensen each double-tapped him. He toppled sideways and fell over the low gunnel, splashing into the dark waters of the lagoon.

The other man stared at the seven brawny men dressed in dark ACUs and armed with sophisticated weapons. He seemed about to reach for the idling boat's throttle. Instead, he froze as Kirkland and Stensen whipped their SIG assault rifles toward him and focused on his center mass.

"*Levanta los manos. Alto*," Whelan said. Put your hands up. High.

The prisoner complied immediately.

Whelan motioned with his head and the Dogs swarmed over the gunnels and into the new boat.

Stone was the first to jump aboard. "What the fuck? You're right, these are no fishermen."

The deck was covered almost completely with large bales wrapped in black plastic and brown tape.

Almeida swiftly whipped out his combat knife and sliced into one of the bales. Whitish powder spilled out. He licked the tip of one finger, touched it to the powder, then tasted it. His eyes opened wide. "This is good shit!"

"Coke, mate?" Stone said.

"Bet your ass!" Almeida said enthusiastically. "There's a fuckin' fortune here. We're gonna be fuckin' rich."

"I read somewhere that the Columbian cartels move tons of drugs along the coasts of Central American and Mexico," Whelan said

"This boat came all the way from Columbia?" Larsen said.

"No. Believe it or not, they're now using submarines to get close to the U.S.," Thomas said. "The lagoon is too shallow for the submersibles, so they transfer the cargo to boats like this one, high speed, low draft."

"Please tell me we're gonna keep this shit," Almeida said pleadingly. "It's better than finding sunken Spanish treasure."

"Toss it overboard, all of it," Whelan said.

Stone, Larsen, and Thomas began to grab bales and heave them over the side.

The surviving drug smuggler lurched suddenly toward the boat's center console, reaching for something behind the ship's wheel. Flame spit twice from the muzzle of Stensen's SIG. The man stumbled backward and fell on some of the bales. There were two bloody holes in the front of his shirt. A rare Trejo 9mm *Modelo quattro* plopped onto a plastic wrapped bale beside him.

"No worries, mate," Stone said. "Live by the sword, die by the fuckin' thing."

He and the rest of the Dogs began tossing the remaining bales overboard along with the crewman's corpse. With the exception of Almeida, who just stared at the bundles as they drifted away. Whelan glanced at him and thought he looked like a man in a deep state of shock. Or mourning.

"Shit, I hate you fuckin' guys," Almeida muttered.

A few minutes later, Larsen took the throttle and the twin Hondas quickly transitioned from idling to full speed. As the boat lifted onto a plane, Stone used a remote to detonate the charges he'd rigged on the remaining inflatable.

———

PURPOSELY HOLDING the speed down to twenty-six knots because of the shallow and unfamiliar waters, the Dogs covered the remaining sixteen nautical miles in fifty minutes. Despite the roar of the powerful outboards, Whelan was able to speak with Christie via the satphone. Christie, tracking the Dogs by satellite and studying charts, was able to guide them around the lagoon's sandbars, shoals, and fish traps to a landing at the place called Losa. Larsen eased the boat through a small break in the low-lying sandbar and beached the craft on the marshy shore. The men clambered out into the waist deep muck and trudged to higher ground. It was mostly barren with clumps of unidentifiable scrubs and stunted trees.

"What the hell is this place called?" Almeida said. "Cosa? That means thing doesn't it? Seems appropriate. There's not a damn *thing* here."

"'Thing' is *cosa* in Spanish. This is *Losa*. I think it means 'flagstone,'" Whelan said. "My Spanish is rusty."

"My ass is rusty from wading through that slimy shit," Almeida said.

"Man, don't you ever do anything besides bitch?" Thomas said.

"You were ass-deep in the same shit. How'd you like it?"

"It beat sitting in a disabled boat in the middle of a big lagoon, waiting for the Federales to come shoot me."

Christie's voice came over the satphone. "From where you're standing, you need to travel sixty-five degrees east-north-east for about eight hundred yards to the grass strip."

"Is it clear sailing?" Whelan said.

Christie hesitated before saying, "Mostly."

"What the hell does that mean?"

"There's a large swampy area near the strip. I've got you lined up with the narrowest part of it. Once you cross it, turn back due east. You'll be about a hundred yards from the strip."

"Speaking of the strip, what are its coordinates in pilot speak?

"Seventeen and thirty-five. According to our information, the prevailing wind is from the east, so it should be landing on what would be seventeen."

"So, it'll land from the northwesterly end toward the south-easterly?"

"Right."

"And what's the situation with the plane?"

"On schedule. Should arrive about the time you reach the strip."

"What is it?"

"A de Havilland Twin Otter."

"Is this grass strip long enough for takeoff and landing?"

"Should be."

"Should be? That's damn reassuring."

"It's a twenty-five-hundred-foot strip. This is a STOL aircraft. It operates effectively in shorter distances than that."

"Yeah? We have seventeen hundred pounds of men, not counting our equipment."

"It's still within the tolerances."

"Easy for you to say. You're safe and sound in Washington."

"Have you forgotten what a dangerous place the Great Swamp is?"

"Yeah? We're covered head to toe in swamp filth, running for our lives from the Federales, and managed to piss off Columbian drug lords in the process. You wanna trade places?"

There was a pause at Christie's end before he said, "You're almost out of there. Just get to the strip as fast as you can." The satphone went silent.

As the Dogs carefully picked their way through the heavily jungled swamp area near the shore, they began to hear a noise in the distance that sounded like powerful engines. Whelan motioned for everyone to stop.

"I don't think that's the plane," Stensen said.

"Uh-uh," Larsen said. "It's coming from the wrong direction."

"Yeah, it's behind us. In the lagoon," Stone said.

"Federales?" Almeida said.

Whelan shook his head. "Most likely it's part of the drug cartel. Buddies of the guys we shot."

"How'd they know where to look for us?" Almeida said.

"They're more sophisticated technologically than most governments," Kirkland said. "Remember, they've got billions to play with."

Thomas took in a deep breath and blew it out. "There was a tracking device on that boat we stole, right?"

"That's the most logical explanation," Kirkland said.

The noise was loud and close now.

Stone looked into the night sky. "Are we going to get to that bloody fuckin' plane in time?"

"Not if we stand around here and jaw," Whelan said. "Nick and Stony are our best shooters. I want them bringing up the rear. Now, let's move."

They broke out of the jungle into a flatter, dryer area with thick patches of scrubs and small trees. Weaving around the vegetation for about three hundred yards, they came to a swampy area. They waded through the chest deep water for about five yards until they came to a patch of higher ground, crossed it, then waded across another thin strip of swamp. From there, it was another two hundred yards to the southerly end of the grass strip.

Whelan looked back up the strip toward the direction from which the plane would come. The strip was badly rutted and, in a few places, he could see that the underbrush had pinched in, narrowing it.

"This strip must not get much use," Larsen said.

"It's definitely been a while," Whelan said, as bullets began whistling through the air above them.

The Dogs all hit the ground in unison.

"You see anything?" Whelan shouted.

"No, and I don't think they can see us yet. Those were just pot shots," Stensen said. "But they've probably been made aware of the airstrip and have to be following the same route we took."

"Then they'll have to cross that same swampy stretch we did. They'll be at a chest deep disadvantage," Whelan said. "Spread out along it. Pick 'em off."

As they scrambled to take up positions, Almeida said, "If they take out that fuckin' plane, we're toast."

"Ever the cheerful soul," Thomas said as he squeezed off a three-round burst on the run.

The seven men lined up about ten feet apart and hunkered down in the tall grass along the edge of the bayou-like area.

Moments later they saw a dozen or so men emerge from the underbrush and begin to wade hesitantly into the marsh.

Whelan waited until they were all well into it, some of them up to their necks. "Now," he said and began squeezing off single rounds.

The other Dogs did likewise and the slugs from their SIG 553s began to eat holes in their victims' skulls. Some of the drug troops quickly ducked their heads under the surface of the green, slimy liquid. The Dogs waited patiently. In a matter of seconds, they resurfaced and met the same fate their comrades had. It was loud, fierce, and over quickly.

"Like shooting fish in a barrel," Larsen said. He smiled his bad smile; people had died.

"Oh, the clichés," Stensen said with a grin of his own.

"Unless my ears are playing tricks," Whelan said, "our ride is about to arrive. Let's move."

"Do you think we got the lot of them?" Stone said.

"Maybe not, but we can't wait around any longer."

"Yeah," Larsen said. "The pilots probably aren't happy about this mission. If they don't see us, they're likely to do a touch and go."

A few moments later, the seven men emerged from the scrubland at the southerly end of the grass strip. The twin engined de Havilland was bouncing wildly toward them. The Dogs waved their arms and the pilot began braking. The copilot dropped the door that was located near the rear of the fuselage. It opened outward and down on two sturdy cables and formed a set of stairs.

The pilot stood on one brake and revved one engine, causing the plane to rotate one hundred and eighty degrees. Its wingtips made a loud screeching sound as they brushed heavily against the tree branches that were steadily reclaiming the strip.

The Dogs scrambled up the steps and the copilot reached for a cable to retract the steps. A piece of his head blew off as a stray shot, part of a sudden fusillade, struck him. His knees sagged and his body pitched forward through the exit hatchway, bounced once on the ground then lay still in a grotesque position.

"Shit!" Stensen said. "This is the nightmare that just keeps giving." His statement was punctuated by additional slugs slamming into the plane's fuselage. "Sven!" he yelled at Larsen. "Grab my fucking belt and keep me from falling out of this crate."

The man-with-no-neck wrapped both hands around the back of Stensen's sturdy, two-inch wide Condor Tactical Belt. He braced his feet in a half crouch and leaned back. "Good to go."

The pilot yelled from the cockpit, "Brace yourselves. I'm gonna taxi to the other end of the strip. It'll be rough."

With unnatural speed, Whelan moved from the exit hatch at the rear of the plane to the cockpit. "No taxi. Take off now!"

"But I have to take off into the wind. Same way we landed."

"Bullshit. It's a crosswind. Doesn't matter."

The pilot started to argue. Whelan shoved the muzzle of his SIG 553 into the side of the man's head. "Take the fuck off. There are at least two of us aboard who can fly this crate. That makes you expendable."

Without hesitation, the pilot reached up and grabbed the throttle on the overhead panel and pushed it forward. The plane began moving toward the other end of the grass strip, picking up speed as it did.

As Whelan looked through the windscreen, the runway seemed much shorter than twenty-five-hundred feet. He glanced toward the rear of the plane and saw Larsen appear to lurch slightly forward, then lean backward and haul Stensen into the plane. Stensen wasn't moving.

"Stonie, get up here and make sure the pilot lifts off by the end of the strip," Whelan shouted above the noise of the twin Pratt & Whitney PT6A 750 horsepower turboprop engines.

The two men swiftly swapped ends of the plane.

Whelan grabbed the cable and pulled the hatch shut. With the speed of the plane, it took more effort than a Norm could have mustered. He knelt beside Larsen who had removed Stensen's body armor and was ripping his ACU jacket off with his bare hands. He tore the unusually durable blend of half nylon, half cotton like it was a paper towel. Stensen lay motionless on the deck, his eyes open but no red dots visible.

"He caught a round," Larsen said without looking up. "In his chest, I think."

"No sign of blood," Whelan said. "His body armor could have stopped the slug."

"Depends on the weapon that fired it and the type of cartridge," Kirkland said, leaning over Larsen from the opposite side.

"We're using the best. Beta models from a Mueller-owned lab," Whelan said. "It's cutting edge, the best there is."

"Yeah," Kirkland said, "ceramic-polymer composite plates wrapped on both sides with one-hundred layers of graphene. As close to AP-proof (armor-piercing) as you can get, but not bullet-proof against all firearms."

"It's unlikely a bunch of narco-thugs would have that kind of weaponry. They mostly rely on sidearms, ARs, and shotguns," Whelan said.

The men could feel the plane begin to rise off the ground. Slugs still clanged against the fuselage.

Larsen had Stensen's ACU jacket off and was examining his chest area. "Got a heck of a bruise forming, but there's no pene-tration."

"Must have just had the shit knocked out of him," Kirkland said. "Might have been an AP round. If he'd been wearing older style armor, he'd be a goner."

Larsen shook Stensen gently. There was no response. He slapped his cheek, gently at first then harder.

Suddenly, a red dot ignited in the center of each eye. He fixed Larsen with a calm gaze and said, "What the hell are you doing?"

"Welcome back," Kirkland said with a big grin. "Thought we might have lost you."

"I remember hanging out of the hatch picking off bad guys." He looked up at Whelan. "Then what?"

"Then you earned a bonus from the Muellers for beta testing their latest body armor."

Stensen touched his chest gingerly and grimaced. "That's going to hurt for a while."

"Beats being a dead motherfucker," Almeida said.

Whelan looked at Stensen. "You feel like anything's broken?"

"Nah, just sore as hell."

Turning to Larsen, Whelan said, "Get him buckled into a jump seat. I'm gonna call Christie."

The plane was capable of climbing at a rate of sixteen-hundred-feet per minute, but Whelan could sense it had leveled off at a low altitude. *Is there an issue with the mechanics? Maybe the pilot is using the ground cover to screen the plane from the drug smugglers' line of fire.*

He went forward, satphone in hand to find out.

"What's the service ceiling for this aircraft?" he asked the pilot.

"Twenty-five thousand feet." The man was sweating profusely, although the cockpit wasn't particularly warm.

Whelan could smell the man's fear. Looking out the windscreen, he said, "You're straight and level just above the treetops. Why?"

"Mexican radar."

Whelan glanced at the instrument panel. "You're on a north-northwest bearing. Why not just head out into the Gulf?"

"The Mexicans claim sovereignty at least two hundred miles out, maybe three hundred depending on what they had for breakfast."

"But if you stay low, you should be okay, right?"

"Hopefully. Based on what I know about your mission and given that hot zone back there, the Federales and the drug cartel will be looking for us with their own aircraft. They'll assume we'll take the sea route."

"What's your destination?"

"A small private strip just over the border."

"Given all the drug traffic at the border, how are we going to slip in?"

"You guys must have friends in high places. I've been assured there won't be any problems."

Whelan nodded. *The Muellers and SAS. And maybe POTUS.* "How far?"

"About three hundred nautical miles."

"Three-hundred-fifty statute miles," Whelan said. "What's your low altitude cruising speed?"

"A hundred seventy knots."

"That's a little under two-hundred miles per hour. We're looking at close to two hours flight time."

"If nothing goes wrong," the pilot said.

"Nothing ever goes wrong," Whelan said with a sardonic smile.

Stone laughed. "Right, mate, and we're currently on exfil Plan D or is it E?"

CHAPTER 50

HIGUERILLAS, MEXICO

It had been a long, painful ride for Turan. Although major Mexican highways were well maintained for the most part, when your broken and battered body is sprawled on the bare metal floor in the back of an old, worn-out commercial van with ancient shocks and springs, the condition of the roadbeds was of little consequence. Turan tried not to think about Carolina, but when he did, the pain was sharper than that caused by his injuries.

The route from Chihuahua to Higuerillas wandered across almost the width of Mexico for twelve hundred kilometers or almost seven-hundred-fifty miles. It ran easterly through the metropolitan areas of Torreon, Saltillo, Monterrey, Reynosa, and Matamoros before turning south for the final leg to Higuerillas.

Saltillo was roughly the halfway point in the journey and the driver had stopped the van there for several hours. He and his partner had rested at the small house of a friend near the center of the ancient city founded by conquistadors. While they did, the friend watched the van and its cargo of five large rucksacks and Turan. He seemed indifferent to Turan's condition and situation, but brought him food and something to drink. The beverage was fresh fruit water known as aguas frescas, a standard drink in Mexico. It was accompanied by elotes, corn on the cob covered with butter, mayonnaise, grated cheese, and chili powder. Despite the pain that motion brought, the temporarily unbound Turan all but inhaled the food and drink. When they returned to the van, the two men from Chihuahua teased him that he probably would get Montezuma's Revenge from the food.

Later, as they passed through Matamoros before turning south, Turan realized he was less than half a mile from the Rio Bravo/Rio Grande that formed the border with the United States. He fantasized briefly that Christie and federal agents might swarm across the river and rescue him. Or maybe they would send those ninja-like killing machines they called the Sleeping Dogs. Then he grudgingly accepted the reality of his fate. There would be no rescue for him. He was a dead man.

The final leg from Matamoros to Higuerillas was partially on Mexican Highway 101. The road was four-laned with a paved median strip. It wound through low hills covered with scattered stands of scrub mesquite, creosote bushes and prickly pear cactus, interspersed with vast fields of sorghum that stretched to the horizon.

The two squat, thick-bodied Salvadorans in the van told him it was called *la Carretera de la Muerte*, the Highway of Death.

"Why do they call it that?" Turan said.

The driver, who said his name was Paco, said, "Keep your eyes open, *chico*, you will see soon enough."

Within minutes they began to pass burned-out vehicles and bullet-riddled trucks on the sides of the road.

The man in the passenger seat, who said his name was Nemesio, said, "A few days ago, those cars and trucks were still full of bodies, most of them with no heads."

"Do the police know who did it?" Turan said.

"Sure, it's the drug gangs and the *loco campesinos* who work for them," Nemesio said. "Listen, *perro*, what you see ain't nothin'. These people stop buses and strip the women and young girls then rape them in front of their own relatives. If anyone objects, well, you know..." He drew a finger across his neck. "Seems like every week the cops find another mass grave around here."

Turan squeezed his eyes shut trying to block out the horrifying images. It didn't work.

"Look around," Paco said. "You ain't seen many cars on the road, have you?"

"No."

"Once, this was the busiest highway in Mexico. Now, few people use it, and nobody uses it at night."

"Are we safe on this road?" Turan said.

"Shit, *perro*, it's those fuckers who should be afraid of us. We fucking MS-13," Nemesio said scornfully.

Paco said, "No worries, *chico*, we do the heavy lifting for all the cartels, as long as it don't involve us in their turf wars. We got free passage throughout Mexico, including the Highway of Death."

They rode on in silence for a few more miles until, cresting a small hill, they saw four SUVs, all gray and with tinted windows, blocking the road a quarter mile ahead. More than a dozen men stood in front of the vehicles. All were armed with assault rifles and shotguns.

Turan was astonished. They had traveled less that ten kilometers from the outskirts of Matamoros.

As Paco slowed the van, Nemesio said, "Now, things gonna get fun, *perro*. You get down low and stay outta sight. Me and

Paco gonna do the talkin.' You don't say nothing." He slapped Turan on the top of the head for emphasis.

The two Salvadorans made it a point to keep their hands where the other men could see them. The images of the burned and bullet-pocked vehicles they'd passed were fresh.

As the van came to a stop about twenty feet from the armed men, two of them stepped forward. One brandished a Mossberg 500 Tactical 12-gauge shotgun. He kept it trained on Nemesio as he circled carefully to the right side of the van. The other man approached Paco, keeping him covered with an AR, a Bushmaster XM-15.

Paco smiled and leaned his head out the driver's side window. He made it a point to display the back of his heavily tattooed right forearm. "*Hola, señor. Hay algún problema?*" Is there a problem.

The man didn't seem to notice the tat and motioned him out of the van with the barrel of his rifle.

Paco's smile vanished. He held up his right forearm and, using the pointer finger on his left hand, indicated a particular tattoo. "No, *ese*, you take a good look at this, then you and your asshole pals get the fuck out of the way."

The man's eyes quickly narrowed in anger, but he stepped forward and studied the tat for several long seconds. Finally, he looked at Paco. The anger at being spoken to so disrespectfully was still in his eyes, but the muzzle of the AR was now pointed at the ground. He turned and yelled at one of the other men. The man climbed into the driver's seat of one of the gray SUVs and maneuvered it off the road, opening a space for the van to pull through.

In moments, Turan and his MS-13 escort once again were bouncing down *Carretera de la Muerte*. In about four kilometers, Paco turned off the Highway of Death and onto *Carretera a El*

Mezquital, a narrow, mostly flat two-lane road. Its sixty miles started off in farm country then segued into scrublands before encountering salt marshes as it began to run south along the Gulf Coast.

Along the way, sensing from the smell of the nearby sea that the journey was nearly over, Turan asked the Salvadorans what the destination was.

"Not that you need to know, *chico*," Paco said, "but it's a place, a fishing village called Higuerillas."

"Do you mind telling me why we're going there?"

"I could tell you to mind you own fucking business, *perro*," Nemesio said. "But at this point it don't really matter."

"Yeah," Paco said. "Me and Nemesio are just the delivery service. We got no dog in this fight."

"For such a young guy, you got some bad people really pissed off at you. It don't look good for you, *chico*," Nemesio said. "We pretty sure they gonna kill you, and it ain't gonna be quick."

They began to pass scattered buildings and an occasional side street. Then they were in a town with regularly spaced blocks and mixtures of residential and commercial structures.

The soaring humidity blended with the one-hundred-degree temperature to create a heavy, wet blanket of air. It made breathing difficult and sweat glands worked feverishly in an attempt to cool the body. Perspiration flowed from the men's pores, the smell mixing with the other long-ingrained odors in the van. The sky was overcast and gray, adding a funereal pall to the atmosphere.

Turan's sense of hopelessness deepened.

CHAPTER 51

SINGAPORE

ZHENG BAO XUN leaned against the balustrade that encircled the one-thousand-one-hundred-twenty-foot-long observation plat-form that was part of the SkyPark, a three-acre facility with swimming pools, including the world's largest infinity pool, as well as gardens and jogging paths. Six-hundred-twenty-seven feet above ground, it connected the tops of three fifty-seven-story buildings that constituted the Marina Bay Sands. The ultra-luxu-rious resort and casino was a jewel in the crown of the Las Vegas Sands Corporation.

Zheng strolled along the balustrade, pausing to sip his kiwi-açaí mojito and admire the bounty of exposed flesh sun-worship-ping in the deck chairs lined up with military-like precision. He smiled and wondered how much scantier bikinis could become. They already seemed incapable of concealing even the most inti-mate of areas. This bothered him not at all.

The air was clean and fresh, scented only with the tropical odors of the various sun screen potions slathered on the sunbathers. He enjoyed the sweeping, unobstructed view of

Singapore's Marina Bay all the way out to the Singapore Strait and the busy shipping lanes. Even more, he enjoyed the resort's four-level casino. The official reason for his visit was to attend the annual meeting of PACED, the Pan-Asian Council on Economic Development. He considered it part of his duties as the minister of finance for the People's Republic of China, particularly when the venue included a casino.

Zheng glanced at his watch. It was almost two p.m. Singapore Standard Time. He walked along the observation platform to a set of stairs and descended to the main area of the SkyPark which included a large bar.

In keeping with his usual punctuality, Andrei Ulyanin was sitting at a small table slightly isolated from the rest of the bar section. He looked at Zheng with an impassive expression.

"What do you think of this resort, Andrei, impressive, yes?"

"It should be. Do you know what it cost to build it?"

"Eight billion American dollars, if my memory is correct."

"For that kind of money, it should be spectacular."

Zheng made a dismissive motion with his hand. "Merely another example of the insanity that is capitalism. Surely, as a Russian, you can appreciate that." He smiled slyly.

"Capitalism is good, Zheng. It offers everyone a chance to succeed, provided they work for it."

"Personally, Andrei, I prefer communism, where being ruthless, greedy, misanthropic, and amoral can take you to the top."

Ulyanin's face curled into an expression as if something had left a bad taste in his mouth. "You didn't have me fly for almost twenty-four hours just to debate economic systems, Zheng. What's on your mind?"

Zheng's sly smile returned. "Debate is good for the soul, Andrei. Didn't you know that?"

"Neither one of us believes in souls. Cut to the chase. I need to sleep for ten hours before my return flight."

Zheng took the chair opposite Ulyanin across the small round table. "Remember when I hired you, Andrei, I told you my ultimate goal was to replace president Jiang?"

Ulyanin nodded.

"As events in China are demonstrating, our president is consolidating power." Zheng sneered. "He thinks he is the second coming of Mao."

Ulyanin said nothing, just kept his eyes locked on Zheng's.

"I fear he is close to becoming too powerful to be challenged, let alone replaced in a coup."

Ulyanin remained silent.

"Before that becomes impossible, I must consolidate my own power."

"You mean it's time for you to take over the Alliance for Global Unity," Ulyanin said.

"Indeed. You will recall when I hired you that it was because you were close to Fairchilde, close enough to kill him when I deemed the moment to be right."

Ulyanin nodded. "I remember."

"I have done enough favors for other members of AGU's power structure that there should be no resistance to my replacing Harland once he's out of the way."

"How do you want his death to occur?"

Zheng shook his head impatiently. "I have never killed a person in my life. Directly. That is entirely your realm. Do it however you choose. Just do it in a way that doesn't implicate me."

"Consider it done." Ulyanin rose. "Now, I'm going to get some sleep."

CHAPTER 52

HIGUERILLAS, MEXICO

TURAN WAS ASTONISHED that he wasn't dead yet. Paco and Nemesio had moved him from the van to a rectangular-shaped two-story building near the waterfront in Higuerillas. He remembered briefly seeing the exterior as he was being moved. It looked as if it had once been whitewashed, but now it was filthy and badly faded. Its plainness was broken by a green, two-foot wide stripe painted near the bottom of the exterior walls and by a row of small rectangular windows about fifteen feet above the ground and just below the flat roof. There was a row of small rectangular windows about fifteen feet above the ground and just below the flat roof. He'd heard Paco refer to it as an *almacen de insumos*, a warehouse.

The interior was much worse. The pervasive smell of industrial fluids mixed with the odors of long-dead sea creatures revealed the operational history of the building. The badly rusted machinery told Turan that the structure hadn't been used commercially in years. There was a staircase at each end of the building that provided access to the second floor.

Nemesio had shackled Turan's hands and feet and left him on the floor near a metal pillar that supported a sagging ceiling. Afterward, he and Paco brought in the five rucksacks that contained the nuclear devices, and placed them on the floor near the middle of the building. An hour later, eleven men arrived. Only their leader, a man who called himself Abdel Sabbah, spoke in Spanish to Paco and Nemesio. The others talked among themselves in variously accented versions of Arabic.

Turan was fluent in both languages and listened carefully to what was being said. It was clear that his MS-13 keepers, the Salvadorans Paco and Nemesio, had completed their work and were being paid off. It was equally clear that the other men made up the two-man teams who would be responsible for transporting the bombs to their respective target cities in America and detonating them.

Using his smart phone, Paco was able to determine that the expected funds had been electronically transferred into the appropriate bank account. He motioned Nemesio toward the entrance. Nodding at Sabbah, he said, "I'm gonna say goodbye to the kid, 'cause we sure as hell won't be seeing him again."

Sabbah shrugged. "Whatever. My instructions are to make him witness the bombs beginning their final journey. It will drive home the point how totally his treachery failed."

"And then," Paco said and drew his finger across his throat.

"Of course, but it won't be anything that kills him quickly. His 'caliph' wants him to die slowly, screaming all the way to the end."

"*No hay problema*, amigo. Do what you wanna do," Paco said.

He walked over to where Turan sat on the hard concrete floor that was stained and sticky with decades of filth and spilled fluids. With his back to the others in the room, Paco carefully fished something from a pocket in his cargo pants.

"Well, *chico*," he said softly so that only Turan could hear him. "Looks like you're on your own from this point. But you never know, things might take a turn for the better." He showed him the object he'd taken out of his pocket. It was a cell phone.

It looked to Turan like the one that had been taken from him on Isla El Idolo.

PACO STUCK the phone back in his pocket and, with his back still to the others in the building, winked at Turan. "*Adios, chico.* Take care of yourself."

Once he was outside, Paco looked casually around. Seeing no one other than Nemesio, he dug the phone out again, slipped a battery into it, turned it on, and softly lobbed it onto the roof of the old warehouse.

As they drove out of town, Nemesio wagged his head back and forth. "Why you helpin' the kid? What the fuck is he to us?"

"Maybe it ain't about the kid."

"Yeah? Then what is it about?"

"I don't like those Arab motherfuckers. They gonna destroy the United States. We got family there, maybe in the cities they gonna bomb."

"Yeah," Nemesio said. "I see your point."

"Also, with no United States, who the fuck's gonna buy drugs off the cartels. Those *perros* pay us well, amigo. Remember, it's always about the benjamins."

CHAPTER 53

WASHINGTON, D.C.

THE WEATHER in Washington was typical for winter. The sky was barren and gray. The air was frigid. The urban pollution was already turning the overnight snowfall black. The city's infamous traffic jams were on full display. On the sidewalks, crowds of people bundled in dark layers plodded along, heads down partly because of the weather and partly because, in an urban environment, eye contact can lead to unwanted hostilities.

Whelan was one of the few exceptions. On the northeast corner of G Street Northwest and 11th Street Northwest, he exited the chauffeured black Suburban that Mitch Christie and the SAS had provided for his trip into the city. The other six Dogs were recovering from the mission to Isla El Idolo at the Lodge sixty miles away in Fairview, Virginia. Whelan, head up and alert, strode north on 11th Street through the frozen throngs. He took care not to collide with the fragile Norms who were plunging blindly forward, focused solely on getting to a warm office. With seemingly effortless grace, he moved smoothly around the fragile creatures. In short order, he came to a pair of large sleek metallic and glass-skinned office buildings known as CityCenterDC. He turned right and walked down Palmer Alley, a pedestrian-only lane that separated One CityCenter from its twin, Two CityCenter. At the end of the alley, he turned north again and entered One CityCenter.

After passing through security, a spotless chrome elevator whisked Whelan to the fifth-floor offices of Castlebaum, Weintraub, Arcaro & O'Malley. He was quickly shown to a richly appointed conference room where Christie, Tomas Mueller, and Levell's attorney, Irv Weintraub, and one of his young associates were already seated.

"Am I late?" Whelan said.

Christie glanced at his watch. "Nope, right on time. We were early. Had some things to discuss in advance of meeting with you.

As Tomas Mueller did the introductions, Whelan shook hands with Weintraub and his assistant, a bookish-looking young woman with thick, rimless glasses and the sniffles. And she was having a bad hair day. He took a seat near the middle of the table. "Not to be rude, but we need to get started. I've got an unruly bunch back at the Lodge. Best not leave them alone too long."

"Agreed," Mueller said and looked at Christie. "Mitch, would you like to start?"

Christie nodded. "To cut to the chase, Irv and his legal team have come up with a plan that could get Cliff Levell released. But it does have a loose end." He looked at Weintraub.

"We're going to file a petition for writ of habeas corpus…" Weintraub paused. "Are you familiar with the term, Mr. Whelan?"

"Yes, it's from the Latin and literally means 'produce the body.' It's a means of recourse to free someone who is being unlawfully detained or imprisoned."

"Very good, sir. I'm impressed."

"You needn't be. I'm a graduate of the School of Law at Trinity College in Dublin."

Weintraub, short and heavyset with a perennially sad smile, shook his balding head. It caused his heavy jowls to quiver. "Then I apologize for not ascertaining your credentials before we started."

"No problem. But it's my understanding that Cliff's being held in contempt of the grand jury because he refused to testify under subpoena after the GJ granted him immunity from prosecution. How does habeas corpus apply in this instance?"

"Under a long line of cases from various federal courts including SCOTUS, even in grand jury situations, a prisoner cannot be detained where there is a lack of evidence to show that his withheld testimony is germane to the case. It will require David Farmer to produce such evidence, and we're gambling that he doesn't have any."

"Not yet, anyway," Christie said.

"Meaning?" Whelan said.

Tomas Mueller said, "Speaking hypothetically, if Farmer believes Cliff has knowledge that POTUS is involved in a conspiracy to use private operators to invade foreign sovereign soil and conduct military operations, he had to have gotten that information from someone other than Flagler or Cliff."

"In other words, a third-party co-conspirator," Whelan said. "And if such a person exists, won't Farmer produce that person's testimony in response to your petition?" Whelan said. "In fact, why hasn't he done so already instead of screwing around with Cliff?"

"Because," Weintraub said, "either that person doesn't exist or, what's more likely, Farmer made a deal to keep them out of it, if possible."

"But that person has to exist, otherwise Farmer wouldn't have had a lead on Cliff," Christie said.

Whelan leaned back in the ridiculously overstuffed conference room chair. "So, you're going to call Farmer's hand. And if he does produce that other person?"

"If that proves to be the case," Weintraub said, "Cliff is screwed."

ON WHELAN'S return to the Lodge in Tidewater Virginia, the Dogs had assembled in the wine cellar hidden beneath the library. Whelan, Thomas, Kirkland, Stone, and Stensen were drinking beer. Larsen was nursing the usual diet cola.

Almeida had brought an all-in-one waiter corkscrew he'd pirated from the Lodge's kitchen. He prowled the racks for a few minutes then sat down at the large mahogany conference table with a dusty bottle of wine. The others watched in amusement as he uncorked the bottle and raised it to his lips. He took a deep gulp. His eyes opened wide and for a moment he seemed frozen. Then he yanked the bottle away, turned his head and spit a huge mouthful of red wine all over the stone floor.

"Jesus Christ! This is the worst shit I ever tasted. What the fuck is it?" He held the label up for Thomas to read.

"My God, you cretin. That's a 'ninety-two Screaming Eagle!"

"Yeah? Well, I think it's gonna give me the screaming shits."

"Do you have any idea what that wine is worth?" Thomas said.

Almeida shrugged. "Ain't worth shit to me. How much?"

Thomas stared at him open-mouthed for a few moments then said, "Seventy-five hundred to ten thousand dollars."

Almeida showed shock. "For one fuckin' bottle?" He squeezed the cork back into the bottle then replaced it on the rack. "Who decides what's good wine and what ain't? Must be some kind of dumb fuck if he thinks it's worth that kind of bread."

Stensen said, "This from a guy who thinks wine is only good if it comes in a carton."

Whelan shook his head. "Alright, the entertainment is over. Let's talk." He spent several minutes relaying to the others what had been discussed in Weintraub's office.

When he'd finished, Stone said, "If there is a third party, they'll have to testify to the grand jury right, mate?"

"He or she will have to testify at the hearing on the petition for habeas corpus, or at least submit an affidavit," Whelan said.

"So," Kirkland said, "I take it this means their identity will be revealed?"

"Yes," Whelan said, "but it's doubtful Farmer will let it become public knowledge. He only has to show the court that there is credible evidence showing that Cliff knows the president is a party to the conspiracy."

"Shit," Almeida said. "How's that gonna get Cliff outta hot water?"

"Farmer, the special counsel, was appointed by the Department of Justice. The DOJ is monitoring his proceedings. Christie has contacts in the DOJ and thinks he can get that person's name."

"Why do I have a feeling something bad's going to happen to the s.o.b.?" Stensen said. He grinned a hawk-faced grin made more frightening by the glowing red dots in the centers of his eyes.

"Because that's exactly what is going to happen," Whelan said. "Are you volunteering, Nick?"

"Wouldn't miss it for the world."

Larsen smiled his good smile. "That's only fair. Nick hasn't killed anybody since that El Idolo thing. What was that, almost a week ago? He's gotta be getting antsy."

LITTLE MORE THAN A WEEK LATER, Mitch Christie was standing in line to place an order at a Starbucks at 1100 Pennsylvania Avenue Northwest. It was about a block from the FBI Headquarters Building. The man standing in line in front of him was tall and broad-shouldered with a thick neck, yet moved with the ease and grace of a jungle cat. Each man placed his order then moved down the bar to wait for them to be filled. To any observers, they were just two strangers exchanging a few words casually while they waited.

"Good day for hot coffee," Whelan said to Christie.

"Good day for a cushy government job in a warm office."

"Any particular bureaucracy come to mind?"

"A White House job would be nice. Something like a special advisor to the president. Maybe like that guy who's Flagler's counterterrorism expert."

"Yeah, I can't think of his name."

"Trupockitt. Billy Trupockitt."

"Right. How could I forget a name like that?"

"On second thought," Christie said, "I wouldn't want to be that guy. I heard he has a drinking problem."

"Yeah?"

"They say he can be found almost every night bellied up to the bar at a place called Swinton's."

"Yeah, I've heard of it, but don't remember where it is."

"In Georgetown, just off Wisconsin Avenue."

BILLY TRUPOCKITT GOT lucky and found a parking place in the middle of the block on N Street Northwest. It was less than four hundred feet from his favorite watering hole, a small restaurant and lounge called Swinton's. He nudged the tires of his Lexus LC hybrid against the curb of the narrow street and unfolded his tall frame from the tight confines of the driver's seat. Emerging from the warm interior of the car, the gusty, frigid air was a hard, unexpected slap across the face.

Even with Daylight Savings Time, darkness had set in early. The dying light of the day was shrouded by a heavy cloud cover. Snow was beginning to fall in large flakes. Trupockitt knew from his days in the Air Force that snowflakes become larger as the humidity increases. This means that the temperature in the upper atmosphere was warmer than at lower levels and slightly above freezing. It was an indication that snow may be about to mix with or change into sleet. *All the more reason to hunker down at the bar and get cozy.*

He had hustled about fifty feet from the car in a half-trot, half-walk, when a man wearing a fedora low over his eyes stepped out of the shadows and blocked his passage. The stranger was not as tall as Trupockitt, but his overcoat couldn't hide the fact that he was powerfully built. There was a fitness center in the three-story brick and glass building he was passing, so Trupockitt assumed the man was a muscle-head who had just finished a workout. The red brick sidewalk was wider at this point, and Trupockitt started to go around the stranger. But the man moved over and continued to block the passage.

Trupockitt straightened his back and squared his shoulders. Maybe this guy just didn't realize that Trupockitt was physically taller. By a couple of inches. "Is there a problem, buddy?"

In a soft voice that Trupockitt had to strain to hear, the man said, "I'm looking for Billy Trupockitt."

"Yeah? Why? Do I know you?"

"We have a mutual friend."

Trupockitt was becoming exasperated. "Look, pal, I don't have time for this shit. I'm freezing my ass off and I need a drink. You got something you want to talk about, do in the bar."

He started to go around the stranger again, but again the man moved to block his way. Angry, Trupockitt lunged out with both hands to shove the man aside. It was like trying to push a freight car. Uphill.

The man slowly tilted his head back until the brim cleared his eyes. The last thing Billy Trupockitt saw in this lifetime was a pair of glacial blue eyes with the fires of hell raging in their centers.

CHAPTER 54

LONG ISLAND, NEW YORK

FEW THINGS in life gave Harland Fairchilde IV as much pleasure as owning things others couldn't afford in their wildest dreams. His one-of-a-kind Bubinga wood desk was an example. It was entirely handmade without use of screws, nails or metal objects other than the solid gold handles on the drawers. The rare and expensive wood had been grown in Equatorial Africa and hand-rubbed with tung oil to bring out the deep tones of the wood. He believed that a man of his means, who could afford anything he wanted, should have exactly that. Anything.

Fairchilde was sitting behind the desk sipping Louis XIII de Remy Martin Black Pearl Grande Champagne Cognac from a rare and delicate snifter he'd bought for two thousand dollars. He'd paid almost thirty thousand dollars for the cognac. It wasn't the most expensive item in his collection. He also owned two bottles of Château d'Yquem 1811 for which he'd paid one hundred twenty thousand dollars apiece. Fairchilde had no intention of drinking them. The joy of wealth wasn't in consumption.

It was in possession. Possession was proof of wealth. You had it, they didn't.

The estate sprawled atop one of the highest points in Brookville, the poshest address on Long Island. It was accessed by a long, winding driveway that twisted through a thick copse of trees, terminating in the estate's enormous motor court. No less than seven individual garage doors lined the court. The manor house rose three stories into the night sky, looming over the motor court like an enthroned royal. Its stony vastness spread far to either side of the massive double oak entry doors that topped a series of granite steps.

Tonight, Fairchilde awaited the arrival of Andrei Ulyanin who had just returned from a meeting in Singapore with the Chinese minister of finance, Zheng Bao Xun. Ulyanin had phoned him during an almost two-hour layover in Frankfurt. Out of respect for the abilities of Chinese hackers, Ulyanin had been close-mouthed about the subject of his requested meeting. But Fairchilde knew it must be important if the Russian wanted to see him immediately after a twenty-three-hour flight rather than first get some sleep.

Ulyanin displayed his usual punctuality, arriving precisely at eleven p.m. He was shown to Fairchilde's den by a servant who closed the door and left.

Fairchilde waved him to a chair. "My, but you do look fatigued, Andrei. Whatever it is you want to tell me must be quite significant."

The Russian settled into his chair and unleashed a deep sigh of exhaustion. "It is."

"As a good host, I must inquire whether you would like something to drink. Vodka, perhaps, although I should think coffee would be a better choice under the circumstances."

"Maybe some of whatever it is you're having."

A smug smile crossed Fairchilde's lips. "I'm afraid this Louis Thirteenth Cognac is not for the hired help. Why don't you just get directly to the point of this meeting."

If the remark offended Ulyanin, he didn't show it. "Sometime back, we had a conversation in which you were concerned about my loyalty as your employee."

"Yes, I remember it well. You were in my employ, but also accepted compensation from minister Zheng to report my activities to him."

Ulyanin nodded.

"I was able to disabuse you of that behavior and you agreed to let me know when his treachery blossomed to the point of a physical threat."

Again, Ulyanin nodded.

"As you've just met with the good minister in Singapore and have come to me immediately upon your return, I presume he's decided the time has come for me to 'be removed from the scene,' shall we say?"

"Yes."

"Do you recall what I told you when we originally discussed your disloyalty?"

"Yes, that you had a dossier on Zheng's actions and intentions to displace the Chinese president, Jiang Qui Xing."

"Indeed, I do have such a dossier. I'll be sending it forthwith to President Jiang. If I know my Chinese politics, and I do, our friend Mr. Zheng will quickly disappear. Forever. And to think, he recently had been appointed vice premier and charged with overseeing all of China's economic policies and financial issues." A vicious smile flashed briefly across Fairchilde's face. "You see, Andrei, greed can be a dangerous trait."

"Are you sure Zheng is expendable at this point?"

"What choice do I have in the matter, Andrei? He's instructed you to kill me. No doubt he expects you to carry through very quickly."

Ulyanin tipped his head to the side and with a thoughtful expression, said, "You have often told me that your plans have been inconvenienced by Levell and SAS's Sleeping Dogs. You also told me Zheng had recruited and trained their counterparts. With his imminent downfall, what happens to those plans?"

"Fortunately, those plans are far enough along that Zheng is no longer a factor."

"How so?"

"The five nuclear devices are in the hands of Nadir Shah's people in Mexico. They are about to be transported to various locations in the United States. Zheng's group of cutthroats has been assigned to protect them just in case Levell's assassins show up."

"Does Zheng's group have a name?"

Fairchilde smirked. "The Bad Dogs. I suppose that's an Asian effort at irony."

Ulyanin's face was expressionless and he said nothing.

Fairchilde tipped his head back and gazed down his long, thin patrician nose at the Russian. "I'm curious. Why is it you chose to throw your lot in with me and not Zheng"?

"It's a personal thing. I'm Russian, there's been bad blood between us for centuries. Personally, I've never liked the little Asian bastards."

A FEW DAYS LATER, Fairchilde smiled smugly as he read a short item in the World News section of the *Wall Street Journal*. It reported that the Chinese vice premier and minister of finance, Zheng Bao Xun, had been arrested at his office in Beijing and jailed, charged with a number of serious crimes, including treason. Nothing more was ever heard concerning him.

An article on the front page of the same edition was captioned "White House Advisor Kills Self."

CHAPTER 55

THE LODGE

OPERATIONS AT THE LODGE ran on a twenty-four-seven schedule and required a large staff to fill its wide variety of positions. One of the employees, a striking young blonde woman named Ashlee Ericksen, worked the day shift as an assistant manager in Food and Beverage. She had a perfect body, and she knew it. She had her clothes tailored to accentuate her physical charms.

Ashlee's attractiveness wasn't lost on any of the males who worked at, or visited, The Lodge, including the Dogs, especially Rafe Almeida. Today, she was wearing a perfectly fitted Kelly green suit. The skirt's hemline stopped at mid-thigh, showcasing her long, beautiful legs.

Almeida, Stensen, and Thomas were sitting in the large atrium area just inside the Lodge's main entrance, waiting for the other Dogs to arrive. Almeida had just mixed his third rum and coke when he heard the sound of high heels clicking on the stone floor. As if guided by radar, his head swiveled around to follow the sound.

"Shit, I'm in love," he said, as his eyes followed Ashlee's long, rhythmic strides across the atrium.

"Love? Nah, man, you're only capable of lust. Whenever you see anything female," Thomas said, shaking his head slowly in mock disapproval.

"You're old enough to be her father," Stensen said.

"But you look more like her grandfather," Thomas said.

"Great-grandfather," Stensen said.

Ashlee glanced over at the three men and smiled. It was like looking at an orthodontist's retirement plan.

"See! She wants me!" Almeida said. He tossed back his drink, stood, and started to follow the young woman.

"Rafe, leave the help alone," Thomas said.

"Maybe after I'm finished with her," Almeida said with a lascivious grin. He rubbed his crotch for emphasis.

"Okay," Stensen said. "In that case, we'll set our watches for two minutes. That ought to be more than enough time."

"Eat your hearts out, you fucking losers." Almeida turned to follow Ashlee, but she had already crossed the atrium and entered an office on the far side of the room. He took a couple of steps toward the office when he heard a familiar raspy voice.

Levell, being wheeled by Nando, entered the room with Whelan, Larsen, and Liam Stone. Levell sized up the situation in an instant. "Almeida, what the hell do you think you're doing?"

Rafe shrugged sheepishly and said, "I was just gonna go for a walk."

"Walk, my ass. Do I need to instruct the kitchen staff to feed you a steady diet of saltpeter?"

"That's an urban legend and a waste of time," Stensen said. "Just castrate the little bastard."

Everyone laughed except Almeida.

"Okay," Levell said, "fun and games are over. Time for business. Everyone in my office. Now."

A few minutes later, all of the men were gathered in Levell's office. He had Nando purposely position his wheelchair so that the others had their backs to the wide glass wall that showcased the thickly wooded area outside. He didn't want anyone to be distracted from the business at hand. The men had moved some of the furniture so it formed a rough horseshoe facing Levell. When everyone was seated, Nando slipped quietly out of the room. Surrounded by the most lethal group of men on the planet, Levell could afford to give the Brazilian Capoeira expert some down time.

"Sir," Almeida said to Levell, "before we get started, I'd like to welcome you back. It wasn't the same without you. Mitch Christie ain't no you."

Levell winced as if the comment had caused him pain. "Just so you know—all of you—my butt is sore from sitting on a hard metal bed in that damn jail. So, no more ass kissing, understand?" He looked pointedly at Almeida.

"Two things," Levell said. "First, Nick, your handiwork made the front pages. Give us a capsule summary."

"I cornered Trupockitt on a cold, dark side street. Nobody was around. He was freezing and desperate to get to the bar. He wasn't paying attention."

"Sounds like a regular galah, mate," Stone said.

Almeida said, "A what?"

"Fool," Stone said. "A bloke can get gobsmacked when he's got his head up his freckle."

Almeida gave Stone a puzzled look, but Levell spoke up before he could say anything. "Get a damn book on Strine and stop interrupting."

Stensen shrugged. "It was easy. I jabbed four fingers into his throat, crushing its vital parts. He couldn't breathe. I stuffed him into the trunk of a 'borrowed' car. Unable to breath, he was unconscious in a minute or so and dead in another one or two."

"And then you hung him to make it look like the noose had done the damage," Kirkland said. "Smart. That's how I would have done it."

"Who are you kidding?" Thomas said. "You would have minced him with that sword of yours."

"That's why we asked Nick to do it," Whelan said. "We knew it would be neat and clean. It needed to look like suicide, not murder. That would only have worsened Cliff's situation."

"So, you took him back to his own house and hung his body in the garage," Larsen said.

Stensen grinned a raptorial grin, the red dots glowing in the centers of his eyes. "Yes. I thought about hanging him from a tree in Fort Marcy Park over in McClean."

"Where Vince Foster died," Levell said. "You're a scary bastard, Stensen, but not without a sense of irony."

"The important thing is that Trupockitt was the only source the special counsel had who could show that you knew about Flagler's plans. His death was the catalyst that got you released from the contempt charge," Whelan said. "Now, what's that second item on your agenda?"

"Those five fucking nukes in the hands of Nadir Shah's Islamic crazies."

"Yeah," Thomas said resignedly, "wherever they are."

"We know where they are," Levell said.

All of the Dogs except Almeida sat forward *en masse*.

"We've had a young Pakistani kid implanted with Shah's bomb squad," Levell said.

"But, as I understand it, Turan—that was his name—disappeared and was presumed dead," Whelan said.

"He may well be dead, but his phone began sending a signal again. Our people picked it up this afternoon and pinpointed its location," Levell said.

"And that's London to a brick?" Stone said.

"If that means, has it been confirmed, the answer is yes," Levell said.

"Well, don't keep us stonkered, mate. Where the hell are the nukes?" Stone said.

Levell looked at Whelan. "Damn, can't you teach our friend from Oz how to speak real English?"

Whelan grinned. "Better yet, he's teaching us Strine."

Levell sighed wearily and said, "Whatever. Look, the signal is coming from an old warehouse in a small fishing town called Higuerillas. It's on Mexico's Gulf Coast about forty or so miles due south of Matamoros."

"In that case," Larsen said, "shouldn't we be kitting up?"

"Not so fast," Levell said. "It's a little more complicated."

"Meaning?" Kirkland said.

Levell's gray eyes seemed to darken, the set of his jaw firmer than usual. "What would you say if I told you there are others like you?"

"Good lookin'?" Almeida said.

"No, you dumb shit. Like you *genetically*, not like Norms."

"That's not surprising," Whelan said. "You and Buster McCoy originally recruited twenty of us. We're the survivors, but there were others."

"But we only recruited in the States. Horowitz and Nishioshi, who discovered your genetic trait, traced it back to western European Early Modern Humans, who interbred with the Neanderthal. These early *Homo sapiens* ancestors were as large as humans today and were more powerful and physically robust. Plus, their brains were one-eighth larger than modern man's. So, it stands to reason that, among those who have Western European ancestors, there would be more like you."

"Shit," Kirkland said, "Western European nations colonized most of the planet. You're talking about hundreds of millions of people in Latin America, Canada, Australia, and parts of Africa and Asia."

"Blokes like me, mate," Stone said.

"So, who are these guys? How many of them are there? What kind of training have they had? What's their purpose?" Whelan said.

"We don't have a lot of information yet," Levell said. "We first learned of their existence when they showed up for the annual special forces competition in Karaganda, Kazakhstan. They were being trained by Chinese special forces operators under the guidance of the former minister of finance of China, a man named Zheng. Supposedly, he referred to them as the 'Bad Dogs.'"

"Wasn't Zheng a major player in the Alliance for Global Unity?" Whelan said.

"Yes, he was AGU's second in command. Our assets in AGU advised that he seemed to be positioning himself to take control of the organization. Those sources, plus ones we have in China, are the reason we know about the existence of these 'gifted' individuals," Levell said, using the term that was generally applied to distinguish the Dogs from Norms.

"So, why are these guys germane to this discussion about the missing nukes?" Larsen said.

"Because we don't know where they are," Levell said grimly.

"Meaning," Stensen said, "they could be in Higuerillas, which would complicate our operation."

Levell nodded.

"Is there anyone who might know their current where-abouts?" Whelan said.

Levell nodded again. "AGU's head, Harland Fairchilde, worked closely with Zheng. Undoubtedly, he knows where they are and what their assignment is."

"Not a problem," Larsen said, smiling his bad smile. "I'm sure we can get Mr. Fairchilde to sing like a bluebird."

"There's an easier way than that," Levell said, and looked at Whelan. "An acquaintance of yours from your recent misadventure with Maksym probably knows. He works for Fairchilde."

Whelan said, "Does he have a name?"

"Andrei Ulyanin."

PART FOUR

MAD DOGS

"Now remember: When things look bad and it looks like you're not gonna make it, then you gotta get mean. I mean plumb mad-dog mean." –Clint Eastwood (*The Outlaw Josey Wales*)

CHAPTER 56

BRIGHTON BEACH

LEVELL TOLD Whelan and Larsen that Ulyanin, the man who had saved their lives in Ireland, worked for the head of the AGU. And that he moved back and forth between Fairchilde's office in Manhattan and the estate on Long Island. Much of the rest of the time he hung out in a bar in Brighton Beach patronized exclusively by Russians.

"How would you know that?" Whelan asked.

Levell, smiling slyly, said, "What I know shouldn't surprise you. It's what I don't know that should."

WHELAN AND LARSEN had gone out to Brighton Beach and staked out the bar that was three doors off Brighton Beach Avenue on Sixth Street. It was housed in an ancient two-story red brick building with failing shops at ground level and mostly seedy flats above. The bar's door was made of heavy wood that had been painted red countless times, evidenced by areas where some of the more recent coats had peeled off or been chipped away. A small sign in Cyrillic script above the door identified the place as *Таверна Магазин*, the Little Bear Tavern. Whelan wondered if the name was intended to refer to Russia's long-reigning current despot.

There was a lot of street noise and traffic was heavy on Brighton Beach Avenue. The air was filled with unpleasant smells—exhaust from trucks, buses, and automobiles, the aging buildings, unwashed bodies passing by, and the ubiquitous cigarette smoke.

After a long wait on a cold, gray, wet afternoon, the two men spotted Ulyanin walking down Sixth Avenue from the BMT Brighton Line station. The Russian had his long, double-breasted Burberry trench coat cinched tight at the waist and the collar. A fedora shielded his head from the endless drizzle. His hands were stuffed into the pockets of the coat. Although his head was down to protect his eyes from the rain, he appeared to easily spot the two large, formidable looking men approaching him. His right hand began to emerge from the pocket.

Whelan had no doubt that it was wrapped around the butt of a sidearm. He and Larsen held both hands up, palms outward and empty.

Ulyanin stopped under a small tattered and faded awning in front of a deli. His right hand remained half in, half out of the pocket.

The two Dogs stopped two feet in front of him, as Ulyanin stared at them without expression.

"We'd like to talk with you," Whelan said.

Ulyanin said nothing.

"We're grateful for what you did in Dingle."

"You are mistaken. You owe me nothing. I didn't do it for

you. My purpose was solely to kill Maksym to avenge a friend's murder."

"Maybe," Whelan said, "but in the process you not only saved Sven's and my lives, but also my...former wife's and my sons'. I'm grateful for that."

Ulyanin stared impassively at the two men, locking eyes with each for a few seconds. He began to step around them, then stopped. "Perhaps there is something. When you are an independent operator as I am, sometimes you have to have cards in more than one game."

"Are you offering your services to the SAS?" Whelan said.

"It could come to that. I like to know that I have another port in case of a storm."

"That would strictly be Levell's call," Whelan said. "What you did for Sven and me was personal to us and won't carry much weight with him. You'd have to offer him something that has value to him."

"As a down payment, tell Levell that there are five rogue nukes in the hands of Islamic terrorists in Mexico. They are in the process of being distributed to locations in your country."

"That much we already know," Whelan said. "What are the destinations of these nukes?"

Ulyanin shrugged. "I don't know."

"Tell us something *we* don't know."

"Fairchilde heads a group called the Alliance for Global Unity. AGU assembled a group of men very much like you and your comrades. They call them the Bad Dogs, and their purpose is to kill all of you."

"Good luck with that," Larsen said and smiled his bad smile.

It caused Ulyanin's eyes to blink a couple of times. He went on to describe the group of men Zheng had assembled. He finished by saying, "My employer, Harland Fairchilde, told me these Bad Dogs are guarding the nukes in Mexico, a place called Higuerillas." Ulyanin went on to tell Whelan and Larsen everything he'd learned about the nukes while in Fairchilde's employ.

When he finished, Whelan said, "That does have some value. I'll let Levell know where it came from."

Ulyanin nodded curtly. This time he stepped around them and walked toward the scarred red door of Little Bear Tavern.

CHAPTER 57
THE LODGE

ALMEIDA TROTTED down the stone steps that led from the library to the well-hidden wine cellar/conference area below. The other Dogs were already seated around the large mahogany table. Almeida said excitedly, "I just saw that hot chick Ashlee again."

Kirkland grinned. "Not that it will do you any good."

"Yeah, wiseass? It so happens she's going out with me for drinks when she gets off." Almeida paused for a beat then said, "And after that we're both gonna get off." He leered at Kirkland.

"Keep it in your pants, Rafe. We're working tonight," Whelan said.

"You gotta be shittin' me," Almeida said incredulously. "Tell me you're just yanking my chain."

"We're shoving off for Mexico asap. Got a lot of planning and preparation to do. Plant your ass in that chair and pay attention." Whelan pointed to an empty seat at the table.

Almeida sat down begrudgingly. "This sucks," he said with a sullen expression.

Kirkland said, "Why do I have the feeling this next operation going to be another 'Mission Impossible.'"

"Why is it there are never any easy ones?" Thomas said.

"Yeah, we nearly got snuffed in Doha," Almeida said. "And the next one, on that island in Mexico, was even worse. How come nothin' ever goes right?"

"Hey," Stensen said, "remember what Nietzsche said, 'That which does not kill us, makes us stronger.' A little adversity comes along and you start whining like wimps." He smiled. It gave his sharp, angular features a predatory look.

"We get these assignments because we're us. Norms couldn't handle them," Whelan said.

"If they get any more 'challenging,' *we* won't be able to handle them either," Thomas said.

Whelan said, "Here's our chance to find out. The added degree of difficulty on this one is that the nukes aren't on a deserted island this time. They're in a populated area, making infil and exfil more complicated. In addition to the usual jihadi watchdogs, drug gangs are warring over the turf, Mexican Marines are actively engaging the gangs, and AGU recruited and trained a group like us."

Kirkland said, "Are you saying they're...not Norms. They're...gifted."

"That's it," Whelan said.

"That sounds like bloody Rafferty's rules, mate," Stone said.

Larsen scowled. "What does that mean?"

"Chaos, but seriously, no worries, mate. She'll be apples."

"And what the hell does *that* mean?" Larsen said.

Stone grinned. "It'll be all right."

"How do you figure that, Stone? Other than training against each other, we've never encountered anyone like us, particularly not when our lives are on the line," Thomas said.

"So?" Stensen said. "It still goes back to Nietzsche."

Thomas gave Stensen a long, grim stare.

"Do these guys have a name?" Kirkland said.

"Get this," Whelan paused, and with a deadpan expression, said, "They're called the 'Bad Dogs.'"

Thomas said, "What's your strategy for fighting these new guys?"

"They're probably lifelong thugs and killers, but they'll be new at this kind of game. We were recruited, trained, and utilized in intense combat situations when we were twenty-years-old. For the past two years we've been in one hot zone after the other from the assault on Chaim Laski's fortified mansion to the caper on Isla El Idolo."

"Yeah," Almeida said, "and don't forget Doha."

"Plus, the assault on the HAC camp just over the border in Mexico," Kirkland said.

"And kidnapping the leader of the Zetas," Stensen said.

"My point exactly," Whelan said. "This may be their first rodeo, but we've seen this film before."

"Remember the famous quote: 'Let's not be overconfident, we still have to count the votes,'" Thomas said.

"I get your point, and it's valid," Whelan said, "but let's remember what we've always done better than anyone."

"Hunt and kill," Stensen said.

"Right."

Thomas leaned over the table on his elbows. "Yeah, but it's more than a little different this time."

"True," Whelan said. "They're formidable for sure, but they've never encountered anyone like us, anyone with our experience, skill sets, and 'gifts.'"

Thomas shook his head slowly. "I don't know, man."

"Sounds like a worthy challenge," Kirkland said. "When do we start?"

"Tonight. They could move those nukes at any time."

"What's the strategy where the ragheads, gangbangers, and Marines are concerned?" Stone said.

"Butch and Sundance," Whelan said.

"You mean we make it up as we go?" Stensen said.

"Yeah, we don't have the luxury of time to plot out where everyone is, how many there are, or what they're equipped with. We have to move right now and develop tactics as things develop."

"When do we shove off?" Larsen said.

Whelan reflexively glanced at his combat watch. "In one hour."

Almeida jumped up and pounded his fist once on the table. "One fuckin' hour?"

"Forget your rendezvous with Ashlee," Whelan said. "If you're skillful enough to survive the mission, you can ask her for a raincheck when you get back."

"Then I'll opt to sit this one out."

"And I'll opt to ask Sven, Nick, and Marc to change your mind."

Almeida looked at the other three men. Kirkland, with a pleasant smile, had slid his katana from its scabbard and laid it on the table. Stensen also was smiling. And the red dots in the centers of his eyes suddenly blazed like a solar flare. Larsen just smiled. His bad smile. Almeida quickly sat down.

"Alright, mate," Stone said, "what about the minor details such as equipment?"

"I've been over this with Levell. As we speak, a chopper is being loaded in Texas with the gear I think we'll need."

"And the infil and exfil?" Thomas said.

"I'm working on the infil. After that, it's all Butch and Sundance."

Thomas stared at Whelan for a long moment. "We've never operated without an exfil plan."

"We are this time," Whelan said.

"It's different this time, Quent, because of a single word. Nukes," Larsen said.

"It's two words," Stensen said. "Rogue nukes."

Shaking his head, as if in disbelief, Thomas said, "Dear God, it's a suicide mission."

CHAPTER 58

HIGUERILLAS: BAD DOGS I

THE SQUATTER FISHING village of Las Higuerillas was one of the countless settlements scattered around the Laguna Madre that stretched two-hundred-seventy-seven miles from the Nueces River in Texas to the Rió Soto la Marina in Tamaulipas, Mexico. It was four to five miles at its widest, but only three feet deep on average. Because of its shallowness and limited supply of fresh water, it was one of only six hypersaline lagoons on the planet.

The village was about one-and-a quarter miles long and less than one-half mile at widest point. Its population of less than twenty-five-hundred people scraped out an existence harvesting the bounty of the lagoon which included mullet, drum, oyster, trout and sand shark, but most importantly shrimp. In an average year, shrimpers using fixed-net systems called charangas would haul roughly four thousand tons from the lagoon. It was the village's economic base industry, but it didn't pay well. Working fulltime, the average shrimper made about six-hundred dollars a month.

The village was an eclectic blend of mostly old, poorly cared for residential and commercial buildings. Most were made of crumbling unpainted cinder block stained by mold or embraced in a death grip by wild, predatory vines. The few buildings that had been painted hadn't seen a fresh coat in many years. Most of the dwellings had no window glass, only tattered canvas-like material that draped the openings like an ill-fitting garment.

Mixed in at random were a few strikingly well-maintained places of business or homes, some of which were two-story structures with wrought iron-railed balconies. All had barred windows and reinforced doors. These were occupied by the few residents who were making significant money, meaning crime-connected.

While the average temperature was a dry and pleasant 70°F in late January, the air was redolent with the smells of exhaust gases, cigarette smoke, Mexican cuisine, and the nearby Laguna Madre. During the day and early parts of the evening, the ear was assaulted by the sounds of traffic and the hordes of locals milling about the streets and filling the ubiquitous bars, tabernas, cafeterías, and restaurantes.

Although lined with aged cars, trucks, and motor scooters on one side only, the streets were surprisingly uncluttered except for an occasional rusted, fat-tired bicycle blocking a section of sidewalk.

On a side street across from the waterfront was a rectangular-shaped two-story building. It looked as if it had once been white-washed, but now was filthy and badly faded. Its plainness was broken by a green, two-foot wide stripe painted along the bottom of the exterior walls and by a row of small rectangular windows about fifteen feet above the ground and just below the flat roof. The street it fronted on was poured concrete and badly cracked.

Inside, five large, exceptionally powerful looking men were crowded together on overturned citrus crates watching a movie on the tiny screen of an iPad. Each was kitted out with a variety of sidearms and blades. The interior of the building was in worse shape than its exterior. The pervasive smell of industrial fluids mixed with the odors of long-dead sea life revealed the operational history of the building. The badly rusted machinery indicated that the structure hadn't been used commercially in years. There was a staircase at each end of the building that provided access to the second floor. In the middle of the building, five large rucksacks were lined up in a row. Six Middle Eastern-looking men armed with AK-47s were standing guard over them, while warily watching the other five men out of the corners of their eyes. On the floor near the rucksacks was the form of another person, ragged, bloodied, and shackled.

"Hey, Punjab," one of the five large men, Gage Stark, said to a guard. "Get me a fucking beer. And if it ain't cold, I'll rip your fucking balls off." Stark's accent was unmistakably Cockney.

The man sharing the crate with him said, "I'd like it if you ripped his balls off anyway. The fucking raghead." His name was Horst Geissler and he spoke with a heavy German accent.

A man with a shaved head was sitting on another crate and looked up angrily. "You call my brother Muslims 'ragheads' one more time and I'll rip your fucking balls off." This man's name was Mehmet Karga and he was a Turk.

Yet another of the five, a Frenchman whose name was Alard Deschamps, said "Aw, don't worry about the Turk. He's always got a hard-on about something."

Karga, the Turk, suddenly stood up. "Yeah, Frenchie? Maybe I start with you." He took a step toward Deschamps.

The fifth man, Sergei Kruchinkin, leaped to his feet and in a heavy Russian accent said, "If anyone does ass-kicking, I do it." He looked at the other four and said, "We are needing drink." He motioned with his head and started walking toward the door. The others followed him.

One of the Middle Eastern men yelled after them, "Hey, where do you go? You are supposed to stay here with the bombs."

"Bugger off, bloke," Stark said threateningly.

On the shore of the lagoon across the street from the decrepit warehouse was a small bar with a red tin roof and open-air seating under palm-thatched roofs on either side. It was made of stuccoed cinder blocks and painted red, white, and blue. The name painted across the lintel over the door was "*El Tamaulipan.*" The onshore breeze carried the smell of decaying sea and plant life in the Laguna Madre. The bar itself stunk of mold, wood rot, stale beer, vomit, and an inefficient sewer system. In a corner of the bar, two elderly musicians strummed ancient guitars and sang Mexican folk songs. An upturned sombrero at their feet held a few pesos.

The large five men sat in one of the open-air areas in cheap white plastic chairs around a table made from a large cable spool. Several locals had been sitting at nearby tables. They took one look at the huge, heavily armed men covered with tattoos and frightening scars and quickly moved to the open area on the other side of the small bar building.

Wrinkling his nose, Geissler said, "Fuck! Does no one in this town bathe?"

"We ain't exactly smellin' like no roses ourselves," Stark said.

"In Russia, we are having shit houses that smell better than this," Kruchinkin said.

A young girl who didn't look like she was older than thirteen took their drink orders. She was careful not to make eye contact with any of the men. The Turk stared at her like a hungry puma eying an elk.

"Don't go there, Karga. We don't need troubles with local police," Kruchinkin said.

"Maybe the bloody wog is getting impatient to meet his seventy-two virgins," Stark said.

"Maybe," Karga said, "I am impatient to kill you."

"And maybe," Kruchinkin said, "you are dumbest shits I ever see. Look around you. There is more money here for the taking than any of you have ever seen."

"Whatcha talkin' about, Ruskie? I don't see nothin' here but filth and poverty. It's fuckin' Mexico," Stark said.

Kruchinkin's lips curled back into a cross between a smile and a sneer. "Because you are stupid, all of you. You spend time fighting with each other because you afraid you have smaller cock. Wake the fuck up! There is no money in your cock."

"*Oui?*" Deschamps said. "Then where is this money? It is not in babysitting five nuclear weapons with a group of suicidal camel jockeys."

The other four men all looked at Kruchinkin. "Is true, this town is shithole. But what you see when you look carefully?"

None of the others spoke.

"Is not all slum. You see very nice house, very expensive auto. These things take money, real money, not fucking shrimp." Kruchinkin said 'shrimp' like it was the most derogatory of words. "What else you see if you keep eyes open? Boats! Boats come in full and dock day and night. They *unload* cargo, not put on shrimp. Cargo loaded onto trucks. Then trucks go north. What is north?"

No one spoke for a few moments, then Geissler said, "*Americanische.*"

"*Da!*" Kruchinkin said and pounded the top of the table with his fist for emphasis. "*Amerikantsy.*"

"Drugs," Deschamps said.

"Of course, is drugs," Kruchinkin said.

"What that has to do with us?" Karga said in broken English.

"What we are doing best?" Kruchinkin said.

"Stealing," Geissler said.

"Killing," Karga said.

"Criminal behavior," Deschamps said with a sly grin.

"Yes, all that and more. It is who we are," Kruchinkin said. "And we are unlike everyone else. We are supermans. Why we work as hired guns for some fucking missing Chinaman, when we can make real money?"

"The bloke's not missing," Stark said. "He's bloody dead."

"How you are knowing he is dead?" Kruchinkin said.

"It's bloody China. If you're missing, you're dead. That's how it works."

"Is no matter," Kruchinkin said. "The ragheads load bombs on boat tonight, then we get paid by Abdel Sabbah. After that, we are taking over drug business."

"Ah, *mon ami*, I am thinking the drug lords may not be eager to cooperate," Deschamps said with a patronizing smile.

"Including the five like us who are on the other shift, we are ten special peoples" Kruchinkin said. "We are killing the local gang leaders and taking their business. The cartels will deal with us or we will kill their leaders too. Who can stand against us?"

Karga said, "That is five too many."

Geissler agreed. "*Ja,* we don't need to share the money. I say we kill the others tonight."

The other four nodded slowly, thoughtfully.

"And," Kruchinkin said, leaning forward and staring at the other men for a few seconds each. "We are actually sitting on another way to make big money and do it now."

"I, for one, hate suspense," Stark said. "Tell us what the fuck it is."

CHAPTER 59

HIGUERILLAS: INFIL

A SUBSTANTIALLY MODIFIED black Sikorsky Sea King rose slowly and quietly from the isolated airstrip near the Mexican border in South Texas. At cruising speed, the two General Electric turboshaft engines would have Whelan and the other Dogs at their objective in less than thirty minutes.

The modifications not only damped the chopper's noise significantly, they also reduced visual, radar, infrared and acoustic signatures. It also featured a digital camouflage system. The result was that, unlike typical choppers, this bird emitted very little noise, making it the perfect delivery vehicle for the mission at hand.

The Dogs sat in jump seats behind the pilots, three on one side of the aircraft and four on the other. They were wearing black, two-millimeter, highly flexible wet suits specially designed for combat conditions. All means of identifying the source of the clothing had been removed. None of the men carried any identification. The exposed areas of their hands and faces had been covered with camouflage face paint.

They were equipped with the same type of enhanced night-vision goggles, or ENVGs, that they'd used on Isla El Idolo. The ENVGs fused image intensification technology with thermal imagery for optimal night operations and incorporated the latest in augmented reality technology. The AR-enabled display could overlay images from a satellite or overhead drone directly onto the Dogs' field of vision. In an urban environment, it could superimpose maps, blueprints and directions as they stalked a quarry in an unfamiliar area. A representative of the Mueller brothers' lab had told Whelan and the others that by combining image-recognition software with AR, it would soon be possible to focus on someone and instantly see information from their Facebook, Twitter, Amazon, LinkedIn or other online profiles. Another pending application would enable pointing at a building and immediately getting its floorplans and schematics.

The men kept to their usual pre-combat routines. Kirkland quietly honed his already razor-sharp katana. Thomas meditated. Stensen and Stone catnapped. Almeida bitched to himself about missing the date with Ashlee Ericksen. Larsen and Whelan discussed the plan of attack.

The pilot curved out over the Gulf of Mexico after takeoff then came back over land once they were below the border. He kept the bird fifty feet above the surface as he headed south across the endless salt marshes that fed Laguna Madre. When the marshes opened into the lagoon itself, he swung the chopper around and came in from the west toward Las Higuerillas, settling the amphibious craft carefully into the water on the back-side of the middle of three small spoil deposit islands. They had been created from the materials dredged to deepen the shipping channel along the town's waterfront. Bushes and small trees had already begun to grow on them in the humid, tropical environment.

The seven men swiftly unloaded their gear, including three DPVs, newly developed by a Mueller brothers' armaments lab. The DPVs used two independent steerable, low noise electronic thrusters with a separate lithium-ion battery powering each. The electric motors and batteries were encased in pressure-resistant, watertight casing.

The chopper was unloaded in a matter of minutes. The pilot had been instructed to keep the bird in place pending the Dogs' return. Whelan reminded him they might be coming in hot and the copilot needed to be ready to man the M60D machine gun mounted at the starboard side forward door.

"How far are we from the town's waterfront?" Larsen said.

"Less than one-hundred yards away," Whelan said. "But that's as the crow flies. Our route will be closer to four-hundred yards."

"We're using rebreathers and diver propulsion vehicles to cross the channel?"

"Yeah, Drägers and DPVs."

"How deep's the channel?"

"The Mexican government is in the early stages of developing Higuerillas into a major port facility. In preparation, the channel recently was deepened to thirty feet."

"Is there a tide, current, or boat traffic to consider?"

"It's slack tide and there shouldn't be any traffic at this hour."

"Why is everything we do always at zero dark thirty?" Almeida said.

"What, a bit too early for you, mate?" Stone joked.

All seven Dogs slipped on compact closed-circuit rebreathers, in this case manufactured by Dräger. They would emit no telltale bubbles. Whelan, Almeida, and Stone were the most experienced divers. Each took control of a DPV. Kirkland and Stensen each grabbed a line trailing off Almeida's. Thomas attached a semi-buoyant watertight bag of gear to a line from Stone's DPV then grabbed the other line. Larsen did the same with Whelan's craft.

With Whelan in the lead, the three DPVs rounded the islet and submerged in the deeper water as they headed into the channel. The submersibles had been specially modified to accommodate the loads they were carrying. But the size of the men and the weight of the bags made for slow going. There were two small lights on the rear of Whelan's DPV. While shielded from view from the surface, they were there for the other two submersibles to follow in the otherwise blackout conditions.

Because of the murkiness of the water and absence of light, there was a row of slightly illuminated instruments easily readable by the pilot of each craft. One was a compass. Another was a highly accurate depth gauge. The third was a navigation panel featuring a moving map display along with data from a bottom scanning SONAR.

It took almost fifteen minutes to travel from the islet to a point on the seawall just north of the now-closed *El Tamaulipan* bar. It was fifty yards from there to the warehouse where the signal had been sent by Turan's phone. While Stone took sentry duty, the men tied the DPVs under a wooden pier that extended out thirty feet from the seawall and stashed their rebreathers under a joist. They removed body armor, weapons, spare magazines, ENVGs, and comm gear from the two watertight bags. Each man strapped ceramic-polymer composite body armor wrapped on both sides with one-hundred layers of graphene over their combat wetsuits.

When they finished checking their weapons and comm gear, Whelan said, "This is our last chance to get those nukes. Failure is not an option."

CHAPTER 60

HIGUERILLAS: BAD DOGS II

KRUCHINKIN and his four comrades finished their drinks at *El Tamaulipan* and walked back to the warehouse across the street. He had explained to the others his second scheme for making easy money. And a lot of it. Only the Frenchman, Alard Deschamps, had been skeptical. But even he was seduced by the prospect of countless millions, and it sounded more realistic than the proposal that they take over the drug business.

With their extraordinary speed and power, Kruchinkin and the others quickly and brutally overpowered Abdel Sabbah's six mujahidin guarding the nuclear devices. They bound and gagged them and closeted them in a small room under the staircase in the rear of the building.

Thirty minutes later, Sabbah arrived in a battered white Ford extended-length cargo van. He left its engine running as he hurried into the warehouse. He sized up the situation immediately. "Where are my men?"

"They take coffee break," Kruchinkin said with a cold-eyed

smile. "We," he motioned to include his other four colleagues standing nearby, "have business deal for you."

"What is this?" Sabbah said. "You are getting greedy? No, we already have a deal."

"That was Chinaman's deal. Chinaman gone. We are making new deal."

"No! You are being overpaid as it is. You do nothing but drink alcohol across the street and belittle my men. They are the true warriors, not you kafirs."

"You better watch your tongue, you fuckin' wog," Stark said.

"Or what? You'll kill me, assuring that you will never be paid?" Sabbah put his hand on the butt of the 9 mm CZ 75 stuffed in the waistband of his jeans.

With a benign smile, Kruchinkin stepped between Stark and Sabbah. "Is not good to get pissed. We have work to do." He pointed to the five large rucksacks and said, "Bombs must be loaded on ship tonight. We are strongest. We will load. You are telling us where is ship."

"No, you will tell me where my men are. We will handle the loading of the devices ourselves. As the American president likes to say, 'You are fired.'"

The smile instantly vanished from the Russian's face, replaced by a snarl. Faster than Sabbah could react, Kruchinkin snatched the weapon from Sabbah's waistband and smashed it across the side of the Arab's head. Semi-conscious and beginning to bleed profusely, Sabbah collapsed to his hands and knees on the filthy floor.

Kruchinkin pointed to Stark and said, "Bring one raghead out here."

Moments later, the Brit returned with one of the bound mujahidin.

Kruchinkin grabbed the collar of Sabbah's shirt and yanked

him to his feet, slapping him hard twice to clear the man's head. "This is your man, yes?"

A free-flowing stream of blood ran down the left side of Sabbah's face from the deep gash above his zygomatic bone. He blinked several times, as if trying to organize his thoughts.

Kruchinkin moved around behind Sabbah and grabbed his upper arms in a grip so tight it made the Arab wince.

"You are watching, yes?" Kruchinkin nodded at Geissler.

The big German slowly pulled a Steyr L-A1 .40 caliber pistol from a holster slung under his right arm. With purposeful slowness, he screwed a suppressor onto the weapon's muzzle. It had a magazine capacity of twelve rounds, but he needed only one to put a slug in the head of the bound man.

Some of the victim's blood spattered on Sabbah. He recoiled in horror.

"Now," Kruchinkin said, as he released the Arab, "you are cooperating, yes? If no, we have five more of your men."

In response, Sabbah spit on him.

Surprisingly, Kruchinkin didn't explode in fury. Instead, he casually wiped the spittle from his face and said, "You are not in negotiating position. You are needing us. Tell us where boat is. We load you, your men, and bombs on board and you give us all your money. Is easy, yes?" He smiled disarmingly. "We even put in something extra. We kill your problem child for you." He nodded in the direction of the still form clothed in bloody rags and lying shackled on the floor near the nukes.

Karga walked over to the person and began urinating on him. He looked back at Sabbah and said, "See, maybe we drown him." When he was finished, he savagely kicked the person he had just peed on.

ABDEL SABBAH STARED at the massive Russian for several moments. He looked around the warehouse space as if hoping to find an alternative to his situation. Instead, he saw five large bodies stacked in a dark corner. He realized they were the other five men Zheng had trained. Sabbah recognized he was in a no-win situation. The words of Nadir Shah ran through his head: "Westerners cannot be trusted. They all are greedy demons." It definitely was greed that had caused his current conundrum. He could refuse to renegotiate the deal with Kruchinkin and his comrades, in which case they undoubtedly would kill him and his mujahidin. The result would be the nukes would never achieve Shah's goal of destroying the West's will to fight.

The only alternative would be to accept Kruchinkin's offer and hope the Russian carried through on it. Shah liked to say that the only person more treacherous than a Chinese was a Russian. On the other hand, it was the only alternative that offered any hope for completing the mission. If the bombs weren't detonated in American cities, Shah and the caliphate were doomed.

"Alright. I agree to the new terms."

"Now, that's a good wog," Stark said. He nodded at Geissler and they grabbed a rucksack in each hand and carried them to the van. Deschamps picked up the last one and followed them. The three of them returned to the spot where Kruchinkin and Sabbah were standing.

"All that is left is knowing where boat is and you pay us, then we kill prisoner over there." He jerked his head toward the shackled, now-wet prisoner.

Sabbah realized that once the Russian knew where the transport ship was docked, he and his mujahidin were expendable. "My men and I will show you where it is. Let's all get in the van."

CHAPTER 61

HIGUERILLAS: INSIDE THE WIRE

As THEY MOVED out from beneath the pier, Almeida nudged Stone and said, "This is Mexico. We're all gonna get the screaming shits from being in this water. Probably gonna die from it before anybody can shoot us."

"Nah, mate, it's ocean water. The cut's just around the bend there," the Aussie said with a grin.

They spread out along the seawall, picking their way carefully through the rocks and other non-biodegradable debris that had been discarded over the decades. When there was about ten feet between each man, they paused as if on cue.

Whelan carefully raised his eyes above the cap of the seawall. The area between it and the warehouse was mostly open space except for two small open-air tiki huts. The warehouse was aglow with interior lights, its doors wide open. To Whelan, there was something sinister about the scene, like an emotional trigger in an M. Night Shyamalan movie.

He slid below the seawall's cap. Using his comm gear, he

said, "Something's going on. The place is lit up like a church on Christmas Eve."

"Maybe we've caught them in the process of moving the nukes," Thomas said.

Stensen said dryly, "Like they say, timing is everything."

"We're goin' inside the wire. This is where the pucker factor starts," Almeida said.

Whelan turned toward Kirkland. "As we expected, there are CCTV security cameras in the corners of the building, and they undoubtedly have cell phones. Work your magic, Marc."

Kirkland held up a black device that was about the size of a smart phone, but twice as thick. It had two short antenna-like projections at the top. He pressed a button on the side and a small, bright green light came on near one of the antennas, indicating the device was operational. He pressed a rocker switch on the bottom left side of the device, then another rocker on the bottom right. The first switch caused the device to emit a low frequency signal, 16kHz, that scrambled the signal from the cameras to the monitors inside the warehouse. The second switch activated another signal that interfered with cell phone operations within a radius of three hundred feet without affecting the comm gear the Dogs were using.

On Whelan's signal, the seven men swiftly and silently scaled the seawall and sprinted toward the warehouse. Spreading out as they went, every fifteen feet two or three of them would drop to a knee, weapons at the ready. The others would race fifteen feet forward then follow suit. They used the leapfrog technique all the way to the shelter of the warehouse walls.

With their Augmented-Reality ENVGs, they were able to see satellite images of the warehouse and surrounding area projected on their faceplates like a "heads-up" display, or HUD, on an automobile's windshield. Using a single finger with a plastic-like cap, they could move the image around as well as zoom in or out, isolate on an image and expand it.

Kirkland and Whelan approached the wide main entrance to the building and pressed against the wall on either side. Glancing inside for an instant, they saw five men who, physically, looked surprisingly like the Dogs themselves. The men were standing in a cluster and appeared to be having a discussion.

Larsen and Stensen took up positions where they could surveil the front of the warehouse and either side. Whelan directed Stone, Thomas, and Almeida to the far end of the building where they found another door. It was locked.

"Stonie, blow it but wait for my signal," Whelan said. He reached high above his head on the frame of the entranceway and, using high strength double-sided adhesive, affixed a high-resolution two-millimeter lens to it. The lens was attached to a flexible fiber-optic cable that fed into a small device that emitted a clear video image that was displayed on the Dogs HUDs. Kirkland attached the device to the wall just outside the entrance.

In a cursory sweep of the interior, they noticed the bodies of five men who appeared to be as large and powerfully built as the men who were having the discussion.

Checking the surrounding area again on his HUD, Whelan saw an extended-length white cargo van approaching on the street that ran along the side of the warehouse. He said "Company's coming." Motioning to Kirkland, the two men moved away from the entranceway, taking up new positions just around the corner where they'd be out of sight from anyone entering the building.

The driver pulled the van to the curb near the entrance and got out, leaving the engine running. He was a tall Middle Eastern-looking man with a trimmed beard and a decidedly hooked nose. He wore faded blue jeans, badly scuffed engineer boots, and long-sleeved shirt in a faded blue plaid. The newcomer strode into the warehouse like he owned it, then stopped and looked around as if puzzled.

The Dogs watched their displays in silence as Kirkland manipulated the lens to reveal the activities inside the warehouse.

They saw the newcomer begin arguing with the five large, powerfully-built men. Their apparent leader pointed toward five large rucksacks lined up on the floor of the warehouse. The newcomer yelled something at him. The leader instantly snatched a weapon from the newcomer's waistband and smashed it into the side of his head, felling him.

"What the fuck's goin' on in there?" Almeida whispered into his comm gear.

"Looks like a dick measuring contest," Stensen said.

"Zip it," Whelan said as they watched one of the big men walk to the far end of the building and return a moment later with a man who was bound and gagged. The leader yanked the injured man to his feet and slapped him twice.

They watched as one of the other five men pulled a weapon from a shoulder holster and shot the bound man in the head. In response, the man from the white cargo van appeared to spit on the leader.

"That was stupid," Kirkland said.

As the newcomer and the leader seemed to discuss something for a few minutes, another of the five big men walked over to what had appeared to be a bundle of clothes lying on the floor near the rucksacks. He spent a few moments urinating on it then gave it a savage kick as Kirkland focused the camera in on the scene.

"Shit!" Kirkland said. "That's a person."

The newcomer seemed to come to an agreement with the five men. He shrugged his shoulders and nodded, as if in defeat. The man who had just shot the bound man nodded at another one of the five. They walked over to the rucksacks and grabbed one in each hand. A third large man picked up the last one. They carried them out to the van and stowed them in the cargo area.

"Their next stop will be a loading dock somewhere nearby. Probably have a ship and more armed men there. We've got to stop them here," Whelan said.

The satphone in a special compartment of Whelan's combat wetsuit began to vibrate. He unfastened the opening of the watertight pocket and fished it out.

Levell said, "The satellite is picking up additional heat signatures clustered near the rear of the building. There's a lot of motion, like they're struggling. It looks like they may be confined in a tight space. Can you see them?"

"No, just the five big guys and the Arab in the middle of the room. I think there's a seventh person trussed up near the nukes, but he may be dead."

"No, we're getting that signature too."

"Stone, Thomas, and Almeida are at the far side of the building, but they're outside waiting for my signal to blow the door."

"We see their signatures. The ones I'm talking about are inside the warehouse."

CHAPTER 62

HIGUERILLAS: DOG FIGHT

THE DOOR to the space under the stairs burst open and five heavily bearded mujahidin tumbled out one after the other. They stood still, trying to adjust to the light.

Kruchinkin swore and looked around at his other men. "Who is dumb shit that not tie them securely?"

Then the mujahidin saw Kruchinkin and his comrades staring at them. They charged the Russian and the others in unison, screaming "*Allahu Akbar.*"

"Blow the door, Stonie," Whelan said into his throat mic.

Sabbah moved quickly, sprinting toward the van.

Kruchinkin yelled to his men, "Kill the ragheads," and took off after Sabbah. He caught up to him at the van and both jumped into it with Sabbah driving. The tires squealed against the pavement as the aging truck spun a U-turn and began accelerating down the street that paralleled the waterfront.

"Nick," Whelan said, "can you get a shot at the van?" Instantly, he heard the noise of several suppressed shots followed immediately by the sounds of slugs tearing through metal and glass in the distance.

An explosion erupted in the back of the building just as the angry mujahidin threw themselves at the four muscular men who, along with Kruchinkin, had previously tied, gagged, and stuffed them into the space under the stairwell. Simultaneously, the door at the rear of the warehouse slammed inward from the blast. Stone, Thomas, and Almeida charged through the opening. Whelan, Kirkland, and Larsen burst through the front entrance. All weapons were focused on the carnage occurring in front of them.

Even with their strength enhanced by the high levels of adrenaline caused by rage, the five mujahidin were still Norms, and no match for the four massive scarred and tattooed men they'd attacked. In mere seconds, Karga, Deschamps, Geissler, and Stark literally had torn the Arabs to pieces with their bare hands. The four men stood, covered in their opponents' blood and scraps of body matter, staring at the Dogs.

"You have guns. We do not," Geissler said in his thick German accent. "Put them down and fight like men."

Whelan sent a slug through the massive calf of Geissler's right leg. The German screamed in pain and collapsed.

"Tie these motherfuckers up. Real secure," Whelan said. "And Stonie, if any of them give you any reason at all, shoot them in the head. Several times." He turned to Stensen, who had just trotted up. "Were you able to stop the van?"

"Negative."

"Shit! The nukes are in it." He yanked the satphone from its compartment in his wetsuit and spoke into it. "Do you have a satellite bead on that van that just left here?"

Levell said, "Yeah, it's stopping about a quarter of a mile south of you."

"What's there?"

"Looks like a small seafood processing facility. There's a pier extending out. A ship, maybe seventy-five or eighty feet, tied up. Lot of activity right now. Looks like the ship could be about to sail."

Whelan stuffed the phone back in its pocket and turned to Almeida. "Rafe, you've got a history of stealing things. Think you can rip off one of these local scows?"

"Piece of cake," Almeida said with genuine pride. "How big?"

"Big enough to haul our guys, these four scumballs, and whoever that is on the floor over there."

"What about you?" Thomas said. "Aren't you coming with us?"

Whelan shook his head. "No, Sven and I are going after the nukes."

"But how are you going to exfil? If the Mexicans get you, you'll never see the light of day again."

Whelan and Larsen were already in motion. "We don't have time to discuss the finer points of extraction," Whelan said over his shoulder.

"It's the Butch and Sundance thing," Larsen said with a smile. His bad smile.

WHELAN AND LARSEN ran the five hundred or so yards from the warehouse to the seafood processing plant full out, as if the devil were chasing them. Considering their goal, he may have been.

They lurched into the parking lot on the verge of breathlessness. The van was facing the lagoon, its lights still on and doors open. The two men took a quick look inside. It was empty except for the corpse of Abdel Sabbah. The Arab was slumped over the steering wheel. There was what appeared to be a bullet hole in the back of his head. The dash and windshield were sprayed with blood and brain matter.

"There," Whelan said, pointing toward an eighty-five-foot steel-hulled trawler at the end of a concrete pier. It was no longer tied up and was pulling slowly away into the channel. He and Larsen sprinted down the pier, intending to leap the widening gap and board the ship. Their plans were interrupted when they had to throw themselves full out on the pier's deck.

Kruchinkin was standing at the rail amidships firing at them with an assault rifle on full auto. The slugs chewed pieces out of the concrete pier very close to the two Dogs. They quickly returned fire and the Russian ducked out of sight.

Larsen looked at Whelan. "Got a plan, Butch?"

"We've come too fucking far. Let's finish this." He pulled the satphone out again. "Send that chopper asap."

A few minutes later, the stealth-modified Sea King was hovering above them. The copilot tossed a line out. The two Dogs scaled it faster than most Norms could have rappelled down.

As Whelan scrambled toward the cockpit, he saw the M60D machine gun at the starboard side forward door. It had spade grips and an aircraft ring-type sight and was fed from a 750-round box affixed to the floor. Attached to it was a canvas bag designed to capture ejected casings and links, preventing them from being sucked into the rotor blades or an engine intake.

He stepped into the cockpit and said to the pilot, "Our target is a big commercial trawler heading for open Gulf."

"Roger that." The pilot swung the nose of the bird south in the direction of the inlet or *ensenada* that connected Laguna Madre to the Gulf of Mexico.

By the time they reached the inlet, the trawler had entered it. Once it cleared the reinforced jetty at the inlet's mouth it would enter the open waters of the Gulf. Whelan directed the pilot to hover above the ship, signaling that he and Larsen would rappel to the deck. But an instant later, people appeared on its deck and began firing at the chopper. The pilot instinctively veered the bird away from the ship and off to a parallel path a quarter of a mile away.

"Isn't this bird equipped with protective armor against small arms fire?" Whelan said.

"Affirmative, but it's not completely impervious. We're carrying four Mark 46 torpedoes. Shall I launch one of them?"

"No. There are nukes onboard. Plus, the Mexicans will go batshit crazy if we plug their channel with a sunken ship."

"That's assuming we get caught," Larsen said.

"Won't matter. Uncle Sam's the most logical suspect in a caper like this. The president has enough problems south of the border. He needs as much plausible deniability as he can get."

"So how do you want to handle it?" the pilot said.

Whelan looked at the M60D. "Make a run back over the ship. Sven will light the deck up and I'll rappel down."

"Not happening," Larsen said. He looked at the copilot. "You know how to operate the M60D?"

The copilot's head bobbed up and down.

"You better be damned accurate." It came out in a low growl, punctuated by Larsen's bad smile.

The copilot wet himself.

The pilot swung the nose of the chopper back toward the ship. As the bird closed in, individuals, Whelan presumed they were mujahidin, scrambled back on deck and began firing automatic weapons at it. The copilot sprayed errant slugs everywhere except the trawler's deck. Larsen gave him a brutal shove that sent the man tumbling over his armored seat. The über-powerful Dog handled the weapon as if it were a peashooter. The cabin began to fill with smoke and the acrid smell of burnt gunpowder and hot metal. 7.62 mm slugs tore up the ship's deck and churned through flesh and bone. All but one of the surviving men on deck threw down their weapons and leaped overboard, preferring the treacherous currents of the inlet to certain death from the barrel of the machine gun.

The one man who didn't run was standing on the docking bridge, raising an American-made FIM-92 Stinger to his shoulder. The portable surface-to-air missile had been used during the Soviet invasion of Afghanistan and proved very effective at downing the invader's helicopters.

The last slug exploded from the muzzle of the M60D and the gun fell silent. Larsen looked at Whelan. "Now what's the plan, Butch?"

"Make sure the pilot holds the course."

With a noticeably strained voice, the pilot said, "No, that fucking thing will blow us right out of the sky!"

"Hold the course or I'll throw you out myself," said the man-with-no-neck.

Whelan braced himself in the cargo door and drew a bead on the rocket man's center mass. Whelan exhaled slowly and gently pressed the trigger. Given the circumstances, the shot was high. It hit the rocket-bearer in the throat. His shoulders and head snapped backward as his knees crumbled. He toppled forward triggering the launcher as he did. The warhead tore into the ship's deck below the docking bridge, resulting in a fiery explosion.

It must have affected the engines because the trawler began slowing and its wake flattened out. It appeared to be settling in the water as if seams in its hull had opened.

"Come on," Whelan said to Larsen. "If the bombs go down with it, Mexico gets to join the nuclear club."

"Bad idea," Larsen said and turned to the pilot and copilot. "Keep this bird right over the ship. If you don't, I'll find you and kill you and everyone who's ever lived within ten miles of you." He smiled his bad smile and both of the pilots wet themselves.

Whelan and Larsen rappelled down the rope to the deck of the trawler. To a Norm, it would have looked as if they simply dropped out of the sky.

On deck, the two Dogs unshouldered their SIG 553s. Whelan nodded at Larsen and pointed at the bridge then, tapping himself on the chest, he pointed below decks. Larsen flew up the ladder four steps at a time. Whelan cautiously raised a hatch cover over the fish hold, leaning away from it. A weapon on full auto spit a string of slugs through the opening.

"Okay," the big Irishman muttered, "we'll do it your way." He pulled a M84 flashbang grenade off the utility belt at his waist, triggered it, and dropped it into the hold. There was the obligatory flash and bang followed immediately by the sound of Whelan's rubber-soled feet landing at the bottom of the hold.

Through the smoke residue he could see five large rucksacks stacked against a far bulkhead. Kruchinkin struggling to get to his feet, both hands clamped on his deafened ears. The blank look evidenced the temporary blindness caused by the grenade's shock to the photoreceptor cells in his eyes. Whelan swiftly shouldered his SIG then spun the dazed Russian around and slammed him hard into the bulkhead. He pulled Kruchinkin's arms behind him and slipped double flex cuffs over his wrists, purposely tightening them to the point where they were constricting the blood flow to the Russian's hands. He swept Kruchinkin's legs out from under him and flex-cuffed his ankles.

Larsen dropped into the hold and took a long look at

Kruchinkin. "I know this guy. It should be fun watching him try to climb the ladder out of here."

"He goes last. The nukes have priority."

Larsen grabbed the handles of three of the rucksacks in one hand and scrambled up the ladder like a monkey climbing a coconut palm. He dropped back through the open hatch a few moments later. "I tied them to the line and signaled the boys in the chopper to haul them up." He grabbed the two remaining rucksacks and repeated he process.

In less than a minute, Larsen's head appeared in the hatch opening. He stretched a massive arm down. "Pass screwhead up to me."

'Screwhead' was the about the strongest epithet Whelan heard Larsen use. The Irishman grabbed Kruchinkin's thighs and hoisted him up. Larsen grabbed the Russian under his right arm and yanked him through the hatch opening. Whelan scrambled out behind him.

Larsen scaled the line first then hauled Kruchinkin up. Whelan was last into the chopper. He looked back at the trawler. The surge of the incoming tide had broached the ship and it had begun to heel heavily. After a few moments, as it continued to fill with water, it capsized.

Whelan muttered to himself, "So much for leaving a zero footprint."

WHELAN DIRECTED the pilot to return to the lee side of the small islet, one of three just off the Higuerillas' waterfront. They could see that the town was aglow with activity. Lights were on everywhere. Vehicles with flashing lights surrounded the old warehouse. More were converging on it. Men in uniform and armed civilians, presumably gang members, were searching the area around it. Whelan realized there had to be more Mexican police and military on the way, including aircraft. Time was critical.

The other five Dogs were standing in the shallow water. A twelve-foot overturned skiff beached behind them. A sixth person was sprawled on its hull.

The pilot set the bird down on its pontoons and the other Dogs piled into the chopper, obscured from the town by shrub-like flora, a solitary seagrape, and scattered juvenile buttonwood trees. Stone carried the sixth person aboard and placed him gently on the deck.

As he did, Whelan said, "Where are the other four bad guys?"

"That's a story best told over a cold frothy, mate." Stone winked conspiratorially.

Whelan knelt beside the stranger. He looked like he was barely more than a kid. His breathing was ragged and shallow. Deep cuts and ugly bruises covered his face. A couple of front teeth were broken. Whelan assumed the rest of the body was as badly beaten. The injured man's expression confirmed the degree of pain he must be suffering.

Whelan slid over next to Kirkland. "Did you have a chance to take a look at him?"

"Yeah," Kirkland winced and shook his head. "Someone all but beat the life out of the poor kid."

"Think he'll make it?"

"Depends on whether we get him to a medical facility in time. Got any idea who he is?"

"Yeah," Whelan said. "I think his name is Turan."

CHAPTER 63

THE LODGE: DOG-EAT-DOG

Cliff Levell's office in The Lodge seemed luminous in the sunlight flowing through an exterior wall of glass. Dust motes sparkled in its brilliance. The entire Lodge basked in an aura of immaculate freshness and pleasant smells that joyfully teased the senses. It was a universe away from the old warehouse in Las Higuerillas.

Clean and rested, the seven Dogs sat on two sofas and matching chairs facing Levell. The furniture was covered with a rich grade of distressed leather the color of an aged saddle. From the potted cactus in a corner behind Levell's desk to the Navaho throw rugs to the Remington reproductions on the wall, the office décor spoke admiringly of the Old West, and not subtly. Levell, behind his desk and looking more like Clint Eastwood than Whelan could remember, surveyed the slice of Americana and his seven hulking charges arrayed in front of him.

"It goes without saying, you did a good job…this time." He paused for effect. "I think."

None of the Dogs spoke. To a man they recognized this as the closest Levell ever got to praise.

"Now that you've gotten your beauty sleep and washed some of the smell off, let's tie up some loose ends."

Whelan and the others knew Levell had a process and objective in mind. Best to let him talk.

"Intel showed there were ten of those guys originally. They were genetically different, like the seven of you. What happened to them?" He looked directly at Whelan.

"To tell you the truth, Cliff, in all this excitement, I kind of lost track myself."

Levell snarled. "Spare me the film dialogue, Dirty Harry. What the fuck happened to them?"

Whelan smiled. The Old Man was always the Old Man. It was reassuring in a mostly chaotic world. "I know what happened to some of them, but," he looked at the other Dogs, "later it became an individual thing."

Levell said nothing. He was sitting back in his wheelchair, chin down, staring squinty-eyed at Whelan from beneath shaggy eyebrows.

"When we got to the warehouse, we saw five large bodies piled in a dark corner. Five more guys, just as large, were standing nearby. Looked like the live ones killed the other five. Probably out of greed. One of them got away in a van with the five nukes. Sven and I went after him."

"That would be Kruchinkin, the Russian," Levell said.

Whelan nodded.

"You got the damn nukes, you must have got him too."

"Yeah, we did."

"Well, where the hell is he?"

Whelan glanced at Larsen and said, "That's a story better left until the end."

Levell appeared to mull that over for a few moments then said, "That leaves four. Where are they?"

"Dead," Quentin Thomas said.

Levell thought about that for a few moments too. "Those men were like each of you. Stronger, faster, part of a new breed and deadlier than *Homo sapiens*. Must have been quite a challenge for you, I mean, confronting your own kind for the first time."

Whelan said, "It was an individual matter. Sven and I weren't there." He looked pointedly at Stone.

"Well, Cliff," the Aussie said, "my mate Rafe here was unable to nick a tinny big enough to get the five of us across to the island, along with the injured lad and those four bruisers. They kept asking for a fightin' chance, so we made what you Yanks call an executive decision."

"You killed them in cold blood." Levell actually seemed disturbed at the thought.

"Naw, Cliff, we gave them what they asked for, a fightin' chance."

"That's the worst 'executive decision' I ever heard." Levell slid forward in his chair. "Why the hell would you do that?"

"How often do blokes like us get a chance to have a real barney with our own kind?"

"I think the question is 'why in the hell would you want to?' So, what happened?"

"There was a big Kraut, called himself Geissler. He was the mouthiest, so we matched up against him first."

"There were five of you and four of them. This isn't Quentin's kind of thing, so he must have been odd man out. Who matched up with whom?" Levell's piercing eyes flickered across the assembled faces.

"Nickie went first," Stone said.

Levell looked in astonishment at Stensen then back at Stone. "*Nickie*? He lets you call him Nickie?"

"He's my mate. And he volunteered faster than any of us," Stone said.

"Obviously you were successful," Levell said. "But you were limping when you walked in here. Geissler do that?"

"Naw," Stone said. "Bren had shot the Kraut in the calf to stop his yammering. So, first off, Nickie shoots himself in the same leg and says to Geissler, 'Stop whining, you pussy.' It got real from there."

Levell looked at Stensen. "Tell me."

Calmly, as if he were discussing a church picnic, Stensen said, "He was strong. Stronger than I am. And a dirty fighter. Tried to gouge my eyes. It was close for a while." The bright red coals flared in the centers of his deep-set blue eyes as he began to warm to the tale. "But he wasn't as dirty as I am. I pinched off his windpipe. When he was nearly unconscious, I kicked him into the wall."

There was silence for several moments, then Levell said, "So, what happened next?"

Stensen shrugged. "There was no 'next.'"

"That's it?" Levell said. "You just slammed him into a wall?"

Stensen grinned and his hawk-like features combined with the red glow in his eyes to give him a demonic look. "There was a jagged piece of pipe sticking out of the wall. It impaled him."

Levell actually shivered. "Jesus, you love to kill in the most bizarre ways." He turned back to Stone. "What about you?"

"One of the blokes was a Limey. Name of Stark. In Oz we have long memories. Don't like the pommy English bastards."

"What happened?" Levell said impatiently.

"Oh. He was quick. And strong too. Maybe the strongest bloke I've fought except for sparring with my mates here." He looked around at the other Dogs. "But he was a drongo, stupid as fuck. Judgin' from the vegetation around his eyes and ears, he must have been a boxer, 'cause he tried boxing with me."

"That must have been interesting," Levell said. "You were a hand-to-hand combat expert in Tag West. A master of Krav Maga, as well as other styles."

"Stark tried to use brute force, not realizing I was as strong."

"Not to mention in better shape and much more skilled. How did you handle him?"

"Easy, he was trying to use boxing techniques. I just moved in close where he couldn't get a punch off, then used head butts, elbow strikes and my knees. It didn't take long. I kneed him in the balls and he reached with both hands to cover his crotch. That exposed his throat and I used a knife-hand strike to kill him."

"Sorry I missed it," Levell, the old Marine, said almost wistfully. He looked at Almeida. "Frankly, I'm surprised you survived. Was your opponent comatose?"

"Naw," Almeida said. "He was French."

Levell shook his head in disbelief. "Tell me about it," he said with an amused expression.

Almeida seemed to swell with pride. Or self-importance. It was hard for Whelan to tell. "I was great. I hate Frenchies, so I started kicking the shit out of him from the get-go."

Levell held up a hand, halting Almeida's narrative. He looked at Stensen. "What really happened?"

"There are some subtle differences from Rafe's version. For one, Deschamps, the French guy, took it to the runt from the beginning. Had him on the deck, choking him. But Rafe managed to get his hands around Deschamps' head and tried shoving his thumbs into his eyes. The Frenchman jumped off him and started rubbing his eyes. Rafe scrambled to his feet, grabbed a length of rusty pipe from the floor, and swung it.

Deschamps put an arm up to block it and got a shattered ulna for his troubles. With the second swing, Shorty crushed the French-man's skull."

"I thought it was supposed to be mano-a-mano?" Levell said. "You cheated. Why am I not surprised." It was a statement and not a question.

"Well, shit, I couldn't let the motherfu—" Almeida stopped as Levell waved him to silence.

Levell turned to Kirkland. "Why do I suspect that sword of yours was involved? What do you call it…?"

"*Doragon no chi.* Dragon's Blood."

"Yeah, did you use it?"

Kirkland smiled slyly.

Thomas said, "It's like his American Express card. He never leaves home without it."

"It's not your style to fight an unarmed man," Levell said. "So, what happened?"

"He was a Turk," Kirkland said. "A weightlifter and wrestler. Very strong, very quick. Probably could have handled a kilij or scimitar very well. But we didn't have one handy, so I tossed him the three-foot length of pipe Rafe used on the Frenchman."

"Obviously, by your presence here, it wasn't enough," Levell said. "How did you end it?" He glanced at Thomas and saw the other man was ill at ease.

"Fighting is all in the footwork and that's telegraphed by what the center of gravity does. No one, no matter how skillful they are, can defend their entire body at one time, particularly when attacking. So, I visually divide an opponent's body into quarters with the lines intersecting at the navel. Then it's just a matter of waiting for the opening," Kirkland said.

"And?" Levell said.

"I saw his attack forming before he launched it. He wanted to jam the end of the pipe into my solar plexus. From a *jodan* stance, I slid to the left as he lunged. Using a *hidari kesa giri*, a downward cut from left to right, I severed his arm near the shoulder. Then I used a *hidari ichimonji giri*, a horizontal cut from left to right, and decapitated him.'"

Levell shook his head. "Nice work, but next time explain it in English."

"And that brings us to the main event of the evening," Whelan said. He looked at Larsen. "Sven?"

The man-with-no-neck shrugged his massive shoulders. He had always been a man of few words.

"Dammit, Larsen, what happened?" Levell said.

"I killed him."

Levell snarled with impatience. "For the record, could we have some details?" He looked at Whelan as if for support.

"When the chopper landed back at the staging area in Texas, Sven and I took the Russian to a nearby building, a small concrete block structure. It was empty and looked like it had been used for storage. I went in with Kruchinkin and cut the flex cuffs off of him. I told him he'd get the same deal the others got. A chance to fight for his freedom. He asked if that meant he would have to fight both Sven and me. I told him no, only one of us. The sonofabitch thought it was going to be me and actually sneered at me. He said, 'Then I am free man.'" Whelan imitated the thick Slavic accent. "Killing him would have been a pleasure, but there was a kind of a history between him and Sven."

Levell looked at Larsen. And raised an eyebrow.

"He reminded me of Maksym," Larsen said. "I had tracked Kruchinkin to Alaska. A contest called The Baddest Badass. Before I could finish him, the cops raided the place and he got away."

Levell turned back to Whelan and motioned with his hand for him to continue.

"I went over and tapped on the door. Sven came in. Kruchinkin figured it out in a heartbeat. A change came over him. He looked genuinely frightened, like he was haunted by the memory of whatever happened in Alaska. Last I saw of him alive he was pressed against a wall trying to stay as far from Sven as he could.

Whelan smiled at the memory. "When I left the room, I couldn't resist a chance to gig Sven. I said, 'Let me know if you need any help.'" He paused for a beat and his smile broadened. "He growled like an angry Grizzly and slammed the door in my face."

Levell looked at Larsen. "What happened next?"

"I killed him."

"Dammit, Larsen, I asked you for details."

The man with no neck smiled his bad smile. "I snapped his spine, then crushed his skull."

Levell sighed in frustration. "Alright, I'll settle for that. For now."

PART FIVE

CHANGES

"Things are not always as they seem..." —Phaedrus

CHAPTER 64

WASHINGTON, D.C.

WHELAN WAS in the rear seat of a Federal Bureau of Investigation gunmetal gray Jeep Grand Cherokee. Levell sat next to him. Nando was in the front passenger seat, Christie was driving. Whelan had opposed going to this meeting with the president. He didn't see any benefit, only a downside. But Levell had insisted, practically begging him to go. They had argued about the wisdom of producing one of the Sleeping Dogs in the flesh. Their greatest advantage was operating in the in the world of anonymity. Outing them, even one of them, stripped away the mythology, the aura, the mystique of the unknown and the fear it generated in those who intended harm to America, whether homegrown or foreign.

Levell was adamant that the president wouldn't relent in his demand to meet the Dogs. He wanted to thank them personally for finding the five nuclear weapons. In fact, Flagler initially had insisted that all of the Dogs must attend the meeting. Eventually, Levell was able to pare the list down to only the leader, Whelan. It was that or there would be no rescission of the outstanding decision directive issued by a previous president, calling for the immediate execution of the Dogs. Whelan felt he owed it to the others to see that the directive was rescinded.

"I hope we don't end up regretting this meeting," Whelan said to Levell. "This city is full of CCTVs, and the White House is too. Your people will never be able to scrub my likeness off all the servers and backups."

"We'll see about that. Don't sell the SAS hacker squad short. Besides we really didn't have any other option. Let's face it, it's not a perfect world; shit does happen." Levell seemed particularly grumpy today.

They passed through a security checkpoint and Christie stopped the Jeep under the covered portico of the West Wing entrance off West Executive Avenue NW. Nando got Levell situated in his wheelchair as a Secret Service agent drove off in the car. Two other agents escorted the four of them into the White House and ultimately to the Oval Office.

President Fred Flagler was standing at a window looking out at the Rose Garden when they were shown in. He turned, hands behind his back, tilted his head back with its oddly coifed blondish hair, and regarded them silently for several moments. He beckoned to them in an almost regal manner.

Extending his hand to Levell, he said, "Good to see you again, Cliff. I wish I could simply have pardoned you and kept you out of the pokey, but my advisors nixed it."

Flagler looked at Mitch Christie for a moment. "You're the FBI guy that works with Cliff."

Christie smiled and nodded.

"You done good, as they say, while ol' Cliff was doing time. Good job."

The president turned to Whelan and extended his hand. When Whelan grasped it, Flagler attempted to pull him off balance. Whelan anticipated the move and instead pulled POTUS to him.

Recovering, Flagler said, "This big son of a gun must be one of the fabled Sleeping Dogs."

Whelan nodded.

The president sized him up from head to toe. "Nice stick pin," he said indicating Whelan's necktie. "But you don't look like a suit kind of guy."

Whelan started to say that the stickpin was Levell's idea, but instead just smiled.

"Are you as strong and fast and deadly as rumor has it?" Flagler said.

"The word 'rumor' usually speaks for itself, Mr. President. Most myths have a strong element of fantasy."

"Fantasy? Ol' Billy Trupockitt wasn't killed by some fantasy, that traitorous bastard."

Whelan smiled. "I understand he hung himself."

Flagler stared at him for a few moments. "I hear you're an Irishman."

"Dual citizenship. Irish and American."

"Yeah?" Flagler squinted his eyes and pursed his lips. "Say something in Irish."

"*Deir roinnt daoine go bhfuil tú lán féin.*" It translated as 'Some folks say you are full of yourself.'

"Hmmm," the president said. "What does that mean in English?"

"That the other Sleeping Dogs and I are proud to serve such a decisive and action-oriented president," Whelan said without a trace of irony.

Flagler literally swelled with pride, squared his shoulders and jutted his chin out. He was a man who *was* famously full of himself. Never more so than now.

"It's the nation that should be proud of you, all of you." He looked around at the others. "Recovering those nukes. Killing the bad guys who had them. We're all very proud of *you*. Well, of course, nobody else really knows about it. It's doubtful most Americans could handle knowing how close we came to a nuclear holocaust. But this nation owes you a very big debt of gratitude. And I won't forget that."

"Hopefully that includes the presidential decision directive," Levell said.

"Absolutely. It's on my desk. I'll sign it before you leave."

"Just out of curiosity," Whelan said, "what happened to those five nukes?"

"They're inside a big-assed mountain in Nevada. They've been disassembled, the parts destroyed, and the fissionable materials stored in the mountain with other nuclear waste."

Flagler paused and glanced at Levell and Christie then stepped up close to Whelan. The president was tall and used to using his height to intimidate others. But he was not as tall as the Irishman. He rose on his toes to try to get to the same eye level and leaned in until he was almost touching Whelan. "You and your boys are a hell of an asset. We need to discuss your future operations."

"Future operations?" Whelan said.

"Sure, we need to foment regime change in Iran, Turkey, Venezuela, Cuba, lots of places. Then there are assassinations like that little Hermit King and the Russian tyrant, those are just for starters. Then there's sabotaging China's industrial, technological, and military buildup."

"I'm aware of the concept of fake news, Mr. President," Whelan said, "but legitimate sources are reporting that your administration is actively engaged in discussions and negotiations designed to address some of those issues."

"We are, and if that works out that'll be fine. But we need to have a Plan B. Always got to have a Plan B. And C and D too. That was the key to my success in business." He tapped his skull. "Always got to be thinking ahead."

Levell and Whelan exchanged glances. The Old Man made a barely perceptible motion with his head signaling that now was not the time object.

Flagler made a statement by looking at his watch.

"Mr. President," Levell said, "we're grateful for the time you made to see us today. But we know you have a full schedule."

Flagler shook hands with each of the men, Levell's last. "Cliff, I believe this is the beginning of a beautiful friendship."

An amused Whelan grinned at Levell and mouthed the word "Casablanca."

CHAPTER 65

WASHINGTON, D.C.

THEY WERE HEADED BACK to The Lodge in the gunmetal gray Grand Cherokee with Christie driving and Nando in the front passenger seat again. Whelan and Levell rode in the back.

"Was that guy serious?" Whelan said.

"Flagler? Yeah, he's serious about everything, but it changes from moment to moment." Levell said.

"Regime change? Political assassinations? Those are suicide missions. What the hell does he think we are, the Impossible Missions Force on steroids?"

"He's the president. He's entitled to have his pipe dreams."

"Not if he tries to act on them. Remember, they've been filming me on CCTV, probably since we entered the city."

"Yes, I know that. But much to their disappointment your facial features were blocked electronically."

"How does *that* work?" Whelan said with skepticism.

"One of the Mueller brothers' high-tech labs came up with a device that interferes with CCTV cameras. You're wearing it."

Whelan reflexively touched the stickpin in his tie. "I know

there are devices that interfere with signals from wireless cameras. But many of the CCTVs we encountered are wired."

"Oh, ye of little faith," Levell said. "Leave it to the Mueller organization to stay out in front of everyone else's technology. The device you're wearing creates a force field that distorts the image the cameras pick up."

"Sounds like Star Wars to me." Whelan shook his head and smiled.

"And there's a Plan B. We know which agencies operate the cameras and where the signals are sent. My tech people assure me that hacking into those servers and destroying the recordings is a breeze. Relax."

From the front seat, Christie said, "The rest of the team is still back at The Lodge. Will they stay together this time or go their separate ways?"

The two men in the rear seat glanced at each other. Whelan shrugged but said nothing.

After a few moments, Levell said, "I wish to hell I knew the answer to that. They're the hardest bunch of bastards to deal with I've ever known. And considering my years in the Corps and the Company, that's saying a lot."

"Is there something in particular you'd like to use them for?" Christie said.

"Yeah, among other things, that fucking Nadir Shah has caused enough problems but he's nowhere near done. The best policy would be to take him out along with his high command."

"Even though his 'caliphate' has been destroyed?" Christie said.

"It hasn't been destroyed. He's just lost physical territory and taken the organization underground. Like all jihadi groups, his will continue to butcher innocent souls for a long time to come."

They were southbound on 14th Street NW, approaching the

intersection with I Street NW. Whelan glanced out the window on Levell's side of the Jeep and saw a large dump truck eastbound on I Street. He made eye contact with the driver. An alarm instantly went off in his mind. The truck had a red light, yet it wasn't slowing down. In fact, it seemed to be accelerating. Whelan instantly calculated where it would be when the Jeep was in the middle of the intersection. "Brake!" he yelled at Christie.

The FBI agent stomped on the brake pedal and yanked the steering wheel to the left. Nando saw the truck too and the agile Capoeira expert literally flipped over the seatback, landing in the middle of the rear seat between Whelan and Levell just as the truck rammed the Jeep's right front quarter panel instead of T-boning it. The truck careened to the right, crossing the intersection at an angle. It destroyed a police cruiser parked at the curb and barely missed two cops standing on the sidewalk. Several other pedestrians weren't as fortunate. The truck demolished a covered bus stop and traffic directional sign before slamming sideways into the wall of a twelve-story building and coming to a stop, pinning the driver's door closed.

The Jeep spun a 360 in the intersection and hadn't quite stopped before Whelan leaped out and raced to the truck, shoving bystanders out of his way like a giant racing through a field of weebles, except these weebles didn't immediately bounce back up.

The driver was struggling to climb out of the window on the passenger side. Whelan leaped onto the truck's running board and grabbed the driver by the throat, yanking him savagely from the cab. He slammed the driver's head on the truck's doorjamb, knocking him unconscious then yanked up his shirt. He was relieved to find the man wasn't wrapped in explosives and packets of shrapnel.

The two cops, one black, one white, materialized next to the car. Their weapons were drawn and shaking badly from their near-death experience. "Put him down and get down off the truck," the black officer yelled to Whelan.

"I'm not your problem. This guy is." Whelan shook the body of the unconscious man for emphasis.

The black cop said, "I'm not gonna tell you twice to get down here. And keep your hands where I can see 'em."

Christie came running up. He quickly showed the officers his FBI creds and, nodding at Whelan, said, "This man is with me. Put your weapons away before you hurt someone. This is a federal matter now. We're taking the suspect into custody."

The white cop said, "Wait, I'm not sure this is a federal offense. I need to check with Metro."

"Don't go getting your ass in hot water," Christie said. "The Bureau's been after this guy for fleeing prosecution on a series of federal charges in Virginia."

Whelan was impressed at how smoothly, convincingly Christie could lie.

CHAPTER 66

THE LODGE

ALL OF THE Dogs were in the Lodge's cocktail lounge, a clubby environment of dark woods, polished brass, and subdued lighting. Levell was accompanied by a beautiful red-haired, green-eyed woman of a certain age, Maureen Delaney. She was chief executive officer of one of the world's leading technology companies, a member of the board of SAS, and Levell's long-time love interest. Almeida had managed to get a seat next to her and, between shots of tequila, was eagerly working his charms on her. Such as they were. Levell kept a wary eye on him.

Mitch Christie arrived a little late for the meeting because he'd been delayed by Washington's infamous rush hour traffic. He didn't come alone either. His fiancée, Camila Ramirez, younger than Maureen Delaney by twenty or so years, was stunning. It was the first time Whelan and the other Dogs had seen her, a raven-haired beauty with long, shapely legs, flawless olive skin, and dark eyes shaded by long, thick lashes. All of the Dogs, Almeida in particular, had difficulty keeping their eyes off of her.

After introductions, Whelan said to Christie, "What's the situation with that young guy we rescued at Las Higuerillas?"

"Turan Salam," Christie said. "He's at the San Antonio Military Medical Center, formerly Brooke Army Medical Center. He's going to make it."

Camila smiled and said, "There's a love story involved too." Her eyes seemed to glow with genuine warmth. "It took some doing, but we were able to convince the young lady's mother to allow the daughter, Carolina, to visit Turan in the hospital. That, more than anything, including medical care, seems to be helping him recover from those terrible beatings."

Levell gruffly said to Christie, "Enough romance." Then, turning to Whelan he said, "Tell Mitch what you learned from that sonofabitch who tried to kill us today?"

"It didn't take long to break him. He's been singing like the proverbial canary."

"And?" Christie said.

"He admitted he was on a suicide mission."

"No shit," Levell said testily. "He tries to crush us with the damn truck. Tell him something he doesn't know. Like who sent the sonofabitch."

Camila seemed amused by Levell's crustiness. Christie, Delaney, and the Dogs were used to it.

Christie grinned and winked at her, as if to assure her that the Old Man's bark was worse than his bite.

"Were you aware he was on a mission for HAC?" Whelan said.

"Nadir Shah? That figures," Christie said. "I'm sure he's incensed that his plans for the nukes were foiled and wants revenge. But how did he know who was behind it and where to find us?"

"He didn't have an answer for that," Whelan said. "But I can think of a source. AGU, particularly the guy who runs it, Fairchilde."

Levell nodded thoughtfully. "That makes sense. Although analysis revealed that the nukes were Russian originally, intel shows that, along with an untold number of others, they were sold to the Chinese after the Soviet Union collapsed. We know China's long-range plans to destroy America involve using Islamic terrorism. Those plans were in the late Zheng Bao Xun's wheelhouse. He provided six nukes to Shah, including the one that destroyed Los Alamos. Zheng was a member of AGU and together with Harland Fairchilde realized the need to stop the Sleeping Dogs from screwing up Shah's plans for the remaining nukes." Levell paused and looked around the room. "Hell yes, it had to be Fairchilde who told Shah who was responsible and where to find us."

"There's a bigger problem," Whelan said. "There's no way the truck driver was operating alone today. For the timing to work, others had to be involved because the truck driver would have needed someone tailing our Jeep, to advise him in setting up for the collision."

"Correct," Levell said. "Thanks to Fairchilde, I've raised the level of security at The Lodge. Fairchilde doesn't know what you seven look like." He motioned toward the Dogs. "But he and I go way back, so he probably knows about Maureen, Mitch, and Camila. Be very careful."

Larsen, who was sprawled on a sofa between Stone and Kirkland said, "What, if anything, does this have to do with us?" He made a sweeping gesture that encompassed the other Dogs. "Because I thought we were done once the nukes were recovered."

A couple of the other Dogs nodded their heads. They all looked at Levell.

"What?" the Old Man said. "Like you have something better to do? Let me be blunt. You're a different breed in every sense of the word. You don't fit into the world of Norms. As a result, you're loners. Not exactly misanthropes, but reclusive. Outside of your existence as members of the Sleeping Dogs, you have no lives. So, where are you going to go? What are you going to do other than fall off the grid, hole up in some wilderness area and live empty lives of solitude until you die?

"Face it, this is the life you were born to lead. You're adrenaline junkies. You have abilities needed by this world if there's any hope for its survival."

There were several long moments of silence then Whelan said, "That was a little cold even for you, Cliff. Each of us had lives before the Sleeping Dogs were reunited. Four of us were married, some with kids. We all worked at jobs just like most Norms. The only difference was that we had to conceal our genetic gifts. Are you asking us to live solitary lives, like eremites, just so we can serve SAS?"

"No, not at all," Levell said quickly. "If you can develop interests, pursuits in the world of Norms without disclosing your special abilities, more power to you. What I'm saying is that the good people on this planet still very much need your services."

"What have you got in mind?" Stensen said.

Levell smiled a leathery, squinty-eyed smile. "There will always be evil in this world. No one is better equipped to fight it than you seven. I believe it's your mission in this life."

"I dunno," Stone said, "If you're proposing a constant diet of it, I'm out."

"Me too," said Thomas.

"And me," Almeida said.

"Let's not make decisions in haste," Levell said. "You men have earned R and R. Take some time off to celebrate the success of the mission. Then we'll get back together and discuss what the future may hold."

CHAPTER 67

DINGLE, IRELAND

COMPLIMENTS of one of the Mueller brothers' diverse and far flung business interests, Whelan flew the pond in a new Gulf-stream 650. With a favorable tailwind, it covered the roughly twenty-nine-hundred nautical miles from Dulles to Kerry Airport at Farranfore, Ireland in less than six hours. From there, he hired a car and driver to take him the final fifty-five kilometers to Dingle.

Although the distance was less than thirty-five miles, it took an hour or so to cover it. The route was primarily over narrow country lanes, shoulderless and barely wide enough for two vehicles to pass. Whelan had been in the States for a while and it took a minute or two for him to adjust to cars being driven on the left side of the road. He settled in and enjoyed the scenery. The roads were lined with hedgerows and low stone walls, many indeterminably ancient. They sectioned off lush, verdant fields with snow white sheep grazing peacefully under low cloudy skies ever-pregnant with the promise of rain. He passed clusters of small homes and the occasional long driveway leading to a large manor home with barns and outbuildings. Whether tiny village or modest town, there were the ubiquitous Catholic churches and ancient, well-kept graveyards. Unlike the States, with the exception of the occasional small town like Farranfore and Castlemaine, there was no commercial usage.

When they reached Boolteens, at the base of the Dingle peninsula, the road angled to the southwest and flirted with Dingle Bay on the left. To the right, loomed the green and brown fastness of the Slieve Mish Mountains that formed part of the rugged spine of the peninsula. The terrain was very familiar to him now. Just beyond a wide spot in the N86 known as Annalack, he passed the turnoff to Mare's Castle, the crumbling ancient fortress where his brother Conall, who called himself Maksym, had nearly succeeded in killing Whelan, his family, and Larsen. His mood turned somber. That was the event that had started the disintegration of his marriage to Caitlin.

Moments later, as the car passed through Lispole, Whelan realized he was only eight short kilometers from home. The thoughts of Caitlin persisted. He told himself he wasn't coming home to Dingle because of her. But as intimate memories surfaced, he wasn't so sure. He wondered how she would receive the news of his being home again. He also wondered how he would react. A relationship that had seemed perfect, unassailable, had somehow crumbled. Her actions had seemed unforgivable at first, but now he had at least some understanding of how it had happened. Perhaps he had the babbling Brooke to thank for that bit of insight.

Knowing that Caitlin had moved back into the Fianna, Whelan had reserved a room at the Dingle Bay Hotel, an aging structure on the waterfront near the center of town. But just before the N86 entered the town it passed right by the Fianna.

"Wait," Whelan suddenly said to the driver. "I want to stop at this B and B."

"Do you want me to wait for you? You said you were going to the hotel in town."

"Yeah, I won't be long."

The driver pulled into the motor court and stopped near the large wooden front door.

Whelan got out and used the large iron knocker on the door.

After a few moments, a stocky young man opened the door. He looked at Whelan for an instant then shouted, "Da!" and wrapped him in a surprisingly powerful embrace. Whelan hugged his son Sean just as tightly. Although Whelan hadn't been gone that long, Sean had grown and noticeably added muscle.

A woman's voice came from inside the inn. "Who is it, Sean?"

"It's Da, he's home," Sean said excitedly.

"Well,…I'm not really living here any—." Whelan saw Caitlin and never finished the sentence. She had always been the most beautiful woman he'd ever seen, but now she looked prettier than ever. Somewhere, he thought, Aphrodite, Helen of Troy, Cleopatra and other famous beauties of legend must be having jealous rages. He felt an odd sensation in his chest, like a pang, but not a painful one.

Caitlin looked at him and seemed to light up. She took a quick step toward him, as if she were going to run to him and hug him. But caught herself and blushed instead. "I don't know what to say."

"For starters, 'hello' would be okay."

There was a period of silence then Sean said, "You *will* be stayin' here, won't you, Da?"

"No, actually I have a room reserved at the Dingle Bay Hotel."

"You'll do no such thing," Caitlin said. "The Fianna is your home as much as it is mine. You'll stay here." She made a shooing motion toward the driver.

He looked questioningly at Whelan, who walked to the car and handed him several euros. Grabbing his suitcase from the car's boot, he walked back to the front door.

Sean grabbed the suitcase. With a big grin, he said, "I'll take this up for you, Da." And he was gone.

Whelan looked at Caitlin. "This will mean there's one less room to rent to paying guests."

She smiled at him with a sly twinkle in her vivid, opalescent green eyes. "We've been separated, but we *are* still married, you know." She took him by the arm gently, but firmly, and led him toward the stairs to the upper floors.

"If you're thinking what I'm thinking," he said, "how will this arrangement affect the boys, given all that's happened? And your parents? And the towns folk?"

She paused and looked up at him and with a tease in her voice said, "If you can forgive my being a 'tainted woman,' everyone else will be delighted to see us mending our fences."

"Acceptance is a two-way street, Caitlin. Otherwise, eventually we could find ourselves having issues again."

"I do accept you, Brendan Whelan. For reasons known only to her, God created you and your friends for special purposes. It's who you are. It's part of your unique nature. I understand that now." She paused for a moment then said, "And I love you unconditionally."

He kissed her, softly at first and then with passion.

She took his hand and led him up the stairs.

. . .

DEAR READER,

If you enjoyed reading *A Deadlier Breed*, please leave a favorable review on Amazon.com, Apple Books, Barnes&Noble/Nook, Goodreads, or Google Play. Reviews not only help writers succeed at their craft but also provide valuable information for prospective readers. Thank you.

John Wayne Falbey

PREVIEW OF THE DEVIL'S LITTER, A SLEEPING DOGS THRILLER

THE DEVIL'S LITTER
A Prequel to the Sleeping Dogs Series

A quantum leap in human evolution is a good thing ... right? Or is it?

Meet the most fascinating and unforgettable characters in modern fiction. America's top-secret military and intelligence operations discover a small group of unique individuals. They mold them into the deadliest, most formidable black ops unit in history. Nicknamed the Sleeping Dogs, their objective is to hunt and kill America's most dangerous enemies. Their training is so challenging they barely survive it; their missions are extraordinarily dangerous. Imagine their reaction when the government that created them betrays them.

OTHER BOOKS BY JOHN WAYNE FALBEY

THE SLEEPING DOGS SERIES: The Far Left has succeeded in undermining the America of freedom and opportunity as we knew it. Their goal is to destroy our democratic, capitalist system by eradicating the middle class. In its place, they are establishing a New World Order based on radical socialism that consists of them as the elite and absolute rulers over an enormous mass of poor and struggling souls who have no freedom of speech, expression, even thought. But a small group of patriots well-placed in politics, industry, and the military fight back. They bring back a forgotten band of exceptional warriors who purposely have been in hiding for almost twenty years—the Sleeping Dogs special operations unit. The Far Left is about to find out why, as Chaucer noted so long ago, it's a bad idea to wake a sleeping dog.

The Devil's Litter, a Sleeping Dogs Thriller
The People's Republic of America, aSleeping Dogs Thriller

The Quixotics: Three disillusioned special ops veterans of the Vietnam War run guns to anti-Castro forces in Cuba. And find more than they bargained for.

The Taxman Cometh: A rogue IRS agent leads a raid on the wrong house and destroys Finn O'Casey's world. A sympathetic neighbor who is also the leader of organized crime is not who he seems. He and the IRS agent thought O'Casey was a mild-mannered accountant. They thought wrong. O'Casey, a former member of an elite special operations unit, goes dark and joins his warrior comrades to wreak vengeance. The moral: *Be careful who you choose as a victim.*

ALL BOOKS ARE AVAILABLE in digital versions at Amazon/Kindle, Apple Books, Barnes & Noble/Nook, Google Play, Smashwords, and all online booksellers. Available in print versions at Amazon, Barnes & Noble, and can be ordered at bookstores everywhere.

ACKNOWLEDGMENTS

No one writes a novel, let alone several of them, without a lot of help from many other people. I'm especially grateful to you, my readers. I write for you. Your support and enthusiasm continually inspire me. Thank you for buying my books, recommending them to other readers, posting reviews, and helping to spread the word.

I also appreciate the input and encouragement I've received from other writers, including Lee Child, Steve Berry, Doug Lyle, and many others I've met through International Thriller Writers–ITW.

My thanks also to the past and present members of law enforcement and the United States military. Your efforts, bravery and sacrifices keep all of us safe and free. Thank you.

Many individuals have contributed significantly to this novel. It's blessed with another great cover from the amazing Tatiana Villa at Vila Design. Tatiana has designed the cover on every novel I've written.

No novel is ready for the editors until it's been reviewed by qualified beta readers. In my case, I'm fortunate to have the finest group of thriller readers to rely on for their input on what works, what doesn't. I'm deeply grateful to Jim McGowan, Rich Burns, Geoff Kelly, Gary Maxey, Frank Zulys, Karen Heney, and Art Burch for their time and suggestions. A special word of thanks to Howard Giordano, a top-notch thriller writer in his own right and a master at critiquing thrillers. I highly recommend Howard's novels; the latest is *The Dark Side of the City*; it's *The Godfather* on steroids. Howard's and the beta readers' incisive critiques made *A Deadlier Breed* a far better book.

Finally, I am most appreciative of all for the support of my family, especially the warm and wonderful girl I married, "Annie." Thank you, sweetheart, for your ever-positive, unwavering support and faith in my efforts. I believe if we "keep the faith," we will see the success we're working so hard to achieve.

A NOTE FROM THE AUTHOR

This novel is a work of fiction and isn't intended to advocate for, nor to praise or condemn, any specific political philosophy. As a work of fiction, it's just a story intended to meet a writer's foremost responsibility—to entertain the reader. It was fabricated, however, on events occurring in the U.S., and globally. It tells the story from the diverse perspectives of various fictional players. Consequently, any resemblance to persons living or dead is purely coincidental.

What is not fictional are some of the underlying storylines. American and Western culture and civilization have been badly eroded over the past several decades, and the pace seems to have been accelerating lately. The elected governments have weakened the military and intelligence communities. A great many citizens seem to be unaware, or simply don't care. But make no mistake—human beings are the deadliest and most dangerous species ever to have inhabited this planet. Few, if any, other animals kill, torture, and imprison solely in a lust for power, wealth, glory, and dominion. Think about the history of civilization—a kaleidoscope of empires built upon war, conquest, torture, and subjugation. Nothing's changed: today you have Russia, China, North Korea, Iran, and other would-be conquerors. Greed and the lust for power are still in mankind's DNA. And always will be. It's who and what we are. As Pearl Buck wisely noted, *"When good people in any country cease their vigilance and struggle, then evil men prevail."* Do you believe the pen is mightier than the sword? You bring your pen; I'll bring my sword. Care to wager on the outcome?

What also is not entirely fictional, is the theory of genetics explored in the books in this series. It's based on considerable research, but necessarily includes a certain amount of speculation. It is a fact that scientists have determined that persons with Western European bloodlines have some Neanderthal DNA. The European Early Modern Humans, or EEMH, interbred with the Neanderthal. These early Homo sapiens ancestors were as large as humans today, and were more powerful and physically robust. Intriguingly, their brains were one-eighth larger than modern man's. Sound like Whelan and his colleagues?

My personal philosophy as a writer of fiction, a teller of tales, is that my first obligation to my readers is to entertain them. A second important duty is to be authentic. In fantasy or science fiction, the author has free rein to shoot from the hip. But with fiction that is based on the world we live in today, places and objects should be accurately described and depicted. This is why I exercise a ratio of 4:1—research to writing. If I describe a weapon, vehicle, or any other object, I want readers who are familiar with them to be satisfied that I nailed the description. Likewise, with locations, I want my readers who have visited those locales to think "that's exactly how I remember it."

The fiction writer also has an opportunity to educate the reader. Not glaze their eyes over, but present them with facts and information that help broaden their knowledge, all within the context of the storylines. One of my undergraduate majors was History. Most people seem to loathe taking those courses because of all the names, dates, and places that have to be memorized for exam purposes. But to me it was a fascinating panorama playing out chronologically on a global stage. I could see the "players" and places in my imagination. That thirst for knowledge about the "world out there" remains as strong as ever. Consequently, when I write, I research to learn about the people and the places that are woven into the storylines. When I read other writers' works, I like to be educated as well as entertained. I try to do the same things in my books.

ABOUT THE AUTHOR

John Wayne Falbey writes thrillers set in the contemporary world of international espionage and geopolitical intrigue. His debut novel, *Sleeping Dogs: The Awakening*, became an international best-seller. He followed it with *Endangered Species, Year of the Dog, Dogs of War, A Deadlier Breed, The Devil's Litter,* and now *The People's Republic of America.* All are thrillers in the Sleeping Dogs series.

He's also the author of *The Quixotics,* an action/adventure Vietnam-era tale of gunrunning, guerrilla warfare, and suspense in the Caribbean. His most recent non-Sleeping Dogs novel is *The Taxman Cometh,* a mystery/thriller in which a CPA accused of murdering IRS agents must dodge local, state, and federal law enforcement agencies until he can find the real killer.

Wayne is a native Floridian, transactional attorney, real estate investor and developer, and reformed academic. His wife likes to say, "Wayne has more degrees than a thermometer (four)," including a law degree and a doctorate in business. In addition to practicing law and developing real estate, he spent five years in academia, creating and chairing a Master of Science program in real estate development at a graduate school of business in Florida. But writing has always been his first choice.

CONNECT ONLINE:

I hope you enjoyed reading *A Deadlier Breed* as much as I enjoyed writing it. I invite you to connect with me at:

www.falbeybooks.com

where you can find discussion guides, sign up for my occasional newsletter announcing publication dates, signings and appearances, and other matters relating to my Sleeping Dogs thrillers and other novels. I also invite you to connect with me through any of the social media below, and look forward to hearing from you.

http://Twitter.com/jwfalbey
https://www.facebook.com/wayne.falbey
falbey@sleepingdogs.biz

www.ingramcontent.com/pod-product-compliance
Lightning Source LLC
Chambersburg PA
CBHW030542020726
47494CB00005B/1456

* 9 780999 861173 0 *